The ISIS Affair

Putting the Fun Back in Fundamentalism

By

David Rich

Copyright © 2018 by David Rich, Rich World Books.
ISBN 978-1-7322534-1-4

Other books by David Rich:

Sail the World? – An Absurdly True Story, Prequel to RV the World

RV the World, 2nd. Ed

Myths of the Tribe - When Religion and Ethics Diverge

Scribes of the Tribe - The Great Thinkers on Religion and Ethics

Antelopes - A Modern Gulliver's Travels

THE ISIS AFFAIR

The ISIS Affair

CHAPTER ONE – A PIECE OF CAKE

"Piece of cake," said Ralph as he punched a bony fist in the air and threw a half-full garbage bag over his shoulder. "We snuck into Syria." He broke into a shuffling jog toward the van for Aleppo, which sat at the end of a very long parking lot.

Doug sped ahead. "I'm a dunce to go along on this crazy trip, even to steer clear of my conniving kids. And mark my words, it won't be a piece of cake, because you always get into arguments about religion."

Doug's posh British accent was as thick as syrup, which he considered license to say anything and get away with it. "Aleppo isn't going to be as easy as Mr. Mustafa said," he added stuffily, "even with the so-called safety guarantee. And you don't have to run for a bus in this part of the world. They never leave until the next one shows up."

"Unless a bomb goes off."

"Then we really don't want to hurry."

At eighty years old, Ralph was unable to keep more than a foot ahead of speed-walking Doug, who was a mere whippersnapper at seventy-nine.

Doug sniffed. "I do so enjoy watching you carry your stuff around in a garbage bag. You can be an embarrassing sort of chap to travel with."

Ralph gasped, trotting to keep up with Doug. "No decent packs in Antioch. And you bad- mouthed the one with the nice camera compartment in Baku. Could have been a souvenir of the disaster in *The World Is Not Enough*. Surely you remember that James Bond movie?"

"I do not," Doug said, snorting. "Real Brits don't watch that James Bond claptrap."

Doug's stiff upper lip dissolved in a sneeze as he sped into the edge of a whirlwind swirling across the Syrian side of the Bab-al-Hawa border crossing. Their Columbia travel togs flapped like loose sails in a gale, making them look like stick figures on the back of a soccer mom's van, tall Doug and stumpy Ralph.

The dust devil churned bags of paper and plastic into a whirligig of grime, making Doug duck and weave, buffeted by the wind. He walked hunched over with the top of his huge orange pack high over a white mop of hair, his mournful brown eyes tearing as the dust cut visibility to inches. The parking lot of little white Ladas and Toyotas had disappeared in the choking dust, the kind they hadn't seen since day thirty-seven of forty-four days by camel from Zagora, Morocco to Timbuktu.

Ralph rasped, holding onto his hat as he spat

blindly. "The Marine will lead us free of this pestilence."

"If you'd keep your mouth shut, you wouldn't have a problem, ever," snapped Doug, wiping his face with a grimy sleeve. "And you're not a Marine." Doug was calm and carrying on, though his huge backpack was being whiplashed by the mini tornado as they dodged around cars in the endless parking lot. "You're a dope, telling that chap in Yerevan you were a Marine. He only admired your pathetic crew cut to sell you a rug. And now you're a Marine?" Doug laughed. "You have a delusion of physical fitness or old-timer's disease. Eh, you're probably just sliding toward senility." A gust tossed Doug and his pack sharply sideways, but Doug swiveled right back on course.

"Okay," said Ralph, taking a deep breath. "The Marine has led us clear of the twister." He pivoted a few degrees to the left, on a straight shot for the van to Aleppo.

Ralph took off his glasses and wiped his eyes. "Buses always make me run." He whipped off the baseball cap with *Arizona* written across it and wiped his forehead below a scraggly white crew cut in the process of disappearing. "If we don't catch the next bus, we'll have to walk miles and miles." Ralph puffed, rubbing his face in a smear on the yellow sleeve. "And don't give me any crap. I paid the baksheesh to the border guard, and as usual you didn't spend a cent."

"You're on assignment. You can expense it.

Anyway, it's your turn to gift a fiver to the cause."

"Me? You're a royal cheapskate!" He glared at Doug. "From now on we're splitting everything half and half."

Doug and Ralph were in a partnership of penny pinchery to stretch the dollar further than it had ever been stretched before. Ralph was a travel writer and self-proclaimed expert in theology while Doug was a globetrotter dedicated to outwitting his grasping children. It'd be easy to imagine them standing under the wobbly gunpoint of a mugger, holding their chins in their hands like Jack Benny, deciding between their money and their lives.

Doug swept along in a speed walk. "The so-called Marine crew cut is nigh nonexistent. But I assume that's why you wear the silly baseball cap. Though at your age, baldness is hardly premature."

Ralph considered Doug's diction his only redeeming quality, which Doug took as an admission of British superiority over the uncultured American dialect, which had obviously emerged from the ill breeding of former colonists.

At Doug's glare, Ralph said, "I know you'd rather walk to Aleppo. But when you walk I have to run to keep up. Kids these days have no respect for their elders, driving the wisest in the clan to exhaustion."

"You poor old codger," said Doug. "I'm not

4

convinced you're actually older than I am. You probably just look older because you're out of shape. Otherwise you wouldn't have to run to keep up."

They were yards away when the front door of the van opened, and the driver emerged in a grubby white robe split to his armpits. Ralph ran furiously as the driver started to close the sliding door of the minibus, pulling ahead of Doug at the last second. The driver jumped out of the way as Ralph pivoted and jumped, agile as an old goat, landing inside the jam-packed van.

Cracked black vinyl covered ancient bench seats topped by tube like roll bars. The two front benches were full, black-clad ladies of ample girth filling the front seat while the second bench contained a skinny woman smushed by two vast figures in full-length black niqabs.

Heads turned and eyes peeked through narrow black slits as Ralph scrambled inside. A rainbow of tassels was thumb-tacked to the ceiling of the van and green plastic grapes garnished the dash where two Barbie dolls were propped. The dolls wore headscarves and full-length black robes with only their wee faces visible.

Seven males were crammed into the two back benches. Three wore luxurious beards while the other four were beardless—a plump young man, two teenagers, and a glowingly cute kid about twelve years old with a cherubic face as smooth as a baby's butt.

The plump young man's clean-shaven face

glistened above a grape-colored scarf with a matching white-and-purple-checked turban that complemented his lavender robe. He smirked at Ralph and patted his lap as Doug swung in behind Ralph.

"This van is too full already," said Ralph. "I know the border guard said it's not safe to stand while the bus is driving and you must have a seat, but I'm not sitting on that guy's lap."

Doug looked at the black-costumed women, whispering at Ralph, "You still have the safety guarantee, don't you? You didn't forget that."

"For Christ's sake, of course I have the safety guarantee. I'm not completely senile." "Just checking in case you forgot something, again," said Doug as he surveyed the crowd. "Assuming the border guard was right, which lap do you prefer? Otherwise we'll have to wait for the next minibus. And what happens if someone checks our passports properly this time? They might notice we've been to Israel and deport us."

The bus driver slammed the sliding door against their skinny butts, forcing them inside. "If we waited for the next bus, we'd get decent seats," said Ralph. "This one won't leave until, like you said, the next one shows up, which could be any second. I'd rather wait than have to sit on that guy's lap. Or maybe the border guard was bullshitting us, because I can't remember a single country in this part of the world where folks don't do standing room only."

"On the other hand," said Ralph, "Assad's goons will march us to the border at gunpoint if they find out we've been to Israel."

The bus driver opened his door and climbed languidly behind the wheel. Doug's eyes glazed over. "You sit on that nice gentleman's lap. You've always been good with gay guys, like the one in Borneo who had the hots for you." Doug chuckled. "I suspect he was legally blind."

The women were frozen in their turned-around positions. They had pulled their eye slits wide open to watch, while the men sat and stared. The chubby chap with the purple scarf had a goofy smile splashed across his face, patting his lap again as he flipped the scarf over his shoulder.

"I don't see a single person whose lap I'd sit on for two seconds, much less an hour," said Ralph.

"We should be able to shuffle these guys around." said Doug. "Maybe the guy in the back, the one who looks like a skinny old farmer, would let one of the kids sit on his lap. He looks like a harmless fuck," Doug said, enunciating the most regal "fuck" ever.

"Everyone smells like a dusty puppy, except ..." Ralph turned. "One of the ladies up front must have really sloshed on the perfume. Her, I think." He pointed at the skinny figure who was fingering her eye slit even wider.

The bus driver started the engine and turned around, motioning for Doug and Ralph to take seats.

Doug directed. "I'll sit on the farmer's lap. You take the nice chap with the scarf." "These guys look like the usual suspects," said Ralph. "Even the kids look dangerous.

Well, except the little kid with the red beret and the bright blue eyes. He'd get a million likes on Facebook. I'm not so sure about the farmer and the guy next to him looks real dangerous. Let's stack these kids up and make some butt room."

Doug bowed to the cute kid with the red beret. "My good man, do you think you might sit on that gentleman's lap?"

Doug pantomimed the kid moving to sit on the lap of the man who looked like a farmer. The farmer stared at Doug without a clue what was going on while Doug nodded and smiled enthusiastically, like anything he said was a done deal.

"And that skinny boy over there, you." Doug pointed and then beckoned at a teenager with a fuzzy beard, blue turban, and cool sunglasses. "Come on over here." He pointed at a spot on the closest bench. "Hold the child on your lap, and I'll scrunch into your space. Okay? Okay."

Doug held his head high, eyebrows arched over wrinkled cheeks, willing immediate obedience.

8

The really cute kid stared at Doug in disbelief as the teenager with the blue turban jumped up and said, "Okay, my ass, walking in here like you own the joint, bossing folks around. You must be ugly Americans."

Doug yelled, "I'm not a bloody American." Ralph stuttered, "Your English is very good..."

"Isn't everyone's English very good?" asked the kid, pushing mirrored sunglasses down on his nose, looking around the van.

Half solemnly shook their heads, saying, "Yes, yes, yes, yes, yes," overlapping like a whisper of adders. Three women tittered, shushed by a harridan in black who sat in the front passenger seat.

The slender lady who'd fingered her eye slit wider practically ripped it open, peering at Ralph while the passengers started talking at once. The cute kid said, "He thinks I'm cute. What a moron."

The skinny farmer on the back bench picked up a bowl and placed it on his lap, bewildered as he said, "What say? What say?" apparently exhausting his English.

"You'd better know I'm dangerous," came from the back bencher with the leather jacket. The older stubby man with a henna beard said, "Welcome to Syria, gentlemen. We don't wish to be unfriendly." He smiled. "At least we don't wish to be unfriendly yet."

The pause was ominous as the man adjusted his

9

sinuous gold-and-beige turban and briskly rubbed his hands. His deeply lined face was ringed by a firecracker-red beard and seemed genial as he yelled at the driver. "Get going. The next bus is coming up behind us."

He turned to Ralph. "My name is Fahd. I'm from Gilgit. We must take a seat."

CHAPTER TWO – THE RIDE

Ralph schmoozed. "I'm Ralph, and this is Doug. I lived in Gilgit for three weeks when I hiked around K2 and Nanga Parbat before heading to Karimabad."

Doug and Ralph loved meeting new folks because they'd never met anyone who came from somewhere they hadn't been. Meeting someone new was like old-home week, reminiscing about the most wonderful people and attractions where the new acquaintance lived, which was always someplace Doug had traveled and Ralph had written a travel story, and everyone they met loved it. Usually.

Ralph's face lit up with the joy of an addiction. "I crossed into China from Passu on the way to Kashgar. I love Pakistan because it has the world's most fabulous mountains, better than Nepal."

Fahd shook his head and said sharply, "Sit down." He scooted over to make room for Ralph and Doug.

The teenager with the cool sunglasses crowded into the back while the other teenager with the fuzzy white turban scrunched his face up like a prune, sitting gingerly on the lap of the chubby guy with the purple scarf. The van started with a jerk as the cute kid perched on the lap of the tough-looking man on the back bench.

Ralph threw the black garbage bag under the seat,

and Doug grunted, pushing his huge orange pack into the corner. The minibus swayed as Doug and Ralph rushed into the narrow space between Fahd and the chubby guy. Ralph swiveled sideways to fit into the seat, feeling the garbage bag to confirm the presence of his camera.

They had barely scooted their skinny butts onto the seat when a *whoomph* from behind hit the minivan like a giant hand. An ear-piercing percussion threw the van forward like a whip, fish tailing the van and throwing the passengers onto the floor as the driver yanked the steering wheel, trying to keep the van from skittering onto its side. As Ralph fell sideways a ball of sun- bright yellow could be seen through the shattered back windows, curling like an atomic cloud, followed by glass raining on the heads of the shrieking passengers. Smoke billowed through the van. The minivan arriving from Aleppo had exploded in a fireball behind them.

The back windows behind the farmer and macho guy had imploded, cascading over the men and boys like a sparkle of diamonds. The women screamed continuously as everyone scrambled back onto the seats and they careened down the middle of the highway like a bucking bronco.

"Wow," said Ralph on top of Doug, coughing as the smoke began to clear, blindly feeling around for his glasses. "It's a good thing I made us run instead of waiting for the next bus, like some folks who don't care about—"

"My arse," said Doug, shifting Ralph's bony butt. "You're only alive because I move with such rapidity that you have to run. I saved your miserable life, you decrepit pansy. If we'd waited for the next bus like you wanted to, we'd be smithereens." Doug smirked. "Of course, then you wouldn't need glasses."

"Oh my God, my glasses," shrieked Ralph, holding them up as he scrambled back onto the seat. "The left lens is shattered. I won't be able to see anything."

"For pity's sake," snapped Doug. "You have another pair in that garbage bag of yours. Don't be such a wuss."

Ralph's face reddened, and he avoided looking at Doug as he pulled the garbage bag to his chest and began searching for his spare glasses.

The minivan's rear windows were missing, but the side windows and tires were intact. They dodged street vendors running toward the border, traffic rushing in all directions on and off and across the highway in chaos. Two women were still screaming as the driver finally steered down the proper side of the road, east toward Aleppo. The explosion had shaken dust from the ceiling, sifting beige powder over the black-clad ladies in front and causing a fit of sneezing.

The skinny lady, who had pushed her face halfway out of the niqab, was staring at Ralph and Doug. She flipped off her hood, baring her head and revealing eyes like black olives. She stared them down, looking like Salma Hayek on meth as dark hair swirled around her shoulders. "You two are dumb as a box of rocks. I can't imagine why they let you across the border."

The other women shrank in their costumes, except for a shrouded hulk in the front seat who turned around, opened her mouth slit with two dainty fingers, and screeched, "Shut up, Marcy, and cover yourself. Put the niqab back on. Now!"

Ralph and Doug slid down in their seats as Marcy shrugged. "Fuhgeddaboudit, I don't do niqabs." She turned away from the men with her nose raised at an angle, staring down the mother superior who turned back toward the front, intent on inspecting the Barbie dolls on the dash.

Except for Ralph and Doug, the men sat with open mouths, horror on their faces as they gaped at Marcy practically disrobing and speaking publicly to a man, showing her long hair to non-relatives, and sassing the matron. Such harlotry was unheard of in a strict Islamic country. They sat glassy-eyed, like they'd been hit by an earthquake on top of the explosion.

Fahd sighed, saying nothing. Marcy's face was set like a cigar-store Indian's, carved in wood and unyielding. An ancient fire engine clanged past them toward the border crossing, the shrill siren scaling up and abruptly down as it passed with revolving red lights.

"You're the one with the perfume," Ralph said. He gingerly brushed shards of glass off his Arizona cap, blinking furiously to get used to the old prescription in the spare glasses. "Are you from New York City?" he asked the back of Marcy's head.

She muttered without turning around. "Nosy American. I'm from Joisey, across the Bridgegate, land of the fat Philistine." Marcy turned around like she was spoiling for a fight. "I prefer Sharia law, better than Joisey law anytime." She smiled at their incredulous stare.

Ralph ignored the hint of allegiance to ISIS "There are bad laws in all countries. The only question is the percentage, which varies…" He trailed off.

Doug also ignored the elephant in the van, turning to Fahd. "Kind sir, thank you for helping with our seats, and especially for expediting a timely departure. It was almost like you knew—"

"My pleasure," said Fahd as the passengers continued to pick bits of glass off their head gear and hair, in shock from the fireball and Marcy's explosive mouth. "Though it wasn't my intention to save two elderly infidels." He smiled like a wolf. "If not me personally, someone will leap to acquire two Western hostages for the glory of the caliphate. For the glory of the Islamic State."

Fahd held his arms high, the men cheered, and Ralph fisted his breastbone to restart his heart as the elephant in the van climbed onto the center of his puny chest.

Fahd bowed deeply, smiling at their incredulous looks. "Only crazy al-Qaeda uses indiscriminate suicide bombers, like back there. I'm not in contact with al-Qaeda."

Fahd did a double take at their surprised looks. "Al-Qaeda blows up Sunni Muslims, the chosen, while knocking off very few infidels and Westerners. I don't know whether al-Qaeda is unlucky or stupid. You know the difference between Shiites and Sunnis, don't you?"

"I don't know why the Sunnis are chosen or why ISIS cares," Doug said loftily. Fahd smacked his forehead with the palm of his hand. "Marcy is right. You are dumb as rocks."

Marcy smiled prettily, showing her dimples, an act sufficiently risqué to snare the rapt attention of the tough guy on the back seat. Whether his interest was in seducing Marcy or executing her for apostasy was unclear, perhaps one followed by the other.

Fahd frowned at Doug's blank look. "We will exterminate al-Qaeda because it is insane. ISIS suicide bombers only kill Shiites and infidels." He bowed. "ISIS are the good guys because Westerners are way down our list of enemies. We target Shiite apostates and Muslim governments from Saudi Arabia to Malaysia. Westerners are a distant third."

Fahd assumed a kindly smile. "ISIS actually likes

Westerners because they bring bounteous ransoms, look good in orange jumpsuits, and their videos go viral on YouTube. We hope against hope that the videos and suicide bombers will entice the Americans into our war." Fahd smiled, his tanned face crinkling in merriment as he slashed a finger across his throat.

"I can understand that," said Doug poshly, studiously ignoring Fahd's rude gesture. "The best way to win a war is to lure the Americans in on the other side. Let's see now, this has been true for the last..." He paused, doing the math. "For seventy-some years, the Americans have lost every war."

It sounded like a BBC pronouncement, devastating news for the former colony. "That is very not nice," stuttered Ralph, patting his throat to confirm it was still intact. "You might come up with some cockamamie argument, but that would be most unkind. Besides, we beat the stuffing out of Grenada and Panama. The world never appreciates how much we sacrifice to police the world for the benefit of ingrates." Ralph placed a hand over his heart, looking suitably patriotic.

"The playground bully is often resented," said Doug. Ralph ignored Doug. "Why does ISIS want to knock off Sunni governments?"

Fahd shook his head at the ignorance. "Ninety percent of Muslims are Sunnis and natural allies of ISIS But secular governments are abhorrent to the Koran which mandates a caliphate. The Koran allows no separation of mosque and state."

Ralph cleared his throat. "Don't confuse our governments with us, the unlucky peons under their thumbs. Minions are us," he said, waving to include everyone on the bus. "We're like apprentices under Trump."

"No one messes with Trump," said Doug, laughing. "Parliament debated barring Trump, but it just gave him more publicity. And then look what happened!"

Fahd cut in. "Why did you two idiots hop on a bus to Aleppo?" He stared at them. "ISIS is just east of Aleppo, and most of these fellows"—Fahd swept an arm to encompass the men— "are on their way to join up with ISIS." He pointed up front. "And the ladies too. Though Marcy isn't exactly a mainstream lady in a niqab."

Fahd bowed in her direction. "Marcy is a wonderful asset for ISIS. She graduated from law school in Newark and aced the advanced course on Sharia law."

Fahd clapped his hands and bowed toward Marcy. "Except for the gentleman you called a farmer and a harmless fuck, everyone else is joining ISIS. The farmer's name is Islay, a Yazidi who went to Turkey to raise funds to ransom his daughter from ISIS."

Fahd smiled with his teeth. "This makes Islay a fundraiser for ISIS and a very lucky man. If ISIS hadn't declared the Yazidis heathens instead of deviant Muslims, the family would have been executed as apostates. You two are the only ones not serving ISIS; at least, not yet. You are truly the only worthless fucks on the bus." Fahd smiled widely as if he might be joking.

Doug gave a pommy shriek. "You mean everyone except the farmer is joining ISIS and that you might join ISIS too, Mr. Fahd? Are you fuddled, Mr. Fahd? ISIS is a bevy of lawless thuggery." Doug made "lawless thuggery" sound noble, rendering the meaning perceived by speakers of English as a second or third language, equally noble.

"Plus you'd be gormless as planks to take us hostage." Doug shook his head as if the very idea were unthinkable. "We're penniless old granddads with no one to bail us out. My worthless children lack both funds and clues and are fully occupied with begetting more worthless children. Our governments wouldn't pony up a quid for two old farts like us."

"Old farts" sounded like British nobility as he placed a hand over his heart. "They don't give two hoots about us." He blinked away tears in a performance to rival Sir Richard Burton in *Hamlet*, or perhaps *Night of the Iguana*.

Fahd smiled and tilted his head. "I could tell at first glance that you're worthless. Whoops," he said as the van dodged an ox cart and they sprawled against each other. They'd passed a few cone-shaped houses and were now wheezing by dusty fields. "But you have excellent potential in public relations for ISIS."

Fahd held up his hands as if framing a picture, distracting Ralph, who sometimes did the same thing. "Imagine an American and a Brit, which is what I'm guessing you are."

Fahd spread his hands as if envisioning the scene. "Heads lopped off on YouTube. It would be a sensation. You'd be the number one story, fifteen minutes of fame until the next big story, like Kim Kardashian nude."

"That wouldn't exactly be news," said Doug. Fahd said, "I may not be a member of ISIS yet, but I am its number one recruiter in Pakistan. And you know how I did it?"

Ralph and Doug shook their heads, waiting for the punch line.

Fahd obliged. "Miss Kardashian is my brilliant key to recruitment." Fahd pounded his chest for emphasis. "She moves my imbecilic flock to fully comprehend the Islamic heaven promised to brave ISIS warriors who expire in battle, the reason for the overwhelming numbers flocking to ISIS from Gilgit. I slip the boys the right Kardashian photo, or maybe a really wrong one, and they, shall we say, eat it up." He elbowed Ralph as if he'd just told an inside joke.

Fahd continued for the crowd. "The river of new ISIS recruits is flooding from the Middle East and Africa,

20

even North America."

Fahd exploded fists into fingers in front of their faces. "Recruits like the fine gentlemen in the back and the ladies up front." Fahd smiled broadly at the women. "The ladies are a reward for our brave ISIS warriors. We are proud of Islamic women stepping up to do their part in the war effort."

"More like lying down," muttered Doug. "And likely a propitious circumstance that finds their faces and bodies concealed."

Fahd caressed the tip of his hennaed mustache, contemplating the possibilities. "I assure you, Mr. Doug, that's it's quite the opposite. I can testify that many beautiful women wear the niqab, hijab, abaya, chador, khimar, and burqa. You never know whose charms may surpass those of Ms. Kardashian, especially if you like them ample, like I do." He gave them a greasy smile.

"So," said Doug, placing his fist as a make-believe mike in front of Ralph, "do you object to losing your head, or would starring on YouTube be the logical culmination of your travel- writing career?" Nervousness had crept between the plummy syllables.

Ralph shrugged. "Not to worry, because these gentlemen aren't ISIS. They're just joining up."

Fahd high-fived Ralph. "You got it. We're all on their way to join up, though I haven't decided yet, which means none of us are a threat to errant Westerners. We

21

first have to be interviewed by the Judge, who isn't really a judge. He interviews recruits and assigns military specialties. Except for Marcy, who for some reason will interview with the caliph." Fahd looked puzzled.

"That's what I thought," said Ralph, shaking his head at Doug's naivety. "These guys are our new friends until way later in the week. Anyway, you know me. I don't worry about things like ISIS. Everything is *que sera*."

Doug groaned. "You are so full of it. Fahd's finger across his throat turned you as white as Mr. Magoo. You were snarfeling out of his hand like a boot-licking sycophant. For a second I thought you might give him a smooch."

Ralph waved Doug off. "Stop that. My complexion is naturally pale. I was having difficulty visualizing seventy-two Kardashians *at one go*." He shakily prodded the floor of the van with a pretend cane.

Doug laughed heartily. "You'd have a heart attack if you saw a Kardashian ankle, even the one who got the sex change."

"Don't get me wrong on the theology," said Fahd, waving his hands, stubby fingers flashing like semaphores. "The seventy-two virgins' story is made up. The idea originates in a Shiite Hadith, which Sunnis regard as heretical. The Hadith doesn't specify the number of virgins, and in any event, only brave warriors felled in battle are eligible. We observe the Hadith for purposes of recruitment only."

The driver swerved again, avoiding two white pickups pulling across the highway without looking. The window curtains swirled gray dust, and a doll bounced against the passenger-side window, rattling onto the floor.

Ralph winked at Fahd like he was an old buddy. "You can't beat the serenity prayer, which pretty much covers any situation, anywhere, anytime, like right now. You'll understand because it begins with God."

Doug groaned. "I must warn you, Mr. Fahd. Ralph's philosophical depths are truly astounding, so hold on to"—Doug smiled—"your turban."

Ralph ignored Doug, reciting like a little old man. "God give me the serenity to abide the stuff I can't change."

Ralph looked serene, but the blank faces of the audience made him grope for a common reference. "I visualize what the Dude who abideth would do. You know, stay relaxed." That didn't seem to ring any bells.

"Or what Larry David would do." Surely if everyone on the bus spoke some English they must have a smattering of pop culture, but that didn't seem to be the case. The guys sat without a glimmer in their eyes, puzzled, but it was better than slicing motions.

"Ohmigod," said Marcy without turning around. "*The Big Lebowski* and *Seinfeld*? That's your life's guide?

Maybe you've had all the life you deserve."

"You nailed Ralph, ma'am," said Doug. "His philosophical depths may be truly amazing, but he deserves as much life as anyone else."

Marcy laughed, turning around. "I think he's real close to his use-by date."

Ralph sighed. "The next part is to have the balls to change the things I can, and the last part is having the smarts to know the difference." Ralph bowed to the audience but only got blank looks.

"It's like inshallah or *que sera*," said Ralph. He closed his eyes. "I can visualize having my throat cut by an ISIS executioner without cringing." He cringed, his face light green.

Doug folded his hands together, long fingers beating a nervous tattoo. "We've been perpetually delighted by the hospitality of the lovely Islamic folks we've met from Uzbekistan and Kazakhstan to Pakistan and Azerbaijan, and everywhere in between." Doug's look at Fahd begged the good luck to continue.

Ralph gulped, going for a self-fulfilling prophecy. "I'm sure these fine gentlemen are our friends, though I'm going to have a stomachache if the safety guarantee doesn't work. Well, worse than a stomachache." He gave a brittle laugh. "Meanwhile, I'm awestruck, meeting ISIS in the flesh, even if you're not quite ISIS yet."

Ralph looked at the men. "I've written stories

about a hundred countries and the pageantry of different religions—Hindu temples in pastels from India to Kuching, Buddhist golden temples from Kathmandu to China, and the Sikh Golden Temple in Amritsar. Muslims worship a meteor in Mecca, and I'm sure some of you have attended the Hajj. The Mormons have a choir and the Adventists their Saturdays. Each champions right against wrong, somewhat differently defined."

Doug put a hand on his forehead, channeling some ancient seer, soothsayer, and sage. "An obscure travel writer pontificates on his tedious obsession with theology." Doug ended with an artificial burp. "Instead of BSing, we should get the hell out of this van and catch the next one back to the border."

Ralph pushed the Arizona cap back. "The devout are usually admired, like pacifist Quakers and whirling dervishes in Konya. ISIS is super devout, but it's the Rodney Dangerfield of the religious world. You get no respect, and no one likes you. The world's most devout religion is totally despised."

"So wrong," said Fahd. "Look around and count the admirers in this one small van.

Hundreds heed the Koran and join the caliphate. We're spreading to Nigeria, Chad, Somalia, and Libya, all around the world. ISIS is superbly admired."

"You can't call ISIS devout," said Doug. "They murder folks willy-nilly unless, of course, they have a safety guarantee." His teeth chattered lightly.

Ralph ignored the interruption. "ISIS observes every murderous jot in the Koran, literally. If devout is a good thing, then ISIS is tip-top, king of the hill, head of the list, cream of the crop, and top of the heap."

Fahd and Marcy clapped and shouted, "Bravo." Marcy seemed to recognize the lyrics while Fahd and everyone else simply believed. Even the tough guy in the back managed a couple of half-hearted claps.

"Other religions are politically correct," continued Ralph. "They ignore the naughty bits of books written when barbarity was fashionable. Only ISIS enforces everything in the Koran. Christians, Jews, and Hindus ignore verses that give the *Good Housekeeping* seal of approval to slavery, beheadings, and other delicious diversions."

Doug sniffed, having never met a religion he liked. "Religion is a barbarous relic invented before the Dark Ages, the opposite of morality. And ISIS is the black sheep of religion." Doug looked to see whether they'd been seduced by the voice or actually understood the words.

The men sat puzzled by the spitfire English but enthralled by the back and forth, turning like spectators at a tennis match as Ralph went on. "Catholics and Orthodox, Sunni and Shiite, and dozens of Protestant sects have splintered when they tried to ignore the ghastly parts of their scriptures. In a few decades Islam will be the world's largest religion. Observing every word in the Koran could easily unite Islam under ISIS and render it schism-proof."

Was ISIS schism-proof and the future of the planet?

Ralph looked sick to his stomach, his skinny little face and ears white as milk. He wondered whether like Doug said, he might be getting senile. How could you tell you were getting senile if you already were? The conclusion that ISIS was schism-proof seemed inescapable, but if he was getting senile, then logic was evaporating. Or was it?

"Oh my God," said Doug, pounding his forehead with a fist. "No one would revere ISIS as the world's most devout religion. If religion is morality, then ISIS can't be a religion, even to a deluded mind. I use the word 'mind' carelessly." Doug tossed a hand.

Fahd stuck a fist in Doug's face, enthusiastically twisting it an inch away from mashing Doug's nose. "ISIS is the only morality because it has reestablished the glorious caliphate. So Professor Ralph got it right, and you, my not-so-good man, are a Western boob."

Fahd gasped at the effort it took to regain his composure. "But you are still our guest." He dropped his fist.

Doug's jowls trembled as Fahd reached over to

shake Ralph's hand. "My Gilgit buddy."

Ralph happily took Fahd's hand, shaking the limp fingers madly as a talisman against the removal of his head from his shoulders. "What did you do in Gilgit, Mr. Fahd? It's one of my favorite places in Pakistan. The Karakorums offer the world's most incredible hiking, the world's greatest mountains, better than Nepal." Ralph couldn't stop jabbering. "Upper Baltit, Fairy Meadows, the great polo games…" He stopped, breathless.

"Pay no attention to him," harrumphed Doug. "Every place is Ralph's favorite place." Fahd paid no attention to Doug, "I am the imam of the great Gilgit City Mosque on Airport

Road. I took leave to decide whether I'm needed more as part of ISIS in Syria or in Gilgit for recruitment, which is going great guns."

Ralph still jabbered, fluttering his hands. "I stayed at the Riviera Hotel in Gilgit, close to City Mosque. Your loudspeakers used to wake me up before dawn, and again at sunrise. You have a very active mosque. It's like we know each other," Ralph said, wide-eyed and wheezing, losing grip on the serenity prayer.

Fahd beamed. "Yes, the Gilgit City Mosque is a credit to the caliphate, which will extend to Gilgit and beyond." He smiled warmly at Ralph. "Schism-proof, encompassing countries such as Egypt, where the kid you call *cute* is from."

28

Fahd stood and turned, stroking his beard, reverently laying the other hand on the kid's slender shoulder. "This is Psar. His father is an ISIS colonel, a leader of the Muslim Brotherhood before Mohamed Morsi was so rudely deposed. Psar's father rots in an Egyptian jail, imprisoned at the filthy hands of the secular infidels."

Fahd patted Psar's red beret. "He is Islam's Pupil of the Month. He recited the Koran perfectly from memory on his twelfth birthday, completing his schooling. He has earned the title of hafiz at a most tender age. Look at that face, and you know he's destined for greatness."

Fahd turned forlorn. "I can no longer recite the Koran from memory. I am forgetting verses." He looked Psar in the eye. "Recite your favorite verses for these fine gentlemen."

At Psar's look, Fahd patted his red beret. "These are our guests… for now."

CHAPTER THREE — THE RECITATION

Psar was uber cute with big brown eyes full of mischief. Curls peeked from under his jaunty red beret, and he looked like he could dance with the stars.

Psar inclined his head the slightest bit, forced to acknowledge the infidels. He said stiffly in English, "The punishment of those who wage war against Allah and make mischief in the land is only this:"

Psar shook his arms wildly and stared over their heads, shouting in a piercingly pure voice like a siren.

"They should be murdered or crucified or their hands and their feet should be cut off on opposite sides or they should be imprisoned. I will cast terror into the hearts of those who disbelieve. Therefore strike off their heads and strike off every fingertip of them. O Prophet! Urge the believers to war; if there are twenty patient ones of you they shall overcome two hundred, and if there are a hundred of you they shall overcome a thousand of those who disbelieve, because they are a people who do not understand."

"Well, I understand," said Ralph as the men applauded with gusto, chanting, "Bravo, Psar. Bravo, Psar. Bravo, Psar."

"Yes, I'm certain I understand too," said Doug

with a stricken look on his face. Psar took a bow, another bow, another bow, doffing his red beret, glowing with the serene smile of the virtuous at heart.

Ralph yelled over the din. "Of course, Doug and I aren't waging war against Allah, so we're good to go." He turned to Psar. "Keep up the cuteness, kid, but don't take yourself too seriously. Disbelief is the same as belief in something else."

"I assume that's a quote I have to write down," said Doug, "if only I knew what the hell it meant. Now you're Yogi Berra?"

Psar interrupted with a recitation. "People of the Book, go not beyond the bounds in your religion, and say not as to God but the truth. The Messiah, Jesus son of Mary, was only the Messenger of God, and His Word that He committed to Mary, and a Spirit from Him. So believe in God and His Messengers, and say not, 'Three.' Better is it for you. God is only one God. Glory be to Him—He is above having a son."

It was apparently a popular verse, because Psar bowed to tumultuous applause.

"Whoa," said Doug. "That was a dastardly slam on the Christians. You are good, Psar." Ralph, cut in, 'I always thought the Christian *three* was a quaint state of affairs. Not the father and son but the Holy Ghost part, which I always pictured as Casper with a halo. It seemed quite funny at the time…"

31

Doug interrupted back. "But don't you think that it's frightfully anti-family, Ralph, for Allah to put himself above having a son?"

Ralph ignored Doug. "Religion, Psar, may be the lodestone of morality, but don't forget there's more than one religion."

Fahd put a hand on Ralph's throat, less than gently. "There's only one true religion. All others are false." Fahd smiled. "Any religious person knows this fact in his heart. Only ISIS is honest enough to say it out loud. But as far as you two being good to go, surely you've heard of Iraq and Afghanistan."

Fahd let go of Ralph's throat but got in the boys' faces. "The US and the UK have been waging war against Allah for centuries. The US began with Jefferson and the Barbary Wars. The US and UK will never stop waging war against Islam, and I'm guessing they issued your passports." He smiled and held his arms wide like a showman. "How am I doing?"

Doug was livid, and he semaphored his arms for an immediate time-out. "This cute kid wants to cut off your hands and feet—not even from the same side but on opposite sides—and you excuse this superstitious rubbish as devotion? At least put in a bid for something other than amputation or beheading. Maybe a short imprisonment would be enough." Doug bowed to Fahd. "Better yet, we formally invoke the safety guarantee."

"What is this safety guarantee you keep talking about?" Fahd asked. "Maybe you are saying you go scot-free. I frankly don't see you leaving Syria alive."

Ralph and Doug cringed as Fahd added, "Not that I plan to have anything to do with that.

I'm just being realistic, boys." Fahd raised soothing hands as if blessing them.

"We have a safety guarantee from ISIS," said Ralph. "It assures our safe passage to Aleppo, where I'm writing a story on the bombing of the National Museum of Aleppo. We will leave Syria immediately thereafter." Ralph raised his hand. "We promise."

"Can I see?" Fahd held out his hand.

"Well, sure, I guess," said Ralph, opening the garbage bag. "I keep it right on top in case we need it." He pulled out a stiff plastic envelope, loosened a string securing the lip, and pulled out a folded page, spreading it open to reveal a fancy manuscript in two sections. The bottom was covered with ribbons and two gold seals, looking as important as the Declaration of Independence.

"It's kind of important to us," said Ralph, protecting it with both hands. "Is there enough light to see?" It was late afternoon and still dusty in the van. "Maybe it's too jouncy to read."

The van hadn't stopped bouncing, swaying, and swerving since the back windows blew out. The driver dodged potholes as insane traffic hurtled toward them, from bicycle taxis to motorbikes and trucks. The only traffic traveling toward Aleppo was two hay wagons lumbering on the shoulder of the road.

Fahd looked closely at the certificate. "This is a very nice job. The green seal is signed in blue ink, which is required for all ISIS documents." He pointed. "It's in Arabic and English, but I've never heard of ISIS doing something like this. Of course, I'm not officially joined up yet.

I'm just a humble recruiter."

The plump guy and the teenager on his lap peered over Ralph's shoulder as Fahd handed back the safety guarantee, which Doug grabbed.

"I'll take care of that," said Doug. "It's too important for a garbage bag."

Ralph didn't say a word as Doug folded it, slipped it into the plastic envelope, and stowed it in the top of his big orange pack, giving it a pat for good luck.

Psar pointed at Ralph and Doug. "ISIS would never give a safety guarantee to infidels.

There's no safety guarantee in the Holy Koran. It's an obvious fake."

"Hey, kid," said Doug, "how do you know the Koran isn't just another book or that your version of Islam is the one true religion, the only right one out of—how many religions are there, Ralph?"

"Depends on how you count," said Ralph. "Over

four thousand with Protestants from Baptists to Unitarians, different kinds of Muslims, Jews, Hindus, Buddhists, Sikhs, and many others. There's no reason to distinguish because they're all branches on the tree of morality." Ralph swept his arms wide to encompass the infinite religious wonders.

A slap, like a challenge to a duel, caught Ralph by surprise. He rubbed his cheek where Fahd had smacked it hard, leaving a red handprint.

"Apostasy," said Fahd softly, thrusting his nose in Ralph's face. "Sunni Islam is the only true religion. And the only true Sunnis are those who join the caliphate. All others are hooey." He spat at Ralph's foot. "Apostasy. The Prophet has spoken."

Ralph shifted his foot. "You're dehydrated and best be drinking some water, because your spit didn't even hit the floor, and you're flat wrong on apostasy. It would only be apostasy if I were a Muslim. But I'm not. I'm a student of the wonderful religion of the world, but I couldn't choose among them because their roots are the same. You can't choose between them. Not if you understand."

Fahd bowed and looked Ralph in the eye. "Of course. You are correct. You are not a Muslim, so you cannot commit apostasy. Please forgive me. You are our guest. And you have a safety guarantee. Elementary, my dear Watson."

Fahd kissed the knuckles on his right hand and brushed them lightly across Ralph's cheek. "But you are wrong about being unable to choose among religions. Everyone must choose and make the right choice. But that's your problem." Fahd shook his head at Ralph's folly. "It's not my problem."

Doug butted in. "That's balderdash, Mr. Fahd. You can choose to have no religion, no superstition, no claptrap, and no reason to knock off the vast majority of mankind because they belong to a religion other than your own."

Ralph hushed Doug. "Of course you're forgiven, Mr. Fahd, if you don't kidnap us or anything like that."

"No," said Fahd. "We're not going to kidnap you because we're not ISIS. Not yet."

The tough guy pushed forward, swatting a teenager out of the way. "Don't promise not to kidnap these two idiots."

"Hey," said Ralph, "no standing when the van is in motion. Remember?"

Marcy turned around and jumped up on her seat, yelling as she towered over the boys. "Stop the van now. I will wear the executioner's hood for these two. I will wield the sword."

Her niqab was up to her waist, revealing form-fitting Levi's as she pulled a long knife from its sheath and slashed it through the air. "There is no need to kidnap them. I will cut them now. I am so sick of that one's mouth." She pointed at Doug, who smiled gently as if anointing her with the indulgence of aristocracy, but his stiff upper lip was telltale trembly.

Marcy laughed at Doug and Ralph's horrified faces, flipping the long knife back into its scabbard. "You two are such weenies. Safety guarantee, bah." She spat and sat down.

"Well," Fahd said, "you've met Marcy, or encountered Marcy, I should say. I arranged Marcy's transportation to Pakistan and now to Syria. But let me introduce you to the fine gentleman you said looked dangerous. This is Muath from Jordan. He's a pilot and will set up the new ISIS air force."

Muath was the Tom Cruise type, a handsome hotshot at five foot seven with a bristly crew cut and jauntily worn garrison cap. He looked like a block of granite wrapped in a scuffed- leather jacket, a back-alley type who lifted weights and liked a tooth-and-nail scrap. His eyes drilled through them without the shadow of a smile.

"So pleased to meet you, too," said Ralph sarcastically.

Muath shook hands with Doug and then crunched Ralph's hand like a cardboard cup, sending Ralph writhing to the floor as he said, "You are our guests, and besides, kidnapping you would be more trouble than it's worth. We'd have to tie you up and carry you around until we get signed up with ISIS. Of course, should the kidnapping whimsy strike, we reserve the right to change our minds."

"That is most ungracious," said Doug snootily. "Kidnapping a guest is contrary to traditional Islamic hospitality, Mr. Muath, and you should be ashamed. However, it's not all your fault. Obviously the so-called Marine named Ralph started out on the wrong foot with you, a fine air force officer."

Ralph rubbed his forehead like a tension headache was coming on.

Muath looked Doug up and down. "Actually, I have already changed my mind. It'd be no trouble to tie two rickety old men up with a piece of twine. We could set a ransom deadline of three days and then, wham, whether we get a ransom or not."

He karate chopped the seat behind Marcy, shaking the van as the metal tubing on top of the seat became a U. Muath turned the edge of his hand and kissed it, eliciting a chorus of Inshallahs.

The women giggled, except for Marcy, who said loudly, "Big tough guy."

Muath flashed the women a toothy smile. Two roly-poly figures wriggled and cleared their throats as their costumes radiated heat waves like a mirage in the desert.

Fahd gently patted the back of an ashen Doug. "He's just messing with you. You have your safety guarantee, for what that's worth. More importantly, you are our guests." He bowed.

"How long do we remain your guests?" asked Doug.

"Until you aren't." Fahd smiled. "By the time we receive our orders from ISIS, you'll be somewhere else, completely out of our clutches." Fahd held his hands up like claws.

"So you won't come looking for us until we're gone," said Doug. "I must write that down."

"You never introduced me, Imam Sahib." simpered the man with the purple scarf. "I would love to come looking for Mr. Ralph and Mr. Doug before they are gone."

"I don't introduce fags," said Fahd. "You are an abomination, no matter how necessary the caliphate thinks you are. There should be no *so-called* hero exemption."

"How is he necessary?" asked Ralph. "He looks perfectly expendable, nothing like a hero."

The plump man huffed. "Well, my name is Slim, and I'm from Tunisia."

"I love Tunisia," said Ralph.

"You love everywhere," said Doug.

"No, really," said Ralph. "I spent a month driving

down the gorgeous east coast to Djerba, into the desert, and through the underground cities where the *Star Wars* movies were filmed." At Doug's questioning look, Ralph added. "Well, the first *Star Wars* movie."

"How cute," said Slim. "I'm necessary because I'm the foremost cosmetician in the Arab world and the hero who blew up the synagogue in Djerba."

"Blowing up a synagogue sounds like essential training for a makeup artist," said Doug sarcastically. "I can't believe you did it without assistance."

"The Djerba synagogue reopened when I was there," said Ralph. "I have a great photo of a rabbi reading the Torah." He fumbled for his camera, and Doug slapped his hand.

Slim eyes twinkled. "I filled a tanker truck with fertilizer and blew the synagogue to bits, along with a load of German and French tourists. Boom!" he yelled, making them jump.

"ISIS is paying me big money to make captive women look beautiful. They hold a giant fair every Friday after mosque. Brave ISIS fighters can take their pick to marry, or tarry by the hour."

Slim inspected Doug and Ralph. "You two will end up as domestic servants, also called slaves. Or wives." Slim laughed, slapping his leg.

"Hilarious," said Ralph. "Like we say in Arizona, you're all hat and no cattle."

The skinny teenager with the white turban waved his hand, and Fahd said, "Go ahead, Nuriddin. And you too, Gallouz. These children are from Uzbekistan and Morocco."

"We're not children," they said almost in unison, stamping their feet.

Gallouz wore a pale blue turban, a tacky robe like a street urchin, cool sunglasses, and a barely discernible mustache that might have gone unnoticed if he didn't stroke it continuously.

Nuriddin had a baby face with a petite nose, little lips, and limpid blue marbles for eyes. His turban was striking, covered with curls the color of rich cream.

"I'm pretty sure I know you," said Ralph excitedly, pointing at Nuriddin. "Where are you from in Uzbekistan?"

Nuriddin's eyes bugged out as he screeched. "Why must we put up with rude tourists? Always pointing! I say push them out the door. Defile this sacred van no longer." Nuriddin paused. "I am from Khiva, why?"

"You can't waste perfectly good hostages," said Fahd. "Pushing them out the door would violate the most basic principle of conservation, to always preserve your resources."

Ralph soldiered bravely on. "I thought we were your guests."

41

"You *are* our guests," Fahd said, "but it's becoming difficult to avoid thinking of you as equally wonderful hostages." He smiled cryptically.

"Gee, thanks," Ralph said, and he turned to Nuriddin. "You've grown in the eight years since I saw you in Khiva, where Shem, son of Noah, dug his famous well. I love Uzbekistan.

And you haven't really changed, except for losing the rocking horse."

"Ah, yes," said Doug dryly. "You made me read your syrupy piece in one of the lesser American e-zines, the undoing of Alexander the Great, trapped into marriage by lust, the World Heritage cities of Khiva, Samarkand, and Bukhara, the crispy draft beer, the sidewalk cafes."

Ralph ignored Doug, smiling at the baby-faced teen. "You rode a rocking horse and wore a curly white turban like Genghis Khan." He touched Nuriddin's turban. "You have the same curly turban, except nicer. Here, I took your picture..." He grabbed the garbage bag from under the seat, evading Doug trying to slap his hand.

Ralph fiddled with a tablet, swiping through photos.

"Peckerhead tourists," said Gallouz. He wore gold-colored sunglasses with silvered lenses, reflecting the row of black costumes in the front of the van, stroking his thin mustache. "I am from Chefchaouen. Tourists have ruined our beautiful city. They wander up and down, walking into our homes, taking pictures, never asking permission." Gallouz gnashed his teeth, bobbing the cool glasses on his nose, shimmering the reflection of the women in black.

"You made me read that one too," said Doug. "Most striking city on the planet, exotic houses in every shade of blue, labyrinth of alleys, better than Jodhpur in India. Okay, you're not full of crap all the time."

"Geez," said Ralph, rolling his eyes. "I have some nice shots of Chefchaouen too." He continued fiddling with the tablet. "It's probably my favorite in Morocco, well, along with Essaouira, Marrakesh, and the desert towns down south like La Kasbah d'Aït Benhaddou and Zagora, and..." He straightened up. "Here's Nuriddin in Khiva," he said, holding the tablet for all to see.

Nuriddin peered, stunned.

Ralph was practically jumping for joy. "Here's Nuriddin on his rocking horse with the curly turban." The men stared, nodding somberly as the women turned around to look.

Ralph swiveled the tablet so the women could see. "And here's some from Chefchaouen..."

"You piss me off so much," shouted Gallouz, jumping up in the rollicking van, practically hysterical. "This is why we fight for ISIS, to make the world safe for modest Muslims in modest homes away from immodest tourists, safe from nosy Westerners looking for the beer

43

depot, taking photos everywhere. Mr. Ralph took these pictures, and I bet he never asked permission. The world would be better off without terrible tourists." Gallouz pushed the golden sunglasses high on his nose, his fingers back to looking for a mustache.

Doug was incredulous. "You'd sit on one little patch of desert and never go anywhere. You'd read a single page in a world with two hundred marvelous countries, paraphrasing St. Augustine." He looked around at the men. "Sorry about the Christian-related quote. I don't mean to offend delicate sensibilities."

Gallouz lifted his head high. "We don't want to bother anyone or anyone to bother us. Leave us alone with our caliphate, restoring the glory of Islam throughout the world."

"You have a funny way of wanting to be left alone," said Doug. "You kill hostages on YouTube, chase the Yazidis up Mt. Sinjar, sell women as slaves, rape, and pillage. You're no better than savages—"

Muath's beefy hand closed around his windpipe, lifting Doug off the seat.

"You push our hospitality, infidel. How did you live so long without keeping your mouth shut?" Muath shoved Doug away in disgust, onto Ralph's lap where he landed with an *oof* from Ralph.

Ralph shoved Doug aside and jumped in Muath's face. "At our age, we've earned the right to say what we think." Ralph shook his finger. "Otherwise we may never have the chance." He glowered at Muath as his little white face turned pink. "Will you be able to say what you think, ever?" Ralph raised his hand, taking a vow. "From now on I'm saying exactly what I think. This is my creed."

"Diplomacy," hissed Doug. "Try diplomacy if we have the remotest chance of survival."

Muath smirked. "Mr. Ralph's chance to say what he thinks may slam shut faster than he can imagine." Muath slapped a hand on his chest. "And I am truly offended. ISIS doesn't rape and pillage more than anyone else. The sultanate is well within the bell curve on this one."

He looked at Doug and Ralph sternly, daring a challenge. "I mean, why have a war if you can't have some fun? We get the babes because women are groupies. They love the uniform and the flag." He held his arms high like he was five foot eight. "We are studs."

"It's the same everywhere," said Doug. "The lower kind of women flocking to men in uniform." Doug turned a regal profile.

Marcy swiveled and hissed at Doug. "I will have your head, disparaging these fine ladies. And you're no better with your cockamamie religious ideas." She glared at Ralph as she bowed her head. "Allah, grant me the joy of their imminent demise..." She waved a hand in disgust. "You're too old to worry about."

Ralph sighed. "I'm a fan of pacifist theology, the one-species thing instead of war against everyone else."

"So you're a pansy who disapproves of ISIS tactics," Muath said menacingly, raising a fist like hoisting a blackjack as the van swerved to avoid a child riding a bicycle. Once the driver reacted, he deserved a medal for reflexes, swerving smoothly, throwing the middle two benches in a heap, bodies stacked against a sliding door that might fly open at any second.

The men scrambled back into their seats, nursing body parts and watching big women unscramble as Marcy kicked out from underneath them. The women hoisted themselves onto the seats with difficulty, using elbows to covertly check bruised and battered parts for damage, like Moe, Larry, and Curly in black tents.

An exasperated Muath thundered, "I declare Sharia law."

Marcy looked at him disdainfully, sneering. "Muath probably can't even spell Sharia law."

Doug sniffed. "Sharia law is barbarous—stoning adulterers; cutting off hands, feet, fingers, toes, extremities of extremists; enslaving women. I'm surprised Marcy puts up with the way ISIS treats women."

Marcy hissed. "Don't worry about it. I put up with nothing. And do not fear Sharia law.

At your advanced ages, what mischief could you get into?"

"We're not really knocking Sharia law," Ralph said soothingly. "Pre-Dark Ages holy books are naturally savage and brutal. The beauty of religion is its evolution to civility as a beacon of morality."

"I am going to puke," said Doug, rubbing his throat and glaring at Muath.

"I understand ISIS is obeying the letter of the Koran and that ecumenicalism is a sham because religions can't really stand each other," said Ralph. "The Christians make it their First Commandment. The most important commandment in every religion is to tolerate no other gods."

"The superstitious are uniformly intolerant of gullible others identical to themselves, rendering ecumenical nonsensical," said Doug. He whipped out a pen and wrote it down. "That's a great new quote."

Ralph turned to Fahd. "Making war against other gods is frowned on. Tolerance is the theoretical word of the day. We've progressed beyond a religion that literally believes everything in its book, trying to wipe out other religions."

Wham! A pickup nudged the side of the minivan, and their driver swerved, gray curtains swishing, but the pickup stayed close, scratching and scraping the side of the van. A soldier manned a fifty-caliber machine gun in the back of the pickup. He peered inside the van, wearing a baseball cap on backward as he swiveled the muzzle of the machine gun inches from their faces. Six-inch cartridges dangled from the gun, and every fifth cartridge was painted red. They could be wiped out with the flick of a finger.

"Duck down, ye people of the Book," yelled Fahd. He pushed Ralph and Doug out of sight as the man scratched the gaping mouth of the gun across the glass.

Fahd slipped a Koran from his robe and placed it against the window. "You never know who is on which side." Fahd smiled. "Of course, no one is on your side."

"See," croaked Ralph. "Other guys wear baseball caps too."

"Righto," said Doug. "The baseball-cap brotherhood consists of a cretin mesmerized by theology and a ruffian bearing a weapon of mass destruction."

The thug in the pickup glanced at the Koran and tapped his driver's back window. The pickup burned rubber and screeched down the highway in front of them, headed toward Aleppo.

Ralph's laugh stuck in his throat, coming out a sigh as he climbed back on the seat. "Sorry, Fahd, but we're not people of the book. We're neither Christian nor Jew."

Doug's eyes bugged out, and his cheeks rippled as he swiveled his head from side to side, shrieking, "Dear God, Ralph, old buddy, old friend. Please try to be cool."

Ralph frowned, determined to say exactly what he

thought the rest of his natural life, however short. He shook a finger. "Come on, Doug. What dear God would you be conjuring? You're agnostic at best."

"We will win the final war against filthy agnostics and other religions," Fahd said softly. Doug snapped, "Stop eavesdropping. We don't need to get in any more trouble."

"But boys," said Fahd, "you funny Westerners are the on-board entertainment, isn't that right, gentlemen?"

"Hear, hear," said Muath, chuckling like a grizzly. "Speak up so we can hear you."

Marcy turned around. "You are lucky our polite ISIS recruits understand only the occasional word of your ridiculous ramblings."

"Lord, grant me serenity…" Then Ralph switched subjects abruptly. "Anyway, Fahd, I'm writing a piece on the bombing of the museum. The curator of the Antioch museum gave us the safety guarantee in case we ran into ISIS, but he said the war was way east of Aleppo. We have no interest in politics."

"Oh, goodness," said Fahd. "ISIS does like American journalists. They look super in orange."

"I'm not a journalist," said Ralph impatiently. "I'm writing about the archeological museum, not wars and the sort of things that would concern ISIS."

"We'll see about that," said Fahd. "And you, Mr. Doug. Are you out of your mind like Mr. Ralph? Why are you here?"

"Well," Doug said, looking at Ralph, "my ne'er-do-well children have a subpoena out to rape my estate, so I can't go home. And I'm writing a book."

"A book about the Aleppo museum?" asked Fahd.

"Oh, heavens no," said Doug. "The book is *The Great and Not-So-Great Quotations.* I distill the wisdom of the species into working propositions, like the Augustine thing, though the exact wording escaped my recollection. Maybe I'm losing my memory like Ralph." Doug's eyes widened like saucers. "Horrors!"

"Mr. Ralph's reason is pretty lame, but you, Mr. Doug, have no reason at all."

"You are absolutely right, sir, and I am ready to return to Turkey forthwith," Doug said like snapping a salute. "I don't know why I'm so patient with Ralph. He always gets me in trouble, and I certainly don't have to travel to Aleppo to distill the world's knowledge into a modest tome of unparalleled erudition."

Ralph looked at Fahd. "His book has been in the planning stages for some years now because he'd rather walk than write. The rumors of such a book ooze from a single source." He pointed at Doug. "He's a lot to put up with."

"You put up with me for the same reason I put up with you," said Doug, wagging white eyebrows at Ralph.

"We require someone to split the cost of a room,"

said Ralph. "It's one reason he's off to Aleppo, though we're tired of each other after a year on the road."

Doug ran his fingers through luxurious hair. "There's another reason. Ralph is starting to forget things, so I have to protect him from con artists and fancy women. He's like you, Mr.

Fahd. You can't remember every verse in the Koran, and one of these days Ralph is going to forget how to get home, if he had one."

"Oh my God, that is wrong on so many levels," said Ralph. "One time I was an hour late fetching you at the Almaty Airport. One time!"

"So I had to find a hotel and pay for a whole room myself," yelled Doug. "And how about your lapse yesterday?"

Ralph shrugged. "Okay, I forgot the guidebook, left it at the museum in Antioch, Antakya, Hatay, or whatever is the right name for that place. You blow everything out of proportion."

"Never mind, gentlemen," yelled Muath from the back. "Here's the checkpoint."

Doug and Ralph froze, and then Doug whispered, "We'll make sure they look at our passports more carefully. We should be escorted back to the border. What do you say? Point out the Taba stamp."

"That's the best idea you've ever had," said Ralph as the driver rolled to a stop beside a green pickup with two soldiers dressed in ghastly green, holding medium-sized machine guns. The inspector of passports wore a pale blue uniform with a matching round hat like a French gendarme.

Feverishly fingering his passport, Ralph said, "See if you can find your Taba stamp..."

CHAPTER FOUR – THE CHECKPOINT

The inspector wore an enormous gun on his hip and a nametag that said "Capt Ocean Palkha" in tiny letters under an Arabic scrawl. The tall handsome captain peeked inside the van with a nose that looked like it'd gone through a growth spurt.

"Passports," he said with an accent.

Everyone held their passports out except Islay, who kept patting his pockets, finally locating a ragged square of paper.

Islay held the paper out gingerly, and the captain batted it away. "Yazidi, okay." He glanced at the passports from Islamic countries, not bothering to look inside. Then he turned with a smile to the Western passports of Marcy, Doug, and Ralph, drawing the enormous gun from his holster, swinging it lazily in their general vicinity.

"We do not want Westerners in Syria," he said, beckoning for their passports. "Fabulous," said Ralph, all smiles, holding his passport open to a particular visa stamp, beating Doug by a hair. "Westerners are happy to be excluded. We are ready to leave this very second."

Before the captain could inspect their passports, Muath stood up, sticking his chin out, unflinching as the captain swiveled the gun toward him.

"You want Madame in Syria," said Muath curtly, indicating Marcy. "She's an expert in Sharia law in Syria by invitation. And you may avert your weapon." Muath pushed the muzzle back toward Ralph and Doug while Marcy remained uncharacteristically quiet, her face and hair completely covered.

"Maybe by invitation of your lot," said the captain, holding the gun on Ralph and Doug. "I'm sure Madame didn't enter Syria at the invitation of my lot."

Ralph gulped. "Who exactly is your lot, sir? I apologize for asking, but I can't rightly tell from the uniform."

The captain turned slightly, striking a pose, elevating his nose, shaking the big gun like a flour sifter, and turning Ralph's face even whiter. "It may not be government issue, but don't fret. Have you seen the Syrian Army uniforms? They're a ghastly green like the Syrian flag, and I can't tolerate ugly, even from the flag." He thumped his chest with the gun. "Though it's above my pay grade to say so." He swung the gun back on Ralph, jerking the muzzle to indicate Ralph's turn to talk.

"Captain, sir," said Ralph, his tongue stumbling all over itself, "you are so right. That green is ugggly. As a photographer, I appreciate your taste in color." He was clearly saying whatever came into his head.

The captain held up a hand, stopping Ralph. "The

government is a little short on funds, like for buying uniforms, though I'm not allowed to say that either. I bought it on eBay. Nice color, eh?"

"Bubble delicious," said Slim, "and a fantastic shade of, I'd say... robin's eggshell blue." "Cut it out, Slim," said Ralph. "Just because he has taste doesn't mean he's"—Ralph searched for a word—"available."

"Captain, sir, there's no reason to get sidetracked," said Fahd. "Madame entered with an invitation from the Sunni faithful who attend mosque faithfully and observe the holy law."

The captain shifted the gun at Fahd again, who shrugged. "By invitation of the Grand Aleppo Mosque. She deserves the respect of the Syrian government."

"What about these two?" asked the captain, grabbing Ralph and Doug's passports.

"We can wait right here for the next bus back to the border. Just take a look at this stamp," Ralph said, smiling like the most harmless old fart on the planet.

The captain's smile mimicked Ralph's. "Surely you've noticed the traffic. There was an incident, and the border has been closed. But I'm wondering why you came to Syria, and now I'm wondering... why are you so anxious to leave?"

Ralph grimaced. "We were part of the border incident. Look at the back of the van, charred with the windows blown out."

Ralph whipped out his camera, trying to run the telescopic zoom in and out to impress the captain, but it wouldn't turn on. "Oh my God, my camera is broken."

Ralph rubbed the camera furiously, pressing extra hard on the on button, smacking the body, tearing up before it finally blinked on. He cursed under his breath, surprised when the handsome captain turned to feature his nose, like a poster for Scaramouche, and the camera actually worked.

"You turned..." Ralph said.

"I'm not ashamed of my nose." The captain sniffed as if to show it off, turning back and forth for a panoramic view. "My nose is an attraction for the ladies." He smiled lasciviously, running a finger back and forth along his proboscis, holding the gun steady in his other hand.

Ralph managed a weak smile, bowing to the captain. "I appreciate the photo-op, but that's really too much information, sir. Getting back to business, the Aleppo museum was bombed last week, but there's no verification...,"

Ralph trailed off. One of Assad's barrel bombs had reportedly damaged a wing of the museum. "But we've been to Israel and must be ejected right away."

The captain shook his head, holstering the big gun. He pasted on a movie-star smile and opened his arms as if to embrace Ralph and Doug. "I'm so happy to meet anyone concerned about the museum. See? The gun is put away. I apologize for the Syrian Air Force, which everyone knows is incompetent."

"ISIS will kick their butts," Muath hissed.

The captain slapped a hand on the big gun, giving Muath a cold stare. The captain looked more closely at the passengers, at Muath, the teenagers, and Fahd, who could only be an imam. Then at the flock of women, probably half with long knives.

The captain's fingers beat a tattoo on the butt of the gun as he focused on Ralph and Doug, snapping the holster flap closed in dismissal of Muath. "The Syrian Air Force couldn't hit the right suburb, much less a designated target but the Syrian Army." He stuck his thumbs in his armpits. "We're the best. So why the hell are you here?"

Ralph gulped. "The Aleppo museum asked me to photograph the surviving inventory and write one of my inimitable stories to rouse the passion of Western opinion, spurring donations to rescue Aleppo's treasures before they're destroyed by war." Ralph flashed a goofy smile, perhaps his impression of celebrity.

Doug gave a polite barf, which Ralph ignored.

The captain tipped the powder-blue hat back an inch, peering to see Ralph better. "I'm so happy you've come to Syria to help save the museum. I've been on the museum board for two years." He beat a fist on his chest like a bass drum. "I am devastated by the bombing. My

57

duties have kept me from Aleppo, but I hope to return tomorrow to find out the extent of the damage."

Suddenly the captain saluted Ralph. "For your bravery, you deserve the commendation of the Syrian Government. I am recommending that you, an American national, receive the al-

Assad Badge of Foreign Service, our highest civilian honor, for traversing a war zone to rescue the sacred treasure of Mesopotamia and Ancient Samaria, land of Gilgamesh, Sargon the Great, Hammurabi, Cyrus, and Darius."

Ralph held up a hand, trying to stop the captain from getting off point. "But we realize we should immediately be removed from Syria, see," said Ralph, leaning forward and pointing at the Taba stamp in his passport. "We lamentably visited Israel. And my traveling companion also has a Taba stamp. We feel terrible that we forgot to tell the border guard."

Doug pasted on his most winning smile, laying on the British accent. "So we volunteer to catch the next bus back to Turkey, unless you would be so kind as to spring for a taxi."

At the captain's glare, Doug added, "Actually, we'd be happy to walk. We wouldn't want to burden Syrian hospitality with miscreants who have"—Doug gave a polite gasp as he covered puckered lips with three fingers—"visited Israel. We are tainted. We volunteer for immediate deportation." Doug held his wrists out for handcuffing, the sooner the better.

The captain shoved their passports back. "I personally do not give a damn about the Israel thing. But saving what's left of the Aleppo museum ranks up with winning the war. As a patron of the museum, I sincerely hope the *Rams in a Thicket* are safe. They're the most important treasure from ancient Samaria, the land of Nebuchadnezzar and the great Mesopotamian kings in the land of the golden crescent formed by the Tigris and the Euphrates. I look forward to reading your story and feeling the swell of world opinion." The captain pumped a fist in the air, ready to release the van.

Doug choked, again offering his passport as he peered at the captain's nametag. "Now wait a minute, dear Captain Ocean, sir. Ralph writes little travel pieces no one reads, in e-zines no one has heard of. There will be no swell of publicity. He'll be lucky if his Aunt Mabel reads

it, because by the time it's published, she'll be too blind to read anything." Doug steadied himself. "It would be a far better thing if we immediately returned to Turkey so we can spread the word about the risk to your invaluable Syrian treasures, preventing the loss of world patrimony in this tragic war." Doug warmed to the topic. "Ralph and I will generate worldwide publicity." He ended by whamming a fist into the palm of his hand. "We know lots of important people…" There was an awkward silence as Doug tried to think of one.

The captain started to back out of the van as Doug yelled, "Wait, wait. We are infidels!" Ralph gasped. "Don't you need my name and address for the commendation?"

The captain patted the huge gun, shrugged as he executed a military about-face, and stepped outside. And the van of happy people, save two, lurched forward down the empty highway toward Aleppo.

Ralph slumped in the narrow seat, putting away his camera. "My stomach feels like it's full of cement."

Doug sat stunned, moaning. "You've killed us. You deserve a stomachache. That was our last chance."

Ralph sat up in the seat. "I am the senior adult here, and I'll get us out of this little problem."

At Doug's sour look, Ralph said, "Don't worry. Be happy and…" "We stop here," Muath shouted. "Driver!"

"That guy is dangerous," Doug said shakily. "He's going to get us yet."

The driver swerved, bouncing along the edge of a pothole before slowing and looking back.

"Keep your eyes on the road," Marcy said.

Marcy pointed at a wide stone platform sheltered by pine trees as Muath bellowed, "Pull over by the altar, driver."

At the driver's hesitation, Marcy screamed,

"Now!"

The driver rolled to a stop in front of a pile of bricks the size of two picnic tables. "Okay, everyone out," said Muath. "We have a sacrifice to perform." He looked at Doug and Ralph as if it might be a fun ceremony, leering, "Come along, boys."

CHAPTER FIVE — THE
SACRIFICE

"Don't forget we're your honored guests," said Doug shakily. "Right," Ralph said, his fingers patting his throat and then his camera.

"Everything is not about you," said Fahd. "This is our ceremony, though you are welcome to take part if you have the balls." He smiled a dare. "Just looking at you, I'm guessing you don't."

Fahd slapped Ralph on the back. "Come witness the dawning of a new world."

Fahd stood and led the men off the bus, followed by the six women. Ralph, Doug, and Islay stood behind the other passengers, who fanned around the stone platform, women on one side and men on the other. The altar stones were black and covered with ashes and colorful bits of fabric that smelled like burnt cardboard.

Fahd raised his hands joyfully. "Let's do it!"

The men shouted hoorays, pulling passports from pockets and waist wallets as the women patted delicately inside their gowns. Marcy ripped open Velcro to retrieve a passport from a pocket in her blouse.

Doug muttered to Ralph, "I can hear you now, writing this up. 'Madame thrust open her robe and withdrew an American passport from her heaving bosom, undeniably qualifying as a breast pocket. She was fashionably clad in a darling rose-coloured—make sure you spell it with a 'u'—blouse accented at her lovely throat with a velvet choker tastefully encrusted with zircons.' Does that sound about right, dear Ralph?"

"A little description goes a long way," said Ralph. "But I've never written anything that flowery bad."

"My treat," said Muath, pulling a handful of BIC lighters from his bomber jacket and handing them around to the men, leaving a pile for the women to select.

"Do you want lighters, too?" Muath asked Doug and Ralph snidely. Doug grabbed a lighter. "This could come in handy. Thanks."

"The lighter is only for burning your passport," said Muath. "If you don't burn your passport, you have to give it back."

"That's an American passport you're burning there, madame," said Ralph to Marcy. "You won't be able to go back to the States. You'll be stuck in this hellhole."

Marcy laughed mockingly. "Bye, bye, American pie. Bye, bye Joisey. Bye, bye, Bridgegate, and bye, bye, passport." Her black-olive eyes flashed in her oval face.

"I hope all that Joisey perfume isn't flammable…" Ralph yelped.

Marcy snarled at Ralph as she flicked her BIC and fanned open the pages in the blue cover. One page caught fire, and she methodically lit the others, holding the blazing mess with her fingertips until forced to drop it on the platform. The blue passport was a molten char faintly showing an eagle with claws. The stench of cellulose filled the air as passports flared and smoldered.

"Get it all," said Fahd to Slim, who was busy with a video camera. "This is important." "Well, me too, then," said Ralph. He smacked his camera to make it come on and switched to video, recording as Gallouz unsheathed a long knife and severed his flaming Moroccan passport in midair. "This is super stuff."

The men yelled excitedly, posing for the cameras as Doug stood transfixed and Islay stared in wonder. The men struck warrior poses, chanting admonitions and mottos to inspire the folks back home.

Muath kicked his feet in the air, nimble as an acrobat—which was remarkable for a blocky guy—as he burned his Jordanian passport. "Attack our enemies. If each of you poisons just one enemy of Allah, we will prevail." He rushed the cameras with his flaming passport, thrusting it forward for a vivid close-up, chanting, "Until you too can join us, do your part for the caliphate. Poison one person who lives in a country that would allow cartoons of the Prophet." He shook a finger at the cameras, looking like an *Uncle Sam Wants You* poster.

"Poison a tourist for Allah," said Gallouz joyfully, poking his Moroccan passport with a long knife as it burned to ashes. "Poison is our friend."

"Wonderful stuff," said Ralph, dancing around.

"Poison is so easy," sang Muath huskily, shaking a fist at the cameras, alternating with his face. "Poison is easily disguised in food or slipped into a beverage, and if each of you slaughters just one enemy of Allah," Muath shrieked, pumping his fist in the air, "we will prevail. We will prevail!"

Psar looked straight at the camera and recited somberly, holding Gallouz's long knife high, its serrated teeth glistening in the glow of burning passports.

"I will cast terror into the hearts of those who disbelieve. Therefore strike off their heads and strike off every fingertip of them."

"You said that before," Doug pointed out. "Don't you have any new material?"

Psar scoffed. "Hold out your hand and I'll sever your fingertips." Psar sliced the knife through the air, through his Egyptian passport. "See how clean she cuts?"

Doug jumped back, saving his fingertips from Psar's next slash, and Ralph caught it all on video.

Muath roared as his blue Jordanian passport vanished. "The ISIS air force is born. We will meet the crusaders on the plains of Dabiq and fulfill the Prophecy. The Holy Caliphate forever!" He held his arms high in a big V for victory, like his mission had already been accomplished.

"An air force would be a waste of ISIS resources,"

Marcy muttered. She stared at Muath belligerently. Muath stared back as Ralph panned the camera from one to the other.

"Run them over with your cars, your pickups, trucks, and SUVs," screamed Nuriddin as his Uzbek passport spluttered and then flamed. He shook his head so fast his curly turban looked like little yoyos. "Obliterate the enemies of Allah. Join M-A-T!" He pumped a fist in the air.

"What's that?" asked Ralph, peering around the camera at Nuriddin. "What's the M-A-T thing?"

"M-A-T is Muslims Against Tourists," said Nuriddin, patting the turban curls back in place. "I am founder, and Gallouz is other member on Facebook. You and Mr. Doug can join and read my wonderful blog. Just send a friend request to M-A-T, Muslims Against Tourists."

"I'm just aching to read the translation of an Uzbek blog," said Doug sarcastically.

"Oh, no," said Nuriddin. "I blog in English. I reach the masses. You no need translation." "You're not burning your passport," said Ralph to Fahd. "So you haven't decided where you're most needed, whether to stay or whether to go?"

Fahd smiled mysteriously, fiddling with the orange and yellow coils of his turban. "How about you, Slim?" Ralph asked. "Are you going to burn your passport?" Slim was dancing around with his passport in his hand, graceful as a baby hippo, resplendent in the purple-checked turban and lavender robe. Slim attacked his passport, holding it open, tugging at a page as he danced around. "I want to keep a souvenir, one page from my passport with the stamp for the sacred Levant, land of the caliphate. But the page…"

"For God's sake," said Doug, snatching the passport from Slim and tearing out the page and handing it back. "I hope you're happy now," he said as Ralph filmed away.

Slim smiled fetchingly, swirling the purple scarf around his neck. "Thank you," he said, smirking. "Can you burn it for me too? I'm not good with fire. I am only good at making up babes and blowing up bombs."

"No." Doug shook his head with mock sadness. "I am not burning your passport, silly boy. I'm sure one of the big brave men can burn it for you, like Muath"—and at Fahd's sharp look—"or Fahd."

Marcy leaned against the stone platform, impatient at the chatter. "I know Fahd is trying to decide whether to join ISIS, though he's far more valuable as a recruiter in Pakistan. But Muath has no reason to be here with his pitiful idea of wasting ISIS assets to found an air force."

Muath walked straight up to Marcy and ordered, "Hide that face with your niqab, woman. You are

67

indecent." He shook a finger under Marcy's chin, puffing up his chest under his leather flight jacket and sticking out a belligerent lower lip.

Marcy smiled and grabbed Muath's finger, bending it sharply backward, sending Muath sprawling as she screamed, "Fuck you, buster. I will wear what I will wear. Don't you ever tell me what is decent, you fake flyboy."

Ralph whispered to Doug, "Jersey girls are unparalleled."

Muath jerked his hand free, rushing back at Marcy. He stopped an inch away, his face at Marcy's chest. "I will not strike a woman."

"You won't strike a woman in public, you mean," said Marcy. "Where someone might see you. Otherwise…" She shoved him backward. "Get your face out of my tits and go sit down."

"I will not sit down," said Muath, scrambling back a few discreet inches. He puffed up like a horny toad, looking very short with his eyes slightly crossed by Marcy's perfume.

"Then stand," said Marcy, shaking her mane.

"Child," Fahd said soothingly to Marcy, calming the waters with a soft hand, "you should dress modestly and decently, as ordained by the Prophet."

"Don't give me any BS, old man," said Marcy. "Thank you for helping arrange my journey. But you should know I am here for a reason far beyond the authority of a local imam. I was recruited by Abu Bakr al-Baghdadi himself."

She smiled at the reaction to the jaw-dropping revelation. The men were stunned, and Ralph kept filming. "I'm sorry you didn't know," she said, though she seemed so happy to tell them. "But the caliph said you didn't have a need to know." She smiled, drunk on power. "My new position will be based on my skillset."

Fahd stammered, "I brought you here and you know the caliph himself...?"

Marcy laughed at his discomfiture. "I don't know the caliph personally, but he sought me out, asked me to join the caliphate after he saw my photo on Facebook. You have heard of the Lincoln Lawyer. I will be the Sharia lawyer."

She smirked as the men shrank back. "The Prophet said dress decently, and I am dressed quite decently"—she passed her hand in front of the burqa—"except for my Victoria's Secret, which is none of your business." She gave them a look to put them in their place. "Welcome to my world. I will administer Sharia law for ISIS, for the entire caliphate, so I outrank you all." She looked at Fahd and impatiently tapped long fingers on the stone platform. "We will proceed to Aleppo as soon as Muath gives me a better reason for being here. ISIS will never waste money on an air force, not on my watch."

Doug whispered at Ralph, "I swear she has the hots for Muath."

"They'd make a cute couple," said Ralph, sidling around for a better angle on their faces. Muath slapped his chest. "We will have an air force, but I could be your man on the side, helping enforce decency for Madame, who should at least wear a scarf, dear future boss." He gave the last word a little twist. "Of course you won't get away with a scarf under ISIS, which requires all women to wear full body armor, an extra layer of veils concealing the face."

"I assure you I am not all women," spat Marcy.

Muath smiled wider. "I'm sure I'd have wide discretion enforcing Sharia." He looked her up and down. "My x-ray vision *penetrates* body armor. You will love me. And I will love you very much. We will pencil in a whole week."

Marcy was livid but under control. "Allah preserve me." She closed her dark eyes and muttered, "Oh, Muath, if you only had a brain. One thing's for certain, many will be unable to live in the same caliphate. It will be interesting to see what happens to whom." She smiled sweetly at Muath. "Now, to Aleppo."

They straggled back to the van where Ralph filmed the back end covered in soot and the window frames fringed with tiny triangles of glass like jagged smiles.

The women lumbered in like Stepford Wives, followed by Marcy wrapping a scarf around her neck. She swirled her glossy black hair like a shampoo commercial, waiting patiently for the scooting of ample behinds onto narrow seats.

Muash returned to the back bench with his jaws clenched, obviously plotting revenge against a mere woman who would dare... who would *dare*... Muath's face was filled with rage as the driver pulled back onto a highway bordered by millions of acres of nothing. Dull hills lay behind jagged cliffs to the north, and a desert stretched south.

Ralph asked the back of Marcy's head, "If you like Sharia law, why didn't you go to Saudi Arabia years ago? Or do they have too many dust storms? In Arizona we call the big ones haboobs."

Marcy turned around, twisting a curl of licorice-black hair around a long finger. "You big religious exper: know nothing about Sharia. Saudi Arabia is a poor shadow of Sharia," she said, jeering at him.

"Wow," said Doug. "I never realized they were the enlightened ones. If whippings, beheadings, and amputations are Sharia lite, we'd better skip the real thing."

Marcy sniffed. "Sharia is not just cutting off the hands of the corrupt, a few lashes here and there, or stoning philanderers, which is where Muath is headed.

He'll receive a good and proper stoning," she hissed. "I see a massive boulder landing on his face." She held an invisible rock over her head and let it go, and everyone visualized the explosion of Muath's head.

Muath swore in the back as Marcy pulled herself back on point. "The fat old doddery Saudi kings are heretics. We will destroy their rotten kingdom."

She smiled sweetly at the boys. "Of course, you're welcome in the caliphate. Ralph can write travel stories and Doug can compile inane Western quotations, though I can't see your stuff appealing to the ISIS market. We only need one book."

Marcy said, "Your ultimate disposal will find a much wider audience than your writing. Viral on YouTube worldwide, inshallah." Inshallahs bounced around the van like arpeggios, with even Islay contributing a bewildered inshallah.

Ralph sagged. "We're not looking forward to Aleppo, but we're happy you fine folks are pre-ISIS. Besides, we have a safety guarantee."

"Gentlemen," said Marcy like a wicked stepmother, "I haven't reviewed your safety guarantee, but it's interesting that you're concerned for your safety." She smiled with teeth. "The safety guarantee could be… defective."

Doug laughed shakily. "Oh, Marcy, if you don't scare us, no evil thing can."

Psar fluttered long eyelashes as he whipped off his red beret, placed it over his heart, and recited.

"And tell believing women that they should lower their glances, guard their private parts, and not display their charms beyond what is acceptable to reveal; they should let their headscarves fall to cover their necklines and not reveal their

charms except to their husbands, their fathers, their husbands' fathers, their sons, their husbands' sons, their brothers, their brothers' sons, their sisters' sons, their womenfolk, their slaves, such men as attend them who have no sexual desire, or children who are not yet aware of women's nakedness; they should not stamp their feet so as to draw attention to any hidden charms."

"Thank you, Psar," said Doug. "However, a child may not appreciate the attraction of a naked woman. Maybe you've been too busy memorizing the Koran. But I'm shocked that Muslim women are allowed to perform strip-teases for nephews and uncles, or even for men with no sexual desire like us."

"Speak for yourself, eunuch," said Ralph. "I'm waiting for Marcy to stamp her feet and draw attention to her not-so-hidden charms."

Marcy jumped up and stomped Ralph's instep. "Is that good enough for you, infidel?"

She peered down at Psar. "Kid, you don't have a clue. The scarf covers my neckline, and you're another rock in a box like Ralph, who thinks he knows so much about religion. He may know about unimportant religions, but he knows nothing about the only true religion. What is the name of the ISIS newspaper?" She stared Ralph down. "You don't know?"

Ralph stammered, "I don't know all the little details…"

"You know nothing," screeched Marcy. "Dabiq, Dabiq!" she shouted. "Calm down, girl," said Ralph. "You're going to have a heart attack."

Marcy spat. "I say that to a heart attack. I am calm." She took a deep breath. "Dabiq is north of Aleppo, near the Turkish border. ISIS conquered Dabiq to fulfill the Prophesy, where Islam will defeat the West in the final battle."

She looked at them triumphantly. "Dabiq is like Armageddon for Christians, located at Megiddo in Israel. It's interesting that Megiddo and Dabiq are a mere hundred miles apart. Final days, boys. The West says this is not a religious war. I say bullshit. This is the final religious war."

She gave Doug a genuine smile. "The last seventy years have proved that luring the Americans into a war means the other side wins. I hadn't thought of that. Thanks."

"You're not welcome, and you're entirely on the wrong track," said Doug. "The West is through with silly religious wars. Europe learned after hundreds of years how absurd it is to fight wars of superstition."

"No basis in fact," thundered Fahd as Psar began wailing, "Infidel, infidel."

"The Koran is the word of Allah. This is the most important fact." Fahd emphasized with a finger in Doug's face. "Everyone knows this except infidels."

"Poor Psar," Ralph said. "He only knows one old book."

Fahd placed his hands over Psar's ears. "Calm, my son. Westerners have crackpot ideas." "That's why we join ISIS," said Marcy. "To rid the world of Western ideas." She patted

Psar on his beret. "In time you will get over these terrible slurs." She flipped up her niqab and unsheathed a long knife, pressing the tip under Ralph's chin.

"Now, now, Marcy," said Fahd, escorting her back to her seat. "These gentlemen are our guests. I realize that's not part of Jersey culture, but hospitality is the first duty in Islamic lands. Only when they cease being our guests..." Fahd zipped a finger across his throat.

"All I can say," said Marcy as she was placed firmly in her seat, "is that extremism in the defense of religion is no vice."

Ralph rolled his eyes. "And you're no Barry Goldwater." At the reappearance of the knife, he muttered, "Okay, you are."

Muath said to Ralph, "You forget that Madame, no matter how rude, is always correct." He waved his recently mangled middle finger, which was why Marcy mangled it. "Our great mercy is decapitating the infidels, striking terror into their hearts so they run away. Terror speeds victory and sheer terror prevents a long war, which is surely a merciful thing. I will name my air force squadron, ISIS the Merciful."

"Isn't that just dandy?" Ralph whispered.

Fahd used his calming voice. "They are difficult guests, but we will cut some slack for old farts with nothing to lose and not much time left to lose it in."

Ralph said in awe, "If ISIS conquers the world, there'll be no more religious wars. ISIS the Merciful and the schism-proof."

"Of course," Doug said, "ISIS will eventually win. They breed like rabbits, tons of wives and heaps of kids."

"Excuse Doug, please," said Ralph, smiling. "Four wives and a dozen or so children. Islam will win the numbers race hands down, simple math, especially since once a Muslim always a Muslim."

The minibus jolted to a stop.

"Oh my God, we're here," yelled Ralph, shaking as he spotted a big white sign with huge red letters in Arabic, and on the bottom, a small blue banner that said: *Aleppo Station.*

CHAPTER SIX — ALEPPO

The minibus crept through a fence topped with razor wire and pulled into a cratered parking lot behind the crumbling Aleppo bus station, which was surrounded by battered apartment buildings. A gray cloth covered three stories of one building and another looked like it'd been sliced in two with a meat cleaver with half reduced to rubble. They passed a large bus burned to a skeleton and parked between rows of white Toyota vans.

Fahd was the first one out, anxiously rubbing his hands like he was worried about herding cats. Ralph and Doug jumped out behind Fahd. The dust from the traffic on the big street in front of the station smelled metallic with a back taste of glass.

The passengers trickled off the van and gathered around Ralph and Doug as they busily checked their belongings.

"We're surrounded," Ralph hissed at Doug as he swung the garbage bag over his shoulder.

"Don't be silly," whispered Doug. He tossed the huge orange pack over his head, and as it descended, thrust his arms through the shoulder straps, hoisting the weight and snapping the buckle tight.

A big new black bus glided into the lot, rolling to a silent halt behind the van. "Pretty nice, eh? ISIS has bales of money," Fahd said, rubbing his thumb and fingers together.

The door of the bus opened with a whoosh of new-bus smell. The driver plunged outside with a flourish, wrenching open three spacious luggage compartments. He wore black pants, sweater, and balaclava.

"Yep, ISIS is rolling in it. We have a forty-minute drive tonight, and we're off to Raqqa tomorrow. ISIS will probably attack Aleppo tonight," said Fahd, dropping the information with a thud. "Where are you two heading?"

"Back to Turkey on the next va—"

"Look at that," Ralph said, pointing across the fence. "Aleppo isn't safe. Mr. Mustafa was a lying sack of shit."

A mosque across the street began a mournful, piercing call to prayer as five men in grimy shirts ran with a boy on a stretcher. The boy's face was like chalk. One leg was missing a foot, and his ankle was wrapped in a blood-soaked tourniquet. The men ran into a ground-floor apartment that displayed a white flag with a red crescent. The building as mostly rubble.

Shaken, Ralph said, "There's a war going on."

"There's been war in Aleppo for months," said Muath. He hoisted a blue bag on his shoulder. "You two are utterly stupid. Here's hoping I catch you in my gun sights." He peeked through a thumb and forefinger like a bull's-eye, smiling as he slapped them on their backs.

"Hope to see you soon." Muath threw his duffel in the luggage compartment and climbed aboard the bus.

"We have to stop by the Aleppo museum before we go back to Turkey," Ralph said as the others gathered around, saying goodbyes.

"Horse pucky," said Doug. "We take the next bus back to Turkey. We'd be insane to stay in this dreadful place a moment longer, definitely not for a ridiculous story."

"Bye, stupid tourists," said Nuriddin, his fuzzy turban quivering.

"Yeah, death to tourists," said Gallouz, shaking their hands. "Don't forget to send us a friend request and a *like* for M-A-T."

Ralph beamed. "Well, by gum, I'll do that. You never know when you might need a friend in Morocco or Uzbekistan." He gulped. "Or Syria."

"I really look forward to seeing you two again," Marcy said sarcastically, pulling out what looked like an oversized Pez dispenser in brushed aluminum. "Bye, boys." She laughed, snapping the dispenser and flipping it back in her pocket. She waved cheerily, striding onto the big black bus.

"I asked around," said Fahd. "The van that blew up was the last one back to the border.

You'll have to find another way." He flipped up a sleeve and checked his watch as the loudspeakers of a dozen mosques wailed out of sync. "That's the sunset call to prayer. It'll be dark soon, so you'll have to stay the night. Where will you go?"

"Oh, no," said Doug. "Then you'll know where we are. Then, presto, ISIS will acquire two star hostages. Anyway, we don't have a clue."

"You mean like usual you don't have a clue," said Slim, flicking his scarf at Doug's scrawny butt.

"Behave yourself, Slimbo," Doug said.

A side window of the van splintered, and a bullet plunked into the corner of the van, inches from Ralph's ear.

"Sniper!" Fahd screeched. "They're all over Aleppo. Get on the other side," he yelled at Doug and Ralph, yanking Slim behind the big black bus. "Watch everyone," warned Fahd. "With a half dozen sides in this war, everyone's a target for someone."

"The curator of the Antioch museum told us Aleppo was safe," said Ralph, "but then he gave us the safety guarantee."

"So where will you stay?" Fahd asked again.

Ralph frowned. "The place in the guidebook is hopefully still standing, but I don't exactly know how to get there."

Doug sneered. "*Someone* left our new guidebook in Antioch, just walked off and forgot it."

"I have a friend who used to rent out a room near

the museum," Fahd said, stroking his beard. "He's a shirt-tail cousin by marriage. I could put you in touch."

"And set ourselves up like sitting ducks, hostage-wise? No thank you, sire," said Doug, emphatically shaking his big orange pack from side to side.

"Wait a second," said Ralph. "Fahd is trying to help. If we took the room, we'd still be his guests, right? I mean, if we were staying with your cousin, we'd be under your protection."

"Of course," said Fahd, bowing. "You would remain my guests." Psar was tugging at Fahd's robe.

"Let's slow down here," said Doug. "Some rooms can be real pricey. How much does this one cost?"

"Yes, Psar?" said Fahd.

"Infidels no more guest," said Psar and belligerently recited over their heads.

"Kill the infidels wherever you find them for disbelief is worse than killing, fight them until there is no more disbelief. Worship is for Allah alone."

"He's just a kid," said Fahd, patting him on the head.

"He may be just a kid, but he could o-ccas-ion-al-ly let it go," said Doug. "He doesn't have to be a smartass all the time."

"Psar can be grating," Fahd said, "but there's a season for everything, and that particular season has not yet come." He playfully boxed Psar's ears. "Meanwhile, you may continue as my guests." He punched a number on his cell phone.

Psar shrugged and said a quiet "Bye," giving a tiny wave as his red beret bobbed onto the bus.

"Are you mad? Staying with Fahd's cousin?" Doug said to Ralph. "We'd be sitting ducks."

Fahd overheard. "We're friends who disagree about one thing only, which is more than you can say about most friends. One thing doesn't have to be fatal." He stopped to murmur into the phone, something beginning with *yet*.

"Got it," said Fahd, snapping his phone shut. "I'll write down my cousin's address. His name is Richard," he said, pronouncing it Reee-shard. Fahd drew a rough map. "Safe journey, *i*nshallah."

"Righto," said Doug. "That's a big inshallah."

Fahd turned and waved as he boarded the bus, which slid off smoothly with Doug and Ralph hugging its rear bumper as it rolled past security onto the noisy Asia Road.

"You watch the rooftops on the north, and I'll watch this side," said Ralph, rushing to keep up with Doug. The wide boulevard of Asia Road was packed with locals fleeing the city, toting their earthly goods on handcarts and in the back of ancient pickups.

Doug stuck out an arm, stopping them short as a tank clanked by, nudging traffic aside, caving in the

82

fender of a battered green car driven by a little old man in a turban, who downshifted and spurted away.

Treads screeched like steel fingernails on a rusty blackboard as the tank turret swiveled wildly. Ralph sidled over to pose in front of the tank, holding his arms high in mock surrender as he positioned his camera for a selfie, edging around to get the turret in the photo.

Doug yanked him away as Ralph exclaimed, "I haven't seen a tank this close up since the Golan."

"Heavenly days, I saw dozens in Bangkok the last time the military took over," Doug bragged as they flew down the sidewalk. "If you're so into tanks you should join the Marines for real."

"An hour ago you were begging to be handcuffed. You'd buckle if anyone said *boo*." Ralph gasped, trying to catch his breath. "Thai revolutions are so much fun, big street party with tanks, cute Thai girls with orchid necklaces attended one back in aught six."

Doug snorted, pulling ahead of Ralph. "It wouldn't take a boo for me to tell everything. I'm an open book, nothing to hide, and I don't do pain."

Aleppo looked like the whole city was packing up and leaving en masse. They met a cluster of four men with cheap suitcases leading wives in black who were yanking toddlers behind them. There were groups of men with guns, eerie figures in the dark as shadows shot toward them and receded when they passed the occasional working streetlight. A breeze swept the street, ruffling canvas covering blown-out windows.

"Aleppo probably always has rumors that ISIS is invading," Ralph said. He stopped short as an armored car swerved onto the sidewalk across the street. Six policemen with heavy pads swarmed out like black bumblebees wearing Vader-visored helmets and wielding bludgeons.

The SWAT team surrounded an unshaven old scarecrow with a head of patchy gray hair. He was carrying a paper bag. A cop pulled a long knife and held it to the old man's throat while two policemen grabbed his arms, making him drop the bag, which hit the sidewalk, and a Luger skittered into the street.

The old man's mouth opened in a silent scream as a cop ran to pick up the Luger. Doug rushed up, slapping the cop across the top of his head. "What are you doing to this poor chap, you big bully?"

Shocked, the cop jumped up and peered at Doug like he was insane. The cop pulled an enormous serrated bayonet and waved it at Doug, shouting in rapid-fire Arabic that sounded like the immediate removal of sensitive appendages was imminent. He laughed as Doug jumped back, bending to retrieve the Luger.

Ralph pulled at Doug, yelling, "No sense getting thrown in jail or worse, if there's anything worse than a Syrian jail."

"Righto," said Doug, shaking. "But if an old guy can't carry a gun in a war zone, what chance do we have?" He turned on the charm with the cop. "Come on, kind sir. A little civility is all we ask." At this, the cop tried to backhand Doug with the bayonet.

Doug jumped back with ease, swiveling the pack between them. The bayonet sliced mostly air along with the tiniest bit of the pack.

"Truce," yelped Doug, speed-walking backward like he'd been yanked by a bungee cord. Ralph punched Doug on the arm. "You shouldn't be messing with guys like that."

"Your principles are in the crapper," said Doug loftily. "I, for one, will continue to stand up for the less fortunate."

"You won't get away with it here. The cop wasn't impressed with your pommy accent." Ralph tried to give Doug the evil eye, but Doug ignored him, inspecting his precious pack.

Ralph tried humble. "We could buy a safe hotel room and save our miserable carcasses, or is it carci? I could skip the museum, forget the article, and we could tuck in safe without further risk on the street. Unless, that is"—he pointed a finger at Doug—"it would interfere with your principles. But you probably feel obliged to rescue the Aleppo treasure and all that rot."

Doug sniffed. "Anywhere can get hit by a stray

bomb. We can check out Reee-shard's since it's close to the museum, convenient for your big story," he said, with *big* inhaled through his nose. "If you'd put some starch in those old legs, we could be there in a trice. We'll get the hell out of Aleppo first thing tomorrow. Before daybreak would be good."

Doug shifted into full-out fast with Ralph trotting to keep up, instantly behind. Doug stopped suddenly. "That's the first butcher shop we've seen. They usually have sardines on offer. I'll pick up a tin for later."

Ralph nodded. "I am getting hungry."

"You're forever thinking about food. You're a perfect candidate for a typically obese American."

Ralph tightened his belt, hoping his pants wouldn't fall off as they peeked through a window where flies romanced a red plastic bin heaped with bones.

"I don't know how you can stand going in there," said Ralph, "even if your nose doesn't work so well. What brought on this out-of-character splurge?"

"The possibility of a long night, based on our tendency for chances to be taken. Don't forget Home Scout training. Oh, yes, your chaps are Boy Scouts—kids' kind of stuff, but you should be prepared."

Ralph numbly shook his head and took a deep breath as he followed Doug inside the butcher shop, ducking through a door draped with plastic ribbons in primary colors. A large man with a blood-splattered apron stood at the end of the counter where a dangling light reflected off his head like a halo.

A shelf above the bones held six cans of tomato paste, four sardine tins, and a basket of bread that looked as dry as wood. Doug rushed the sardines, elbows flapping as flies exploded into the air. "I'll have two tins," he said, as if it were an occasion for champagne.

Ralph shooed flies with one hand. "All that extra weight and twice your daily food allowance. We're off to the clinic with you." He choked as he took a breath of rotten air, coughing as his stomach went to spin cycle.

Doug patted Ralph on the back like humoring the hysterical, placing the tins on the counter and smiling at the butcher for a price.

The butcher stirred from a trance, fingering a filthy calculator and flipping it around.

Doug's hand gripped his throat as he peered at half-formed numbers. Three hundred. Not possible.

"That's Syrian pounds," said Ralph. "With a hundred fifty to the dollar, it's only a couple of bucks. Not bad for a war zone."

"It's a little expensive," grumped Doug as the hand slipped from his throat to caress his neck-wallet. His hands shook, unable to unzip the zipper, buggering it before he made himself dig out one British pound. "Here." He thrust it at the clerk.

The clerk stood, shaking his head repeatedly.

"Give him some real money instead of a crappy British pound," said Ralph. "It isn't worth a buck and a half any more, much less two dollars. Pounds are good on one small island in a remote corner of Europe. The rest of the world uses dollars."

Doug gritted his teeth, turning to shield the neck-wallet from view, leafing through packs of banded currencies to find two bedraggled dollars. He tossed them on the counter, rezipped the wallet, and tucked it inside his shirt.

The butcher stood looking at the crumpled bills, shaking his head in wonder at foreign- born idiots. He flattened the bills with the palm of his hand, held them up to the light and looked skeptical, laying them back on the counter.

"No fresh bread?" asked Ralph, plopping a rock-hard roll and the last two cans of sardines on the counter. He pulled out a five-dollar bill, slapping it down like a big spender. "Don't worry. Doug's money is good. It may be worn out because he tries to keep it forever, but it's the real thing. See, I'll take the old ones in change, and you can keep the nice new five."

The butcher held his palms out, begging them to leave. Ralph whispered to Doug, "Look at his eyes. He's scared." Doug was already out the door.

Ralph slipped the sardines into the garbage bag and threw it over his shoulder as he chawed at the bread, which crumbled like dust. He choked as he stumbled through the curtain, took a deep breath, and dropped the bread to chug his water bottle.

"You'd better lay off the water or you'll be looking for a loo," said Doug. "Now we're in trouble," he said, eyeing a horde of kids. "It must be a school."

The butcher's shop sat next to a dirt lot split by a fence, ragtag girls on one side and boys on the other. Doug and Ralph edged along the sidewalk, facing away from the children. They were mobbed anyway, two boys yelling "hey mister, hey mister" while others screamed "candy, candy," jumping up and down like pogo sticks.

The girls stood demurely, shifting from foot to foot, murmuring "Pens, pens," shyly holding out their hands as the boys demanded loot.

"Now, children," said Doug, bending over the chattering heads, "you know candy will rot your teeth. Let me see your teeth, young man." He stared down at a yowling child with a dirty face and the eyes of a juvenile delinquent.

"Come on, open up," ordered Doug.

The kid mischievously pursed his lips and then opened wide.

The kids hushed, crowding around as Doug stooped to check teeth that had never seen a toothbrush, jerking back at the kid's breath. "My good sir, I find you've missed your biannual cleanings for… How old are you?"

The kid held up two hands with the fingers proudly extended.

"No dentist for ten years," Doug said. "If I were so lamentably unkind as to give you candy, your already cruddy teeth would surely fall out. Can you imagine? No teeth? Then you couldn't eat and would die an agonizing death. I simply cannot allow such fine children to die of starvation. Sorry, wish I could." He smiled obscenely. "But this nice gentleman will give you pens," he said, pointing at Ralph.

Doug speed-walked away, leaving the melee behind as Ralph screeched, "Someday I'm going to kill you, Doug, you skinny-ass son of a bitch."

Ralph was mobbed by children chanting in unison, "Pen, pen, pen" as a small girl tugged at his trousers. "You poor kids," said Ralph as he tore himself away from the screaming horde, jogging to catch Doug.

Ralph yelled at Doug's departing back. "Come back here, you S.O.B." He dodged around a row of carts, suddenly catching up, stopping just in time to avoid flattening his face on the back of Doug's pack.

"Where have you been?" asked Doug. "Follow me, and I'll show you where to turn."

Ralph gasped. "I know where to turn," he said, his breath in puffs. "I remember the map too." He dodged a three-wheeled cart stacked with yellow boxes of crackers.

"No, you don't know," yelled Doug as they flowed across Asia Road, "because we turn here."

The four lanes were clogged with handcarts stacked high with lumps eerily lit by flickering kerosene lights that smelled oily like diesel.

"That's the Grand Aleppo Mosque," said Ralph. The square minaret was a hundred fifty feet high, towering at the end of a side street. The roof was covered with curly tops that looked like orange sherbet, and the main entrance was crowded with men in robes. Women streamed into a separate entrance, segregated behind a high wall. The mosque shimmered in a rainbow of Christmas-tree lights strung under the curly tops, attached to rebar with twisty ties.

They followed a stream of men slipping off their shoes and rinsing their feet, slip- slapping their way across a marble floor. Half carried automatic weapons.

"Let's take a closer look." Ralph patted his camera case, getting excited. "Machine guns in a mosque might make National Geographic."

Doug pulled a mournful hound dog look. "For chrissakes, we'd have to take off our shoes."

"So you're aromatic," Ralph shot back. "Wearing socks in the shower and calling them laundered. Then stay outside." Ralph dropped the garbage bag, dancing around to untie his shoes, muttering about there never being a place to sit in a mosque. He slid like-new Asics into one of a hundred battered cubicles, then grabbed his black bag and joined the line under the arches.

Doug sighed. "Too much trouble."

Ralph tiptoed into a room filled with two lines of men funneling into a courtyard the size of a football field. One line moved rapidly into a large open square with rows of prayer mats while the other moved slowly with men checking their AK-47s, receiving a chit in return.

The attendant was a skinny guy with horn-rimmed glasses who might have weighed ninety-eight pounds. He hung each weapon on numbered pegs covering a wall the size of a barn, rushing from chit to patron, hanging AK-47s as fast as possible, but the line moved very slowly despite his effort.

Ralph yelled back at Doug. "Come on. Hurry up already. You've got to see this." He'd unpacked his camera and was shooting away.

Doug clumped down the big orange pack, muttering, levered off his shoes, swung the pack back on, and strode toward the anteroom. His face was skeptical as he stuck his head in the door, but he exclaimed, "By Jove. You have me this time."

The pegs held dozens of weapons, and the wall contained hooks for a hundred more. Doug added in a merry whisper. "See the little door under the pegs? It's good to know how to acquire a free Tommy gun. In a pinch," he added, snorting as if he'd made a brilliant pun.

"I'm sure you're an expert with an AK-47." Ralph shook his head at the impossibility. "Have you ever fired one?"

"Good grief, no," said Doug. "I'm not a crazy gun-slinging American. But anyone can pull a trigger. If those brats on the street can, we can. I'm getting excited about this whole adventure."

"We can do anything if we have to." said Ralph as they backed out of the anteroom. They retrieved the only Western shoes from cubicles full of flimsy slippers and pungent sandals, balancing on one foot, tugging their shoes on as men streamed inside. Doug and Ralph drew laughs as they danced around men filling little plastic pitchers and sprinkling their feet with water.

Ralph leaned against the wall, cursing mosques with no place to sit. "I'm glad you're getting into the adventure."

"The Museum should be at the end of the block," Doug said. "Right across the street." And he was already out the door.

Ralph strained to catch up but was jostled by men with grim faces, rushing to avoid a scolding from the mosque disciplinarian who was hissing what must have been Arabic *bedamn*s at the tardy.

Doug raced around the lofty minaret and down the deserted backside of the Grand Mosque, stopping short at the back corner as Ralph puffed up behind. They stared at the catastrophe across the street, the grotesque scene faintly lit by a flickering streetlight.

"Half the museum is gone," said Ralph.

CHAPTER SEVEN – THE ALEPPO MUSEUM

The three stories of the east wing had collapsed into craters of blackened bricks. A marble sign with a corner of its Arabic script missing said "Aleppo Museum of Ancient Art" in tiny English letters. Piles of bricks cast oblong shadows that shifted with each blip of the streetlight, and yellow tape encircled two dark tunnels that disappeared into the ruins. A guard loitered in front, wearing a turquoise shirt and a black-and-white checked scarf.

The west wing was undamaged except for windows covered by metal plates. Soft yellow light filtered from two surviving windows bordered by great stone shutters. The entrance was flanked by enormous statuary—stone men with tall hats standing on lions carved from ancient basalt. The soaring stone hats supported the west half of the roof. The east door hung on its hinges, revealing a wasteland of tumbled bricks behind.

The guard watched them, stroking a bushy brown beard as they walked slowly across the road to peer at a pitted brass plate listing museum' hours and the price of admission.

"A thousand Syrian pounds is seven dollars,"

griped Doug, turning his back on the guard and crossing his arms. "I'll wait here."

"Good grief, Doug. They won't charge admission after closing time and certainly won't charge someone giving them free publicity."

"That's you, not me." Doug pouted, following Ralph as he pounded on the massive bronze door.

"Very nice door," said Ralph, tracing the intricate bronze design with a finger. "Nice, except for being closed," Doug said.

Ralph pounded again but it stood as stolid as the Rock of Gibraltar. The guard ambled over. "We've been closed since the bombing."

"Well, yeah, I figured that," said Ralph, rubbing his fist. "I'm supposed to meet Mr.

Jerash, the curator. I'm writing a story about the bombing."

The guard beamed, his big brown eyes shining. "You don't say." He pulled a radio from his belt and clicked it on. "Alistair, Alistair. It's Jeffrey. You have visitors. Do you read?" Static and silence.

"Have you had looters?" Ralph asked.

Jeffrey shook his head proudly. "Syrian people do not loot. We are proud to preserve our heritage."

Doug scoffed. "If ISIS invades tonight, you won't have any heritage left."

"We're packing up the museum and shrink-wrapping what we can, using the thing from the airport that they wrap luggage with." Jeffrey looked at his watch. "Our friends and relatives will help defend the museum."

"Wow," said Doug sarcastically. "That should be quite an army." Doug nodded at Jeffrey's sidearm. "Like a handgun against an AK-47."

Jeffrey jutted out his chin. "We have no choice. Assad only cares about his own survival. Our heritage isn't even a blip on his radar. We'll smuggle out as much as we can. Mr. Jerash is organizing a convoy to the border tonight, hopefully saving the Rams and the Ugarit treasure."

At their blank looks, the guard said, "The museum billed the Ugarit exhibit as 'the world's oldest treasure displayed in the world's oldest city.' It includes bronze and gold weapons and jewelry, and the basalt friezes from the Hittite temple at Ain Dara, the model for Solomon's temple. The friezes are too big for shipping containers, so ISIS will get those. The Rams in a Thicket are even more valuable. I'll try again." He lifted the radio.

"I know how to defend the treasure," said Ralph, waving his hand. "You can get as many AK-47s as you want for free."

"What?" said Jeffrey incredulously. "For free?"

"Well, yeah," said Ralph. "We just came from the big mosque, and there are a hundred AK-47s hanging on the wall. But you'll have to hurry before prayers let out."

"Are you crazy? Do you know what would happen if you stole someone's AK-47?"

"But they wouldn't have anything to shoot you with," said Ralph. "I know they might get upset, but that's only if they find out who did it. Stealth works best."

Jeffrey was struck dumb, stunned by the logic.

Ralph shrugged. "Don't worry about trying the radio again. I'll knock on the window." He headed for the yellow light around the corner with Doug and Jeffrey following behind.

Ralph peeked through the window at a grand mahogany desk. "This looks like reception. There's a lady at the desk." He tapped energetically on the window, shrilling, "Ma'am, ma'am. Can you let us in?"

A superbly coiffed lady stilted around the desk in high heels, wearing a tailored blue suit, her hand at her throat, startled out of her wits.

Jeffrey waved frantically, shouting. "There's no problem, Helen. Don't worry. These gentlemen are here to see Alistair." He turned to the boys. "Helen's a little flighty, but she's very knowledgeable. Educated at the Sorbonne."

"So she's French," said Ralph.

The guard smiled, shaking his fingers, ooh-la-la. "Exactly. A very nice lady. It was great talking to you. I'll see you when you leave." He waved as he ambled back to his spot in front of the ruins, lighting a hand-rolled cigarette. Sweet-smelling smoke sucked their way as the big bronze door swung open.

Ralph whispered, "Smells like a joint." He waved goodbye to Jeffrey as they walked inside.

"This is a joint," said Doug, looking down the enormous first-floor gallery with the ceiling open to the third floor. The place was packed with swaddled statues from the petite to the humongous, including four giant horses wrapped like mummies. The closest galleries were filled with enormous stones the size of a barn, the Hittite Temple friezes with winged lions carved in red basalt.

"Hello," said Ralph, sticking his hand out to the lovely Helen, a petite beauty who nervously swung the door closed and strained to lift a massive steel bar. She managed to slide it through metal brackets before presenting an elegantly limp hand.

Ralph bowed. "I'm Ralph Charlton," he said, taking the limp hand halfway to his lips. A forty-year age difference never bothered Maurice Chevalier. "I'm the writer from the States. Your curator, Mr. Jerash, is expecting me."

Ralph beamed, and Helen looked at him blankly. Ralph belatedly let her hand go. "I'm here to write a story on the museum."

She happily repossessed her hand. "Thank you, monsieur."

"Forgive him, madam," said Doug. "He's just an

old duffus, and I don't mean descended from the venerable Lord Duffus of Scotland, while I"—he curtsied, showing off—"am Douglas Kirk, descended from the famed protectors of French and Norman kings. But dash the formalities. You may call me sir."

Helen curtsied back, and Doug acknowledged her bow with a slight nod.

"Come this way, gentlemen." Helen led them to the polished reception desk like she was baffled that Mr. Jerash had failed to mention Ralph, the famous writer. "I'll let Mr. Jerash know you are here," she said, rivaling Doug at his snootiest.

They looked around as Helen whispered into the phone. The museum was in shambles, a topsy-turvy mass of wrapped enigmas and roughly bricked-up galleries in the collapsed east wing. Suddenly the museum turned magical as a dapper gentleman dressed entirely in yellow glided up to the front desk, a new-and-improved version of Doug, but even shorter than Ralph.

"I'm Mr. Jerash, and I am so pleased you have come," he said, bowing, hand over his heart, the genuine article compared to Doug's tramp aristocrat.

Mr. Jerash bubbled happily with tension in his voice like fingernails about to be yanked out. "Please call me Alistair," he fluttered, "and I abhor nicknames, such as shortening Alistair to Ali." He held up an instructional finger as if to stop them right there.

Doug and Ralph would always remember him as Ali. They stood stupefied at the sartorial shades of yellow, from the palomino shoes and a blond mustache with crispy rolled ends to a mop of yellow hair and a corn-silk yellow vest etched with ochre under a canary-yellow jacket.

Ralph sidled around to hold his shirt sleeve alongside Ali's jacket. "We do like our yellow. Your jacket and my shirt are the same shade. Except for a little mud here." Ralph scratched at a splotch on the sleeve. "No problem. It'll wash right out."

Ali stared down his nose. "Well, of course it does. We recommend nylon for our laborers."

Ralph stuck out his hand. "I'm J. Ralph Charlton, call me Ralph. Mr. Mustafa phoned from the Antioch museum and mentioned my name. I was there when he called you."

Ali smiled, shaking Ralph's hand. "Mr. Mustafa is a most interesting gentleman. Such a crafty one."

Ralph introduced Doug, who bowed. "Pleased to make your acquaintance, my good man." They shook hands with a double pump that looked like a secret handshake among a certain class of Brit.

"Likewise, I'm sure," said Ali, entering the bowing competition.

"The shades of yellow will make fabulous photos among the antiquities," Ralph gushed. "It'll be a doozy of an article." He sighted through a thumb-fingers rectangle. "Of course, it won't be as dramatic with everything wrapped." Mummy-like figures stretched to the end of the mirrored corridor.

"The museum was counting on your story to spur the rescue of the Syrian patrimony," said Ali, "but it's too late now. There are other pressing issues, like why Mr. Mustafa sent you."

"Mr. Mustafa sent us?" said Ralph, scoping out photo ops. "I don't understand." "We'll get to that," said Ali, oscillating toward Doug.

"I must say your wardrobe is amusing," said Doug.

"Well, yes," said Ali. "Yellow is my talisman against depression. Come on back."

Ali whisked them through a gallery filled with statues in shrink wrap, from winged lions with human heads, bearded like ancient kings, to a trio of nymphs and warriors with bronze swords.

"We'll have drinks," said Ali, welcoming them to a sumptuous office at the end of the first gallery.

One side of the office was glassed, providing a panoramic view of galleries stuffed with enormous white wraps. Ali waved them into comfortable chairs in front of a finely-grained redwood cabinet next to a sprawling desk, raising an eyebrow as Ralph dropped his garbage bag on the floor.

"We moved hundreds of pieces to the Topkapi Palace and Museum in Istanbul. Obviously with the civil war." He shrugged, shot his cuffs, and paced.

"Then Assad dropped two barrel bombs on the east wing. Son of a bitch," Ali cried, running nervous fingers through his hair. "Assad buried half the collection, which we've been trying to dig out before ISIS shows up. Much has been reduced to bits of marble and bronze. But we salvaged the Ugarit treasure and the Rams."

"'Before ISIS shows up' sounds particularly ominous, but in any event, I need to take some shots to go with the article," said Ralph, plucking the camera from his bag. "I really love the bowler." A bowler hat in canary yellow that matched Ali's jacket was propped on an antique wooden hat rack. "And I'll need photos outside the museum too."

"We haven't wrapped the Ugarit treasure, which was recovered today. The wrapping crew will be back"— he shot a cuff and glanced at a yellow wristwatch—"in a few minutes."

"Your outfit is perfect," said Ralph, twirling the camera. "What will you do if ISIS takes Aleppo?"

"Today is special," said Ali, ricocheting around the office, poking at photos, touching plaques, as hyper as a prairie dog. "I dressed up to commemorate my last day as curator." He flipped open doors on the beautifully grained liquor cabinet. "Gin and tonics," he said, nodding

103

at Doug. "Is that okay with you, Mr. Charlton?"

"Perfect," said Ralph as he and Doug cracked ear-to-ear smiles.

Ali bustled around the polished redwood cabinet, extracting chilled glasses and ice cubes shaped like fat little saucers, pouring Booth's gin and adding Schweppes tonic, talking nonstop.

"I am informed—unreliably, I hope—that ISIS will take Aleppo tonight." Ali shuddered, shaking his head like a tambourine. "ISIS steals and destroys ancient relics, partly financing the caliphate by selling antiquities. If it's too big to move, they'll blow it up like they did in Mosul, which always goes viral on YouTube."

He put a shaking hand over his heart. "We won't be able to move many priceless Assyrian and Persian treasures. And there are hundreds of small items, mosaics, ancient jewelry, golden statues, all priceless."

Ali composed his face, still fluttering over the drinks, fiddling with limes, knives, and oversized glasses. "They blew up Palmyra and killed Khaled al-Asaad, an old friend of mine. He was the curator at Palmyra for forty years, devoted to antiquities his entire life."

Ali handed them elegant crystal beakers with a slice of lime, holding his up for a toast. "To Assyria, the Middle East, and the end of war. As usual, too late for my friend, Khaled al- Asaad."

They swooped their glasses high and drank deep.

"I must say I'm glad you came," said Ali, "even though it is the middle of a war."

"Mr. Mustafa said the war was way east of the city," said Ralph. "That it'd be easy to hop into Aleppo and get a great story, and he gave us a safety guarantee from ISIS. We're leaving as fast as we can."

"The safety guarantee might not work with ISIS," said Ali. He stammered, "In fact, I don't see how it could."

Ralph and Doug stared, unable to move their eyes from Ali.

"Does this have something to do with Mr. Mustafa being crafty?" asked Ralph.

"It's partly my fault," said Ali. "I asked Mr. Mustafa to do whatever it took to get you here. I know your writing, Mr. Charlton. I need your help, though it's too late now. I mean, how long would it be before an article could appear? I'm sure it won't be before tonight.'

"I said call me Ralph."

"In these circumstances, I can't really call you that," pleaded Ali. "I feel too bad about Mr. Mustafa luring you to Aleppo." Ali looked like a yellow submarine, scuttled.

"An article can go online instantly, like that would do any good now. So, what's wrong with the safety guarantee?" asked Ralph, draining his gin and tonic, setting the glass on a coaster carefully, like trying to stay

105

serene.

Ali bent toward them conspiratorially. "Do you know Jürgen Todenhöfer, the German journalist?"

They shook their heads.

"Mr. Todenhöfer received a safety guarantee from ISIS. As far as I know, it's the only one ever issued. Your safety guarantee is a blueprint-quality copy with Mr. Charlton's name substituted for Jürgen Todenhöfer." Ali shot them an apologetic look'. "Mr. Mustafa makes copies all the time. A fresh safety guarantee takes five minutes and is indistinguishable from the real thing. They're handy for people smuggling antiquities to Turkey."

Ralph stared at Doug, who opened his pack, pulled out the clear plastic folder, and set it on the desk. "You can see through the plastic, or I can take it out…"

"No, that's fine," said Ali, pulling the folder around. "Oh, yes. This is the Todenhöfer safety guarantee with your name inserted. Perhaps there's nothing to worry about. Only the caliph and a few of his lieutenants would know whether it's genuine. The odds of meeting such exalted persons are slim to none. You might pull it off."

"That is so heartening," said Doug. "We might pull it off. I must write that down." He handed the big crystal glass back for a refill.

"Oh, geez, I'm out too," said Ralph, pushing his empty beaker forward. "I find I'm developing a thirst for

106

anesthetic."

"Sure," said Ali, starting another round of drinks. "But you'll be happy to hear that no one smuggling antiquities has had a safety guarantee challenged."

"Because ISIS checked it out and it passed or none have been challenged?" asked Doug dryly. "It might make a difference."

"Actually, both," said Ali, bustling around, sloshing double measures. "Think positively. If you run across ISIS, like say tonight, flash the safety guarantee with confidence." Then he added, almost too low to hear, "Though it didn't work for old Jürgen."

"We'll be fine because we have contacts," said Ralph. "Look at this." He turned the camera around, smacking it twice before it would run the video. "These are our buddies, new ISIS recruits burning their passports, and we're their guests. There's Doug cowering behind the big stone platform, and that woman is from New Jersey. We're the guests of Imam Fahd from Gilgit, and if we can't get out of Aleppo tonight we're staying with his cousin a few blocks from here."

"I must say," said Ali, "I am happy you came. I commend you for being…" He paused, searching for the right words.

"Brave beyond belief," said Doug as Ralph said, "Dumb as a box of rocks." "According to our ISIS friends," explained Ralph, "we're dumb as a box of rocks." He toasted Ali. "To Alastair, our best bet for a ride to Turkey. Maybe we could join the convoy tonight, escape all the tanks and AK-47s in town. An armored car stopped and kidnapped an old man right in front of us. Surely you're leaving too."

"I cut a deal with Assad, the FSA, and ISIS to remain here," Ali said sheepishly, "protecting the World Heritage collection. I've had to consort with all sides to buy time, digging out whatever survived after the bombing so I could sneak it to Turkey."

Ali stuck thumbs in his vest pockets and looked pleased. "I moved half the inventory to museums in Ankara, Istanbul, and Antakya. Mr. Mustafa has been exceedingly helpful."

"Impressive," said Ralph, chugging the dregs of the beaker. "Can we take a few photos while you fill us in?"

"We only have a few minutes," said Ali. "Leave your things here." He again eyed Ralph's garbage bag before leading them into the long, brightly lit corridor. "Most of the pieces have been wrapped. When we return to my office, I'll show you two special items."

Ralph shot artsy photos of shrouded figures ranging from winged lions to men with tall hats knobbed at the top, placing Ali in the photos as garnish, like a portly lemon with a mustache.

"Don't you think we should be getting on?" Doug

grumped. "It's well past your bedtime."

"Don't be silly. This is great photography. Take a look at this, Alistair," he said, holding the camera for Ali and then for bored-out-of-his-mind Doug.

Doug waved each photo away with a flip of his hand. "Oh, that is so very lovely. Oh, that is so very lovely."

Alistair moaned. "Thanks to Assad's utterly incompetent pilots, that's all that's left. The idiots were aiming at an FSA stronghold a mile south. Of course you can ride with the convoy, assuming the trucks they promised me actually show up. Assad's ministry promised three eighteen-wheelers, but two were commandeered to move arms to the front. They couldn't say when the remaining truck might arrive, and I'm sure it won't."

"I believe we caught the drift," said Doug. "You're light on trucks, would like us to smuggle a few small things, and in return, you'll help us get to Turkey, hopefully tonight, which is only fair, since you got us into this in the first place."

"You could conceal important items in that big orange pack," said Ali. "Let's go back to the office." He herded them along, bowing for them to enter.

Doug grabbed his pack off the floor and held it high with a spindly arm. "I'd have to discard valuable items, shoes and socks, my coffee press, and my special coffee…"

"British Hero Rescues World Heritage," said Ralph, hands framing headlines in the air. "You'd have a story to tell, condescendingly, as only a Brit can, casually revealing your sparkling repartee with the Queen during the knighting ceremony. You could become an actual gentleman."

Doug rolled his eyes.

Ralph nodded with mock sympathy. "I know it might be too much to ask that you serve your country and relinquish your ruffianship. But just think, you'd get back at your worthless kids. They wouldn't dare mess with Sir Doug, which would keep them from looting your modest estate."

"You don't drink tea?" asked Ali, as if Doug might be an actual ruffian.

"I despise the poor weak stuff," said Doug. He dropped his pack clanging on the floor, thinking about a knighthood. It might be the lowliest of titles, but "Sir Doug" *would* fall lightly on the ear, *and* the kids would be electrified.

Doug looked at Ali. "If you can get us out of Syria forthwith, I might be able to make room in my pack for something small and extremely valuable, though there's not much I can leave behind. Everything in my pack is absolutely necessary. Although I'm sure Ralph would compensate me for the value of the necessities that must be removed from my pack"—he finished, stammering—"and left behind forever." Doug was compelled to wipe a dry tear.

Ralph rolled his eyes. "Doug's definition of 'compensate' means luxury replacements for shoddy goods bought from bargain tables all over the world, but yes, I will. I'll reimburse poor impecunious Doug for those things that he must remove from his pack in order to rescue the world's heritage. But what happens if ISIS, or the FSA, or Assad, or a Turkish border guard catches us smuggling antiquities?"

"I would so appreciate ensnarement by a Turkish border guard," said Doug, sensing money was no longer an issue for Ralph. This was a seismic shift in bargaining positions, exposing Ralph's gleaming white underbelly. "I would let you pay for everything in my pack if we could get nabbed by a Turkish border guard in the next hour or two. But what do you care since you have the serenity thing? A coward dies a thousand deaths while you soldier gamely onward, against all odds, que sera."

"I've always emphasized the part about *the balls to change the things I can*," said Ralph, shaking hands with Ali. "We'd love a ride to Turkey tonight. But what does happen if we get caught?"

"The art would be confiscated," said Ali. "What happens to you depends on who catches you. Syrians take the removal of their heritage seriously, even if Assad

111

doesn't really give a damn."

Ali shook his head. "Maybe the task is too dangerous for the elderly. Of course, being a certain age could be the perfect camouflage for smuggling valuables. And Doug, imagine.

Knighted by the Queen."

Doug stiffened his upper lip and stuck out his chin, holding his nose high like he was passing in review before the Queen, flinching as an imaginary sword touched his shoulder. "But I don't know that I could lower myself to a mere knighthood," Doug said with a sniff. He swept the icy crystal beaker high as a toast. "However, notwithstanding my complete lack of interest in the Queen's Honours List published every New Year's and on her birthday in June, I selflessly volunteer my services to Her Majesty the Queen."

Ali sighed. "I'll do my best but would be deeply beholden if you would carry two golden statues. We'll figure out how to get you out, later." He turned to a wall safe and cranked it open, revealing two figures wrapped in sky-blue silk. Ali set them on his desk, where they shimmered in the light. They were as tall as Hollywood Oscars, but with outstretched arms.

Ali unwrapped one slowly, revealing a golden goat on its hind legs. Golden leaves jutted from golden boughs around its shoulders, and looked nothing like an Oscar. Ali couldn't resist rubbing a golden leaf with the sleeve of his yellow jacket.

"This is Sumerian," he said, "2500 BCE. Isn't it beautiful?"

They stood enthralled for a full second before Ralph whistled. "Hey, Doug. That would fetch a pretty penny on eBay. It might be worth more than a measly knighthood."

Ali gave a hearty ha-ha-ha, then said "Don't you dare," as if they were naughty chaps that he'd shake his finger at if they weren't in an old-boys club together. Instead, he sighed. "The statue is gold and lapis and was known from antiquity. Tales of old called it *Ram in a Thicket*.

They're priceless twins, the best-preserved relics to survive Babylonian Mesopotamia, from the age of Gilgamesh. These were the first gods in human history and were found in the Great Death Pit of Ur."

"I think the golden balls are a nice touch," said Ralph.

The goat was solid gold from its head to hind legs, standing like a randy Pan. The goat rested its golden hooves on a bouquet of flowers in intricately cast gold with four boughs spiraling from either side, decorated with lapis lazuli. A tube of gold protruded from the shoulders of the goat, suggesting it may have supported a bowl.

Ali carefully rewound the scarf around the Ram

and indicated the second object. "This is its twin."

"What is priceless?" asked Doug. "Is this gewgaw worth someone's head? And does that depend on whether it's your head or someone else's?"

"The curators of antiquities are unqualified to answer your question," said Ali, "the same as everyone else." He smiled as he selected a large meerschaum pipe with eagle's talons from a mahogany rack of astonishing pipes.

As he filled the pipe, he said, "The more urgent question is how to get you to Turkey, assuming transport doesn't work out." He lit the pipe with two puffs of aromatic cherry. "The shortest way is north to A'zaz on the border with Kilis in Turkey. Museum patrons will load personal vehicles with whatever we can fit inside and take that route. Of course, we may have to head west to Antioch, which is farther. Whatever we do will be by the seat of our pants."

"So north would be the shortest route if, for example, everything falls through and we have to walk," said Doug, "which would be my preference." He waved smoke away from his face.

"A trail parallels the road. Younger men have carried antiquities in backpacks larger than Doug's by far, though we've never had any carried in a garbage bag before. Unfortunately, the movable inventory would fill seven of my nonexistent eighteen-wheelers." The pipe pulled down the corner of Ali's mouth as he wrung his hands like a little yellow windmill.

Ali scraped out the meerschaum pipe and placed it back on the rack. "There will be ample reward for those who assist. May I henceforth refer to you as Sir Doug?"

"Don't give him ideas," said Ralph, setting the empty glass down like he was feeling good, "because ever one Ram is too wide to fit in Doug's pack. The boughs stick out a foot. They'd have to be bent flat to fit in any bag."

Ali shuddered at Ralph's bag. "I would normally be aghast at such a suggestion, but that's how they were found—the stems flattened against the body from the soil in the Death Pit. I'll bend them into the smallest package possible. You go ahead and take a few photos outside while I make a few phone calls and secure the Rams. We have to hurry because at midnight the Turks start shooting at anything that moves."

"I have to leave my pack here?" asked Doug, stopping short at Ali's raised eyebrows. "What do we do with the Rams if we get them out? I mean, besides eBay," asked Ralph. Ali rolled his eyes. "Any museum in Turkey will take care of them, from Antakya to Ankara to Istanbul. They're insulated from government corruption. Of course, any curator would recognize the Rams."

Doug inclined his head. "And what if we keep one as a souvenir for our trouble?"

"If I get you out of Syria and save you from ISIS, that wouldn't be very gentlemanly," said Ali, his jaw rigid from how far the old-boy's circle was stretching.

Doug laughed at his discomfiture. "I'm not a gentleman yet. Anyway, you'll have to give me a few minutes to inventory my pack so Ralph knows what he has to pay for when we get back. And I have to decide which stuff Ralph has to help carry…"

"Like the French press you got for free?" Ralph huffed. "A story I heard a dozen times, and the two kilos of coffee you got a deal on in Tbilisi, that you've been carrying around ever since."

"And my toothbrush," said Doug snootily.

"I'm not carrying an electric toothbrush. Or that metal-loop thing you use to heat your coffee or any of your other weird stuff. You should learn to pack light like I do—one toothbrush, a change of clothes, and essential electronics. A much lighter way to go."

As Doug started to open his mouth, Ralph said, "Remember the knighthood, Sir Doug.

And let's skip Reee-shard's. He could be an ISIS sympathizer ready to grab us."

"Not possible," snapped Doug. "Fahd's on the up and up. I'm a better judge of character than you'll ever be. But I agree. There's no reason to go to Reee-shard's. I'm ready to walk to Turkey. You know we can do it. How far is it, Ali…er, stair?"

"Fifty K," said Ali.

"A measly thirty miles," said Ralph. "You're right. We could do it overnight, assuming I don't have to carry extra weight. I'm not taking one pound of your stuff no matter how essential you think it is. It'd take me all night to walk thirty miles with an empty bag."

"You are a bit slow," said Doug, "and getting slower." He shook his head. "Age catches up with everyone, faster for some. In a year you'll be too knackered to walk around the block. So there's apparently no choice but to walk, Ali"—he choked—"stair."

Alistair let them out the front door and Jeffrey gave them a tour of the east ruins while Ralph snapped dark photos of rubble, and in a few minutes they worked around the back past a wide door lit by a brilliant rectangle of light above a loading dock with four cars and two vans lined up.

Doug yelped. "We don't know those people inside. I have to go check on my pack." He scooted between two cars, stopping short at the red sign on the front door of the museum:

CLOSED

"You think that son of a bitch Ali just wanted to steal my pack?" screeched Doug as Ralph and Jeffrey huffed up. "We haven't been gone five minutes."

Ralph scoffed. "The sign is new. And no one would steal a pack full of worthless crap, so don't worry

117

about it." He pounded on the beautifully embossed front door of the museum.

Ali answered the door. "Everyone's inside crating and wrapping, for all the good that's going to do." He took an anxious breath. "None of the big trucks are coming, not a single one.

We're cramming personal vehicles, but it's hopeless." He gestured them inside like a whirling yellow dervish. As they sidled by, Ali said to Jeffrey, "Stay alert. It's going to be a long night."

He pushed the mighty door closed, lifting the steel bar and sliding it through the brackets. Doug and Ralph stared at the brilliantly lit museum. A dozen men had formed a chain, passing items to the loading dock in the back corner.

Ali wrung his hands. "It's the last closing time, I'm afraid. And I am afraid." "Where's Ms. Helen?" asked Ralph, glancing at the vacant desk. "Did she get safely home?"

"No," said Ali. "Helen insisted on staying. She's still wrapping items in the back, but she has to leave soon."

Ali fretted, hands doing pushups against each other as he paced. "I haven't gotten the Rams packed," he said, flitting around like a sunbeam. "I've called around, but I've had no luck getting you a ride. Everyone is leaving or already left. We don't have room for the more important pieces, and our few vehicles probably won't make it to the border. We've had better luck with men on foot. If ISIS takes Aleppo, we'll lose everything. Yes, I am afraid."

Ali was shivering, twirling his mustache with his fingers. "I'm afraid for the museum, for myself, and for you because you're on your own getting out of Aleppo. I don't know what it looks like outside, but it looks like a full-blown war between the Kurds, FSA, ISIS, the regime, and splinter groups, every one of them with tanks and bazookas. The regime is firing missiles and dropping barrel bombs. There are rumors of poison gas, which would be Assad's style."

"We're ready to hit the road," Doug said, waggling his eyebrows. "We'll be stopping at the mosque on the way out, maybe say a prayer or something. As soon as I grab my pack, we'll be on the road again." He grinned, happy as a geezer.

Ralph nodded. "We should stop by the mosque. Sometimes chances must be taken, even if an AK-47 might be too heavy to lug thirty miles." Ralph held up a finger to deflect Doug's interruption. "Walking is the easiest option, though I'd rather find a motorbike so I don't have to run all the way to Turkey."

"I'm not riding on a motorbike with you," said Doug. "And anyway, it would cost way too much to rent a motorbike. Everyone in town wants one."

"What's your crinkly old skin worth compared to the price of a motorbike? Get us to Turkey, pronto!"

"You're trying to kill me. I couldn't bike a block without crashing, much less fifty K." At Ralph's withering look, Doug muttered, "Maybe if we went slow," he said, pausing, "but slow enough wouldn't be as fast as I can walk, and I prefer to walk."

"So why don't you look where you want to go instead of where you don't want to go? Let me put it this way." Ralph put a fist under his chin. "Your life or a motorbike; which will it be?

We don't have much choice, except walking all night. That would screw up my neck worse than it already is."

Doug waved Ralph away. "A Marine must develop a high pain threshold, a threshold so high that pain does not exist. Get over it, soldier."

"AK-47s aren't heavy," said Ali as he led them back to his office.

The lights silhouetted men carrying pieces to the outside loading dock, casting shadows that painted the museum a surrealistic sepia. Ali flipped a switch on the intercom and glided behind the big desk. "If they're ready, Helen, bring them in," he said, toggling off.

They could hear a sudden tap-tap-tap-tap on the marble floor, fast like a geisha in high heels. Helen swerved past the big picture window, awkwardly balanced with her arms out wide.

She carried two figures draped in blue as she turned through the door sideways, setting them on the desk. Golden branches like wings showed faintly through the silk. "I haven't wrapped them yet, and I still think it'd be safer—" She stopped abruptly at Ali's frown.

Ali said in a measured tone, "Thank you, Helen. You must leave now. Don't keep putting it off."

"Be safe, Alistair. And good luck to you two," she said, head held high as her heels beat a staccato retreat and the boys said goodbye, waving at her back.

Ali nervously adjusted his yellow tie. "It's going to be tough to get to Turkey without running into trouble or getting lost. You'll have to dodge militias in the dark." He paused, looking at them. "You will definitely run into trouble."

CHAPTER EIGHT — ESCAPE FROM ALEPPO

The last vehicle had left, and the museum was still full of antiquities when Ali finally got around to folding the glittery golden boughs of the Rams.

"This is the way they were found," said Ali, sighing.

"They look better that way but too heavy to carry thirty miles," said Ralph. "I'm not sure I can do it."

Ali wrapped the diminished Rams in the layers of blue silk. "This will help cushion them.

I worry about you getting lost."

"No way," said Ralph. "We're geniuses at maps and directions. We never get lost." He paused. "Well, we got lost once in Brussels. But we only have to glance at a map and we can go anywhere, find anything. Would you happen to have a spare map?"

"Not a problem," said Ali, opening the top drawer of his desk. "I keep maps for visitors." The boys sighed in relief, gathering around as Ali spread the map across the desk, rubbing the creases flat. "We're here, of course." He pointed at the big red star labeled Halab. "The province is Halab, and Halab means Aleppo. You can see it's farther to backtrack west to Antioch. Due north is closest, so always bear north and west." His finger traced the route.

"Be careful, because this takes you close to Dabiq." Ali pointed at a small red dot barely east of due north. "Dabiq is controlled by a nasty branch of ISIS."

"Every branch of ISIS is nasty…" Doug muttered.

"Oh, yeah," said Ralph. "We got the Dabiq story in Technicolor from our Jersey friend, the Sharia lawyer. We definitely want to stay away from Dabiq."

They pored over the map as Ali traced the route. "Aim for Kaljibrin and work north from there. None of the secondary roads cross into Turkey. You'll have to sneak across an unfenced part of the border, if you can find one. The main crossings are guarded by the Turkish army, and the rest is razor wire."

Ali handed the map to Ralph, who folded it into a square and stowed it in his back pocket.

Doug propped his big ugly orange pack on Ali's desk and flipped open the top. "What were you saying about AK-47s, Ali…stair?"

"An AK-47 weighs two to four kilos, depending," said Ali. "The new ones are lighter.

It's the ammo that's heavy."

"Wow," said Ralph. "You sound like an expert."

Ali shrugged. "It's basic survival. I have two AK-47s at home. They're easy to fire but hard to control."

"Great," said Doug, "the gun is light but the ammo is too heavy to carry. Big help, that." "I have a Swiss Army knife," Ralph said.

"You are so lazy," said Doug. "You have a change of clothes, a toothbrush, a Swiss Army knife, and now a road map."

"Plus two cans of sardines, my tablet, and camera," said Ralph. "You even ran out of toothpaste. You borrow everything from me."

"I only borrowed toothpaste that one time in Sevastopol," said Ralph. "Boy, you never forget some things, but you always forget I can't carry a lot of weight." He rubbed his neck theatrically.

"Your whole body should be condemned…"

Ali held up his hands. "Please, gentlemen. Remember, Doug could become a knight." Ali smiled. "I would recommend a knighthood for any British person who single-handedly saved the Rams, which are among the most valuable of the world's heritage."

Doug scoffed. "We only said we'd carry the Rams if you found transportation, and you didn't."

Ali put his hands out. "Queen and country calls. You're my only chance of getting them out since everyone else has left. You have to try."

"We don't have to," said Ralph, looking resolute. "But Alistair is right. No one else can do it but us, and we did sort of promise we would. I will fight through the pain, like a Marine."

Doug stood with his chin in his hand, looking like Jack Benny, weighing a knighthood against a world travel kit, a life as Sir Doug against the irreplaceable contents of his pack. He clutched his throat, thinking about his deadbeat kids and how a knighthood would protect the few assets he had left.

"I'll do it," he said valiantly, like a hero. "We will rescue the Rams."

Ali sighed. "You'll have to dodge ISIS, the FSA, Assad's cutthroats, bandits and ragtag militia, random missiles, bombs, and trigger-happy renegades. But Mr. Mustafa says you've been everywhere and are quick on your feet, or at least you walk fast."

Ralph pointed at Doug. "He walks *real* fast."

"There's still the problem of fitting a Ram in my pack," Doug said.

"Just see what you can do," said Ali, handing one to Ralph and the other to Doug.

Ralph hefted his Ram. "Wow, it's a heavy little bugger, isn't it?" He set it on the desk. "It weighs more like a Rambo in a thicket, so Rambo it is." He opened his garbage bag, wrapped a spare outfit around the Ram, and dropped it inside. Ali winced.

Doug rummaged inside his pack and removed a large aluminum cook set. "For Rambo to travel, I fear I am obliged to abandon my plates and utensils." He easily fit the Rambo inside the pack. He turned to Ralph. "Do not forget. That was specially reinforced aluminum," he said, pronouncing it al-lu-*min*-um. "You owe me forty quid."

"You've never used that cookware in your entire life, you pirate," said Ralph. "And you've never spent forty quid on anything except a plane ticket. You don't cook, so that was extra weight you should have been abandoned years ago." He looked up as if picturing the future. "Doug owes me heartfelt thanks for relieving him of an unnecessary burden and therefore cancels the forty-quid debt I never had."

As Doug began an eloquent response, Ali held up his hands. "I've got to get out of this place if it's the last thing I ever do, so stop it. I thank you, and I thank you," he said, turning to each in turn, "for taking the Rams, and I hope the map helps."

Ralph started to ask if the map might not help but said, "You'll love the story on the museum when we get out. If we get out."

"We'll email you first thing from Turkey," said Doug. "Then you can start the paperwork for the knighthood." He beamed and headed out.

Ralph groaned, hefting the bag over his shoulders, gritting his teeth as the Rambo poked his neck. He tottered out of the office to find Doug lifting the steel bar from its brackets and pushing on the massive front door, which swung open to an inferno.

The mosque was engulfed in fire a short block away. The wind whipped flames the length of the minaret.

Orange and red tongues licked the walls from tiny windows near the top. A fire truck bumped down the street toward the mosque with four men on the back but the intense heat forced them to stop short.

"This is our big chance to nick an AK-47," Doug yelled. He took off like a shot, skirting the chaos of worshippers pushed outside when a bomb or missile had interrupted the last prayers of the evening.

Ralph yelped. "My pack is way too heavy, man. I can't carry a Rambo thirty miles. We have to get a ride. Anyway, how can you nick an AK-47 from a firestorm?"

Doug didn't appear to hear him. "Wait the fuck up," Ralph screamed at Doug's rapidly disappearing back, clenching his teeth and running as Doug ducked around the side of the mosque. They headed for the miniature door that opened into the check-room filled with guns.

Ralph caught up as Doug edged into the sanctuary on tiptoe. From a distance, firefighters shot a puny stream of water at a wall of flame shooting up the minaret.

"Shoes," hollered Ralph. "We could get in trouble if we don't take our shoes off." "Dim-witted American," screeched Doug. "Come on, here's the little back door." He punched it with an elbow, and it swung open easily. Doug peeked through. "Hurry up. Three gentlemen were in a real hurry and left three lovely AK-47s."

Doug wriggled through the small door as a firefighter entered the hall from the rear, yelling

127

something that probably meant "thief, thief."

Doug's pack swung wildly from side to side as he ran back toward the little door, dragging a newly acquired AK-47 behind him, knocking Ralph down as Ralph tried to step through the door at the same time.

Doug held the gun by its sling, yelling back at Ralph, "Get up you dozy-poke, and run as fast as you can."

The fireman sprinted in their direction, pointing at Ralph and yelling at another fireman behind him. The firemen were interrupted by intense heat surging in waves as the flaming minaret shuddered and collapsed in slow motion. They ran for their lives as Ralph staggered to his feet and scooted through the miniature door, breaking into a desperate run, holding his pants up with one hand, the bag in the other, and yelling at Doug as the minaret crashed in an explosion of bricks.

Ralph rolled up the waist of his pants as he ran. "You're getting way too bossy, but it does my heart good to see you running for the first time ever."

Ralph's arms and legs pumped like a rocket as he tried to keep Doug in sight around the side of the mosque.

"Stop, stop!" Ralph yelled as Doug ran across a wide parking lot filled with dozens of motorbikes. "Look at this motorbike." Ralph's finger shook, and his chest heaved as he stood pointing at a battered bike.

Doug pivoted back. "You can't possibly fancy that

bike. It's a rust bucket. We'd die on that."

The bike was a rainbow of ugly from its rusty fenders to faded green gas tank, a dull wreck in the orange light of the fire. Doug shook his head. "I hate bikes, and this bike is worse than any bike I've ever seen. And here comes the fireman who was pointing at us..."

Ralph gasped. "My bag's too heavy to carry, but you'd rather get shot than ride a motorbike with the keys in it, ready to roll." He jumped on the bike, tied the garbage bag around his waist, turned the key, and kicked the stand up, searching feverishly for a starter button.

"Maybe someone removed a doohickey so their bike doesn't get stolen," said Doug, swinging the AK-47 off his shoulder. He climbed on the back. "And I got no room with your garbage bag in my lap, but you damn well better hurry up and figure it out."

Ralph frantically searched the instrument panel, which consisted of a tiny window with needles labeled *petrol* and *batt.*

"Get a move on," yelled Doug. "That fireman is almost on us. This thing is so old it probably needs a crank." Doug started to swing his leg off. "We have no time..."

Ralph sighed. Spotting the kick-starter, he flipped it down, kicking viciously. The bike coughed anemically. Ralph held tight onto the brakes, revving the engine as it caught.

The fireman threw himself at the motorbike the same instant that Ralph let off the brake. The bike surged forward like molasses, and the fireman landed on his face, inches behind the back wheel as they putted slowly onto the street with Doug halfway on.

"Watch out! Hello, Ralph," yelled Doug as Ralph slid the bike into traffic, pulling too wide, sideswiping a pickup with a machine gun mounted on the back, scraping his rear bumper. The gentleman manning the gun shook a fist at them.

"Christ, watch what you're doing. You'll get us killed," yelled Doug, grabbing Ralph around the waist and holding on tight.

Heavily laden carts moved jerkily down Asia Road, most pushed by hand. Their side of the road was filled with pedestrians and motorbikes while more pickups with machine guns careened past them in a convoy.

Ralph swerved. "Don't hold on to me. Grab the side handles over the back wheel." Ralph hit a pothole as Doug shifted radically on the back.

"Watch it buster," Ralph yelped, desperately sliding to rebalance after the near upset. "Like I could do that with a big pack and a machine gun, and I don't balance awfully well anyway. Maybe you shouldn't have sideswiped that pickup because it seems to be suffering road rage."

The pickup had made a U-turn and was roaring up behind them. Doug panicked, jumping like a cat and losing control of the AK-47.

The gun somersaulted off Doug's back, hitting the road behind them as the armed pickup closed in on the motorbike. A dozen spits of orange fire erupted, *rat-a-tat-tat*. A random shot exploded a front tire of the pickup, and it veered into the other lane, knocking over a pushcart and crashing into the front of a public urinal. A solar light illuminated a small sign over the urinal that said in small English letters "Entrance, men only."

Ralph's teeth chattered as he screeched, "We turn here and go north, only north. North..." He turned the rickety motorbike onto another wide street jammed with vehicles as Doug smacked him on the back of the head.

"Not that way. That's northeast. You know we can't go northeast. We'll end up in Dabiq."

"You lost our precious AK-47, and now we're easy prey for every hooligan in Syria." Men with guns loitered under streetlights as the explosions in the southeast moved toward them faster than the motorbike could putt.

Doug stuck out his bony chest. "I shot the tires off that pickup truck and braved enemy fire. If I were with your lot I'd get the Congressional Medal of Honor."

"There's probably no fuel in this thing so watch for a gas... petrol station..." Ralph screeched to a halt.

Traffic was blocked by a tank painted in camouflage like no one would notice it. Soldiers herded trucks, pickups, bicycles, and hundreds of motorbikes in a continuous river of traffic to the right of the tank. Everyone honked and spewed exhaust under the glare of the turret pointed down their throats.

"We need the road behind the tank." Doug pointed. "Otherwise we'll have to turn around and cut over to go northwest."

They looked at each other, thinking the same thing, but Ralph said it first. "Real men don't backtrack."

"Unfortunately, everyone has a gun except us," said Doug. For the first time ever, he hung his head. "I shouldn't have dropped the gun."

"Wisdom will someday come, maybe," said Ralph. "Of course, wisdom often arrives late for those from countries suffering a loss of empire." He laughed. "Such a loss can retard the spirit of an entire population. But buck up, and let's talk to that spiffy-looking sergeant."

A big man with three yellow stripes on his sleeve stood at parade rest. He wore a green helmet that matched a sharply pressed uniform and a tiny mustache on an olive-complexioned face. But no one in their right mind would laugh at an Arnold Schwarzenegger lookalike, even wearing white tennis shoes. In their minds, they had already nicknamed him Arnie.

Ralph revved the engine and slid the motorbike up to the sergeant, who looked like he got it on with barbells. The sergeant stood ramrod straight, looking at them icy-eyed as if to say, "How dare you come unbidden into the presence of the lord of the universe?"

Doug lumbered off the back of the bike, leaned his pack against the tread of the tank, and stretched theatrically. "Good sir, we have come on a mission from the Aleppo museum and are headed to Turkey. Could we please pass in that direction? Purty please?"

Doug pointed behind the tank at the northwest fork of a beautifully dark and empty road, looking peaceful and quiet compared to the rest of Aleppo.

The sergeant relaxed and shook his head as if he'd placed them as harmless fucks. "If you were allowed to go down that road there wouldn't be a tank stopping you." Arnie patted a tread. "That's the whole point of this baby. To keep refugees out of Turkey."

Arnie bent and whispered to Doug like he was doing his civic duty. "We're paid by the Turks. Erdoğan wants to keep the riffraff out of Turkey. The only reason to take this road is to sneak into Turkey illegally. Sorry, gentlemen." He pointed west. "Try west toward Antioch. That border is still open."

"Yeah, yeah," said Ralph. "We know it's open because we came in that way. But Antioch is twice as far and would take hours in traffic, blockades, checkpoints, explosive devices. And besides, what's the difference? Either way is Turkey. Why block a road that would take no time compared to making us suffer on the other one for hours, if we're lucky?"

The sergeant shook his head at their naivety. "I'm paid to block this road. I'm not paid to block the other road."

"We're obviously not refugees," sniffed Doug, raising his eyebrows regally and laying on the syrup. "So there is no reason to shuffle us the long way around, especially in the middle of a war. That would be most unkind."

The tough sergeant smiled. "I do what I'm paid to do."

The point dawned on Doug and Ralph simultaneously. They began staring each other down, eye-wrestling to see who'd contribute to the sergeant's retirement fund.

"I'll give you fifty bucks to let us take that road," Ralph said to Arnie. "Oh, and I need a gallon of petrol, gas for the bike. If you could throw in a few liters of fuel, it wouldn't cost you anything."

The sergeant smiled with Arnie disingenuousness. "One hundred dollars including a liter of petrol." He tilted his helmet back to take a closer look at them.

"Sure," said Ralph. "That's easy. Fifty bucks from each of us."

Doug reached for his neck-wallet, but his fingers trembled, and he couldn't make his hands work. He clutched the shirt over his heart and mimed a death spiral, an apparent goner with his time utterly up.

The sergeant laughed. "There is a big cheapskate like you on the new American program we get, called Jack Benny." He couldn't stop laughing. "Your friend is even worse than Mr. Benny."

"He is miles worse," said Ralph.

"He's a funny old bird. I'll let you have the road and the fuel for seventy-five dollars." Doug had twenty-five dollars out of his neck-wallet and the wallet restowed before Ralph or the sergeant could move a muscle. He held it toward the sergeant. "If you'd rather, I could do another impression. I'm sure one of my famous soliloquies would bring you more joy than wrinkly pieces of paper. After all, what benefit doth lucre hold compared to hilarity for a man?"

Doug started to pull the currency back, but the sergeant was quicker, grabbing the twenty-five dollars.

"Maybe next time," said the sergeant, holding his hand out to Ralph.

"Now, wait. That's thirty-seven fifty each," said Ralph. When Doug just stared at him, he sighed, handing over fifty dollars. "You are such a cheapskate."

Arnie led them behind the tank. "Prop the bike here." He shook his head as Ralph searched the motorbike for the fuel intake. "The gas cap is next to the seat." Arnie hefted the huge metal can like a feather, pouring a thin stream of gasoline into the tiny opening, stopping abruptly as it overflowed, slopping down the side of the bike.

Arnie tried not to laugh. "It didn't take much."

Doug was aghast. "It sure as hell didn't take much." He glared at Ralph. "I should get a refund for the petrol, my twenty-five dollars back."

Ralph ignored him and hit the starter. The engine caught, sounding like it was full of mud.

***

The motorbike's dim headlight showed ridges of grass growing through the broken pavement while the buildings on either side cast long fractured shadows from ruined brick walls with empty windows.

"I was defrauded by your failure to determine the state of our petrol, paying twenty-five dollars unnecessarily," Doug groused. "And this road doesn't seem to go anywhere. Where are we, and how does this fit with the map?"

"You should occasionally look on the bright side. The fuel is topped up, and we're headed in a direction that feels like north. And look, we're out of town. We escaped Aleppo."

"But in the dark, who knows which direction

we're really going? The road could curve either way, and we wouldn't be able to tell." Doug squinted for stars, but they were hidden by billowing clouds, and the wind was rising. Explosions in the southeast were fainter, the occasional burst reflecting off of clouds.

After an eerie half hour the headlight picked up a chain-link fence ten feet high with five strands of barbed wire on top, crowding both sides of the road. The headlight bounced in a sudden dip, shining off oversized barbs as the road changed from potholes to brand-new pavement.

Their balance bordered on the precarious as the motorbike toiled up a very long hill, underpowered and overwhelmed, moving even slower as they neared the top, which was edged with a halo of light. The sides of the road had narrowed, hemmed in by the claustrophobic fence. They inched to the brow of the hill, the motorbike huffing into a jerky chug on top where the glow resolved into a regiment of klieg lights spread out for miles below, turning night into day.

The bike plunged into a vertiginous downhill swoop, seeming to reach the speed of sound. Far below them, a lit-up military base stretched for miles, bordered by the fence that had funneled them there. As they careened down the hill, they could see barracks jamming the west side of the base. The east was split into two crisscrossed runways, one twice as long as the other. They clung to each other, frozen on the bike as it catapulted down the hill. As one jet landed on the long runway, another wheeled into place and squealed off.

The road at the bottom of the hill was barred by a chain-link gate in front of a wooden sentry box. Ralph skidded sideways, sliding to a desperate stop in front. Inside stood a very young soldier with a rifle topped by a long bayonet. Doug toppled onto the sidewalk with his big orange pack, jumping up in front of the peach-fuzz face of the guard.

A beautifully painted sign was lettered in big Arabic and small Roman letters. The legible part at the bottom said: Minakh Air Force Base.

CHAPTER NINE—MINAKH AFB

Ralph recovered from the near crash, flipping the guard box soldier a crisp salute. "Greetings, fellow Marine."

The guard snapped to attention, lifted his rifle, and did a maneuver like a college ROTC squadron. He flipped the bayoneted rifle in the air and caught it before saluting. "Sirs. The entrance to the Base is off the other highway. The road you came from is closed, and this gate is no longer open. I trust you have not been inconvenienced."

He shifted the rifle to an at-ease position. "Sirs," he said as he slammed the butt of the rifle on the concrete. His nametag read something in Arabic, and under that it said "Najd."

Ralph peeled the map out of his back pocket and saluted again. "At ease, Najd," he said, tripping over the pronunciation so it came out Najed. "Er, my fellow Marine."

He unfolded the map, and Doug stabbed at an intersection in north Aleppo. "That's where the tank was. We took this road. There's no air force base in the way."

Ralph pored over the map, looking for the copyright. "Crap. This map is ten years old." He looked at Najd. "How long has the base been here?"

"I was told two years, sir." Najd snapped to

attention. "How did you get here, sir? This road is closed. If you go back five kilometers, another road will take you around the base, then toward Turkey, if that's where you're headed, sirs." Every time he said "sirs," he clomped the rifle butt on the concrete, bouncing it back up into his hand.

Doug rolled his eyes as the kid exchanged salutes with Ralph. "Why would you salute this old man? He's a civilian. He doesn't even have a proper hat. Look at it. It says Arizona. It doesn't say Marines or Air Force."

"I'm new," Najd stuttered. "I haven't had basic training. No time in the middle of a war. I was told I was the lowest of the low and to salute everyone. It worked all week…"

"Don't pay any attention to him," said Ralph soothingly. "He's jealous of everything military, Najed."

Najd flinched every time Ralph massacred his name but smiled when Ralph said, "You'll be a fine soldier." They exchanged fresh salutes.

"I wish you'd get over your military delusion," said Doug. "We were cleaned out and badly used by Sergeant Arnie of some military or other. You owe me twenty-five dollars, sucking my money into a scam like that."

"It's entirely your fault," said Ralph. "My part of the deal was not just the fuel but getting us past the tank, which was worth seventy-five bucks by itself."

The kid soldier stood at attention, staring over their heads as if he couldn't hear a word.

At Doug's incredulous look Ralph added, "It was worth every penny if we'd needed the fuel. You had as much responsibility to check the fuel level as I did, but no. You've been no help getting us to Turkey. I've been doing it all."

"I'm not a motorbike expert, but you pretend to be an expert at everything when you didn't even know about the starter or the fuel tank. You're Walter Mitty Magoo, always trying to palm your mistakes off on me," said Doug. "You must learn to take personal responsibility for your actions. At your age, there doesn't seem to be much hope, but right now that's not important." He looked at Ralph as if to say "so I'll have to be the adult here." "The question is, what now? We can't go back."

Ralph looked inquiringly at Doug the grump. "What? Yes, right. We can't go back." It was good to agree on one thing, that real men did not backtrack, waste fuel, and meet back up with Arnie again.

Doug looked at the kid. "Can we walk around the outside of the base?"

"Well, you could," said the kid, lowering his gaze. "But the perimeter is mined."

"How about a pass so we can cut across the base and go out the other side?" asked Ralph, flipping a crisp salute.

141

The soldier shook his head. "Well, sir, I can't rightly do that." His return salute was notable for its lack of enthusiasm. "I don't know which Marines you're with, but it can't be any Marines we have reciprocity with. The Syrian Air Force doesn't have reciprocity with many other Marines. Actually, none, I think, sir."

At that second, a jeep roared into view, careening toward the gate.

"Oh, shit, sir," Najd said hastily. "It's time to change the guard. You might want to backtrack... Oh, I guess it's too late."

The kid soldier's rather large replacement exited the jeep and unholstered a firearm. "Who are these intruders?" the new guard demanded.

The nametag under the squiggly part said Zamoode, but the brute in ugly army green looked like his name should be Unjolly Green Giant. "Why aren't they under arrest?"

Ralph saluted Zamoode, and Zamoode took the opportunity to press the muzzle of the pistol against Ralph's forehead, right under his saluting hand.

"Why the hell are you saluting me?" Zamoode screamed. "You're not military. Not unless nursing homes are making up battalions these days. And you're certainly not Syrian. You're both under arrest. Get 'em up." He gestured with the gun without removing the muzzle from Ralph's eyebrow.

Ralph jumped, rubbing his forehead. "Let's be careful there. You wouldn't want to hurt someone with thin skin just like your grandpappy."

"You're bleeding," Doug said. A few drops fell on Ralph's grimy yellow shirt. "Maybe you'll get a Purple Heart."

"Oh, my goodness," said Ralph. "I need to rinse the shirt so it doesn't stain. I only have two shirts." He pulled a hankie out of his back pocket, spit on a corner, and dabbed frantically, smearing a liver-like splotch.

"Shut up and get into the jeep, you skinny old wimps," Zamoode said. He pointed at Ralph. "This one is stupid to worry about a little scratch when I might just shoot him for fun." He twirled the gun on his finger like a twenty-first century cowboy, flipping it to aim at Ralph's forehead. "You're like a little girl, going on about a scratch. Get your sorry ass into that jeep," he screamed. "Now!"

As Zamoode herded Doug into the jeep, Ralph gave up on a bad job, folded the handkerchief, and shoved it back in his pocket and yelled, "Stop! I'm not worried about a little scratch. I just don't want to ruin one of my only two shirts. Anyway, I can't leave the motorbike here."

"You most certainly can," said Zamoode, flexing his biceps as he slapped the pistol back into its holster. "Take these two to headquarters, Private Najd."

"Oh, the 'j' is silent," said Ralph.

"I meant to mention that, sir," said Najd.

"Stop calling these clowns 'sir,'" snarled Zamoode. "Yes, sir," said Najd, snapping a crisp salute at Zamoode.

Speaking to Doug, Najd said, "Go ahead and get into the jeep. You, si— Er... mister, follow behind the jeep with the motorbike."

Zamoode glowered, standing with his hands on his hips, watching intently as the jeep and motorbike sped into the lit-up heart of Minakh Air Force Base. The main road bustled with fuel trucks and uniformed pedestrians as they drove between low barracks and administrative offices on one side with runways on the other. The runways were separated from the road by a high- security fence, the scene bathed in blue light that cast flickering shadows and a halo around the razor wire and aluminum posts.

Ralph parked the motorbike next to the jeep as Najd stopped in front of a low building painted a forbidding gray.

"In here, fellows," said Najd. "Come meet the duty officer. He'll decide what to do with you. You're lucky it's not Zamoode."

A young lieutenant stood behind a high desk surrounded by bulletin boards and phones, holding an arm over a register he was reading intently, wearing a nametag that said "Johnny." Johnny was dressed sharply in gabardine, his dark hair cropped short and his face shiny with an almost visibly growing beard that probably needed shaving three times a day. A fan behind him blew wildly, causing the papers to flutter with a large stack secured under a chunk of rose quartz while Lt. Johnny concentrated on the vibrating ledger. The temperature was sweltering, like a furnace was stuck on high.

"Wow," said Ralph. "I didn't know Johnny was a Syrian name."

"Gentlemen," said Lt. Johnny, looking up, "what are you doing at Minakh Air Force Base? Sergeant Zamoode called and said you're spies for the FSA."

A look of disbelief crossed the lieutenant's face as he craned his neck for a closer look. "But that's silly. You're obviously up past your bedtimes. Way past." He laughed at his own joke. "I suppose you thought this was a shortcut to Turkey. Now you know it isn't. Passports, please," he said, holding out his hand, tapping a finger on the counter.

"If you promise you won't keep it," said Doug, digging the neck-wallet from his shirt, shielding it with his body, furtively extracting a shiny red passport, and *zip,* whistling it shut to conceal the contents.

"You're in no position to make demands," said Lt. Johnny. "Go ahead, Private Najd." He jerked his thumb to dismiss Najd out the door. "You're off duty. Report to the chow hall and the barracks."

Ralph started to whip off a crisp salute but dropped his hand, waving to Najd. "Thanks for the help. Best of luck in your air force career, but if you want some real excitement, sign up with the Marines."

Najd started to return the salute, squelched the reflex as Lt. Johnny stared at him, and waved instead. "Good luck, gentlemen. I hope you make it to Turkey."

"And your passport," Lt. Johnny said to Ralph, who was busy digging through the black garbage bag.

"Here, sir," said Ralph, saluting the lieutenant.

"Enough of that nonsense," said Lt. Johnny. "You have no business saluting anyone.

Why are you here? A Brit and"—he looked at Ralph's passport—"an American in the middle of the Syrian civil war? Are you social workers or something? And what's that poking out of, good grief, your garbage bag?" A tiny horn of blue lapis peeked out.

"It seemed like a good idea at the time," said Ralph, handing over his passport, furtively shoving the *Ram in a Thicket* farther down in the bag while nudging the blue shirt and beige pants over the top. "I'm writing an article on the Aleppo museum. Its priceless Assyrian treasures are at great risk of destruction…"

"You're telling me," said Lt. Johnny, slamming their passports on the counter, knocking the quartz rock off the stack of papers. The fan blew papers everywhere.

Lt. Johnny was irritated, snapping off the fan. "I don't have time to deal with trivia, but speaking of priceless Assyrian treasures, let's see what you have there…"

Heat descended like a tarp as the last of the papers fluttered to the floor, ignored by Lt. Johnny as Ralph stood blushing, ears red like he'd been caught doing something bad.

Lt. Johnny sighed as he picked up clumps of papers, bending to retrieve a batch at the boy's feet, slapping papers on the desk, securing them with the block of quartz, and switching the fan back on.

The lieutenant stood grimly with his hands on the counter as beads of sweat trickled down faces and necks, dried, and trickled some more. Doug turned this way and that in the breeze as the lieutenant demanded, "Where did you get it?"

Ralph stood at rigid attention. "I could tell you, but its top secret, so then I'd have to kill you."

The lieutenant had a glazed look on his face, unbelieving. "Are you insane?" Doug started edging his pack toward the door with his foot, slowly, slowly.

Ralph waved his hands in a placating mode. "For your information, this is your entire fault. The Syrian Air Force bombed the Aleppo museum, and the curator asked me to transport this to safety in Turkey. You're the bad guys because you bombed the museum, and I'm the good guy here, so just give me a second."

Ralph sat the bag on the counter, pulling out the *Ram in a Thicket* with the Columbia shirt and pants flapping in the breeze of the cyclone fan. He extracted the statue and set the Ram in front of Lt. Johnny.

Lt. Johnny stared at the Ram, speechless as Ralph neatly folded his clothes and placed them next to the Rambo, wiping his sweating hands inside his pants pockets.

"Kind of nice, isn't it?" Ralph asked.

Doug nudged his pack another few inches toward the door.

"Turkey?" yelled the lieutenant, suddenly aggressive. "Turkey isn't a safe place for Syrian heritage. Turkey has stolen our birthright in the past." He pounded the desk. "You can't trust a Turk."

The lieutenant looked closely at the statue. "A very nice *Ram in a Thicket*, one of two in existence. Syria will never get this back if you take it to Turkey."

"I assume you're not appropriating it for yourselves." He took a fresh look at Ralph and Doug, at Doug standing innocently, shielding his repositioned pack. "No, I didn't think so."

"Well, if I shouldn't take it to Turkey, then you keep the damn thing," said Ralph, wiping his face with a blood-smeared hankie. "It weighs too much to carry around. It's been killing my neck and shoulders, see? Right here." He reached around, showing the lieutenant where it hurt, feeling the damp shirt. "Damn, it's hot."

The lieutenant waved Ralph away, fascinated with the Ram, gingerly touching the radiant blue lapis. "The thermostat is stuck."

Ralph shook his head sympathetically. "I know about military snafus—situation normal, all fucked up."

"No, not really," said the lieutenant, still enthralled with the Ram.

"Well, it was a snafu when you bombed the museum," said Ralph. "Pick it up. See how heavy it is."

The lieutenant hefted the Ram, nodding yes, it was heavy.

Ralph wouldn't let the lieutenant get a word in edgewise, lest he object to keeping the Ram. "It's too heavy to carry all the way to Turkey, and when I run, it jounces, and we've been running a lot lately." He pointedly looked away from Doug inching toward the door. "I'd rather leave it with you, for your Syrian heritage, assuming that's where it ends up."

Ralph looked the lieutenant up and down. "There is one condition. You have to get us a ride to Turkey. It might not be safe for your precious Ram, but it's a whole hell of a lot safer for us. We'd consider that a perfect trade-off. Then the *Ram in a Thicket* is yours, and it wouldn't hurt if you'd turn the fan up a little higher." Ralph mopped his face.

Doug sniffed as if to say only lower classes sweat.

"We can leave right now if it'd be more convenient," he said, already halfway to the door. Then as an aside to Ralph, "You are a right wuss."

The lieutenant turned to Doug, catching him in mid-shuffle, another foot toward the door. "I don't suppose you have a similar item in that big old pack of yours?"

Doug shrugged as the lieutenant picked up a pea-green phone and punched in two digits. At the immediate response, Lt. Johnny barked something unintelligible, then said, "Practice our English, yes, sir. Two intruders smuggling priceless Syrian art to Turkey. Yes, sir, they stumbled onto the base. No, sir, we don't know exactly how. Yes, sir, really priceless. The *Rams in a Thicket*. No problem, sir. They are old."

He hung up the phone. "Your ride is on the way. You can have a chat with the captain. Here, wrap this up and put it in your pack so he can take a look."

Ralph stuffed the Rambo in the bag. "We'll wait outside, and I promise not to salute." He threw the bag over his shoulder with an *oof*, sticking his hand out to shake.

"The lieutenant isn't going to shake your hand, so come on," Doug said dryly, striding to the door with the huge pack already cinched tight.

Ralph dropped his hand. "Thank you, sir. You have been most kind."

Doug had already beaten him out the door, hissing back at Ralph, "Hurry up, old man."

As Ralph ran out the door, Doug was already on the back of the motorbike. "Hurry up. Hurry up," yelled Doug.

Ralph rolled his eyes, standing by the bike, refusing to swing his leg over the seat, though he lazily teased the starter with his toe, and the bike putted like a puddy cat.

"Hurry it up," said Doug.

"Don't worry about it," drawled Ralph. "We're old. We can do what we want. Screw the captain. Screw the lieutenant."

"You're crazy. Let's get out of here before we're kidnapped by a major or colonel and get in real trouble."

"What are you talking about?" cried Ralph as he twisted the right-handle grip, revving the engine to see if it could. The RPMs maxed out at asthmatic. "We can't go running away because we need to stay friends with the Syrian Air Force. Be calm, carry on, and wait patiently for the captain's driver. These greedy bastards will get us out of the country if we give them the Rambos."

"You dumb fuck," Doug said. "Let's go."

"No, we can't go running off. The air force is al-Assad's favorite toy. We don't want to get on the wrong side of al-Assad."

Doug screeched, exasperated, waving his arms

151

like crazy. "Assad will throw us in a filthy cell with ruffians and serve up a firing squad for lunch."

Ralph contemplated. "A firing squad might be better than a Syrian jail. You remember that Turkish jail movie, Midnight something? I've heard that Syrian jails are even worse, and you know al-Assad is an ill-tempered bastard."

Ralph looked at little white cars starting to clog the road. "Anyway, how would we get over razor wire without getting shredded or shot?"

"We're already in trouble with the Syrian Air Force," Doug said, his voice turning to a shriek. "And here comes the fucking lieutenant. Jump on…now," he yelled.

Ralph jumped on the motorbike a little too fast, overbalancing the bike. The shifting weight of Doug's pack pushed them into a near capsize as Ralph leaned to counteract the tilt. The back wheel spun anemically as the bike barely outran the lieutenant onto the main road, dodging a little white car as Lt. Johnny screamed, "You're too old to ride a motorbike…"

The lieutenant stopped short, breathing hard as the bike crept away, dodging a fuel truck as Doug yelled, "Don't hit anything!"

They swerved erratically down the avenue as little white cars honked at them. "Feeble," said Doug. "This motorbike is pitiful. It'll take forever to get up to fifty K an hour. We could get killed."

"Shut up and hold on, and stop leaning in the wrong direction when I have to pass someone."

"You only passed one truck, and now there are cars everywhere. Must be a change of shift."

"Everyone has guns."

"Just like home sweet home," Doug rasped in his ear.

"Everyone has guns except us. We dropped our gun, just threw it away." The traffic was getting worse.

Ralph swerved down the road, dodging drivers pointing at two old guys on a motorbike like they were dressed funny. "See the gate?" yelled Ralph, driving one-handed, pointing with the other. "It goes onto the runway, where the fuel truck is turning off." Ralph jerked the handlebars. "Stop that. You make me have to use my not inconsiderable skills to keep us from crashing, very difficult with an unbalanced passenger."

"I've noticed your attention isn't what it used to be," sniped Doug as they rolled to a stop behind a wall of cars and trucks. "The tiniest thing distracts you."

To avoid the traffic jam, Ralph wheeled the bike onto a footpath along the security fence, jolting along slowly to stay upright, bouncing like a pogo stick as they passed honking drivers flipping the bird at each other.

Ralph nodded toward the gate. "Flight areas are off-limits to foot traffic. We can climb the fence at the end

of the runway and escape because no one will be around."
He almost capsized the bike as he punched a fist in the air
like it was the best plan ever.

Doug's hands were white on the handholds as the
bike rocked and rolled, but he managed to croak, "Yes, I
see the end of the runway very clearly, you doofus."

As they hit a series of bumps, Doug said, "Your
plan is a dead end… steel planks and no way… to get the
bike… over the fence. We'll have to abandon… the
bike… and then we'll be able to walk… I am so happy."

A man with hair like a Brillo pad stuck his head
out of the car alongside them, flipping an energetic bird
with a hairy hand. "Hey, assholes. Get in line like the rest
of us! And by the way, fuck you."

Ralph wasn't in the mood. "Fuck you too. We'd
don't have time for nonsense…" At this point the traffic
started to move, and the gentleman in the little white car
opened his door. Ralph gunned the bike, ramming the
edge of a door that had apparently missed a recall for
defective hinges. The door skittered across the hood of the
little white car and shattered the passenger-side window
of the adjacent little white car.

The gentleman vaulted out of the door-less car,
running faster than the motorbike could bump down the
pedestrian path.

"He's chasing us," Doug yelled. "He's going to
kill us. Go faster."

"I'm going as fast as I can, the path is crappy and you're rocking like Little Richard," said Ralph as the motorbike came to an abrupt halt.

With two big hands the gentleman had grabbed the rear fender of the motorbike, planted his feet, and reduced five miles an hour to zero. In a single motion, Doug pulled the huge pack over his head and swung it, knocking the gentleman sideways and face first into the diamond-shaped grid of the security fence as another gentleman with a checkerboard turban, whose passenger-side window had just been destroyed, scrambled up and began kicking the first gentleman with enthusiasm.

"Hang on," Ralph yelled, revving the motorbike, which leapt like a pregnant walrus toward the wide gate leading onto the runway. It clicked closed in their faces, and Ralph crashed into it at six miles an hour.

Ralph surged halfway over the handlebars, face to face with a keypad next to the hinges of the pedestrian gate. He peered myopically. "Crap, it needs a code." He pushed his glasses back on his nose, yelling at Doug, "Get off so I can push the bike back."

"Righto," said Doug, jumping off the back. Doug pushed on the pedestrian gate, which sprang open as Ralph tried to push the bike backward, finding it weighed more than he did.

"Well, look at that," said Doug as a jeep tore around the corner of the runway, heading directly toward them.

"Shut up and jump on," yelled Ralph as the weight of Doug and his pack smacked the bike sideways.

A soldier with a megaphone stood in the back of the jeep yelling "Halt, halt!" as Ralph scraped through the pedestrian gate, revving the motorbike full on.

Doug hung on like a bat as Ralph turned onto the runway and hit a new top speed of ten miles an hour. The motorbike coughed its lungs out, heading on a collision course with a jet touching down on the other end of the runway—a jet whose approaching bulk filled the horizon faster than seemed earthly possible.

The noise of the jet dwarfed a heavy metal band. "There's a problem besides burst eardrums," Ralph screamed. He pushed his screech above the whine of the engines. "The turbulence will knock us on our butts. We're out of here."

Ralph swerved off the runway into a series of scalloped bays. "These are run-up areas for the taxiways," said Ralph, driving a loop-de-loop through ovals the width of a football field as the jet screeched toward them.

"Just because you used to fly a Cessna doesn't mean you know anything about jets," Doug said.

The turbulence from the jet staggered the bike, sending it teetering. Ralph hit the brakes, dropping the speed to zero and toppling the bike onto its side as they jumped free.

"That son of a bitch is following us," said Ralph as the jeep revved up on the runway behind them. He yanked the bike upright and swung a leg over. "I didn't think they'd cut across a runway. Wait until the Syrian FAA hears about that. That's a no-no. But they just keep on coming."

As Doug clambered onto the back, Ralph kicked the starter, and the bike coughed. Ralph kicked, kicked, kicked before it coughed twice and caught. Ralph twisted the throttle to max and wrenched the motorbike onto the runway as the jeep rolled to a stop on the taxiway behind them and they were engulfed by a brilliant white light.

"Must be the second coming," croaked Doug, hanging on as Ralph steered a loopy course down the runway, but the big searchlight stuck on them like glue.

"It's from the control tower. We can't escape it. Don't you feel like a star?"

"One of the jets is going to take off behind us," said Doug. They could hear the hiss as it turned in behind them, swinging in front of the jeep at the other end of the runway, the jeep squealing off to avoid incineration.

Ralph checked the rearview mirror, watching the jet's needle nose pierce the pale fluorescent sky and stop short, aimed at a spot above their heads as Ralph revved the motorbike to the max.

"Not to worry," said Ralph. "The bike will do better on the runway, and the jet won't risk taking off with us in the way. Air traffic control wouldn't let them do something like that. Not with the spotlight on us."

The roar of the jet was unmistakable as it stood upright on its brakes, engines building for takeoff. The brakes came off, and the jet catapulted down the runway, coming up behind them like the speed of sound and twice as loud.

Ralph gunned the bike off the runway, swooping into a wide ditch as the jet screamed past, the turbulence catapulting the bike toward the perimeter fence, which consisted of three iron rails topped with barbed wire above scrubby bushes.

The bike skidded parallel to the fence along a bumpy dirt road and the spotlight lost them. "They can't see us. We'll find a way out..."

The bike fishtailed, and Doug leaned exactly the wrong direction as Ralph yelled, "The jeep is coming up fast. Hear it?"

The bike slid onto its side and shuddered to a halt, rolling them into the dirt and knocking the breath out of Ralph, who lay wheezing.

Doug paced the dirt track in a frenzy. "Get off your ass, Magoo."

Ralph struggled to his feet, grabbed his bag, and ran to catch up with Doug, who was headed for the darkest section of fence. The big orange pack bounced on Doug's skinny back as he zoomed along the track, peering into bushes on the perimeter, looking for a place to climb.

Ralph moaned, falling behind. "The bag's too heavy, man. I can't do this…"

"Here," said Doug. "This is the best place. The bushes will hide us while we go over the top, nice and dark between the lights. The jeep hasn't spotted us yet. They're still at the motorbike." Ralph struggled up behind him, gasping.

Doug made a face like Deputy Dawg. "You simply must get in shape." He shook his head hopelessly as Ralph panted, bent over, trying to catch his breath.

Doug pointed at the top of the wall, shining a headlamp. "No razor wire, and only two barbed wires left. The other two have gone missing. Flip your bag over the top and you'll scoot over like butter on toast."

Doug took his pack and flipped it around, snapping the waistband around his back. He stood on tiptoes, grabbed the top rail, and was up with little apparent effort. His toes flew on the steel railing as he boosted the pack over the nasty barbs onto the top of the fence. He swiveled, grabbed the pack, and whispered urgently, "Hurry up. The guys in the jeep are looking our way."

"Crap," yelled Ralph as he climbed halfway up the wall with the bag tied around his neck, exhausted. "The Rambo is cutting my chest."

"What chest?" Doug scoffed, and he dropped to

the ground on the other side.

Ralph glanced behind him. The men in the jeep had spotted him and were racing full blast toward where he hung helplessly, halfway up the fence.

"This is bad," Ralph gurgled. "The jeep is coming, and the Marine must get going. Hold on. The Marine, I say. Yes." He pulled his bony torso up to the top, shifting the bag to avoid the Rambo, swiveling and ignoring the barbed wire cutting into his chest, imagining a medal affixed to his uniform. He wriggled helplessly like a pinned butterfly, trying to free his shirt from the barbs.

A flash erupted under the front tire of the jeep, and it skidded onto its side.

"It's a fucking mine," Ralph screamed at Doug. "The guard told us the perimeter was mined, but we forgot." He ripped barbs out of his shirt. "Sometimes it's better to be forgetful, don't you think? Doug, are you there?" Ralph peered into the darkness.

"Jump, jump," Doug yelled, and Ralph jumped, landing square on Doug's face, knocking him to the ground as Ralph stubbed his elbow on a rock.

Doug staggered, throwing his arms up as he balanced the big pack, giving Ralph a hand, pointing. "Maybe we should have stayed inside the base. Unending somethings are bursting in the southeast, maybe bombs, if we believe the Yankee anthem. And way over there," he said, pointing. "You see the big light? Maybe a city.

160

Distances are deceiving in the dark, but that could be Dabiq. The only question is, how close? Think about the map. The only city of any size was Dabiq, eight or ten miles east of our intended route. Right?" Doug seemed a little shaky.

Ralph sadly shook his head, rubbing his elbow, ready to go along with anything. "It depends on whether the lights are a mile away or five miles, which might make them Dabiq. Just a second." Ralph sighted through an aperture formed by a curled-up pointy finger. "The curled- up-finger thing really works. It looks like one big light. I'd guess half a mile."

"Wrong," said Doug. "It's a group of lights. See the individual pinpricks? Oh," he said soothingly, "I forgot your eyes are getting worse. We're probably nowhere near our intended route, so we're probably lost, which is easy at night. That's Dabiq, and it's way too close."

Ralph laughed weakly. "Then we definitely can't go any further east. We might run into Marcy. Or worse."

Bombs burst in the southeast and to the north; a highway blazed with light. They stood next to broken tarmac with no traffic in sight.

"We have to be real careful," said Ralph. "Things get screwy in the dark." He followed Doug, dodging a bush, walking fast through an obstacle course of bushes and sandpits, finally yelling, "Slow down already. The

bushes have thorns, and I can't carry the Rambo that fast."
He broke into a run as Doug turned onto a rudimentary
path, stopping between the wall and a vacant road that
ended in a pile of rubble. A shabby yellow bulldozer sat
on top the pile as if to say, look what I did.

"There's a nice little market outside the main gate,
which is really lit up," said Doug, watching the traffic
move in spurts. "That's the shift change we got stuck in."

Little white cars and trucks flowed out like a river
while traffic entering the base proceeded in fits and starts.
The traffic stopped suddenly, snarling like a colony of
honking seals An MP jumped into the muddle, sorting out
the tangle.

"Base security could be looking for us," Ralph
said. "We can't cross here and risk getting nabbed."

Doug nodded. "We're too easy to spot, a tall,
handsome Englishman with a cartoon character tagging
along."

"I've learned to accept that I look more like Mr.
Magoo than a short Brad Pitt. Someday you'll realize you
look like Huckleberry Hound with a white wig."

"You are distinctive, and I am distinguished," said
Doug. "We'll turn north first chance, away from Dabiq.
We can cut through the outdoor market, which will take
us away from the gate. Come on." And he was off, past
battered stalls offering little or nothing, one with three
brooms, another with a basket of beans, and one with an

162

assortment of automatic weapons.

"Stop!" yelled Ralph at Doug's disappearing back. "Take a look. We might find a good investment..." A dozen machine guns lay on the counter in different sizes, shapes, and designs.

Doug about-faced, striding up with his hand out to a pouty teen in a white T-shirt behind the counter, a swarthy James Dean type with long wavy hair and a hand-rolled cigarette propped behind his ear. "My good man," he said, "is any of your weaponry on sale?"

"I really like that little one," said Ralph, pointing at a miniature. "What's that?"

The teen stared at Doug's hand until Doug dropped it. The teen gave a haughty sniff. "You are foreigners. I have no guns for sale to foreigners, or to the wrong locals."

"Well, fine," said Ralph. "But what is that cute little thing?"

The teen groaned. "That's a mini Uzi. Five hundred dollars, but it's not for sale to foreigners. Go away."

"A mini Uzi would be just the right size. I like it," said Ralph, getting excited. "And what's that one?"

"You can't buy anything, so leave," snarled the teen like he was bad to the bone. He snapped the cigarette off his ear and scraped a fingernail on a match, lighting up in one smooth motion.

"Don't be silly," said Ralph. "I can ask you anything I want. If you don't want to answer, fine, and you're too young to smoke anyway." He waved away the fumes. "Now what kind of gun is that one?"

The kid took a furious puff. "That's a SWAT-K Mini."

"That's cute too, and it looks easy to handle. Don't you have any AK-47s? I thought the AK-47 was the only gun in Syria. They all looked the same to me, but up close I see they're amazingly different."

The teen rolled his eyes with the cigarette lolling out the corner of his mouth. "That's an AK-47," he said, pointing as if they were terminally stupid, which they apparently were.

"That's smaller than the ones we saw in the mosque," said Doug, giving the teen a look that demanded deference to elders. "I'm sure you'd sell a mini Uzi to a couple of harmless old gentlemen. My friend has a hankering for a mini Uzi, and I'm sure he will present you with an extra hundred dollars in addition to your first asking price." He rubbed long fingers together. "Will you take seven hundred dollars cash?"

Ralph's protest was cut off by the teen storming around the end of the counter with the cigarette dangling from the corner of his mouth, very cool as he shooed them off with both hands. "Go away before someone shoots you. Someone like me."

164

"Right," Ralph said. "Good idea, since I'm tapped out and not spending another cent unless Mr. Cheapskate chips in his share." He pulled Doug toward the brightly lit road.

Assorted rowdies with guns hung about in twos and threes, eyeing pedestrians who hugged the narrow strip of sidewalk between irate drivers and ruffians with AK-47s, or whatever they were.

Ralph dodged a woman in black and averted his face from two kids with guns. One twenty-year-old wore a plaid shirt and jeans and a baseball cap that said "NY." He pointed his weapon at Ralph and said, "Hey, you. Your hat is from America?"

Ralph stopped with his hands mentally up and looked at the young man. "Arizona," he said rather too loudly.

Doug headed back but stopped short as the man pointed to his own cap and said,

"Arizona team is…" He stopped to think, the gun muzzle tracing a figure eight. "Rattlesnakes." "No, it's just a hat that says Arizona. It's a state. It's not a sports team." Ralph had developed a tremor.

"That's good," said the kid, dropping the muzzle and pulling the trigger to send a single shot ricocheting. Ralph jumped ten feet as the kid said, "I am Yankee. New York Yankees are the only team that counts." He waved Ralph on.

"Go Yankees," Ralph stuttered. "Nice SWAT-K."
He took his leave and flashed past Doug.

As he swept by, Doug hissed, "Lose the cap.
You'll get us killed."

Ralph pulled the cap off, turned it inside out, and
put it back on. "We need to get away from people with
guns."

"No, lose the cap completely. You don't need a
cap at night. In fact, you don't need one at all, except to
obscure your hairline problem."

"Give me a break, Madame Pompadour."

They careened down the sidewalk, zooming
around a covey of airmen in blue and more guys with
guns, moving so fast the guys with guns almost didn't see
them at all.

Ralph rubbed his neck as he ran. "This bag is
killing me, and I could have gotten shot for nothing.
Someone could shoot us for the fun of it."

"You Yanks enjoy a strange logic, your love-hate
relationship with guns. But I suppose you deserve a break
since you almost got killed," Doug said, dripping sarcasm.

At Ralph's dark look, Doug said, "I came back for
you, but I couldn't do anything against a cowboy with a
gun." He smiled at Ralph like he was bestowing an honor.
"You did well at the end. Sometimes you can move right
along."

"I beat your butt," bragged Ralph.

"God, you'd argue about anything," said Doug, taking off like a roadrunner.

Doug swept along the path as Ralph pushed a towel under the bag to cushion against the Rambo, which felt like a sword in his back.

"Bloody good path, I say," Doug yelled. "Cool desert air." Then he began massacring "The Happy Wanderer."

"Shhh," hissed Ralph. "The Syrian Air Force might still be looking for us." He flinched. "Wow, did you see that?" The sky lit up in phosphorescence in what might be the southeast.

"I'm conserving breath," said Doug, pushing the pace up a notch, punishing Ralph for back-seat walking.

Ralph ran to keep up, finally stopping with a coughing fit beside one of the few trees they'd seen, this one looming out of the dark, silhouetted against a group of lights.

Doug dropped back. "Shhh, the Syrian Air Force might hear you. What a brilliant path. No one around and the lights aren't any closer. You did jolly well, for you." Doug pounded Ralph on the back as he coughed his lungs out. "The lights are miles away."

Ralph stopped coughing and began gasping. "You have to slow down. I can't keep up." He tossed the bag against the tree and it stood rigid as a sword, like a Ram on its hind legs.

"From the halls of Montezuma to the shores of Tripoli," Doug sang. "Isn't it fabulous to be back walking? The path is getting better, and we're staying north of the lights. Are you ready yet?" Doug continued singing. "To fight our countries' battles in the air on land and sea."

Ralph held up his hand. "No more Marine Hymn. You win the race. I have to slow down. I may have to resign my commission."

Doug shook his head in exasperation. "You'd never be an officer. You're too much of a smart aleck."

Ralph ignored him. "I'm at the end of my tolerance for pain." He rubbed his neck. "I won't be able to move tomorrow, and my neck is burning. Here, feel it."

"Gack! I'm not feeling your neck. You're becoming more of a wuss every day. But think about this." Doug shook a finger at Ralph. "If someone grabs us tonight, you may not be able to move ever again. Seriously, you're slowing down. I've noticed a difference."

"So I've heard and heard, though you are right. We have to get going." Ralph sighed. "Turkey or bust."

Ralph swung the bag over his shoulder, following Doug, who pointed at lights that seemed to be on the horizon. "The light is south of us now. We've dropped onto a giant plain. Did you notice?"

Ralph shook his head, dropping the bag on the

ground with a clunk. "Fuck the Rambo. I can't carry it any farther." He cuffed the bag like slapping a face. *Smack, smack, smack.* "I'm sick of this. We can't be very far north."

Two soldiers in black slid silently into the clearing, balaclavas over their faces. They carried assault rifles, one aimed between Doug's eyes and the other between Ralph's.

The man on the left said, "Welcome to Dabiq."

CHAPTER TEN — WELCOME TO DABIQ

"Sometimes you're lucky, and sometimes you aren't," said Ralph. "The first time we were lucky was right at the beginning, when al-Qaeda blew up the van behind us and we got away scot-free. Oh, and this week hasn't been that bad so far."

"Maybe," said Doug. "But the first time we were unlucky was right before that when the border guard let us into Syria. This is the dumbest trip we've ever been on. It's worse than North Korea or Turkmenistan. Or Agdam, where we drank beer with snipers in Nagorno-Karabakh. I'm thinking we shouldn't have come." Doug sighed. "And any second now it's going to get real bad," he said, straining against the loops of rough hemp.

They stood in front of the colonel's beautifully carved desk in a cavernous room with cobwebs in the rafters and their arms tied to posts behind them, awaiting the return of the colonel, who fancied himself the foremost dispenser of ISIS fear and dread.

"Oh, hindsight," Ralph snapped. "Think positively. We haven't gotten blown up, and we escaped Aleppo. You deserve half a credit for getting us out of town with your spastic gun control." Ralph had manipulated the ropes down to his waist, relaxed to the point of almost going to sleep because they hadn't gotten much sleep the last week.

"So we went north and unescaped," Doug muttered. "Maybe we should feel better since it made no difference which direction we went. Anyway, you followed right along with me, so it's mostly your fault." Doug sounded so disheartened that the jibe collapsed dead on the floor.

The impatient stub of a colonel, who they'd come to know far too well, slammed the door with vigor and kicked an ugly gray sofa bed out of sheer cussedness. He scurried into the room with short choppy steps and slapped a file on the beautifully grained desk, easing onto a tall leather chair, sitting with his back ramrod straight.

Colonel Beretta wore a tailored uniform while a fancy Mohawk slithered across the top of his head, looking like a mean Mr. Clean with a head like a Roman helmet with the brush on top. A revolver much larger than a Beretta—in fact, it looked big enough to fell an elephant—sat on the table next to the colonel's elbow, propped on a battered wooden stand, pointed at Ralph.

Beretta pounded the desk with a big fist they'd already seen close up. "I asked a simple question this morning—how you got here—and all I got was a big song and dance…" He shook his head like he was so tired of dealing with them. "You're only alive because Raqqa took eight tedious days to decide what to do with you.

Now I have to send you to Raqqa, where you'll meet the caliph before your abrupt transition to dead meat."

Doug sagged against his bonds as Ralph gulped and said, "Thanks for the week of boredom, and I mean that." Ralph bobbed his head up and down like Tom Lehrer singing "genuflect, genuflect, genuflect," refusing to process the colonel's last statement. "And thanks for letting me rinse my clothes. Soap would have been good, but that's okay. I used Doug's sewing kit to fix the yellow shirt, so that should get me home. I also wanted to tell you that the falafels weren't too bad. Thanks for that."

Ralph could conjure a hundred and one things to thank Beretta for because the colonel otherwise tended to throw temper tantrums, jumping up and down with his little feet, beating his big fists on anything handy, mostly on them, though he was more of a pusher than a hitter.

"You'll have a lot more to thank me for," Beretta said. "New orange outfits and a brilliant road trip to Raqqa, first thing tomorrow." He whammed a big fist on the heavy desk like the whole thing pissed him off. But then, everything pissed him off.

"You only got the kid glove treatment while emails flew between Dabiq and Raqqa—" "I didn't think of you having email," Ralph interrupted. "Could we log on to your Wi-

Fi?" He leaned forward excitedly. "We said we'd let Ali know what happened to the Rambos, and we promised Nuriddin and Gallouz that we'd join M-A-T." He stopped a second. "I probably have a million spam."

Beretta stood. "You are harmless and worthless, and you give me a throbbing pain." He rubbed his forehead theatrically. "I would have loved to see your heads impaled on the city gate. Check it out on your way out of Dabiq. I wanted you behind shiny bars with the other soon-to-be headless wonders, but the caliph insisted on following the Geneva Convention. I trust you enjoyed the bungalow."

"That's why we had the bungalow? Because ISIS follows the Geneva Convention?" asked Doug incredulously. "So maybe we're okay?"

"Not exactly," said Ralph. "The guard smacked me and tied us to these hideous posts…"

"You have no contact with reality, you stubborn old fools," Beretta growled. "Don't you know how you'll end up? This is Dabiq. Do you know what is Dabiq?" His mouth seemed a little foamy.

"Well, sure, yeah," said Ralph. "We got the big lecture on the bus to Aleppo, that Dabiq is Armageddon for Islam, the final war where Islam conquers all other religions and reigns supreme. We know all the stuff about Dabiq."

Beretta leaned forward, irritated. "Allah is in the details, and Dabiq is me. I run Dabiq." "If you run things, then when is the amazing final battle, pray tell?" asked

Doug icily. "I am so unhappy to send you two smart alecks to Raqqa." His big fists clenched in a ripple of white knuckles. "I so wanted you for myself."

The colonel grabbed the long barrel of the big revolver and pounded the butt on the teak desk, solid blows in a cadence. *Boom, boom,* rest. *Boom, boom*, rest. Repeated beyond nerve- wracking. "The most wonderful day in the history of the world has already occurred."

He smiled a cockamamie smile, pounding the butt of the gun again and again. "That was the day the Americans finally entered our war. All that's left is the final battle, which will be soon. The timetable has begun. As the holy book sayeth: Rejoice. The great battle at the end of time cometh."

He stopped the pounding, propped the revolver back on the stand, and swiveled the sweat-covered muzzle to point at the center of Doug's forehead.

"That's not very nice, pointing a gun at a guest," said Ralph, though he was plainly relieved it was no longer pointed at him. "We're not enemy soldiers, you know. We're not enemies of any kind, yet you brandish weapons like a five-year-old child. In the end, Raqqa might cut our throats, but in the meantime, grow up and act civilized."

Beretta sat back abruptly, slid off the chair, walked around the desk, and slapped Ralph. "I said shut up."

Ralph sat shocked, tears drooling out of one eye.

174

He held his breath as Beretta continued in a trance with his hands up, visualizing the final battle, acting it out.

"A third of our brave Muslim warriors will die, a third will run away, but the third that survives will destroy the West, because it says so in the Koran." Each third got its own karate chop.

"That will occur right here in Dabiq, and I will be the one to do it. You are privileged to be tied up in the exact spot where ISIS will conquer the world. You are in the presence of history." He bowed his head reverently. "Inshallah."

"We've had a week to do nothing but look out the window at the unending splendor of Dabiq," Ralph said. "Well, except when you shoved us around." He laughed. "There's nothing here. Dabiq is a dump with crappy little buildings in the middle of nowhere surrounded by ugly desert and littered with garbage. Dabiq is a nothing place. It's worse than Arizona."

Beretta climbed back onto his chair and sat up straight, regal like a chesty little bulldog. "Dabiq may not look like much to you, but let the scales fall from your eyes. I beseeched Allah to allow your martyrdom in this holy place." He bowed three times, hands together. "Imagine your heads on the cover of *Dabiq Magazine*. We ran a special edition when ISIS buried the first American crusader, and we're eagerly waiting for the rest of your army. You've certainly been a bunch of pansies so far."

Beretta beamed a big smile. "Jihadi Jim was on our November cover, holding the severed head of the aid worker we held captive for a year. When the mujahideen reported seeing American soldiers in battle, our ISIS Twitter accounts erupted with pure pleasure, like enthusiastic hosts when the first guests arrive at a party."

Beretta slid off his chair and walked around to sit between them on the edge of the desk, inches away, elbowing the revolver stand to one side. "*Dabiq Magazine* is more prestigious than the *Rolling Stone*, which only has a circulation of a million five. I researched it when we chopped off the head of that journalist and put him on the cover. That issue had a circulation of a hundred and fifty million."

Beretta licked his lips, holding onto the edge of the desk, kicking his little legs between them. "*Dabiq Magazine* is the messenger for two billion Sunnis, so our circulation beats the *Rolling Stone* a hundred to one. I wanted to buy five copies for your mothers"—the colonel looked at each in turn—"with me, holding your heads aloft, on the cover."

Ralph gasped. "That's most unkind for a religion of peace," he said, ignoring Doug mouthing "Show him the fecking safety guarantee."

Ralph was irate. "But you don't have to buy copies for my mother, because she's departed, happily, for us both." He hissed at Doug, "You have the safety guarantee.

Not me." Ralph tried to laugh, which came out as a gurgle. "Anyway, not all heads have hair to hang on to." He gave a sharp nod of his head.

Beretta looked at Ralph doubtfully. "I would be out of luck with you, but the snobby Brit has a mop to hold on to." He smiled at a thought. "I will hold your stubby necks in my hands and direct your sightless gaze at the camera." He held his palms out and swiveled them at Doug and Ralph in turn.

Doug was somber, his speech turned Cockney. "Don't go terrorizing me dear old mum. Me old mum would have a heart attack. Don't you harm a hair on her old gray head." Doug stopped, shaken. "What is there not to love about religion? You're perversely right, Ralph. We should consider all religions the same."

"I didn't mean it that way," Ralph stammered. "You should respect the glory and history of religion, the purity of faith and spirituality. Don't blame religion for the failing of a few outliers, and don't forget ISIS is simply following its holy book. Have respect for the infinitely pious."

"To terrorize me mum?" shrieked Doug. "Where is that required in the Koran?" Beretta grabbed the barrel of the huge revolver and pounded it on the base of the stand. "Shut up, you two."

They snapped to attention as Beretta laid the revolver back on the stand, pointed at Doug. "The caliph promised me that you'd star in a spectacular execution. That was my condition for releasing you. You will long be remembered in the glorious history of the caliphate."

Beretta turned glum. "So I've been outranked, but it'll do my heart good to see how you like Raqqa, briefly, on live television. Of course, you'll live on YouTube forever." He seemed to have recovered his good cheer.

"That would make us immortal, Mr. Beretta," said Ralph. "My two bloodless fingers are crossed behind me, so it isn't going to happen. I say inshallah because it covers heads or tails, keeping heads or losing heads." We have a hole card, Ralph's look said, and we're not telling you what it is.

Doug rallied bravely. "We look forward to the road trip, but we'd actually rather walk. In either event, tear off these ropes, Mr. Beretta. We are harmless old chaps who wouldn't harm a flea. You can't possibly be as backward as you appear." He made it sound simply grand. Doug tossed his head. "You and I and Ralph have had our civil chats. Well, somewhat civil. There is a precedent for no ropes and a modicum of civility."

The colonel called, "Guard."

A scrawny little old man appeared instantly, wearing suspenders to hold up his pants. He saluted and almost knocked off his glasses.

Beretta whipped off a derisive salute. "Untie the infidels and throw them in the new holding cell. No more coddling, you hear?"

Beretta turned back to Doug and Ralph. "That's my old daddy. I got him a job as my bodyguard so he wouldn't starve to death. That's pretty good of me, don't you think? It's a nice retirement for him, and of course, he's the only person I can trust not to shoot me."

Beretta laughed like it was funny. "First thing tomorrow, you get a free ride to Raqqa." He looked at his watch. "You leave at seven a.m. for the two-hour trip, which means you have twenty-five hours to live."

"Thankee, thankee," Ralph said. He raised an elbow in a wimpy toast. "To a long, or longer, life. It was exceedingly kind of you to provide daytime transport." He wiggled to let the old man finish untying him. "We'll be able to see the countryside, and I can pick up some color for my museum story, incorporating the history and myths of the mighty Euphrates River and take a few shots as we go along. Remember the map of Syria, Doug? The Euphrates is like a lake on the road to Raqqa. I might turn this into a book. I'm looking forward to a fun road trip. Dibs on shotgun."

"You're insane," said Beretta as good ole Dad finished untying the ropes.

"Ralph probably thinks insanity is a defense against wearing orange," Doug said. "that it's the new black."

Ralph sighed as he massaged the cramp in his

179

hands. "Doug is just jealous that the colonel got his daddy a job. Doug's kids would rather see him in an institution." Ralph shuddered. "Anyway, we have a hole card that will put an end to this nonsense. Show him, Doug."

"'Bout damn time," Doug muttered at Ralph. He yelled at Beretta, "Bring me my big orange pack."

"Your bags will accompany you to Raqqa along with their interesting contents, which do not include a hole card. I'm not sure whether Raqqa is more excited about two Westerners or two *Rams in a Thicket*."

"That's not what I meant about a hole—" Ralph started.

Beretta roared, his face taking on a volcanic sheen. "The Raqqa bastards. The Rams would guarantee Dabiq's starring role in history. My contacts in North Korea and Pakistan would sell me a dozen suitcase nuclear weapons for a single Ram, which I would place strategically on the plains of Dabiq. We lure in the Americans, and when you land"—he looked at Ralph as he did a big whooshing thing with his hands—"mushroom cloud blows the American army to Antarctica."

Beretta eyes seemed dangerously mad. "I'll protect our forces with a lead shield. I've already contacted China for an estimate on fabrication. We'll recycle the shield over the radioactive remains of the West."

Beretta frowned, mimicking a stupid Raqqa

180

bureaucrat. "But no, Raqqa insists on the Rams for themselves, says they'll pay for months of war against the infidels, for covert operations in the West, suicide bombers at key soft targets." He shook his head ruefully "The Rams are worth more than an oil field and are much more portable."

His face crumbled. "But I lost the tug of war. I will personally deal with Alistair for hiding the Rams from ISIS. We were supposed to have a deal." He picked up the revolver, slapping it back and forth in his big hands.

"Well, say hi for us," said Doug, standing up and stepping out of the coils of rope around his feet, shaking the numbness out of his arms and shoulders. "We liked Ali. He was a colorful chap with colorful promises."

"Mr. Alistair disappeared along with much of the museum, which was the fault of that idiot Assad and his bush league air force. Otherwise, I would be happy to say hi to Mr. Alistair for you. So happy." He twirled the revolver between his hands. "Guard, bring their new outfits, please." Beretta slapped the revolver on the table and held out his hand.

Dad scurried to a bin and hastily removed two orange jumpsuits wrapped in plastic, handing them over. "Here, son."

Beretta looked up at his father, scowled, and pointed. "Look at the sizes. We want these boys to look good." He drew out the last word.

Dad held up an orange jumpsuit. "Your size," he asked Doug. "No," he said, unfurling the other one. "This one's longer."

"Not my color. I'll stick with this," Ralph said, indicating the blue Columbia shirt and beige trousers. "A safety guarantee means never having to wear orange."

Doug harrumphed. "We agree on something, at least. Orange is hideously unbecoming to anyone other than an Irish Setter, and no one looks good in a jumpsuit. So how about the safety guarantee, in the bungalow, with our own clothes?"

Beretta laughed, "Oh, yes, but a fake safety guarantee is not my department. Raqqa made that clear. They said only one safety guarantee has ever been issued, but they'll be happy to take a look at yours. Counterfeiting gets fingernails pulled out before one's execution. Now get the goddamn orange suits on." He pointed the revolver at the floor. *Boom, boom*, splinters flying.

"Shouldn't that be Allah-damn jumpsuits?" asked Doug under his breath. "What did you say?" Beretta snarled.

Ralph and Doug doffed their clothes while Beretta laughed at their scrawny bodies and his father kindly looked the other way. They pointedly bent their butts toward Beretta as they folded their clothes.

"Pretty funny, boys," said Beretta, grating his teeth together as they pulled on orange jumpsuits.

"Do you have a mirror?" asked Ralph, pirouetting. "I'm ready for my bag now. This thing itches, and it's a little big. Where's it from?" He looked at Beretta accusingly. "Did you get these on Alibaba?"

Beretta looked sheepish. "We did. ISIS is internet savvy. We do all procurement online, though some would argue that the Koran requires competitive bidding."

"This does itch," said Doug imperiously. "I dislike it. I beseech you, Colonel Beretta, may we please redon familiar clothing? The cut is dreadful."

Beretta sneered. "You'll receive a personalized cut in Raqqa."

"This really sucks," said Ralph, peering at a sleeve. "Nothing goes with orange." "Guard!" yelled Beretta. His father turned around, looking sorrowfully at the boys as Beretta said, "Throw these two in with the riffraff."

As Dad started to escort them from the room, Ralph turned to Beretta and said, "Thanks for everything. You should join M-A-T, Muslims Against Tourists. We know the founders. And I believe the Koran does require competitive bidding, so what do you say we keep our own clothes until you can get that straightened out? I know for certain"—Ralph paused—"that you wouldn't want to offend the Koran."

"Fuck you," screamed Beretta, grabbing the big revolver. "Get them out of my sight."

Dad pulled them out of the room by their wrists. "You are bad boys," he said. "I have son... have problem but you keep..." He searched for a word that wouldn't come as he hustled them down a green hall with rotten yellow linoleum curling at the edges, pushing them into a rotunda at the end.

The huge room was filled with a shiny chrome cage from floor to cathedral ceiling, completely open without a scrap of privacy, and so new it still had the fresh chrome smell. A narrow walkway surrounded the cage. At each corner sat a guard, four dumb-looking brutes slouched on chairs holding machine guns, checking their phones.

Doug and Ralph stared helplessly at a dozen men in fluorescent jumpsuits identical to their own. The men sat slumped and unmoving, turning around when Dad inserted a large key into the massive floor-to-ceiling door with the bright shiny bars.

Dad pushed them inside. "One night. No problem." Dad was the reassuring fatherly type, closing and relocking the door with a thud, surrounded by dead men sitting.

"Greetings," said Ralph, waving a big hello. "Thank God we're not a bunch of girls, or we'd be mortified wearing the same outfit." No one cracked a smile. "Okay, that didn't work."

"How stupid was that?" said a bald man with curly

whiskers like steel wool. "We're tomorrow's batch Contemplate your life."

At their blank looks, the man said, "Heads on spikes. Surely you've seen the wall at Dabiq's city gate? ISIS marched me by two days ago, and there were thirty-two heads. Welders were adding spikes. Tomorrow morning everyone will admire our heads on shiny new spikes."

Ralph looked guilty, like he was thinking about a road trip. "We haven't seen the city gate, but what did you do to offend ISIS?"

"I did the same as everyone here. We're the wrong people. I'm Bishman," he added. They solemnly shook hands, and Bishman pointed out the different clumps of men in orange depressions. "The Shiite group, some Sunni, two Yazidi, anyone not ISIS."

Then he grimaced, pointing at himself. "Even one from ISIS. I joined up from Tunisia and fought in Iraq. I helped ISIS take Mosul." Bishman ran hands over his bald head. "I hated it. The food was lousy. They threw us into battle with no training. Told us the enemy would be terrified and run away when they saw the big black flag, like the Iraqi army did when it saw a thousand ISIS soldiers flooding into Ramadi."

Bishman sneered. "I was lucky to march in the middle of my unit. My friends were mowed down by the Kurds. ISIS is a bunch of thrill seekers and murderous

185

thieves, corrupt and holier than thou, so I decided to go home."

He sighed. "ISIS tells everyone the same thing. 'You want to go home? Your home is in Heaven.' After your head cures on spikes they ship it back home, propped between your shoulders. This head." He stroked his curly beard. "Sometimes they don't even videotape us for posterity. They just shoot us or cut our throats. I wish I'd died in battle, though Colonel Beretta says not to worry. Tomorrow morning, we get the girls. You know it's over when you can't think about getting the girls."

"I'm sorry," said Ralph. "We met a really flamboyant guy from Tunisia who joined up. He'll end up like you, and he won't be thinking about the girls either. He went by Slim, from Djerba. Do you know him?"

Bishman looked sadder. "He did the synagogue bombing. Sure, I know of him. I met his sister. She slapped me once." He thought for a second. "I'm surprised Slim would come to Syria. ISIS slaughters fags. I wouldn't admit to knowing him, but it doesn't make any difference now." He looked down sorrowfully. "I have difficulty thinking about anything except videos of orange jumpsuits."

Doug chimed in. "I, too, find the orange suit has concentrated my mind wonderfully. Have you given a thought how we can extricate ourselves from this prison? I can't seem to work it out."

"I don't think we can get out of here," said Ralph "The cage is impossible." He shook the bars, and they didn't even shiver. The closest guard looked up from his phone, raising a sneering lip and sharply tapping the barrel of his Kalashnikov on the corner of the cage. The cage rang like a tuning fork, and Ralph put his fingers in his ears.

"Maybe a diversion would work, next time they open the gate," Ralph said. "You might want to think about that, Mr. Bishman. If four doomed men knock out the gunners, that could save ten, er, or a dozen doomed men."

"You don't seem terribly upset," said Bishman, rubbing his ears. "Don't tell me you're not scheduled for tomorrow's beheadings." He stared them down. "You're going somewhere. I can see it. You won't be at the morning's beheadings." Bishman was stricken while others began milling and muttering things like "off with their ears" and worse.

"Okay, now fellas," said Ralph, waving off stares and mutterings. "We have a one-day reprieve. We're being shipped to Raqqa, where we'll get ours tomorrow, just later in the day." There were mutterings about how that made them feel so much better.

"Wow," said a skinny kid with a withered arm twitching in a too-large jumpsuit. "I always wanted to go to Raqqa. It was my Make-a-Wish, to see the glorious

187

capital of the caliphate with my own eyes."

He whipped the little arm in a semicircle, swirling the orange shoulder back and forth. "But ISIS said I wasn't fit and that it doesn't let you make a wish. Instead, I get a shortcut on the stairway to Heaven." He beamed. "So I am pretty happy. I am looking forward to the girls. I never have a girl before." His face was shining.

"I hear Raqqa is in pretty bad shape," said Ralph, trying to make the kid feel better. "The garbage collectors are on strike, so it's worse than Dabiq. You'd probably be disappointed in Raqqa. I know we'll be disappointed. You're better off going for the girls right here in Dabiq. I mean, why wait?" Ralph turned to Bishman. "How do you know Slim's sister?"

"I wouldn't know her anymore." He shook his head as if to clear it. "I can't concentrate. I met her in Djerba, Houmt El Souk, at an old caravanserai."

Ralph slapped Bishman on the back. "I stayed at an old caravanserai in Houmt El Souk, a block from the water and the fish market. It was a wonderful old place."

Ralph looked at haggard faces and blank eyes uninterested in travel tales. "I liked Slim because he was irrepressible. He struck me as innocuous."

Doug harrumphed. "Well, you weren't very nice to him. You refused to sit on his lap. You'd think you were homophobic instead of just being a smartass as usual."

"You know me, kidding around," said Ralph. "I

wouldn't sit on anyone's lap unless she was cute." Ralph sighed. "Slim loved trying to freak me out, but he was tame, nothing like a mad bomber. He'll never survive ISIS."

Doug shook his head. "The life of an ISIS beautician doth be solitary, poor, and nasty, and the half-life brutish and short. By now Muath the pilot may have murdered Slim for his smart mouth. Never insult a tough guy with a thin skin, for he may take you seriously." He waved a finger at Ralph.

"Muath was a practical guy," Ralph said. "He understood that ISIS needs a beautician to pretty up the girls. I hope Slim's sister worked out for you."

"You're joking," said Bishman. "I don't care about Slim or his sister, or girls of any kind. I have prayed to Allah and promised to give up girls if Allah will get me out of here. Inshallah."

Bishman stared at Doug and Ralph and asked tentatively, "What will you think tomorrow when you see my head on a stake? Give me some feeling for how life continues after I die..." He was crying. Embarrassed, he turned away.

The nearest guard yelled something, and a second later the lights went out.

"Lights out at nine," whispered the kid with the wonky arm. "Are you okay, Bishman?" "You two take mats in the corner," Bishman said. "It's not that dark, and

189

I won't be sleeping. No one will be sleeping except you two. We have our last hours. You have a reprieve. We die at dawn." He began gurgling again.

Ralph hugged Bishman. "I'm sorry." He turned to the kid and shook his good hand. "Have a nice heaven."

Doug hugged Bishman. "I'm sorry old chap. We'll get our turn." He clapped the kid on the back, unable to say more.

They groped their way to the corner mats and lay down. "We can't end up like this," Ralph said. "It gives me a stomachache. We'll escape on the way to Raqqa. Tomorrow will be a better day."

The quiet wailing continued around them, rising and falling for hours, whispered conversations flitting around their ears as they fell into an exhausted sleep.

CHAPTER ELEVEN—RAQQA OR BUST

"We're stuck with orange suits the rest of our worthless lives. Give me serenity," said Ralph as the lights came back on, illuminating the boys in the furthest corner, where they were sprawled on mats in rumpled orange jumpsuits. The rhythmic rap of a Kalashnikov on the giant door vibrated the cage as a guard yelled unintelligible instructions.

Doug and Ralph jumped up as the cage door swung open and a mass of orange suits surged forward, desperate men yelling at the top of their lungs.

"That wasn't a plan," said Doug. He dove to the floor as Kalashnikovs laced the men, throwing them around like rag dolls.

The bodies of the prisoners jerked and toppled into bloody heaps, bullets ricocheting off the bars like angry bumblebees. Doug and Ralph lay screaming as a crew-cut guard stepped inside the cage and placed the muzzle of a gun on Ralph's palsied head.

"Don't fucking shoot," said Ralph with his hands behind his head, twisting to see the guard. "We're off to Raqqa!" he said when the gun barrel knocked Ralph onto the mat.

Doug lumbered up stiffly, raising his eyebrows.

"Take us to Colonel Beretta, now. We have an appointment."

The crew-cut guard seemed unfamiliar with the British royal accent. He gleefully clubbed Doug like he enjoyed the exercise, covering them with the Kalashnikov as two more guards rushed in with long knives. They were followed by a cameraman, a scraggy little guy with a goatee who looked like Toulouse-Lautrec. The knives were placed across their throats, stretching their necks upright so that Doug and Ralph stood taller than seemed possible for men their age, as the camera rolled.

"Beretta," they croaked in unison. "Beretta, Beretta." This halted the arc of the knives a split second before their certain demise. Disappointment etched Toulouse-Lautrec's face as he turned the camera to more colorful tableaus. The rich smell of blood choked throats and sinus cavities in a rotunda awash with what looked like pools of paint made black by the fluorescent lighting.

The guards marched Doug and Ralph out of the cage with knives at their throats, past two guards working in tandem with long knives, slicing heads off dead bodies. Toulouse-Lautrec wielded the video camera like he'd done it a lot, zooming in for dramatic angles.

A burly guard wrapped a muscular arm around a forehead and lifted the body, stretching the neck and with a serrated commando knife, severing the throat in one fell swoop, the almost bloodless cut exposing a cross-section of tiny white bones. The guard held the head high, posing as a dribble of blood coursed from the neck and down the guard's arm. He dropped the head, which bounced on the floor as he grasped the next dead body.

Out of the corner of their eyes, they saw a sightless Bishman seized by the forehead. They kept their own heads stock still and high for safekeeping, inspired by the sharp knives as they were quick-marched down the hall.

The guards halted at the sentry posted by Beretta's office door. Doug and Ralph whispered at the same time, "Hi, Dad."

Dad yelled loud enough to blow the door off its hinges. "Colonel! It is Father, sir. The two old guys survived."

"You're older than we are," hissed Ralph as Doug harrumphed his disapproval. They both stood shaking in their boots.

Beretta opened the door, bleary eyed and unshaven in fuzzy blue pajamas, roused from the old gray couch by the door. He pointed the giant revolver in their faces.

"You two!" he screeched. "Why didn't you die with your buddies in the orange suits? Dad tells me the suicide stampede was lost to cinematic posterity. I knew they'd rush the gate. They always do. I'm charging my slug of a cinematographer with dereliction of camera for showing up a minute late and missing the massacre. He will be hanged forthwith."

Ralph stared. "Hang Toulouse-Lautrec?" Ralph blinked. "Can you at least call your goons off?" he asked, stretching his neck.

"Well, he does look like Monsieur Lautrec," said Beretta, surprised. "But his name is Nash. He's Belgian. We have a lot of good Belgians in ISIS, but Nash slept in."

"Who knew the colonel liked post-Impressionists?" Doug whispered.

"Sleeping in is not an excuse," Beretta said. "By the time Nash showed up, the guards had already shot everyone to crumbs." He looked at them. "Except for you two, unfortunately. Losing a potentially viral video pisses me off as much as your continued existence. I so wish I could keep you right here in Dabiq, on the city gate."

Beretta jerked the muzzle of the big revolver, ordering them inside, dismissing their crest-fallen guards. Doug and Ralph rubbed their necks, grateful for existence as they waved goodbye to Dad.

"You're sure grouchy this morning," said Ralph as he stood in front of Beretta's desk, leaning against the familiar post, scrunching his back around, trying to get comfortable.

Beretta stared at them, pointing the big revolver back and forth like playing *Eeny, meeny, miny, moe.*

"You need more REM sleep," said Doug. "You

should probably lose the couch and find a decent bed. I'm sure you can afford one, or is ISIS having trouble meeting payroll?"

"Let's get on with the expedition to Raqqa," said Ralph. "I've been looking forward to a road trip with fresh air. The cage smelled okay to start with but then it was like the worst ever, not that you can blame the poor bastards. I want to soak up local color and do some sightseeing, see the big dam on the Euphrates, take a few pictures."

Doug emphasized, "On foot."

"First we need showers," Ralph continued blithely. At Beretta's put-upon look, Ralph said, "Truly. We haven't had a shower all week."

Beretta flashed an oily smile. "You can shower in paradise. Meanwhile, stand at attention while I call your transport." He kicked the chair for fun and punched in a phone number.

Doug raised his hand just as Beretta said hello into the phone. "Permission, sir, to walk to Raqqa, please, Mr. Beretta, sir. Ralph is right. We've not been getting our exercise, and there's been a dearth of fresh air."

"I'm on the phone here," Beretta spluttered, leveling the revolver at Doug. "If there's one thing I hate, it's being interrupted when I'm on the phone." He punctuated this with an explosive shot into the rafters.

A pigeon clunked onto the desk, twitching. The

warm hole in its breast pumped the last of its life's blood onto Beretta's pristine desk, followed by the last of its life's poop.

"Son of a bitch," yelled Beretta as the door opened.

Dad peeked inside. "Is everything okay, Colonel Son, sir?"

"Everything is fine. Close the Allah yil'anek door." The colonel clenched his teeth. "Close the goddamn door," he sputtered as Dad backed out of the room.

Beretta shouted into the phone. "Of course this is Colonel Beretta, you fool... Caller ID was working yesterday... Yes, I understand things change... Shut up. I called because I need transportation immediately. I have two prisoners for delivery to Raqqa... Just. Shut. Up. That is your top priority." He slammed the phone down.

Ralph and Doug stood at attention, pretty in orange, hands over their mouths as a reminder to keep them closed. They twitched slightly as they stared straight ahead at nothing.

"Here are the pack and the garbage bag. The Rams will accompany you to Raqqa. You'll be tied in the back of the truck and guarded at all times. If you try to escape, you will be shot," Beretta said pleasantly.

"Now wait a minute," said Ralph. "I had dibs on shotgun. I want to see stuff on the way to Raqqa."

"You stupid moron, the driver can't guard you when he's driving," screeched Beretta. "Oh, why do I talk to you?"

Beretta slammed the revolver into his left hand. "The guard won't hesitate to shoot you. Beheadings are often taped after a shooting, as you may have noticed. Either way works for me," He gleefully rubbed the revolver.

Beretta whirled the revolver into his right hand as a vehicle pulled up outside and honked. Beretta barked, "Atten-hut."

They rolled their eyes, and Beretta glared at them "About-face. Forward march." He opened the door to a rising sun that cast a yellow glow over Dabiq, making it look like an old snapshot as pickups and vans swirled in sepia down the dusty street. The magic evaporated as exhaust fumes enveloped them and the unending litter snapped back into focus.

Beretta shepherded Ralph and Doug outside as a tall muscular soldier jumped out of a white pickup and strode forward to salute Beretta. The soldier was sharp in his dress uniform, jaunty garrison cap, and pistol holstered on his hip.

"Rondo." Beretta returned the salute. "Take these two to Raqqa headquarters." He handed Rondo their passports. "Don't hesitate to shoot them, and under no circumstances are you to lose them." He stared at the pickup. "How many men do you have?"

"Just me, sir. We're a little short-handed," said Rondo, shrugging at the empty pickup. "Goddamn it, man," Beretta erupted. "This is unacceptable. Where are Waiti and

Shumati? They should be with you." "You sent them to Aleppo, sir." Beretta looked dazed at the news.

Rondo continued. "Late last night. You ordered Waiti and Shumati to scout out rebel positions, sir." He saluted sharply.

"Right," said Beretta, looking exhausted. "Take care of the prisoners, and don't let them get away with anything."

"You must be kidding, sir." Another salute, which Beretta waved away. "They're old as dust," Rondo said. "I can handle them with one finger."

"Make damn sure," said Beretta, relenting to crisply return Rondo's salute. "The ugly one called shotgun." He pointed at Ralph, who was already streaking for the pickup, yanking the camera out of his bag as he tossed the bag on an old tarp in the back.

"Let's go," said Ralph, swinging open the passenger door. "Come on, Doug. You're invited along even if the colonel didn't order the ugly one who looks like a hound dog to sit in the middle, which you have to do before I can close the door and sit shotgun. We're off to see the wizard."

Doug followed, shaking his head, carefully placing his pack in the back of the pickup away from a suspicious-looking mound of filth. He rolled his pack and Ralph's bag inside the tarp, wedging it in a front corner before climbing into the front seat.

Ralph scooted alongside, closing the door and cranking down the window. "Phew, we need a little air in here. What have they been hauling, hogs?" He scraped his feet on a floor covered with smelly bits.

"Don't get carried away insulting everyone," Doug said. "You know they haven't been hauling hogs. We need a plan for getting the bloody hell out of here. Even you may have noticed that this ISIS lot is completely bonkers."

"I know that," said Ralph as Rondo climbed in the driver's side and keyed the ignition. "ISIS is also completely disorganized, which compounds their nasty habits. They don't know how to run a war."

"And you do?" asked Doug derisively. "The ineptitude of ISIS, Assad, and the FSA is the only thing that's saved us so far. Our mutual incompetency cancels out. This whole affair is getting a bit hairy for my taste."

As Rondo backed out, into early morning traffic, Ralph called to Beretta, "See you later, but hopefully not."

Beretta flipped him off.

"You two behave now," said Rondo, distracted as he pulled into traffic, honking at a guy in a white pickup who swerved to avoid hitting them. This threw the moon-like face of a large female passenger against the side window, her terrified nose and mouth smashed flat against the glass.

"Son of a bitch," said Rondo, swerving in behind the pickup as they sped past low nondescript buildings. They entered a large central square ringed by erratically parked vehicles. Peddlers assembled stalls and slowed traffic to a crawl. The stalls sold dirt-encrusted vegetables and junk that would embarrass a ninety-nine-cent store— ragged spatulas, battered CDs, one screwdriver, a lopsided egg beater, and a pile of grimy rags.

"What's that statue?" asked Ralph, pointing at a twenty-foot figure toppled on its face in the middle of the square. Rusty rebar poked out of a head pounded to fragments. "I mean, who was it?"

"Al-Assad," said Rondo. "The first thing we did was knock down the statue of Assad, the filthy Alawite war criminal."

Rondo sneered, bragging on the home team as they crept around the square. "We'll take Assad's whole country and Iraq too, then the Middle East, and Africa from Egypt and Libya down to Nigeria and Cameroon with Boko Haram and over to Al-Shabaab in Somalia and Kenya." He swung his hand to encompass the world. "This is the bare beginning as foretold in the Holy Koran."

"How'd you get into the ISIS game?" asked Doug.

"You seem a perfectly reasonable chap, though a little overenthusiastic."

"Well, thank you," said Rondo, blushing. "I'm just a simple believer. I'm not a boss. I don't have any say in what happens to you. I mean, for infidels, you seem okay by me."

"Then maybe you could let us walk to Raqqa," said Doug, stretching his arms over his head. "We've been cooped up and need to get on the road and loosen up. Gotta get walking."

Rondo glanced at Doug. "I can't do that. Nothing personal, you understand, just following Allah, staying away from treason." He thumped the perfectly creased gabardine uniform, exactly over his heart.

"You surely know that treason is just politics," Ralph said, "and you shouldn't let politics make you do bad things, like harming two innocent gentlemen who've bothered no one, at least not intentionally. We're no threat to ISIS."

Rondo thought about it, tapping the steering wheel as they crawled along. "That is a good argument, but it doesn't apply to caliphate politics, Allah's kingdom on Earth."

Ralph whistled. "Did you go to philosopher school or something like that?"

"I studied at the madrasa in Mosul." He shifted to second as traffic cleared the square and started moving, a block later slowing for a bottleneck.

"So you studied the Koran, mostly?" asked Ralph. "That's your philosophy."

"I am a hafiz." He bowed his head proudly, pulling ahead slowly. "I memorize the Koran."

"Jesus Christ," said Ralph, pointing with his finger shaking like palsy. "That's what's holding up traffic. They're putting new heads up on the city gate."

Men in black uniforms slid heads onto shiny spikes shaped like little hearts. The heads were framed by rebar, and a decapitated body had been laid below each head. Traffic slowed like it was a road accident.

"Watch out, Mr. Rondo," Ralph screeched. "I think Doug is going to be sick." "Stop," said Doug to Rondo.

"This isn't a taxi," said Rondo.

"Either stop or I'll be barfing all over the truck," said Doug, his voice muffled, hand over his mouth.

"Right," said Rondo, stopping next to the soldiers arranging fresh heads on spikes. "This is a horrible place," said Ralph, climbing out fast. Doug sprawled on hands and knees, upchucking with vigor, hacking and coughing.

"Look, there's the skinny kid with the little arm," said Ralph, staring at the heads with a hand on his throat, looking at people they knew, his stomach roiling. "The kid's eyes are open. I hope he saw the girls." Every mouth was open, but most eyes were closed.

Ralph gasped. "They have the wrong body with the head of the kid with the withered arm." He rushed up to the nearest soldier, pointing. "Sir, you have the wrong body with that head."

The soldier swung around, whamming Ralph across the face with the side of a machete. Ralph hit the ground and skidded through the green puddle where Doug sat trying to catch his breath. Ralph jumped to his feet, swiping at the mess on his sleeve, and bent over, gagging.

"Don't bother the nice soldiers," gasped Doug, wiping his mouth on an orange sleeve. "Let's get out of this in one piece."

"It's too terrible," Ralph said, swiping at the gunk on his chin. "The Koran teaches respect for an enemy martyred in war, but ISIS has no respect for anyone."

Doug scoffed. "You're out of your mind to respect any religion. They're all hypocritical creepy crawly things with bats in the belfry and snakes in the basement. Every one of your blessed religions is holier than the other, and they all hate each other to bits."

Ralph looked at Doug and puckered up his nose. "I hope you feel better, defaming the world's holiest institution while I stand here covered with your upchuck. This is the worst I've ever felt. And don't go starting on the memory thing like I felt worse on a previous occasion."

Doug rolled his eyes. "A Marine who can't handle

a little regurgitation won't last long in a real shooting war. Marine, pshaw."

Ralph gagged again half-heartedly, like he was too tired to throw up. "I need something to clean up with. Maybe Rondo has butt wipes in the truck." Ralph swiped at his mouth, rubbed the sleeve across a splotch on his pants, and wrinkled his nose as he pulled sticky hands across his scrawny orange butt. "Religions must respect other religions because they're based on the same moral foundation. Facts aren't the thing."

"Religions don't do facts, morals, or respect," Doug snapped. "When I was a kid, the Anglican bishops told us Catholics were going straight to hell."

"Some do purgatory…" Ralph said, then he was suddenly wailing, pointing at a head. "There's Bishman! Good old Bishman."

Bishman's mouth gaped below a jagged hole in his forehead. His top teeth were broken on one side, and his curly beard was caked with blood that had drained from an empty eye socket.

"How can you say good old Bishman?" demanded Doug, irate. "He was ISIS, same as the rest of these bastards."

"He was nice to us."

"He was too worried about the morrow to harass us, and he had a right to be worried. Maybe we should worry too."

Ralph shrugged. "Would worrying help?"

Rondo marched up, impatient, slapping his thigh "Come on, boys, if you're through making sick."

"There's your fellow photographer, Toulouse-Lautrec," Doug said, pointing to the head next tc Bishman.

"Ohmigod, Beretta wasn't kidding, and just because he was a minute late. Look at him with his perfect little beard." One eye was closed and the other one open. Ralph was outraged, but suddenly he calmed down. "Maybe he died that way, looking through a camera lens, doing what he loved best."

"Just shut up," said Rondo. "We've got a long way to go. Wipe your chin off." Rondo wrinkled his nose and gave Ralph a pained look, reaching in the back of the pickup and handing Ralph a filthy rag that smelled like crap.

"Look," said Ralph as Rondo slid behind the wheel. "It's a wedding. I've never seen a wedding dress like that. What the hell are they doing?"

As Rondo hit the starter, Ralph waved a hand at him to stay a minute, hoisting his camera, amazed as it turned right on. Rondo sighed as the wedding party blocked the street, banging his head gently on the steering wheel as Ralph zoomed in for close-ups.

The bride was covered in white satin from head to toe with narrow slits for eyes, waddling along with a white satin cushion in one hand and a bouquet of roadside flowers in the other. She was followed by the groom in a dress version of the ISIS uniform with matching black balaclava contrasted by white tennis shoes. The wedding party trailed behind, also in white tennis shoes. They stopped in front of the wall of heads.

"They're posing for wedding photos," said Doug. "Come on, boys…" Rondo said.

"My God, they are," said Ralph, snapping shots. "They're posing with the heads…"

The bride stood under a head while the groom took her picture. Then the bride and groom posed for a selfie. The groom imitated Bishman with his mouth wide open and eyes closed and tapped the Facebook app on his phone.

Rondo honked at a civilian who was too slow letting Rondo into the stop-and-go traffic, and they inched alongside little kids wearing black uniforms like ISIS, from white tennis shoes to black skull-caps.

"The Children's Brigade," said Rondo. "Pretty cool, eh? They're also called the Youth of the Caliphate." Rondo shook his head in wonder as they drove by ten-year-old kids firing pistols at targets on tripods, flanked by kids holding black ISIS flags. "The kids love it. I wish they'd had the Children's Brigade when I was little. It's like Boy Scouts with guns, an idea the Americans might like."

"They all have miniature pistols," Doug said. "Do you know what kind of gun that is?" "We don't know anything about guns," explained Ralph.

"They're firing Berettas, which are small and compact, perfect for a Boy Scout. This would be something the colonel would do, arm the Children's Brigade with Berettas to remind them of their small compact leader," Rondo said proudly, "In Mosul, the Children's Brigade beheaded a thousand Shiite soldiers."

At their aghast looks, Rondo said, "Seriously. The beheadings are on YouTube. Just do a search for Children's Brigade, Mosul, and Shiite. It'll come right up."

Rondo acted like a proud papa, waving at the boys as they inched by. "The Dabiq brigade is coming along nicely. Kids are perfect for intelligence gathering and suicide missions. These boys are a little young, but by age twelve, they really want the girls. That's when they're ready. Did you know our new official virgin is Kim Kardashian?"

"She's not a virgin," scoffed Doug. "And that is so unkind, sending these young sprouts off to die for nothing. Suicide bombers never get the girl because they lose interest when they're dead."

"We wouldn't get many recruits if we didn't tell them about the girls," Rondo said. "Besides, it's not really a lie. The wonders of Heaven are yet to behold."

Ralph said, "I heard from an Israeli buddy that suicide bombers wrap their dicks in tinfoil so their equipment survives to enjoy Heaven."

Rondo pulled a face. "It may sound stupid to you, but yes, of course, all suicide bombers wear tinfoil…"

"Except for the women suicide bombers, I expect," said Doug, smirking.

"Do you remember the British schoolgirls who ran away to marry ISIS?" Rondo asked, looking at Doug. "They joined the Children's Brigade in Raqqa. Perhaps I could arrange for you to meet them."

Rondo steered away from an approaching tank, its treads creaking and clanking down the middle of the highway like a green monster, stamping the pavement into geometric potholes.

Ralph shuddered as it clanked by but grabbed his camera, snapping a straight-on shot of the muzzle and then the sides painted in glowing murals of angels and clouds.

"Why would I want to meet stupid children?" asked Doug, regally placing his fingers in his ears. "I despise noisy tanks."

"A thinking person networks when possible, and besides, most people enjoy meeting folks from back home. The girls were recruited by Jihadi Jim, who you'll meet in Raqqa. So the British schoolgirls might be a super networking opportunity." Rondo looked over, smiling at their reaction. "I deliver Orangemen to Jihadi Jim. That's what he calls them, honoring his Irish roots. Jimbo really hates the British."

Rondo raised an eyebrow at Doug. "Meeting the British schoolgirls might help you with Jimbo, in case you ever need a favor. I'm just trying to be practical," said Rondo, shrugging at their indifference.

"I am so thrilled to hear that," said Doug. "I thought you were the nice mellow type, but you sound bloodthirsty." He gave Rondo the evil eye as the tank squeaked and clanked down the highway behind them, dropping the stare as Rondo concentrated on passing an armored truck.

"The armored truck and the tank look new," Doug said. "Not like the fire engine we saw at the border and in Aleppo."

Rondo looked proudly at Doug. "ISIS has hundreds of new tanks." He glanced at Ralph. "Courtesy of our American friends. They left goodies all over Iraq."

"Since I helped pay for them," Ralph said, "I hope ISIS doesn't remove the tags, 'Courtesy of US taxpayer.'"

"What do you expect?" asked Doug. "You have the dumbest government on the planet. The UK has seen the light. We're out of the world-conflict business."

"ISIS couldn't have conquered Syria and Iraq without the millions of tons of equipment the Americans left behind," said Rondo. "I guess we owe you." He reached across Doug to punch Ralph on the shoulder. "The colonel says America will soon have boots on the ground, bringing even more equipment." He laughed with delight.

"Hey, can you pull over so I can get some shots of these guys?" asked Ralph, swinging the camera around as an ISIS platoon marched briskly down the road toward them, all dressed in black and waving huge black flags, front and back. The men held an AK-47 in one hand and the necks of men dressed in camouflage in the other hand. The captives were bent forward with their arms tied behind them, struggling to avoid tripping on their faces and slaughtered on the spot.

Rondo slowed to a crawl. "That's the latest batch of al-Assad goons, captured outside Aleppo."

"They're just kids," said Ralph, zooming in.

"All enemies are goons," said Rondo, getting excited. "Fresh heads for Dabiq's wall of spikes."

At their aghast look, Rondo said, "Now, now. I didn't say that to freak you out but so you understand. There is ISIS, and there is everyone else. Everyone else is the enemy." He flipped a hand to deflect their glares. "Nothing personal, but I cheer when we win." He smiled pleasantly. "Present company excluded, included, or whatever."

"That's gracious of you," said Ralph, zooming back to capture the panorama of ISIS on the march, herding doomed enemy prisoners.

"I see why the Iraqi army deserted Mosul without firing a shot," said Doug, "even though it outnumbered ISIS ten to one." He stared in awe.

"It's just the black uniform and huge black flag," said Ralph. "They're kids and petty hooligans like you have in the UK, out for the thrill."

"I can't get beyond the religion and the uniform," said Doug.

The leader of the platoon halted the procession. He waved Rondo to a stop and swaggered toward the pickup. The platoon leader was either born with a sneer or had an inch missing from his upper lip. He rapped his gun on the window before Rondo could get it all the way down.

"Merde," said the sneering officer, sticking the barrel of a Kalashnikov inside. "Who are zeez peoples in ze orange suits? I can take ze motherfuckers off your hands. What you say?" He poked the gun at Rondo.

Rondo grabbed the gun by the muzzle, ripping it from the hands of the sneerer, flipping it over and pressing the muzzle into the gap in the sneerer's top lip. "I say no, which I trust you understand." Rondo jiggled the muzzle. "I'm delivering two infidels to Raqqa on orders of Colonel Beretta, so don't be so nosy." Rondo smirked. "Or you could get hurt."

Sneerer held his hands up, whispering, "I don't appreciate you picking on the hare-lip person in front of my troops."

Rondo lowered the gun as Sneerer said, "I was only trying to be helpful. Eez my first command since I join up."

"My goodness," said Ralph. "You're a Frenchie. You're supposed to be lovers, not fighters. Or is that the Italians?"

"I am Belgian fighter." He shook his head and raised his nose. "I plan Charlie Hebdo, but no one want me. I leave Belgium because I cannot be lover. Belgian girls don't look at the ugly guy. But I am the leader of men. I am lieutenant." He stuck out his chest and held out a hand for the gun.

"Your troops may not like a lieutenant who lost his gun," Rondo said, "but do your best." He handed the gun back by the muzzle.

"There's a friend of yours with his head on a spike in Dabiq," Ralph yelled. "Say hi to Toulouse, who you probably know as Nash. He's Belgian too. Was Belgian."

"I know no Nash and no Toulouse. I am fighter," yelled Sneerer, firing the Kalashnikov in the air. "We go." He motioned the troops forward, and they broke into a jog, forcing the prisoners to break into a headlong run toward Dabiq's city gate.

"Stopping is never a good idea," said Rondo. "So don't even think about asking." He pulled back into traffic, which consisted of military vehicles and little white trucks.

"I'm a travel writer and have always wanted to see Qalaat Jaabar Castle," Ralph said. "You know where it is, on the peninsula sticking out of Lake Assad. We go right by it, so it won't take any time to stop for a look-see."

As Rondo gritted his teeth, Ralph added, "Just a short little stop. One photo?"

At Rondo's look that foreshadowed the removal of Ralph's throat, Ralph said, "Right. You're a hard-ass. I get it."

"This is not a road trip. I have to be back in Dabiq this afternoon."

"Christ, it's only two hundred K," said Ralph. "Surely—" He stopped at Rondo's throat- cutting gesture.

Ralph looked at Doug, "*Necessita vamos ahora.*" We gotta get out of here. "*Comprende,*" said Doug. "*Cuando?*" When?

"La curva."

"But the road is straight as an arrow." Doug pointed.

"Sorry," said Ralph. "I couldn't think of the words for 'little parking lot with the broken- down fence coming up on the left.'"

"Don't be stupid, you two," said Rondo. "I'm not slowing down, and if you jump out you'll break every bone in your decrepit bodies. Then, for starters, I'll shoot you."

"Well, okay," said Ralph. "But we're going to have to stop pretty soon so I can pee."

CHAPTER TWELVE – RUN FOR THE BORDER

Ralph stuck his head out the window. "I love riding shotgun. I can see everything. Whoa, look at that," he said, pointing a mile south at a dozen ruined aluminum cones surrounded by wheat fields with swathes burned black. "Assad's flyboys are getting closer to the road, bombing whatever those things used to be."

Rondo was testy. "Probably grain silos."

"Maybe not," yelled Ralph. "Look at your guys in black. They're running from the wreckage. And a fighter jet is coming back for another run."

Rondo whammed the steering wheel with his hand, shoving the pedal to the metal, the pickup taking a chance passing a slow truck, careening back into the eastbound lane. "This is the main ISIS corridor for Dabiq, Raqqa, and Mosul. Cutting the road would split ISIS apart, which is Assad's main objective."

"Maybe it's a former ISIS corridor," said Doug.

Ralph jabbered excitedly. "Look at them run." The jet's cannons stitched the men in black like a fifty-caliber sewing machine, exploding another aluminum thingie.

Doug laughed. "Maybe you could fit a Cessna with a machine gun, ratta-tat-tat, make a flying Marine."

"You can't put any extra weight on a Cessna,"

Ralph said. "It's just a kite with an engine. Any extra weight would make it crash it on takeoff."

"Well, aren't we literal?" mocked Doug as the fighter jet peeled off and fired a volley that punched holes down the middle of the highway. No vehicles were hit, but traffic scattered into chaos, exploding away from the center of the road. A white van ahead of them T-boned the white pickup ahead of it. Rondo's reflexes plunged them off the side of the road, the truck gyrating wildly as Rondo managed to keep them on the sharply slanting shoulder.

As they rolled to a stop beside a burned-out brick building Ralph said, "Okay. Now I really have to pee."

Rondo sat shaking at the wheel, cursing, "That fucker."

"Not Fokker," said Doug drolly, enjoying the whole affair from the safety of the middle. "It was probably a Messerschmitt."

"What the fuck are you talking about?" asked Rondo. "ISIS needs an air force so we can shoot down Assad's crappy Russian jets."

"I have good news," said Ralph, opening the door. "We met Muath the Merciful from Jordan, and he's organizing an ISIS air force. I'll tell you all about him after we finish peeing."

"We don't have time for you to pee again," Rondo yelled. "I have to get you to Raqqa"— he looked at his watch—"in the next half hour."

"Dude," said Ralph, slipping out the door, "you don't have time for me not to pee? It's either outside or inside on the floor."

Rondo unholstered his pistol. "Get back in here, or you'll be peeing in paradise." "Man," said Ralph, hopping around, tap dancing and talking to Rondo. "You haven't peed since we left, and it's been three hours. Besides, it only takes a second to pee." This was a lie. "Come on. Join us. Never miss a chance to pee. Someday you'll understand."

Doug clambered out of the truck behind Ralph as Rondo aimed the pistol at the middle of Ralph's back. The jet returned, strafing down the middle of the truck with the *splat, splat, splat, splat* of wet liver on marble, repeated lickety-split. The percussion knocked Ralph and Doug into the ditch at the bottom of the steep bank, senseless and deaf. They landed on their backs like orange lumps, staring up at a fireplace in the burned-out building that looked like it was flipping them the bird.

"What happened to the truck?" gasped Ralph. "Where's Rondo?" His eyes were glassy and unfocused.

"This is our last chance to get away from ISIS," said Doug, getting up shakily. Rondo lay in a lump halfway out of the pickup with his head missing. Doug looked at Ralph lying on the ground. "What's wrong with you?"

"I think I'm broken," said Ralph. "My head is

bonkers, ringing, ringing." He struggled onto all fours, then stood up and unzipped with speed.

Doug joined him. "Let's see what's left of our stuff. Lake Assad is on the other side of the road?"

"Oh, yeah," said Ralph, grunting. "That's the Euphrates, backed up by the big dam, whatsitsname?"

"Your memory is going. Tabqa Dam. We talked about it when you begged Rondo to stop at Qalaat Jaabar Castle."

Ralph grunted. "I can't even think. I must have a concussion."

"Headline: Fake Marine Receives Purple Heart. Hurry up. We don't have time for your fussy prostate. Look, the bloody jet is coming back." It swooped down the other side of the road, splitting the air like it was breaking the sound barrier, large caliber shells exploding the pavement into geysers. Shells peppered the white van and its former occupants, splattering the highway red. Survivors ran in every direction.

"Right," said Ralph. "Qalaat Jaabar Castle is across the road, on the lake. I should be able to get a telephoto shot." He tucked back into the jumpsuit, zipped up, and limped behind Doug toward the pickup. The fifty-millimeter shells had laced the cab diagonally, splattering the back into neatly stitched islands. Their stuff was untouched.

Ralph shook his head. "I told him he should drink

218

more water."

Doug bowed his head in memoriam. "He was a macho guy with fantastic reflexes, but I'm glad." Doug murmured, "Rest in Peace, Rondo."

Ralph bowed his head too, which lasted a split second before Doug grabbed his pack and threw the big orange monstrosity over his shoulders like it was old-home week, ready to fly. "We have to get cross the road and head north. Folks might find orange suits suspicious, so let's get out of here, get rid of these clothes."

They avoided looking at bloody bodies next to the wrecked white van as they cringed from the heat of a truck on fire across the road. Two men in white robes and a woman in black wandered in shock.

"Just a second," Ralph said. "I have to get my camera." He picked up his bag and promptly collapsed, plopping on the ground with his legs in front of him. He staggered up as Doug dashed over the lip of the bank and across the road through the mayhem, dodging a dazed man in a turban with the eerie white bone of a stick fracture poking through his robe. Doug was across the road in seconds and halfway to the lake before anyone could focus on his orange jumpsuit.

"Wait, wait!" yelled Ralph.

He faintly heard Doug call back. "I've heard you resigned from the Corps, now Marine emeritus, dishonorably retired, unable to cope with active duty, or much activity at alllll..."

Ralph clenched his teeth and limped across the road, ignoring two guys staring at the orange jumpsuit. A burly gentleman with a figure like a wine barrel crooked a finger at Ralph, ordering him over with something that sounded like gibberish. Others turned to watch.

"Piffle, piffle, piffle, piffle," Ralph said, hissing as the large gentleman waddled toward him. The man stood waving his fist as Ralph plunged down the other side of the road, chasing Doug, who'd reached the edge of the vast reservoir and was whirling madly north.

Ralph gasped. "Hey, Doug. Slow down. Just stop, damn it. We made it, and there's a nice reflection of Qalaat Jaabar Castle off the lake. Folks love reflection shots."

"Look how low the water is," said Doug, moseying back. "There must be a drought." "Just a second," said Ralph, pulling out his camera.

"Catch me if you can," said Doug. "I'll be on the low road." Parallel trails followed the contour of the lake like tree rings, each marking a drop in water level. The water was far below the lowest path where Doug whizzed north.

"Wait," yelled Ralph, snapping shots of the faraway castle and puffing like a locomotive to catch up.

"We can make better time on the road along the hill above us," Doug said.

"I can't go any faster. This is fast enough," gasped Ralph. "But maybe we can hitch a ride." He summoned a breath. "It must be thirty miles to Turkey."

"It might be closer to forty," said Doug, shading his eyes from the morning sun. "Are you sure you want to risk hitching? We're in ISIS country, and everyone's out to get us, as usual."

"It'd take me two days to walk forty miles. Anything is better than walking." Ralph was untucked and bedraggled.

"I'd rather walk, but you are a mess. We need to be especially careful who we ride with."

Ralph looked behind them. "There's no one following us." They were hidden from the road by a small hill. Puffs of smoke and mortar fire could be seen further south. "Everyone's too busy saving themselves. We can change clothes."

"Righto," said Doug, dropping his pack on the path and pawing it open. He had the orange jumpsuit off and his charcoal-colored outfit on in seconds. He balled up the jumpsuit and threw it toward the water, but it billowed open and fell short.

"Got it," said Ralph, sliding down to the lake and dunking both jumpsuits.

Doug stepped out briskly, breaking into song. "I love to go a wandering, along the mountain track. Without an orange jumpsuit on my back." They climbed onto the road with Doug yodeling exuberantly.

"There's no traffic," said Ralph.

"It's just a farm lane," said Doug. "We'd be lucky to catch a hay wagon, so keep your eyes peeled."

"Traffic already," said Ralph as a motorcycle roared by, spewing dust. The driver was dressed in antique leathers from helmet to chaps. He nodded as he forced them to the shoulder.

"Here comes an old pickup." Ralph stuck out a thumb as the truck putted toward them. It might have been white at one time. "Two bales of hay in the back. Maybe a farmer."

The pickup beeped and veered wildly, a narrow front tire cutting over the edge of the road as the truck slid to a stop high above the lake. They hurried to the driver's side, standing together by the open window, waving their arms like metronomes.

Ralph bent toward the window. "Hello, sir. My name is Ralph, and this is Doug."

Doug launched into his best BBC voice. "Could we possibly hitch a ride to Turkey, kind sir? My friend here is incapacitated, or at least is refusing to make the effort to place one foot in front of the other. The poor chap can no longer Marine on, worn into sedentary retirement after years of questionable service."

They began waving again, smiling at the wizened little man with wispy white hair who sat unmoving, slumped behind the wheel. The little guy had a white handlebar mustache and wore a black jacket over a white robe. He looked like a dim Albert Einstein, turning to look at them and giving a start like he was stunned by their costumes.

He put up a small hand and waved back. "I am Ishtar. Where in world are you come?" He paused as if pondering the request of the British nobleman. "I go almost to Turkey." He bent his head to Doug as if in fealty. "Are you lost?" Ishtar laid his head on the steering wheel like he was exhausted, turning to look up at them with big brown eyes.

"We could pay for fuel..." said Doug, nodding at Ralph the paymaster.

"We will pay for fuel and help you in any way we can, which of course means I will," said Ralph. "Are you okay? You look plumb tuckered out." Feeling his Arizona, he flipped off his cap and turned it right side out, making the world right again.

"All day I have gone," said the old man, levering his head off the wheel like a lead weight. "All day yesterday I have gone. I have no sleep, but I have gone."

"Can we help push you back on the road?" asked Ralph solicitously.

Ishtar moved like a sleepwalker, ignoring them as he put the pickup in reverse, revved the engine to a cough, and let out the clutch, rocketing back onto the road and skidding as he belatedly hit the brakes, killing the engine. Ishtar restarted the truck and began revving the engine, presumably for takeoff.

"Wait," yelled Ralph, running to the truck. "Can we get a ride for however far you're going?"

"Okay," muttered Ishtar, sticking his head out the window and peering at them like he was confirming something he'd forgotten to remember. He flicked his thumb at the back of the truck where they wedged their stuff between two bales of hay.

Doug slid in next to Ishtar. "How far are you going, my good man?"

Ishtar stared at Doug. "My goodness, you are a British person. I thought I dreamed it. I have passport. No, I no have passport so I can go to Turkey." He shook his head, starting again. "No, I can no go to Turkey. I only go to border."

"My God, you are a fine chap. That's wonderful," enthused Doug, shaking Ishtar's hand. To Ralph he said, "Give him a ten. I'll pay you back later." "I should live so long."

"We must help this fine chap with fuel. Maybe we'd better give him a twenty."

"I should live twice as long, but as no one I've ever known said, it's only money." Ralph shook his head as he extracted his last twenty-dollar bill and pressed it on Ishtar.

Ishtar looked at the money like he couldn't believe he was holding twenty American dollars. He putted onto the road as Ralph said to Doug, "We forgot to get our passports from Rondo. We'll see what happens at the border, but I'm guessing, as Rondo might say, we're fucked."

"The last time I saw Rondo, he didn't look like he was able to return our passports," Doug snarked.

"Well, yeah, I know he's fecking dead," snapped Ralph, "but we could have found our passports if we'd looked."

Ishtar took the twenty-dollar bill and held it up against the light, steering with one hand as he folded the bill like origami and tucked it in the pocket of his robe. They could practically hear him thinking, *ka-ching*.

"The missing passports are your fault." Doug sniffed with his nose in the air. "Rondo went from placid to deranged when you harped on about stopping to see the castle and having to pee. He had our passports in his shirt pocket when we left Dabiq, but he must have hidden them the first time we stopped to let you pee. Which is also your fault because the only reason Rondo hid the passports was because you were nattering on about jumping out and escaping to Turkey, pretending he couldn't hear you talking about it."

"Baloney, salami," retorted Ralph. "We discussed that in Spanish. He didn't know what we were talking about."

"Maybe we should assume that everyone knows what we're saying all the time, except that Yazidi farmer on the bus—"

"What makes you think we could have found the passports? Did you see where Rondo put them? I didn't."

"You don't know what happened, so stop arguing," said Doug. "The fact remains that our passports have gone missing." He stared at the deserted road ahead.

"Syria reminds me of Sudan," Ralph said. "Guys in a truck tooling across the desert, next to the Nile. Here we're next to the Euphrates, and no one else is around."

"I like the no-one-else-around part," said Doug. "No ISIS, no Assad, no Beretta."

"I thank you for big money, sir people," said Ishtar as he concentrated on holding the pickup's skinny tires on the narrow track. "We have same passport problem. Maybe we fix both." He smiled at them, looking smarter now. "I have idea. You help my daughter over border.

She is good girl. Her name is Narin." He swerved around a boulder and bounced back on the rutted track as they sat stupefied.

"You mean marry her or something?" Ralph asked.

"Don't be daft," said Doug. "He just wants us to sneak her across the border, something like that." Doug nudged Ishtar as they chugged up the road, ignoring the sweep of Lake Assad. "What exactly would you have us do?"

Ishtar began sobbing, each sob catching in his throat. "I ransom my little girl from ISIS. She is only fifteen. She is too young to marry and never marry out of caste. Now get her safe since her young mother die on Mt Sinjar. Only way is over border." The pickup hiccupped along as Ishtar wrenched the wheel with each theatrical sob, showering dust on the windshield.

Doug patted Ishtar on the back, shaken. "We'll do whatever we can."

"For sure," said Ralph, at which Ishtar stopped sobbing and gunned the pickup, steering merrily down the center of the dusty track, raising a cloud behind them.

"You buck up fast," said Ralph, incredulous. "Were you putting us on?" "No know what is putting on." He smiled like Peter Lorre.

"Where is she now? This Narin?"

"Narin is at border with other refugee," said Ishtar, shaking his head. "Many peoples. Once a week food and water and let few peoples into Turkey. Not every day. No cover place for sleeping. Whole place big toilet. Sometimes Turkey give water two times one week, little stupid bottles of plastic water. Need money to get over border. Much money. Turkish bastards."

"And you can't cross?" asked Ralph. "Why? You have no money?" "Yazidi no have no money and no

227

passport. Like you."

"Please don't remind us," said Ralph.

"We had a Yazidi chap on the bus," said Doug. "He didn't have a passport either." "He didn't speak English," Ralph said, "but I shook hands with him. His name was... Ilyas. Something like that. No, maybe Islay. Do you know him?"

Doug laughed. "That's like when you were in Ireland and everyone asked if you knew their cousin in Pittsburgh. I stayed with a Yazidi family in Yerevan. The daughter was attractive and very nice. She fixed breakfast every morning and was leaving to go to school in Mosul. Since ISIS controls Mosul, I wonder what happened to her."

"That was only a few months ago," said Ralph. "She's screwed. Probably literally. She's a sex slave if her family didn't ransom her back. The Yazidi are a recognized group in Armenia and there are hundreds of thousands in Syria and Iraq. We meet such interesting folks and never know what happens to them."

Doug patted Ishtar on the back. "What did you pay to get your daughter back?" "Everything," said Ishtar, back to sobbing and driving badly.

"The Yazidi religion is a blend of Islam and Hindu," Ralph said. "Melek Taus is the top angel, the Peacock Angel, and he got thrown out of Heaven. That's all I remember, and that's kind of fuzzy." Ralph frowned, trying to remember more.

Ishtar stopped sobbing, brightening at the chance to tout the merits of the Yazidi faith. "I am from Adam."

"Everyone's from Adam," said Ralph.

"If you're among the gullible who would believe everything you're told," said Doug. "No," said Ishtar smugly. "You from Adam and Eve. Yazidi only from Adam." "That's rather sexist," said Doug, "leaving out Mom, good old Eve. And the apple."

"What got you tossed out of Heaven?" Ralph asked. "I forget that part. Wasn't there an intrigue?"

"What is intrigue?" asked Ishtar. "God tell Melek bow down to Adam and Eve, the new creation. Melek say no. Only bow to God." Ishtar added, "Top angel no bow to parent of lesser mankind." He smirked. "God pissed off." He looked around. "God toss Melek from Heaven. But Melek back later. I am from Melek and Adam."

"Sounds drolly gay," said Doug sarcastically.

"Don't be snide," said Ralph. "Gods and angels are considered sexless." He snapped his fingers. "I remember the problem. Melek wasn't just kicked out of Heaven. He was sentenced to Hell. Melek's tears extinguished the fires of Hell, putting Melek back in God's good graces, and Melek was repromoted to Peacock Angel."

"His tears do not a sexless angel make," Doug said, his tone uppity. "Anyway, it'd take oceans of tears to put Hell out of business." He pointed at the drought-stricken countryside. "Hell hath reopened, and its name is Syria."

The lake stretched behind them, the track bumping along the edge of the blue Euphrates where the sounds of explosions reached their ears, puffs of black smoke like pirate balloons dotting the eastern bank a few hundred yards away.

"Does ISIS control the other side of the river?" asked Ralph.

"Yes," said Ishtar, steering furiously around a disabled tank. "ISIS bad to Yazidi because Melek same name in Koran for jinn."

"Gen?" asked Doug. "General?"

"No," said Ralph. "He means devil. Jinn. I can see the problem when your top angel is a devil in Sunni theology. I'm surprised ISIS let you ransom your daughter instead of killing you as infidels."

"ISIS no final decide. Top ISIS people say kill Yazidi like on Mt. Sinjar. Other ISIS say Yazidi much Islam but also believe reincarnation and caste like Hindu."

"Religion is the most mixed-up mess on the planet," said Doug. "Anyone who's studied the mad menagerie can only conclude that they're all a crock. Where did you go wrong, Ralph?"

"You miss the point, Doug. Religion is freedom of spirituality in various forms and manifestations that culminate—"

"Bah, humbug," grumped Doug. "Tell me about the world's most devout religion, variously named the caliphate, ISIS, IS, ISIL, Boko Haram, Al-Shabaab, and I'm sure there are more. How are they a good thing? You should start taking this personally because they could be the death of us."

"Yazidi are the nice guys," Ishtar said. "You can no be Yazidi. But I make you honorary Yazidi if you help Narin."

"Why don't you sneak Narin into Turkey?"

"I told you. No money. No passport." He began sobbing again. "We almost at bad Turkey border. Many problem there."

Ralph pointed. "The main highway is gridlocked going north and blocked to the south. No one can get on or off."

The dirt track ended at the edge of a highway filled with honking cars and a line of pickups full of squawking chickens in baskets with motorbikes weaving through. But there were no tanks, armed soldiers, or pickups with machine guns in the back. They were all refugees headed to Turkey.

"My good man, what are you doing?" demanded Doug as Ishtar drove the pickup off the edge of the bank and onto the walking paths below.

The pickup careened sideways and then caught,

righting itself on the two lowest trails headed north, a few feet above the rolling river. Ishtar barely missed a southbound truck as he clung to the bucking steering wheel. "Big road is full," he yelled.

Traffic on the steeply canted bank was fiercely competitive. Tilted pickups with impatient drivers bounced along tracks in both directions, kicking up dust plumes. The trails weaved erratically on an angle that left Ralph squeezed against the door and Ishtar and Doug on top.

"You're squashing me," Ralph squawked. "And be careful or we'll be swimming. Slow down." He gasped for breath, trying to shove Doug away to roll up the side window. "Get off me. And that 'good man' crap is terribly repetitive."

"It makes people feel good," said Doug, hanging on to the rearview mirror. "It breaks the ice, don't you see, old man?"

Ralph sounded hurt. "That's the second time you said it to Ishtar. He's probably tired of it too."

"I thought we might fall into the river," said Doug. "Do we live or do we die? That always seems to be the question."

"This is stop," said Ishtar. He'd clipped a crumbling concrete barricade that guarded the river against inattentive drivers, marking the boundary of a vast parking lot.

CHAPTER THIRTEEN — THE BORDER

They were blocked by a sea of badly parked vehicles, dirty white pickups, and little white cars. The spacing was helter-skelter, creating a maze.

Doug jumped out, grabbing the big orange pack and swinging it on with an audible sigh of pleasure.

Ralph was stunned. "This is the most terrible thing I've ever seen, so many poor people, refugees." He tied the garbage bag around his shoulders with the Rambo away from his neck. "You have more stuff than these people," he told Doug.

"Even you have more stuff," said Doug. "We're the one percent."

Acres of barbed wire enclosed unending pallets of cardboard. Hundreds of pallets were crammed together in a field of misery, an area the size of a hundred city blocks, stretching half a mile to the border.

Doug and Ralph followed Ishtar as he fell in behind a tall man wearing a red-and-white checkerboard scarf, dodging along a narrow path through the squalid field. Each encampment contained a large white bag. Some were stuffed with irregular shapes, some looked like bags of flour, and each was guarded by one or more women in black. The children looked oddly sedate. Two small girls in frilly dresses slept inside a cardboard box stamped with big red letters: Made in China.

They met two women carrying babies and small bags of commodities, dragging two toddlers up the foot-wide path. Ishtar and the boys sprawled against a large duffel bag to let the menagerie pass, watched closely by two women in black guarding a big bag of commodities.

The men of the camp paced, smoked, and argued behind waves of razor wire piled next to a fifteen-foot-high border fence of barbed wire with extra-long barbs and more razor wire on top.

Turkish soldiers lounged on the other side of the fence with crazy-looking assault weapons slung across their chests, chain smoking.

Ishtar passed a six-year-old girl holding a baby who looked unconscious. Doug stopped, staring at the baby. "Is the child ill?"

The little girl screeched, running away, bobbling the unconscious baby.

"You scared her to death," Ralph said. "This is the worst place we've ever been. It's worse than Aleppo or Dabiq. It's time to go home and rest up."

"What happened to our Marine?" asked Doug as Ishtar cut through the crowd to the right. They followed each other in a line, like old men playing *Crack the Whip*.

"The Marine will provide a change of scenery on the other side of that fence," said Ralph as Ishtar stopped in front of one cluster of tents out of a dozen that stretched along the Euphrates River, ending a few yards from the border.

Each cluster of ten circular tents surrounded an ablutions tent, luxury accommodations compared to sleeping on cardboard in the open. They were large two-room affairs of white nylon with UNHCR stenciled in large blue letters, a number, and a red crescent moon stamped sloppily on front.

"Just so, we stay on this side of the river," said Doug. "The other side is obviously ISIS."

Three black flags the size of eighteen-wheelers flapped wildly in the breeze on top of thirty-foot flagpoles a half mile away on the other side of Euphrates. The flagpoles stood atop the highest of a series of rolling hills descending to a bank high above the river. On this side, the bright blue water lapped the deck of a battered car ferry that protruded from the shallows.

Shattered concrete and rebar remnants of a crumpled bridge dangled from two giant pylons in the river.

Ishtar ducked into group number two and led them to a tent with the number seven stenciled on the front. He unzipped its flap as half a dozen kids surrounded Ralph and Doug.

"Pens," demanded a snot-nosed boy, hand thrust from a ragged sweater sleeve. Another yelled "candy" at the top of his lungs, jumping up and down. A shy girl in a crimson skirt stood with her finger in her mouth, swishing her hips back and forth.

"Dearest children," said Ralph, slapping an urchin's outstretched palm in a low five, "I am fresh out of candy and pens. And keep your grubby hands off my garbage bag. Now watch it. No messing with the bag. No touching. Yuck. Go wash your hands in a puddle or something." Splotches of water dotted the ground around the tents, drying to mud.

Ralph did a double take. "What's with the puddles? This place is a mud hole. Where did the drought go, the dust storms, and the dust devils?" he said, yelling at the kids as if they were responsible.

A ten-year-old with a hennaed hand assaulted Doug with demands, begging for a gift and utterly ignored by Doug. "Candy, pens, cadeaux, cadeaux."

A wee tot missing a diaper stood with both hands under his fat little tummy, proudly piddling in a puddle next to tent number eight. A woman in black with excellent hearing rolled out of tent eight and grabbed the little guy, pulling him toward the ablutions tent in the middle.

Doug tut-tutted at the kid demanding candy and dodged another kid wearing a knit cap. He danced around a puddle to avoid the invasion of children and skidded on a mud patch with aplomb, making it look intentional, gracefully landing on a dry patch with his pointy finger in the kids' faces. "Now children, I see you enjoy inadequate dental care. Candy would render you toothless…" He was interrupted by Ishtar ducking out of the tent with a woman in tow, shooing away the urchins.

"This my Narin," said Ishtar proudly and with good reason.

Narin wore trendy green moccasins and no scarf. With her long black hair pulled back in a ponytail, she looked like she must be age fifteen going on twenty-five. She carried a cell phone that complimented the blue scallops painted down the front of a white blouse tucked into slender black jeans.

"Hey," she said, waving. "I hear you're smuggling me to Turkey."

Ishtar blanched, shushing Narin and beckoning everyone inside the tent. Thin brown pads covered the floor of the tent, which smelled musty and new at the same time. "Please have seat. I am sorry no chair."

The boys propped their stuff against the tent wall, which sagged under the weight of the Rams. They plopped down on the pads cross-legged, agile as fifty-year-olds.

"Better keep it quiet because you heard wrong," said Ralph, pointing a finger at Narin. "We lost our passports, so we don't even know how we'll get ourselves over the border. I'm Ralph, and this is Doug, who forgot

237

our passports back down the road. So don't get your hopes up. What's with the muddy mess outside?"

"Don't worry," she said. "We haven't had hopes for a while…"

"I'm sure you've already figured out that Ralph was the one who left our passports behind," Doug interrupted.

"Wow," said Narin. "A Brit. I love the accent. I went to a British high school in Mumbai and applied to art school in London before we were chased over Mt. Sinjar. I didn't make it off Mt. Sinjar. ISIS caught me."

At their shocked looks, she said, "No. I wasn't forced to do anything." Narin had a tear in her eye. "Dad saved me from ISIS. Some girls were sold as concubines but not girls from families who paid a ransom. I owe Dad everything, which is what he had to sell. Everything. He sold the oldest carpet emporium in the Middle East. For me."

She pointed a green moccasin at the door, where they could see puddles whipped by the wind. "The water is from refugees getting too rowdy. If we try to push our way over the border, the Turks blast us with a water cannon."

She smiled. "That's the only water we're allowed on any day when we rush the fence. No one wants to do that again, after yesterday. We cut a hole in the fence, but the Turks shot seventeen of us, and ten died."

Narin held out an arm with parallel scabs running from shoulder to hand. "That's from clearing razor wire two weeks ago. We opened the weakest part of the fence for a morning rush."

"Why wait until morning?" asked Doug. "Sneak through at night and be gone with the wind."

"The old ones and kids don't herd well in the dark. They panic at night, especially wives who haven't been out of the house by themselves their entire lives, not without a male chaperone."

"Go away, kids," Ralph yelled at two urchins begging at the door, bright little eyes glistening at the gossip. "We're fresh out of pens and candy." The kids dropped their hands, leaning in to listen.

"If we rush the border at night, they use guns instead of water cannon, which is just as bad as guns. The water cannon throws people backward through razor wire. There are incentives to wait until UNHCR convinces the Turks to let us pass."

"Goddamn borders," said Ralph, livid. "Borders are racist because they exclude folks for reasons other than character. Whether you get into a country depends on where you're from, not your character. That's the definition of racism." Ralph pumped a fist, which might have scared a fly.

Doug raised his eyebrows. "You're stuttering. Calm down."

"This guy, for example," said Ralph, pointing at Doug. "He looks like a bad character, but Doug wouldn't hurt anyone. Borders bar everyone based on where you come from. You have to buy a passport, an expensive visa from a corrupt government, pay baksheesh at the border." He started getting into it. "Rattlesnakes and hyenas can cross any border, but harmless guys like us, phooey. Borders are bureaucratic bullshit." He was getting noisy, enthralling the kids in the doorway.

"I'm disappointed to announce that we agree on something," Doug said, "though no one else agrees with us unless they travel full time. Unfortunately, there's no app for character, and governments use visa games to get back at one another, and I stand corrected. You weren't stuttering, you were spluttering."

"The border is open once a week for those with money and a passport," Narin said. "Daesh took our papers."

"Daesh?" asked Ralph.

"Daesh is the local name for ISIS, the Islamic State. Instead of papers, we carried children over Mt. Sinjar, and Syria doesn't issue passports to Yazidi. Worse, everything we owned is gone, which is my fault for getting caught by Daesh."

"Lalish Carpets," Ishtar said. "We..." He began his famous sobbing.

Narin grimaced as if she were torn between being

eternally grateful and enduring Ishtar's sobbing. "Lalish is the Yazidi capital. Our family owned the biggest carpet emporium in Lalish… forever. For centuries, until now." At their blank looks she said, "Lalish is in northern Iraq."

"Is it big?" asked Ralph.

"It is for Yazidi," said Narin. "Half a million people. The most important Yazidi pilgrimage is to the Sheikh Adi ibn Musafir shrine in Lalish, and we owned the oldest carpet business, across the square from the shrine. We had the location." She snapped her fingers, then remembering it was gone, was crestfallen.

"ISIS destroyed the shrine, and we got out just in time, selling the business. Then ISIS took over and it went bankrupt. That's the only sweet part," she said. "Lalish Carpets had a strict policy against customers losing their heads. ISIS was too drastic a change of management. Dad spent the proceeds from the sale to ransom me from ISIS."

"Tell you what," said Ralph. "You're alive. You got away from ISIS. You're inches from freedom."

"Too many inches," said Narin. "We've been here three weeks, and without money, it's impossible to cross the border."

"Mission impossible, that's us," said Ralph. "We'll bring in the Marines." He hoisted scrawny arms in a body-builder pose. "We'll rescue the damsel in distress."

"Oh, brother," said Doug, eyes rolling back in his

241

head. "She's too young."

"That's a terrible insinuation," said Ralph, miffed. "I'm a people person. You, on the other hand, are an inanimate-object person."

He turned his back on Doug. "Let's go, Ms. Narin. We'll scout out the fence and figure out how to get across. You coming along, Ishtar?"

"I come," he said as they filed outside, threading through neighborhood kids.

Narin pointed a hundred yards west, away from the river. "See that clump of people?" Dozens of families had crowded into a corral of barbed wire next to the border. Rolls of razor wire shimmered in the afternoon light.

"The Turks open the gate on Thursdays. Bring your wallet, your purse, your gold bars, and your gilt-edged securities, and you might get across."

"Well, what day is it anyway?" asked Doug. "Retired means never having to say you're sorry you don't know what day it is."

"Wednesday," said Narin. "They open the gate at ten o'clock tomorrow."

"Turkey is bound to welcome folks like me and Doug," Ralph said, "since we hail from favorite allied nations and are harmless fellows well met. The guards will probably let us in right now, no problem."

Ralph led them on a straight shot toward the

growing crowd, leading like a Marine for approximately four seconds until passed by Doug, who swirled through the crowds like a broken field runner, around mud holes and ragged families, paralleling razor wire where men harangued Turkish soldiers standing on the other side.

A man pushed a wad of banknotes through coils of razor wire, holding a baby in one arm. "I pay. Take baby," he said to a Turkish soldier.

The soldier turned his back.

A man in jeans and a red vest pushed bottles of water through the fence from the Turkish side, offering one to the man with the baby. The wind tore the money from the man's grasp. He tried to retrieve it from a loop of razor wire as the baby began to scream.

Doug deftly threaded through refugees pressed dozens deep in front of a thick steel gate. The gate was notched on the top, where a tank turret rested like a big eye staring at the crowd.

"That's a great place to line up," Ralph said, "in front of a tank."

A skinny soldier with a blond crew cut and a new gold bar on his shoulder climbed on top of the tank. He whipped a red beret the color of the Turkish flag from his belt and perched it on his head. He yelled at the crowd. "Make my motherfucking day."

"Excuse me, my friend," Doug said as he ducked around and through family groups. "Pardon me. Sorry, we're not cutting in line. We'll be going back in a minute. Excuse me."

Doug and Ralph wound their way through the crowd toward the front. The men under the turret at the front of the line swore a fresh string of epithets as they pushed toward the tank.

"Sorry, sir," said Ralph. "We won't be a minute. You have earned your place in line and we are not cutting in front of you, I promise you sincerely."

Ralph made it to the front, thrusting himself back to avoid being pushed into coils of razor wire by the crowd behind them. The razors were sharp and new with a thin blade every couple of inches.

Ralph bent to look. "I could get some great shots off the little razors, reflecting the gate with the tank turret on top, the sun through the dust..."

Doug shouted at the spiffy red beret on top of the tank. "I say, my good man. Might we have a word?"

Red Beret screamed down at them, "Didn't you hear the word I already gave you? Make my motherfucking day."

Red Beret held up a black box with two toggles. "Bring it on. Step right up so I can test my slick new remote control." He fiddled with a toggle and the turret swung abruptly left, scraping across the top of the steel gate, worse than claws across a blackboard.

The vibration of the turret on the gate knocked

Red Beret sideways, and he danced a fine line to keep from teetering off the tank. As he recovered his balance, the crowd broke into derisive applause. "I am so ready to have my motherfucking day made," he screamed.

Ralph waved his hands in simmer-down mode "Relax. You're not Clint Eastwood…"

Red Beret ran back to a machine gun mounted above the turret, swiveled into the seat behind it, clicked off a safety the size of his thumb, and fired a burst over their heads, really getting into it before lowering the smoking gun. He jumped out of the firing seat and ran back with the black box in the palm of one hand. He grasped the toggle delicately with extended fingers.

"Don't trip, bozo," said Ralph as the crowd surged away from the burst of machine-gun fire. "You might hurt someone."

"I will hurt you bad, motherfucker," yelled Red Beret. "If you refugees don't move back, I will blow your heads off." He touched the toggle, clanking the turret, almost falling off the tank.

Doug rolled his eyes. "We're not refugees."

"Maybe you got the wrong toggle there," said Ralph. "Maybe the other one makes it go boom."

"I'll make you go boom, boom." Red Beret cautiously moved his fingers to the other toggle.

"Shut up, Ralph," Doug said. He yelled up at Red Beret. "We wish to pay handsomely to cross the border, cash for a nice chap like yourself, whereupon we promise"—he crossed his heart—"to go directly to the airport and leave Turkey forever. We promise to never become a burden on Turkey's generous welfare system."

"You mean never see Cappadocia again? Or Istanbul?" said Ralph. "Surely we can come back when we get new passports. I love Turkey."

"You love everywhere," Doug hissed. "I don't love Syria," Ralph hissed back.

"Then shut up so we can get *out* of Syria."

Red Beret growled above their heads. "Turkey has nothing for foreigners. No welfare for you."

The crowd along the fence west of the gate was getting bigger and very noisy.

"That's the welfare we promise to forego," said Ralph, raising a finger. "In addition, this nice British gentleman has a wad of money, green American money in large denominations. He would like to donate that money to the charity of your choice if you would be so kind to let us move two feet behind you, on the other side of the fence." He shoved Narin in front of them. "Along with this lovely lady."

Doug experienced an epileptic fit, his lifeless fist clutching spasmodically at his heart as Red Beret said, "She would definitely make my day." He leered down at Narin like a lecherous Dennis the Menace.

"Now, none of that, bully boy," said Ralph.

"We're not bartering for the young lady." He shoved Narin behind them.

"I thought you wanted to donate to the charity of my choice," Red Beret said. "She is the charity of my choice, yum, yum." He licked his lips obscenely.

"Attench-hut," commanded a chubby officer in a hard-brimmed hat and uniform jacket with captain's bars as he clambered onto the back of the tank behind Red Beret.

"Soliciting again?" Chubby said. "I should have you shot." Chubby unholstered a German Luger from his hip. "I would prefer making the solicitation myself," he said, pointing the gun at Red Beret.

"Fifty-fifty as usual?" asked Red Beret.

"Done," said Chubby, swiveling the Luger at Doug's head. "Your money or your life?" "Open the gate first," said Ralph. "We like value for our money."

"Let's see how much American money you have, preferably in large denominations," Chubby said, "and whether it's enough to get you through the gate. Let's take a look at that right now," he said, shaking the muzzle at Doug.

Doug ceased play-acting. Turning a ghastly shade of gray, he slowly raised his hands as if in a trance.

"I didn't say raise your hands," said Chubby, gesturing. "I said hand over the money." Doug was frozen.

"In case you've forgotten," Chubby snarled, "it's probably around your waist or your neck. That's where all the stupid tourists keep their money."

Doug stood with shaking arms, unable to move.

"Have the other one unbutton his shirt," said Red Beret as the crowd noise rose in a crescendo to their left.

"Shut up," said Chubby. He pointed the Luger at Ralph. "Unbutton his shirt."

Besides the fact that Doug would hate him for the rest of his natural life, Ralph looked like having to touch Doug might make him throw up. But without a bribe, they might as well kiss their sorry butts goodbye.

"Yuck," said Ralph, gingerly unbuttoning Doug's shirt.

Doug slapped his hands away. "You can't do this. I will die."

They could hear yells in Arabic and English. "Hole in fence." The crowd surged to the west.

"Go check that out," Chubby said to Red Beret. "And shoot anyone who tries sneaking through the fence."

"Don't forget my half of the money," said Red Beret, saluting. He grabbed a scary- looking assault rifle and caressed the narrow barrel, the serrated body, the ergonomic hand grips, and the gigantic clip as if molesting a maiden. He jumped off the tank in crack paratrooper style. "I finally make my day." He slammed the loading mechanism home and hoisted the gun on his shoulder, strutting off with the excitement of being able to shoot anything that moved.

"Hand it over," said Chubby as Ralph shakily removed the stained white wallet from Doug's neck.

"Don't do this," gasped Doug. "That's my life savings. Me poor mum and me will be destitute."

Chubby fired a shot between Ralph and Doug, splattering dirt and pebbles on their feet, making them jump like marionettes, scaring the bejesus out of them.

Ralph groaned, handing over the grubby wallet. "I'm sorry, Doug. I'm so sorry. This is entirely my fault."

"Like taking candy from children," said Chubby, grabbing greedily at the wallet.

"You owe me forever," said Doug to Ralph. "Forever, should we live so long. Now, my good man with the lovely Luger, may we enter?" He put on a brave front as his life's blood drained from his extremities, squeezed by the iron fist around his heart as Chubby ripped the wallet open with gusto.

Chubby glared at Doug, reluctantly torn from counting Doug's loot. "Please, my good man," Doug added, really laying it on.

"Shut up. I'm counting," said Chubby, flipping through currencies.

The air shrieked with a machine-gun blast—Red Beret with his fun assault weapon. "I don't know won," said Chubby, holding up a sheaf, "or baht, or yuan. This funny money can't be worth much."

There were screams to the west as Red Beret forced illegal immigrants through razor wire back to Syria, and Chubby held up a clump of multi-colored bills. "You think this is enough money to buy your way into the homeland of the Exceptionals, Mother Turkey? Surely you jest."

Single shots as Red Beret picked off running targets, high-pitched pings, but they never heard a thud, only unending screams and pings.

"Use your phone. Check xe.com for current exchange rates," Doug screamed hysterically. "The 10,000 won note is worth a hundred dollars."

Ralph stood stricken, like the wind had been kicked out of him.

Chubby waved Doug away. "There's no phone reception here. Oh, here's some dollars. I know what *they're* worth, which isn't much anymore." He counted laboriously, fumbling, finally saying, "Thirty-two hundred isn't enough to let even one of you into Mother Turkey. The going rate is five thousand a person."

Doug gasped. "The other currencies are worth far in excess of fifteen thousand dollars, so let the three of us across. Now, forthwith, forsooth."

Chubby waved the pistol. "You have no bargaining chips. Go away."

Doug stood holding his breath, turning blue as

Chubby added, "Holding your breath won't get you anywhere. Don't be silly, or I'll have you shot. On second thought," he said as if inspired, folding the wallet full of currency and sticking it in his pocket. "I'll shoot you myself." He leveled the Luger at Doug.

"Don't be a barbarian," shouted Ralph, pushing Doug out of the way. The Luger fired harmlessly into the ground as Chubby grinned like a pumpkin.

Chubby aimed at Ralph, who waved his hands. "Let me say this first, a message for your boss, Mr. Asshole Erdoğan. This is no way to treat the citizens of important Turkish allies, and I am very disappointed in Mr. Erdoğan. Will you tell him that for me?"

"Oh, go away now, far away," said Chubby. "Not that way," he said as they turned west toward the crowd trying to break through the fence. "The other way." He sounded disappointed he wouldn't be able to shoot them. But he squeezed off a volley anyway, making them run for the blind spot at the east corner of the gate. They tucked around the corner and stopped as Narin and Ishtar struggled up behind them.

"That went well," Narin said. "It looks like you won't be getting yourselves across, much less me."

"I told you we probably wouldn't get ourselves across, much less you," Ralph said. "Prediction accomplished." He blinked. "What happened to you?"

Narin's blouse was streaked with dirt, her phone

was missing, and her green moccasins were caked with mud, which she scraped at with her fingernails. "Everyone stampeded when the asshole in the red beret opened up with the machine gun. Didn't you notice?" She pared mud from under a fingernail.

"I thought you were behind us, but we were kind of busy," said Ralph. "Trying to talk our way over the border."

"Busy squandering my life savings," Doug snarled. "Imagine trying to bribe an obvious blackguard. I'll have to cable me mum. She'll be so disappointed."

"Oh, for God's sake," exclaimed Ralph. "I don't want you to cable your mother. If she had internet like everyone else, she could send you some money. But it was my fault, so I'm paying for everything from here on out, assuming they take credit cards."

"I've waited years to hear you say you'd had a fault or would pay for anything," Doug said. "Of course, interest still accrues on the gazillion dollars you owe me."

"I always pay, and you never pay, and 'from here on out' may not be a very long time. Without five grand each there's no reason to wait around until tomorrow. So any ideas on getting over the border, Narin, Ishtar?"

"The river might work," Narin said, "and there are rumors of a gap in the fence, fifteen miles west."

A machine gun began firing over the heads of those trying to widen a hole in the fence. As the barrage arced down, the crowd scattered.

"Great," Doug said, excitedly wiggling his scrawny shoulders at the thought of throwing on the big orange pack. "Fifteen miles is nothing. Let's go."

"What about the river?" asked Ralph. "Can you sail?" Narin asked.

Ishtar didn't seem to be following the conversation. He stared into space, mumbling. "We can no walk that far. We are lost."

"Why not drive?" asked Doug. "You could get everything you own in that pickup." "Only road to here," said Ishtar. "Next road goes to Dabiq and ISIS."

"Of course I can sail," said Ralph. "I lived on a sailboat for two years. I never got an anchor to hold, but I was okay at everything else, except navigation, which I was super good at. But isn't the river mined and strung with barbed wire. You can't sail underneath the barbed wire and besides, there aren't any boats."

"Except for that, it sounds peachy keen," said Doug sarcastically.

Narin smiled cryptically. "Barbed wire can be cut, and I know a guy who hid a Hobie Cat down by the river. His name is Abdul, but he doesn't know how to sail. He said a catamaran can be tricky."

"It's easier than a monohull," said Ralph, "depending on the size. How big is it?" "It's sixteen feet."

"Oh, crap," said Ralph. "The little ones are

finicky. They're fast as the wind unless they're overloaded, and they're easy to capsize. We'd never get four or five people on a sixteen- foot Hobie Cat, which is meant for two people without luggage. The pontoon storage is barely enough for a snorkel and mask."

"You bragged about sailing the Caribbean," said Doug, "but you're always bragging about something, and I don't remember you being the captain." He almost sounded impressed.

Narin clapped her hands in excitement. "Daddy, we have a captain. Mr. Ralph is our last chance to escape Syria."

"I sailed a Hobie Cat down the Sea of Cortez with friends in a sag wagon," Ralph said. "Got becalmed and showed up twelve hours late. The guys had already listed my stuff on Craigslist: *Estate sale for sailor lost at sea.*"

"So you don't really know how to sail, and you got becalmed, and those are your qualifications for drowning us in the Euphrates," said Doug snippily. "This means walking is the only way to go, especially since I hate sailing and love walking."

"But it's our only chance," Narin pleaded, eyes big and brown and shiny, cute as a junior miss.

"The river is the best bet," Ralph said, "and we don't really know if there's a hole in the fence fifteen long miles away. If the river doesn't work, we can walk and walk and walk, though it will finally destroy my neck."

He rubbed his neck as he checked the sun. "It's an hour to sunset, so we have plenty of time to try the river. If that doesn't work it'll be dark, which is a good time to avoid border guards. Though if you think about it, the hole-in-the-fence idea doesn't make sense, or everyone would head that way."

Doug turned to Narin. "Is the river mined?"

"I haven't heard," she said. "But we need wire cutters for the barbed wire. The Turkish stuff is old and nasty with long rusty barbs. We'll have to cut through trash and algae too." She was ready to go.

Doug snorted. "Wet trash and algae breed diphtheria. This is the perfect opportunity to see if our inoculations remain effective."

"Let's go take a look," said Ralph, dueling with Doug for the lead.

They ignored the phalanx of black ISIS flags on the other side of the river, staring at the point where the Euphrates crossed into Turkey. "It looks like razor wire under barbed wire." Doug pointed. "We'll have to cut both."

Ralph said, "Farther out the wire sags below the water. A Hobie Cat has a six-inch draft, so we should be fine. The best part is the wind." Captain Ralph swiveled to check the wind direction. It was blowing from the east, directly at them. "The wind will keep us away from ISIS, and we can easily tack north across the border. It won't take more than five minutes. Should be a piece of cake."

"You know," said Doug, "you've force fed me several pieces of cake, and they've been largely inedible. And I do remember a couple of your sailing adventures, exciting because of your incompetence. You have amazing stories of whatever's the opposite of seamanship."

"It's just a matter of proper planning," said Ralph. "And therein lies the rub," said Doug.

"Stop it, you two," said Narin. "We'll find Abdul. He wants out as bad as I do, and he's a hustler, so he'll know where to get wire cutters. He's the camp's Sergeant Bilko."

"Wow," said Ralph. "You know of Sergeant Bilko? Our childhoods were equally privileged."

"Who's Sergeant Bilko?" asked Doug. "Some slapstick American comic like Jerry Lewis who only the French could love?"

"Nope," said Ralph. "Sergeant Bilko was the typical resourceful American, an army quartermaster able to procure anything."

"I think I have it," said Doug. "The name Bilko comes from the root *to bilk*, illustrating the American delight in the trick, the con, the swindle, and the bamboozle, the means by which my life savings evaporated."

"Oh, Dougy, Dougy, Dougy," said Ralph as Narin

led them past the block of tents. "TV was way better back in our day. Now it's all crap. Back then it was only mostly crap. Bilko and Benny were two of the great old comedians."

"You two are old comedians," said Narin stopping to look at tent numbers. "Abdul's in the next alley over. I like Sergeant Bilko and the Honeymooners. but I never heard of Benny."

"And that, ladies and gentlemen, is the difference between Syria and northern Iraq," said Ralph. "The nuances of TV programming."

"Here," said Narin, stopping in front of tent number two in group ten. She scratched at the flap. "Are you there, Abdul?"

A shaggy old man with scraggly white whiskers stuck his upper torso out of the partly unzipped door. "Abdul at river." He paused, looking them up and down "Back soon. We leave."

"So you found someone to sail the boat?" asked Narin.

"Shhh," said the man. "Boat secret. Did you hear the much shooting? We leave, captain or no captain. Point boat and go."

"Pointing the boat and going is not really the way it works, but yes," said Ralph. "We heard the shooting close up. We can help you escape by boat. I'm Captain Ralph." He shook the old man's hand.

"You are captain!" cried the old man. "I am Ferhad" He unzipped the tent, stepped out, and hugged Ralph.

Doug sighed. "He *says* he's a captain…" "Better than no captain," said Narin.

"Well, thank you, my dear," said Ralph, giving Ferhad a big smile because he looked way older than them.

"We ready to escape to Turkey," Ferhad said. "Is wonderful wind, no?" "I can see this going very badly," said Doug.

"Wonderful wind," agreed Ralph. "So grab some wire cutters, and we'll help Abdul rig the Hobie Cat." Ralph swooped his hand north. "And off we go. Escape to Turkey."

CHAPTER FOURTEEN –
CATTING AROUND

Ten minutes later, they stood around Abdul and the shambles of a Hobie Cat on the edge of the river. Abdul was a twentysomething smooth operator, proudly brushing the last of the leaves off the carcass as he said, "It's a sturdy watercraft."

"My dear God, you know this isn't going to work," said Doug.

The aluminum frame was stretched taut by a splotchy canvas trampoline sprinkled with the fragments of reeds and branches, undersized for six people. The only fortunate circumstance was its location a hundred feet south of the Turkish border, right on the edge of the bank where the river had cut a small cove. It was a tranquil site for launching a boat into a roaring river swept by gale-force winds.

Ralph slipped the mast out of a burlap sack and unrolled the little mainsail, holding it up to the fading light as it snapped in the wind. It didn't look like it'd last a minute.

"And where are the sheets?" Ralph asked.

At Abdul's blank look, Ralph said, "You probably call them ropes." He glanced behind him at the sunset, which seemed a little dusty.

"Red sky at night, sailor take fright," Doug muttered as the sunset turned crimson, thinking about how to handle a big pack underwater.

"Ah, yes," said Abdul. "I kept the ropes underneath." He tugged at an old canvas bag, scattering sand that blew in their faces.

As Abdul opened the bag, Ralph tried to inspect the trampoline. "It's getting dark fast." Abdul was the heaviest with everyone else's weight dropping from there. It was hard to tell if it would hold several hundred pounds for even five minutes.

Ralph put his nose to the canvas and pounded it gingerly. It smelled like mildew. It might be brittle, maybe exceedingly brittle in the middle.

Ralph pointed at the edge of the cove as he said to Abdul, "Let's set the old girl right here. Give him a hand, Doug."

"Yes, massah," Doug said, helping Abdul slide it to the edge of the river.

"Okay," said Ralph, "now point the bow straight out. No, the bow is the pointy end. Yep, it's easy to turn around, only weighs a couple hundred pounds. Push it forward so it's touching the water."

Abdul followed orders perfectly as Doug stood rolling his eyes.

Ralph clapped his hands. "Good. Balancing the boat requires three on each side. I'll man the tiller..." He trailed off. "Now, Abdul, grab the mast, and we'll set it here on the hinges."

Ralph jumped on the trampoline, which unbelievably held the one hundred thirty-seven pounds Doug had starved him down to. He flipped open the mast-step while Abdul carried the mast to the front. The base slid easily into the step, and Ralph latched it down.

He stepped back to take a look. "Maybe this will work. Next, we bend the mainsail onto the mast." He laid the sail on the trampoline, where it flapped madly. "Oh, dear," he said. There was a foot-long tear in the mainsail but no reason to upset anyone.

"Oh, well, we thread it through the slot in the mast and pull it up with the main halyard like this."

Ralph pulled up the mainsail and it began snapping like a cracking whip.

"That looks funny," said Doug. "Are you sure it's right?" Ralph stood back. "It's upside down."

"Why'd you put it on upside down?"

"There's a hole in the sail," Narin said. "And it's getting bigger."

"Give me a break," said Ralph, pulling down the main. He flipped it over and attached the halyard properly, ignoring the growing hole in the middle. "You don't need sails in a wind like this, especially on a catamaran. We could sail under bare poles." It was the captain's duty to protect landlubbers from worrying about the dangers of passage and technical matters like the condition of component parts. Nervous passengers could tip a boat over.

Doug looked at the others. "Are you certain you want to sail on this wreck with this captain?"

They nodded sadly in unison, their hearts not exactly in it. Doug shook his head in exasperation. "Okay. Now what, o captain our captain?"

Ralph hoisted the little jib, and the wind exploded it into a half moon. The bulging jib wrenched the mainsail into the wind, making the Hobie Cat buck like a rodeo bronco.

Ralph hastily dropped the main and the jib, smiling weakly as they stared forlornly at the darkening sky. Even Abdul seemed to have lost his swami enthusiasm.

"Smooth move, Magoo," Doug said.

Only an idiot would hoist the sails before launching, but Ralph's lips were sealed. "Okay," said Ralph, swallowing hard. "We slowly push the cat into the river and load by twos." They looked at him blankly.

"Okay, we push it into the river this far," he said, holding his arms wide apart, "three times." He sighed. "When we push the last little bit and we're floating free, I'll jump on and take the tiller."

Ralph looked them over. "I need the lightest in front, so that'd be, let's see, Narin and Ishtar, then Doug and Ferhad. Doug, you'd better tie my bag and your pack to the mast. Then Abdul gets on, and I'll be right behind to take the tiller."

Ralph blinked, trying to think of what he'd forgotten. "Oops, wait a sec. I need to check the tiller."

Ralph grabbed the end of the tiller, and it swung free. "Crap, the pin's out." He scrambled, twisting open the pontoon hatch, feeling inside, holding on to his hat in the wind. "Here," he said triumphantly, holding up a round piece of metal.

Everyone looked glum as Ralph twisted the pin into the tiller, swinging it as a test. Ralph sang like a conductor. "We're ready so climb aboard," he drawled, tugging the Arizona cap firmly on his head.

"Yeah, right," said Doug as they pushed the bow of the Hobie Cat slowly onto the water. "We're ready to die." Narin and Ishtar scrambled to the front on either side.

As Doug and Ferhad climbed on, Narin screamed, "Haboob coming."

"Oh, fuck, you're kidding," said Ralph as he looked behind them. A wall of dust towered hundreds of feet into a darkening sky, sweeping toward them like an out-of-control locomotive, covering the horizon from north to south. "No wonder it was getting dark."

The haboob hit full blast, flipping the wind direction one eighty degrees from the stiff easterly they'd had all afternoon and dropping visibility to zero with stinging dust that peppered them like buckshot.

Ralph grabbed for the tiller, missed, and hung on as the Hobie Cat shot off under bare poles, loose sails flapping out of control. Ishtar lost his balance and toppled into the water, disappearing in the billowing dust. Abdul missed his footing and also fell in, dapper during the split second before he sank. He bobbed up, waving one arm with his head high before he vanished behind the Hobie Cat.

"Where's Doug?" yelled Ralph, holding the tiller as the haboob whipped the cat from side to side. They could see nothing, shielding their faces from the grit that scoured their skin like sandpaper, making them duck their heads and close their eyes.

"I'm here," said Doug, sounding gurgley. "I'm holding on to the pole. Along with Narin."

"I grabbed him and got him to hold on," Narin said. "He's okay now. That was a close one."

The haboob had thinned slightly, revealing the survivors. Narin was drenched but unflappable. She sat caked with orange sand, cross-legged with one arm around the mast, smiling back at Ralph. Doug lay flat on his face, embracing the pole with both arms.

Ralph laughed. "That pole is called the mast. Keep on holding on. We lost Ishtar and Abdul and Ferhad. So only you and Narin are left. I can't believe your pack and my bag are still tied on."

Doug gasped as they shot into the darkness. "I never saw what happened to Ferhad. So here we are again. Totally fucked."

Doug pulled himself up with effort, catching his breath in the teeth of the wind, patting his pack. "I'll help with the sail thingy," he said, staggering up, rickety as he pulled the main halyard and hoisted the mainsail. Ralph's warning cry was swallowed by chaos.

The haboob caught the mainsail, ripping it through and flipping the Hobie Cat sideways and upside down. They fell spluttering into the dark water of the Euphrates River as the dust storm raged over their heads.

"You dumb fuck," said Ralph said between gurgles. "I got my hat," he said, holding it up, "but I lost my glasses. Quick, grab a pontoon before it gets away, Doug. See, Narin is already on top." He peered myopically, guessing Narin was the shadow perched on the upside-down trampoline.

Ralph squinted, making out Narin's pixie face smiling down. "Why'd you pull the sail up in this wind?" he yelled at Doug.

"Well, you pulled the sail up on land, which was apparently in error. I concluded sails should only be pulled up on water and that you'd probably forgotten to do it since you've been forgetting things. So I assisted a captain whom others must continually rescue." Doug grabbed a pontoon. "I am secured on the large tubular thing," he said as Narin helped pull him back on board. He lay panting, draped like a mop over the top of the pontoon as dust pinged off the hull.

Ralph had climbed halfway on when a gust jerked the hull, spilling him back into the water. As Ralph started to float away, Doug yelled, "Here, take a hand."

"That's called ass-over-teakettle," said Ralph, coughing as he grabbed outstretched hands. "The Marine is coming," he said, grunting to pull himself up. He squinted, trying to see something, anything, without his glasses. "Damn. Where are we? Do those look like hills to you?" He shifted his skinny butt on the underside of the upside-down trampoline, which held water like a wading pool.

"Definitely hills," Narin said. The cat swept forward on a long diagonal toward the shore.

"You have another pair of glasses, don't you?" asked Doug. "You're not going to be any good blind, in addition to your other infirmities."

"Only half a pair. I lost a lens when the Aleppo van almost got blown up. The half glasses are somewhere in my bag, I hope. I'll look when we're on dry land." He shivered from the shock of blindness, though the water was warm.

"Did you see?" asked Doug, pointing straight down. "My pack is still there, and that might be a black garbage bag. They're a bit wet, but they're tied to the pole under this canvas... affair." He poked the trampoline with his finger and it sliced through.

"You did a good job tying them on," Ralph said and patted his hand. "But we have to spread the weight so we don't fall through the canvas. Will everyone we lost be okay?"

"Oh, boys, boys," said Narin. "We're almost on shore. Abdul was standing in the shallows when I last saw him. Nothing we can do about them now so not to worry." She pointed at a looming shape in the haze.

"We might be better off falling through the canvas," said Doug. "Guile is the better part of valor..."

"Is that really a quote?" snapped Ralph.

"I just made it up," said Doug loftily. "True guile would avoid the wrong side of the river, and this bit coming up is definitely the wrong side."

Doug rubbed his eyes, cleared his throat, and spat river water. "We're on the wrong side and coming in fast." The upside-down mast grounded, tipping them forward into the water as the Hobie Cat swiveled on the mast and sent the closest pontoon skittering toward them. Narin calmly rolled off and waded to shore in a blouse washed newly white, jeans stuck to her legs, little green moccasins squishy as she stepped on land, a narrow strip of beach below a steep bank twenty feet high.

"Perfect," said Ralph. "It'll be easy to untie my

bag." They scrambled for their belongings as Narin stood watching.

"What's the big lump?" asked Narin, poking at Ralph's bag as he rolled it over to a gush of water. Doug pushed over his big wet pack, turning it upside down, water streaming out.

"We're in the service of the Aleppo museum, rescuing the *Rams in a Thicket* for some reason that completely escapes my mind," said Ralph, suddenly tired as he shook his head and rummaged in the garbage bag for his glasses. "We thought we were saving the Rambos for posterity and for Sir Doug to achieve his destiny, but now I don't know. I can't believe we're still toting them around."

He rubbed his neck, about to kick the bag when he felt the corner of his glasses case, crushed by the Rambo. He pried the glasses from the shattered case, holding them up. "They're a little bent, but they should be okay," he said, slipping them on. Cockeyed, he tottered onto the sand.

"What's wrong with you, Captain Ralph?" asked Narin, bending over and shaking his arm.

"Oh, nothing," said Ralph, picking himself up, embarrassed. "One lens is missing, and it makes me dizzy to look through just one."

"Marcy was right," gasped Doug, unsnapping the top of his pack, more water dribbling out. "Dumb as rocks."

"Oh, that's Howard Stern's show," said Narin, clapping her hands.

"Dumb as an entire box of rocks," snapped Ralph, worn out from losing the boat and half the passengers, left with half a pair of glasses, blind in one eye, shipwrecked in Syria with a feeling that lowlifes lurked nearby bearing long knives and black flags. He rewrapped the Rambo and fit everything in the black bag.

"Wow," said Narin, impressed. "You're pretty smart because your version is better than Howard Stern's. That's the show when he interviews the hos."

Ralph was aghast, dropping the checkerboard pack on his foot. "I'm shocked to hear a nice Yazidi girl has even heard of Howard Stern. Ishtar would wash your mouth out with soap."

"Don't be silly," said Narin. "You must have heard of the internet."

"Quiet," said Doug. "Do you hear noises? Like someone talking or walking around up there?"

"We'll stay on the beach," said Ralph, "and follow it north to the border fence, though it looks like we lose the beach pretty fast." The beach dwindled to nothing in the dark distance between the river and the high bank.

"One second," Doug said. "I should check the condition of the safety guarantee, in case we need it." He removed the plastic envelope, flipping it open to a sodden safety guarantee. "This won't dry well," said Doug, gingerly pulling it out of the envelope with water cascading. "There's not much left of the seal, but you can still see the writing if you look real close." He waved it to dry it.

"Come on, boys," Narin cut in. "We really should get going." Doug looked up. "It's too late."

Two men in black stood on the bank over their heads bearing headlamps and guns similar to those called AK-47s.

Doug and Ralph slowly raised their hands, blinded by the headlamps as Narin charged up the beach. Her moccasins flashed in the weak moonlight as she sprinted north along the river's edge.

"Get your stupid butts up here," said a silhouette, turning its headlamp at the other silhouette. Both wore black balaclavas. "You go get the girl."

"Leave her alone," screeched Ralph. "And relax up there."

"One moment," said Doug. "I have to dry the plastic before I put this important paper inside, protect our safety guarantee in light of recent developments."

"Bring it up here with your miserable selves," the first soldier said.

The second soldier ran down a diagonal path, his headlamp jiggling as he slanted toward the beach double-quick. Doug and Ralph stood horrified as he crunched

Narin in a flying tackle.

Narin screamed, and the soldier cursed in an unknown language as she slashed his face with her fingernails, rolling on pebbles, kicking and scratching, all Narin.

Ralph and Doug started toward Narin when the soldier above them flashed the light in their eyes and leveled his weapon at them. "She'll be fine, so get up here right now."

Doug swung on his sodden pack, and Ralph grabbed his bag. They watched the action and scoped out footholds, the headlamp above blinding them as they stumbled up the almost vertical bank. Doug climbed with the limp safety guarantee and plastic envelope in one hand, keeping his balance with the other.

Narin kicked and scratched the young soldier, whose headlamp swiveled back and forth as he tried to drag Narin up the path, two steps forward, one step back.

Ralph sounded like he might puke, breathless as they neared the top. The boys peered into the headlamp as the first soldier said, "Fecking tourists."

Doug stopped flapping the safety guarantee, and they stood stock still, trying to place the voice as Narin and the second soldier brawled up the path toward them.

As Ralph started toward Narin, the first soldier said, "We know you, old farts." He pulled off his balaclava and shined the headlamp on his face. Gallouz still wore a minute mustache and now an even punier beard, asking, "Why did you fail us? Why didn't you send us a friend request on Facebook?"

"Hi, Gallouz from Chefchaouen," Ralph said, rushing up to shake hands. "I almost didn't recognize you without the cool sunglasses and the nice blue turban. How the hell have you been?"

Gallouz laughed, snapping on a pole light, flooding the area with a faint glow and revealing a green pup-tent that was surely too small for two teenage soldiers. The rest was bare dirt, a stubby stool, and two rickety chairs next to a scratchy-looking green bush where Gallouz propped his fancy assault rifle. He and Ralph embraced like long lost friends.

Ralph pounded Gallouz on the back. "That's not a very professional way to treat your weapon," he said. The other soldier pulled off his balaclava, trying to hold Narin still with the other hand as she screeched, grabbing and scratching at his face.

Ralph gasped. "And our old buddy Nuriddin from Khiva, land of Shem, son of Noah." The same baby face, button nose, girly lips, and blue marble eyes.

Doug tut-tutted. "Word of advice, Nuriddin. You'd be a lot better off letting the girl go." "She already slap me, scratch like Wolverine," Nuriddin said.

"Let me go," screamed Narin, stuck on replay. "Let me go." She wrenched a wrist free and slapped

Nuriddin again. "Unhand me, you mongrel dog."

Ralph backed away from Gallouz, smiling broadly with his arms held wide. "Well, boys, it's good to see you As soon as Doug dries the safety guarantee we'll let you take a look and we'll be on our way, and you really should let Narin go." Ralph turned to Narin. "He'll let you go if you promise not to run off. Don't worry, you're safe with us."

Narin rolled her eyes. "No one's safe with you two."

"I don't know," said Nuriddin, leaning his assault rifle against his leg and stroking the downy peach fuzz on his chin, holding Narin at arm's length as he looked her up and down. "She is cute, but no can trust."

"Good idea," snarled Narin. "Trust no one, ever, and damn right I can't be trusted." She shifted her tone, simpering. "Let me go anyway. Because trust me, I am cute." She laughed as Nuriddin squinted, puzzling that over.

"Just tell Nuriddin you won't run away, whether you will or won't," Doug said. "If you promise to send them a friend request on Facebook, we can get on with more important things."

"I shoot her if she runs," said Nuriddin the tough-guy cream puff, rubbing his face where Narin had slugged, scratched, and scraped him. "She is bad, bad girl."

"Oh, you wish," snapped Narin. "I don't want to be friends with this sissy brute, on Facebook or any other way. He hit me. He's an ISIS thug."

Ralph sighed. "No, he's not a thug. He's just a kid who hates tourists and is playing soldier. I bet he's already had it with ISIS."

Doug showed the safety guarantee to Nuriddin. "Be careful. It's still wet. And about the Facebook thing, the only reason we haven't sent a friend request is that we've been in ISIS captivity and haven't had Wi-Fi."

At their skeptical looks, Ralph said, "Seriously. We asked Colonel Beretta to let us log on to Dabiq's Wi-Fi, and he threatened to shoot us. So we haven't been able to get online. But we talked about it, didn't we, Doug? We were going to send you both friend requests, scout's honor." Ralph raised two fingers. "Oh, I mean, sir." He unfurled a third finger and saluted crisply like a Marine.

Gallouz took control. "You can present the safety guarantee at headquarters. You showed it to Imam Fahd, and he wasn't impressed. We'd be in big trouble if we just let you go." Gallouz kicked at the dirt. "We've been in trouble ever since we joined up. That's why we're stuck on guard duty way out in the middle of nowhere. ISIS is worse than nosy tourists."

Nuriddin propelled Narin onto the stubby camp stool, pulling a rickety green chair around and plopping down on it, close to Narin, like she was magnetic.

"We told one gentleman about Muslims Against Tourists," said Ralph. "We—" "Everyone stand at attention," said Gallouz. "You must learn discipline."

Doug was irate. "Don't go crazy. Ralph can stand at attention. He likes that stuff but not I," he said haughtily, lounging at ease, shaking his fingers to show how not at attention he was.

Ralph snorted. "Before I was so rudely interrupted and made to begin again, we told Colonel Beretta about M-A-T. He's the head of ISIS in Dabiq. Becoming friends with the colonel would be excellent networking because the colonel sounded really interested. We can probably find an embarrassment of new members. At the first opportunity we'll send friend requests, and when you add the colonel, you'll more than double M-A-T membership," said Ralph. "Just do the math."

Nuriddin jumped periodically as Narin elbowed him for edging his chair too close to her. He snuck glances at Narin's sodden blouse while she laughed out the side of her mouth, men wrapped around her finger as usual.

"Oh, yes," said Nuriddin, dodging an elbow as if remembering to assert himself. "That is good thing for M-A-T, hundred fifty percent explosion of membership." He pumped a pale fist. "We go viral with marketing."

"First we go to headquarters," Gallouz said. "Letting you go would get us the firing squad." He thought for a second, then shook his head. "They wouldn't waste the bullets. Jihadi Jim would cut our throats off camera."

Ralph saluted nervously. "But there's no record that you found us yet. You would save a lot of paperwork. And tell you what." Ralph raised his hand. "We swear on your mama's grave that we will go directly to the first internet café in Turkey and send friend requests and give a big like to Muslims Against Tourists. Okay? Do we have a deal?" Ralph thrust a hand at Gallouz.

Gallouz scratched his head like he was straining for the proper military strategy. "Wi-Fi sucks at headquarters. The major only has dial-up, run by ISIS dumb butts from Nigeria. I told them they can't run a router off Skype unless they have internet in the first place. Catch-22 snafu." Gallouz grinned. "We have to go all the way to Raqqa to get Wi-Fi, but the major won't let us leave the base, and Raqqa Wi-Fi is censored. You only get access to *Dabiq Magazine,* unless you have a special password. I read *Dabiq Magazine* one time, and it's so booooring," he said, trilling it out. "It doesn't have a single video-game review. But I can probably figure out the password, something like 72virgins, and meanwhile, you're our ticket to Raqqa. Of course, we didn't know you hadn't sent us a friend request so you're in real trouble now. Promises are promises."

Narin nudged Nuriddin. "Tell the dunderhead to let us go. Kissy kissy, big boy." She laughed as he blushed.

"Narin's right," said Ralph. "You should stop being hardasses and let us go, because there's a big problem you might not know about, something we can help you out with." Ralph was spinning magic, relaxed as a noodle and out-lounging Doug, his knuckles almost grazing the ground. "Since you're stuck in nowhere land, you may not have heard that ISIS doesn't let warriors go home. Actually, ISIS lets you go halfway home via Paris or Brussels."

Doug rolled his eyes. "That was a little dramatic, don'tcha think? But yes, boys, an ISIS colonel told us that homesick fellows have a choice. You can impress Mom with your head propped between your shoulders or choose the glory of a *suicide gilet martyr*. Only the suicide vest gets you the girls."

Doug laughed at Gallouz's skeptical look. "The colonel bragged about being mentored by the Judge at the school for martyrs. Each graduate earns the Many Virgins' medal, like the Yanks' Congressional Medal of Honor, both posthumous, of course. The Judge wears a suicide vest at all times, which means he doesn't shower. They call him the Judge because he not only decides who lives and dies, but how, and he's quite the creative chap. I thought you had to interview with him to get into ISIS."

"We didn't have to interview with anyone, but we have heard rumors about the Judge," said Gallouz. "No way are we're blowing ourselves up over a few tourists. M-A-T is way better because you can reach a lot more people on Facebook."

"Don't worry about it. I'm a pilot and a sailing captain. We'll sneak you out of Syria, no problem," said Ralph.

Narin choked, but a half second later she was back to studiously ignoring Nuriddin.

"We should team up and help each other escape," Ralph said. "It'd be a piece of cake with our wisdom and experience and your local knowledge. Yep, we'd be a great team."

Gallouz looked skeptical, waving away Ralph's suggestion. "I know a Kurdish soldier who could get Nuriddin and me out of Syria, name of Berfîn. He was in a Kurdish delegation learning the essence business from my father. He was the only good tourist I ever met, present company excluded, of course, since I never met you in Chefchaouen." He smiled like the idea made him dizzy.

Nuriddin eyed Narin, and she swiveled on the stool, turning her back.

"I almost fell over when Berfîn appeared out of nowhere," Gallouz said. "He marched into headquarters wearing a snazzy desert uniform with a boxy cap." Gallouz looked at Ralph. "It made your Arizona hat look ratty."

"The major had just ordered us to carry our gear

all the way out here on foot, punishment for playing video games. You would not believe how much two chairs, a stool and a tent, a change of clothes, and a ridiculous amount of food weighs. It took a day and a half because we had to rest a lot. Nuriddin had to rest a lot."

"Hurry up the story already," Nuriddin said. "Wildcat restless so must hold her." "Oh, you wish," Narin snapped, slamming a vicious elbow into Nuriddin's ribs.

Gallouz waved Nuriddin away. "We were walking out the door when Captain Berfin materialized as a dashing Kurdish commander. I introduced him to the major, sweet revenge for our video-game punishment. That's our boss who hates us. The major screamed us the hell out the door after we'd stayed around long enough to hear the deal. There's a ceasefire between ISIS and the Kurds in the Sarin sector, though they're still fighting around Mosul."

"The major said we had to stay out here until we captured enemies of the Sultanate. So thank you for being you. We won't have to carry all this stuff back, because escorting prisoners comes first. So we're off to see the major."

Ralph lurched for the lethal-looking assault rifle propped against the scraggly bush. Narin pushed Nuriddin away, and he fell on his back with a shocked look.

"Fuck, fuck, fuck!" Yanking the gun free, Ralph

scraped his arm and shredded a shirtsleeve. He peered myopically at the gun, trying to squeeze off a warning shot.

Nuriddin was off chasing Narin, who was headed north down the slanting path toward the beach when Ralph realized the trigger wouldn't budge. He fumbled for the safety, his arm dripping blood as Gallouz stood laughing.

"Ratta-tat-tat, take that," Ralph said as Gallouz took the gun by the muzzle, relieving Ralph of a gun weighing twice as much as the comfy little AK-47 or whatever it was that Doug had dropped in Aleppo.

Doug pounded Ralph on the shoulder. "Good show. You didn't really do anything, but you tried."

Gallouz beckoned to Ralph. "Stand at attention. You need to learn about gun safety. You can't go grabbing a weapon like this. Pay attention, because these guns are special and can be real touchy." He pointed it toward the cliff, squeezing off an ear-crunching volley that ripped the hard pack, spurting earthen geysers down the side of the cliff toward Nuriddin and Narin rolling on the beach, though it was non-violent rolling that resembled slow-mo wrestling.

"I thought you were a Marine and knew how to handle a weapon," said Gallouz the steely eyed disciplinarian.

"I'm a little rusty at pretty much everything," said

Ralph. He shook, blinking madly behind broken glasses. "I'm glad you kept your composure, Gallouz. Things could have gone really wrong."

Doug snorted, raising an eyebrow at Gallouz. "You think? Keep your fingers crossed that things haven't gone really wrong already."

Ralph tried to compose himself. "You're calm under fire, so you'd make a good Marine even if you don't fit in with ISIS. Anyway, I'm sorry. I panicked when you said we had to go to Raqqa, where there's a bounty on our heads." He shuddered.

Doug was getting impatient. "So you admit it out loud. Our death sentences in Raqqa shook you up. That's why you're sweating like a stuck pig."

Ralph shook his head sorrowfully. "I'm sweating because it's hot. I don't know how Gallouz and Nuriddin can stand the balaclavas and sweaters."

Ralph focused on Gallouz. "Taking one's execution personally may not be very Marine- like but hey, no harm no foul? Can we still be friends on Facebook?" He kept it between a question and a statement as he stuck his hand out toward Gallouz.

CHAPTER FIFTEEN —
ASSIGNMENT RAQQA

The major pointed at Doug and Ralph. "The infidels will stand in the back of the troop truck with their hands and feet tied. And don't let them hold on. I want them to fall down a hundred times. *Wham*!" He slammed a hand on his desk. "I want them black and blue by the time they get to Raqqa."

"But it's only thirty K from Sarin," objected Gallouz. "And the road isn't that bad. They probably won't fall down once."

The major lost it with the back talk. "You will supervise them falling down until they can't get up. Do you understand? But you will be careful with the girl. She is known to the caliph as the treasonous Yazidi Joan of Arc, which is another stupid infidel heresy. This puny little girl dressed like a cheap Western tramp"—he waved his palms out at Narin— "isn't worth a flyspeck on a goat's ass," he said mockingly. "But we must keep her safe for the caliph so he can decide what to do with her."

Narin slouched in her chair and casually flipped him off. She was guarded closely by Nuriddin, who pretended to ignore Narin back.

"Boris," yelled the major.

A side door opened, and a giant entered. The

assault weapon across his chest looked like a toothpick. His shaved head was bumpy like a potato.

"Take this sorry lot to Raqqa." The major raised a finger, admonishing Boris. "No funny stuff with the girl, and make sure you knock the old guys around all the way to Raqqa. Do you understand what I just said?"

Boris nodded dumbly.

"Now get out of my sight." He pointed sternly at the door.

Boris hoisted the assault weapon in one hand like a baton, herding Ralph and Doug with rough jabs of the barrel. He ignored Nuriddin and Gallouz as he pushed the boys stumbling through the door toward a troop truck pumping black plumes of carbon monoxide in their faces. Boris stood stolidly as Narin was off like a shot into the bright morning sunshine.

"Come back," called Boris in a high-pitched voice, firing the weapon into the air and bringing the muzzle down, stitching a splatter pattern on either side of Narin. She slowed to a stop with her hands up and goose-stepped back in mock military cadence. She bowed in front of Boris, who stood with his big mouth open like he loved the bewildering variety of whatever happened next. He absently twirled the big gun on a giant forefinger.

Narin followed both sets of boys up a ramp into the back of a big open truck with its canvas sides rolled up. Boris followed them, pulling the ramp up behind. He threw the ramp into the truck, making them jump to avoid the amputation of their feet. Narin stood with her hands on little hips, giving Boris the evil eye as he pounded on the cab.

The driver threw the truck into gear and chugged off at school-zone speed, the little troop carrier that could, crunching over potholes as Doug and Ralph staggered to stay on their feet. Narin sat with her feet hanging over the open back, guarded closely by Nuriddin.

"We've ditched the psycho major," Gallouz said to Boris. "So sit down and relax." "No," screamed Boris in a falsetto to slice steel, his potato head bobbing. "Dance," he said, directing Doug and Ralph with the assault rifle.

"Fall," he said as Doug pirouetted around him like Fred Astaire and Ralph stumbled like he was blind drunk. They turned Boris in circles as Narin kept nudging Boris and the boys toward the back, where Nuriddin stood seriously cool like he was guarding Narin.

The truck turned onto a paved road behind an ancient white pickup that left them in its dust. They passed a string of bare cinder-block buildings and broken-down shops before entering the countryside. The sun rose steadily as they trundled south toward Raqqa with Doug and Ralph playing *Ring Around the Rosie* with Boris.

Boris staggered, gesturing for Gallouz and Nuriddin to take over the supervision of Doug and Ralph, who danced wildly around him. Narin pantomimed for Doug to nudge Boris with his pack, and Boris lurched closer to the open back.

Narin executed a roll as Boris stumbled by, tripping him in a thunderous clap. He hit the floor and fell off the back of the truck onto the pavement, bouncing twice before landing on his head. Boris sprawled flat in the middle of the road, his body spread-eagled with the big gun still belted to his chest. He receded rapidly behind them, then was run over by a little silver car that careened over Boris without stopping, revving to pass the troop truck.

"Help," said Nuriddin. "Boris squashed Narin. Poor Narin."

Doug and Ralph helped Narin up. She was dazed, her ponytail unbound with long hair down to her shoulders. Nuriddin propped her gently behind the cab, the truck chugging along as if nothing had happened. A troop truck of ISIS soldiers roared toward them, waving at Gallouz and Nuriddin.

"Duck," Narin yelled at Doug and Ralph, who promptly fell on their faces until the ISIS truck disappeared.

Ralph jumped up and yelled, "Free at last. We're free at last." He hugged Doug.

"Not so fast, boys," said Gallouz. "We'll get the YouTube treatment if we don't deliver you to the Judge.

But don't worry. We'll figure something out."

"Come on, Gallouz, don't be such a stickler for orders," begged Ralph. "When it's the only way to save yourselves then orders are meant to be ignored. It would be the end of Muslims Against Tourists if something happened to you, so you need us." Ralph smiled. "As usual, I have a plan."

Everyone leaned forward to listen as Ralph said confidentially, "We'll jump off the truck and hoof it to the Turkish border."

"It seems to me," said Gallouz with mock puzzlement, "that you tried that plan twice, and it hasn't worked yet."

"It would have worked if you hadn't turned us in," Ralph cried. "Correct," said Doug. "It's entirely your fault, Gallouz."

"So stop turning us in so we can get started on a slick escape plan. We need to work our specialty: outsmarting other people."

"We haven't outsmarted anyone lately, except yourselves." Narin sighed, brushing the hair out of her eyes. "Consider how fast we're going and how well Boris did leaving the truck at this speed, like not getting up? You'd break every bone in your decrepit bodies and so would Gallouz and Nuriddin. I could do it because I've learned to roll with the punches. But I wouldn't want to abandon you, on your own, stranded in Syria."

"Yeah, by the way, what was the Joan of Arc thing?" asked Ralph. "I'm guessing it has nothing to do with sainthood," said Doug.

"Catty," said Narin, tapping Doug's nose with a forefinger. "The major is guilty of mistaken identity. Narin is a common Yazidi name."

She looked at them. "Okay, don't believe me. I've been chased by ISIS and caught before. But I won't stay caught. Got it?"

Doug and Ralph held up their hands, in unison, "We got it". "You are a tough little thing," said Gallouz.

"Don't call me little or thing," said Narin, "or I'll chop your nuts off." "Whoa," said Gallouz as Nuriddin whistled admiration.

"Don't worry, boys," said Narin. "I know Yazidi in Raqqa. The biggest problem is our bumbling buddies, dear Ralph and Sir Doug. It's going to be tough to get them out of Syria intact. So we'll do a Ralph kind of plan. We'll jump off the truck when it slows down and see what happens."

The truck hit the brakes for a herd of sheep, throwing everyone in the back into a jumble against the cab, like in a cartoon but not as funny. Narin and the young boys were dazed, the older boys cushioned by the pack and bag. A soldier who looked like Tweedledee appeared at the back of the truck followed by one who looked like Tweedledum, twins in black ISIS uniforms who were shaped like enormous pears, standing on tiptoes, peeking into the truck, apparently the driver and his twin.

Tweedledee roared in a big voice, pointing at Gallouz. "Where is Boris? What have you done with our friend Boris? Report, soldier. Where is your weapon? Oh, right, you were court- martialed." He chuckled.

Gallouz sauntered to the back, saluting. "Ha, ha, yourself, sir. Boris fell off the back of the truck. He was twirling around, acting funny."

"Why didn't you tell us to stop the truck so we could rescue Boris?" Tweedledee demanded. "Sacre bleu, we didn't stop for Boris. Boris," he wailed.

"Oh, no problem, sir," said Gallouz. "We yelled at the ISIS truck we met, and they'll report the mishap to the major in Sarin. Boris will be okay, I'm sure. We saw a little silver car get him, might have passed us earlier. He's probably already in Raqqa."

"You poor gentlemen," said Tweedledum, making a dazzling leap and bouncing like a blimp into the back of the truck. Everyone stood staring, no idea how he did it.

"I'm sorry. We had to stop for the sheep." The big pear bent in the middle, politely helping Doug and Ralph up. Then he pushed them against the side of the truck and motioned to Nuriddin and Gallouz. Narin stood slumped against the cab, watching innocently.

Dum tapped the Rambo bump on Doug's pack.

"I'll ride with you and make sure everything is okay. Sit down over there and relax," he said, unsnapping the pistol on his hip and leveling it in their general direction.

Dum yelled at his brother, "Get going. I'll watch 'em the last few K."

Dee drove, and Dum leaned against the cab, staring at them like they'd done something wrong. Dum was distracted by the junky suburbs of the city but a second later yelled, "Stand up. Get your butts up here. You have to see this." He pounded on the cab for Dee to stop, motioning to the boys and Narin, his round face glowing with pleasure.

The truck stopped at a black building with a sign that said "ISIS Officer's Club." Men of all ages were crowded around the base of the building, throwing rocks. Dee pulled the truck onto the sidewalk behind the crowd where the passengers in back enjoyed a panoramic view of the proceedings.

Dum pointed at the edge of the roof on top of the building where feet stuck out, tied at the ankles. Blindfolded men were perched on white plastic chairs tipped halfway over the top, four stories straight up. The excited crowd chanted something as it flowed back into a wide semicircle, staring up. A lavender caftan billowed off a man on a chair high above them.

"We missed the first two," Dum explained. "See?" He pointed where the crowd had pulled back from two bodies with their ankles and arms tied, lying on a concrete slab with mustard-colored rocks surrounding pulped heads.

Dum was excited. "Boy, are we lucky. Every Monday ISIS pushes fags off the top of the officer's quarters."

Men with heads covered by black balaclavas peeked over the top of the building next to ankles protruding from two white plastic chairs. The men tipped a chair forward, saving the chair.

A blindfolded man with gray hair and a curly white beard fell from the chair, his jacket snapping in the breeze. His arms and ankles were bound, and he hit the ground head-first like a watermelon. The crowd surged, throwing yellow rocks with gusto. Stones slammed with dull thuds, and the crowd pulled back for number four.

Dum clapped his hands for the encore, yelling, "Bravo, bravo. The caliphate is rid of deviant vermin, keeping us pure." Then he did some kind of ritual, slapping an arm across his rotundity, then the other arm as the rest of the occupants in the back of the truck stood glassy- eyed. Narin was uncharacteristically shaken, and the others were like jelly.

Ralph pulled himself together, peering up, blind with the missing lens, focusing with the other eye, and suddenly he was screaming. "It's Slim!" He waved his arms. "Stop! It's Slim." He jumped off the back of the truck.

Dee sprang from the driver's seat and grabbed Ralph, cuffing him about the head and tossing him back onto the truck where he landed with a thump. Dee stood beside Dum as Slim started off the roof in his lavender caftan, grabbed at the last second by the men on top. Slim hung by his ankles, and the disappointed crowd chanted louder.

Slim was yanked back and then swung to and fro over the void. Slim moaned, trying for dignity as they lofted him over the parapet and let him go, but he screamed all the way to the ground. The crowd surged forward with rocks and boulders and stones.

"I know obscenity when I see it, and religion," croaked Doug, "is obscene."

"Don't indict all religion," said Ralph, trying to get up, choking. "But that was Slim. He was such a peach."

"Slim was a terrorist," Doug said. "He bombed the Jewish synagogue in Tunisia and bragged about it. He wanted you to sit on his lap. You weren't happy about that."

"He was harmless."

"Hey, you," yelled a big guy wearing a black beret. "Move that piece of junk," he said, looking tough at Dum and Dee. The black beret's little white car was wedged between the truck and a light pole as the dispersing crowd swirled around them.

Dum laughed heartily, holding a hand up to the crowd. "Wait up, gentlemen. I found us another fag. Have you ever seen a real man wear a beret?"

The black beret backed off hurriedly, disappearing, apparently having decided to retrieve his little white car a little later.

"Excuse me, Mr. Big Fat Guy, either one of you," said Narin, raising her hand. "I have a question. Why do you only throw guys off the roof? What do you do with gay women? You know, lesbians?"

"I'll tell you, you little smartass bitch," snarled Dee. "My imam is asked that question frequently, so he put it in the FAQs. Check any mosque website. Gay girls are perfectly fine because they remain virgins, and with seventy-two for every man, we need all the virgins we can get. Plus a recent poll found that eighty-seven percent of men prefer two women. Islam, being a practical religion, knows there's little else for a girl to do. The poor things can't just sit around waiting for a man, so we tolerate it. Nay, we encourage it."

"How remarkable," said Narin. "Who would have thought that of a patriarchal religion?" "That is amazing," said Ralph. "I've never heard of that."

"He's just putting us on," said Doug. "They're pretty shifty for jolly fat guys."

"You filthy infidels really know how to make

292

friends and influence people." Dum swiped a finger below his jiggling chins.

Doug rolled his eyes. "It's quite impossible to make friends with psychopaths and savages."

"Jesus, Doug," said Ralph. "Don't you remember your earlier lecture? Think discretion, spurting carotic arteries, and Muath the Merciful. Look what happened to Slim, a faithful ISIS servant, and poor Bishman, a brave warrior who only wanted to go home. Even if we don't insult them, we don't have a chance."

"Leading to the inescapable conclusion that when the result is the same, go with the insults," Doug snipped. "You are the wimpiest Marine I've ever met. I stand in awe." Doug stood in awe, perusing the heavens, looking for stars in the brilliant noon sky.

Dum yelled at Dee, "Let's go. We're late for a very important date."

CHAPTER SIXTEEN – HERE COMES THE JUDGE

"We quite appreciate that you have a very difficult job, your judgeship, sir," Doug said, peering up at the Judge who stood above them on a high podium.

Everyone stood at rigid attention in front of an ugly metal acreage of a desk in the cavernous Raqqa administrative center, including Gallouz and Nuriddin in their spiffy ISIS uniforms. The only furniture besides the enormous desk was one skinny chair that Narin slouched across.

"Ralph may have occasional digestive issues," Doug continued soothingly, "but society esteems us as elders. Anyway, everything will be fine when we leave."

Narin sat holding her nose, because Ralph had apparently provided proof of the digestive problem.

Ralph stood at attention in his Columbia blue and beige, no part of his body relaxed, embarrassed. He hissed at Gallouz and Doug out of the corner of his mouth, "Sorry about that."

The Judge was livid. "You call me Judge, *sir*," he screamed. The Judge had already ground, chopped, and roasted Ralph, Gallouz, and Nuriddin into cornmeal, and now Doug was having his turn. The Judge hadn't said a single word to Narin.

The Judge pounded the podium as he switched from Doug to Gallouz and Nuriddin. "I'm pleased to announce the life expectancy of the little baby soldiers ends at midnight, when they will be executed for their complicity in the death of the major."

Narin forgot herself, turning to stare at Nuriddin with her mouth open. Everyone knew the Judge could tell the future. When he said something, it happened.

The Judge punctuated the story with little gasps of pleasure. "The Kurdish swine of a captain faked a cease fire and attacked Sarin, killing the major right after you left. The infant soldiers are granted ten minutes of internet access to notify their loved ones of their imminent demise." His grin was as wide as all outdoors. "You'll finally be a credit to your uniform."

"After a few minutes of supervised internet, you two…"

Doug and Ralph pointed questioning fingers at themselves. "No, not you two," the Judge thundered, rolling his eyes to control his blood pressure. "The baby soldiers will return to Sarin at the head of our mighty ISIS troops to battle against the filthy lying shithead Kurds."

Nuriddin and Gallouz stood at rigid attention, sharp in their uniforms as the Judge descended from the vast auditorium's high podium to stand inches from their terrified faces. The Judge's own face was off-kilter, racked by grotesque tics that made him look like a psychotic killer. He smelled like a sewer because he wore his green nylon vest 24/7, slept with it on, and never bathed. The fact he never took the vest off made folks overlook the smell.

The vest's tubular pockets were outlined by yellow seams filled with rows of two-inch metal pipes. The pipes were wrapped with clear plastic packets of steel washer, nuts, and ball bearings on one side. The other side was crammed with four-inch drill-bits. The pipes sprouted colorful red wires wrapped with yellow tape. Not the kind of vest to shower with. Water could ruin it.

The Judge's creativity in executing Westerners had been featured in *Dabiq Magazine* and was known throughout the caliphate, a reputation polished by a *60 Minutes* special featuring the Judge, in imitation of Christian inquisitions, burning a dozen teenagers at the stake for playing video games in violation of Sharia law.

Narin continued to lounge, sandwiched between Nuriddin and Gallouz. She raised her eyebrows as her tongue bulged her cheek. She stared at the Judge until he blinked and suffered a tic, a big one wrenching his face.

Gallouz saluted sharply. "Sir, we have delivered the infidels as ordered." He held Ralph by a scrawny arm as Nuriddin thrust Doug forward. Narin sat with her arms crossed, staring at the Judge like he'd crawled out from under a rock.

Gallouz saluted again. "Permission to go online

for ten minutes to notify our loved ones of our immediate deployment to the front lines to forthwith join the holy battle against the Kurds?" Another crisp salute. "Sir."

"All in good time," drawled the Judge, inspecting the prisoners. He gazed at Doug's pack and Ralph's bag like he'd heard about the contents, lazily looking them up and down, ignoring Narin.

The red wires and yellow tape rustled like dead leaves as the Judge thrust his face at Ralph, who jerked back to focus on the Judge's bushy black beard, holding his breath against the stink as the Judge's black eyes bored into Ralph's watery baby blues.

Ralph peered back. "Nice vest. Did you make it yourself?"

The Judge jumped back like a grasshopper, the vest rattling with heavy pipes clanking against each other, everyone watching for a spark and the end of the world. Surprised, the Judge leaned back, nose-to-nose with Ralph. "No one has taken an interest in the nuts and bolts of my excellent vest. *60 Minutes* never asked me where or how it was made and neither did *Dabiq Magazine*. Are you a journalist?"

Ralph groaned. "Not really." Doug chimed in, "Definitely not."

"A Brit," exclaimed the Judge, shoving out his hand. "You simply must meet Jihadi Jim." Doug froze, and the Judge pretended he hadn't offered to shake hands, waving the hand like he was cool before dropping it.

"But I digress from my wonderful vest, the best one ever made, custom manufactured to my specifications in Kano, Nigeria by Boko Haram. One look at this beauty, and you see that the Nigerians and me, we know what we're doing." He fondled the pipes, tweaking the red wires as a big tic crinkled his face.

"We used Mother of Satan for sheer power." He added at the puzzled looks, "That's triacetone triperoxide, TATP. It's really easy to manufacture from hydrogen peroxide and acetone, available at any drug store. Personally, I prefer hydrochloric acid, though Mosul prefers nitric. I think Mosul just likes the sound of nitric," he said, making "nitric" sound black. "But nitric acid is nowhere near as efficient as hydrochloric. BOOM," he yelled, scaring everyone except Narin. Ralph and Doug jumped a foot as Nuriddin and Gallouz backed toward the door. Narin twiddled her thumbs, looking like she was planning the usual escape.

"It's like *Breaking Bad*," the Judge said, "and we be real bad." He cackled, the pipes in the vest jiggling with each tic of his face.

Then the Judge turned hostile. "Welcome to Syria, infidels. You two are such a deal, valuable hostages for free—"

He was interrupted by a woman in black throwing open the big front doors, rushing in and wailing as she threw her arms around the Judge, poked everywhere by the Judge's pipes.

"Bailiff," yelled the Judge, cornered.

"My son, my son, I have terrible news. We must flee Raqqa."

The Judge's mother rearranged her ample body, peeking through the narrow slit in her niqab. "Don't waste a single minute. We must go now because bombers are on their way.

Russian. American, British, and French jets are coming to bomb Raqqa. We just got the news at the post office. We are doomed. You must leave immediately, my son, because you are a prime target. Take off that ridiculous vest and flee to Europe, your mama says."

Even Narin stood transfixed, her mouth open like there was no reason to go escaping just yet.

The Judge's face was black as storm clouds, jumping with tics. "Mother, you abandoned your official post at the post office," he fumed, the tics making everything come out jerky. "We will return there now. I should never have gotten you a job across the street. Come along, soldiers," he ordered Gallouz and Nuriddin. "Escort the infidels and follow me."

The Judge led them out of the big auditorium and through the front doors into bright sunshine. Narin and the infidels followed without a murmur.

At the appearance of the Judge, cars rushed away

as if they had been sucked into a vacuum. Pedestrians fell all over themselves to escape, then paused, frozen like in a twilight zone, curious as the Judge brusquely pulled his mother across the suddenly empty street.

His mother's niqab fell off her pale pudgy face, and the Judge pulled it back up, whispering in his mother's ear. "It is better that you do not see."

The crowd grew rapidly as the Judge mounted the post office steps, followed closely by Gallouz, Nuriddin, Narin, and the infidels. The Judge stood on the top step next to a scrawny security guard with a prominent Adam's apple and white hair. The guard wore a long knife in a fancy scabbard, which he caressed constantly.

The Judge turned to address the crowd, patting the famous vest he'd trademarked after the *60 Minutes* special went viral. "This is my mother." He held her head up by the hair and niqab, the slit catching on her nose as the crowd hushed.

The Judge shouted for all to hear. "My mother is a traitor. The Holy Koran requires your humble Judge to punish traitors and infidels, such as those who stand before you." He pointed like the Grim Reaper at Doug and Ralph.

He screeched, pounding on the suicide vest. "Hark, the Holy Scripture orders that you *kill the unbelievers wherever you find them*, and that includes traitors! I, the Judge, humbly obey Allah, enforcing his justice on Earth."

Narin hissed up at the Judge. "How do you know Allah isn't a *she*?"

The Judge became livid, looking diabolical as a tic rippled over his face like an earthquake. "Lend me your long knife," he screamed at the guard.

The obviously deaf guard put a hand to his ear, leaning to hear the Judge. "Give me your fucking long knife, old man," the Judge screamed.

The old man stumbled, unable to understand, leaning closer to the Judge, question mark all over his face as the Judge grabbed the long knife and the man's scraggly white hair, and in a single stroke sliced the old man's head off his shoulders, slick as a whistle.

The old man's body cartwheeled down the post office steps like a windmill, blood spurting from between the shoulders. A surprised look was etched on the old man's face as the Judge held the head high by its wispy white hairs, blood dripping onto the post office steps.

The Judge lowered the old man's head to eye level. "Thank you," he said, bowing to it. He inspected the head before tossing it at Narin and missing. The head bounced down the steps and rolled to the edge of the crowd that filled the street below. A ten-year-old boy in a striped caftan snatched up the head and looked into the old man's astonished eyes, and then passed it back for inspection by the silent crowd.

"The infidels must wait patiently for their punishment, because traitors come first. Meet the filthy traitor who ordered me to abandon the caliphate. My mother, the traitor," said the Judge, jerking up his mother's trembling arm, yanking her lopsided.

"My mother is a traitor because she ordered me to flee, treating me like a little boy. Her excuse was typical woman weakness, cowering before the bombers of the great Satan. Now I ask you, are we men or are we mice?" He raised his arm to a disappointing response from a dazed crowd. A tic racked his face.

"Do the forces of Allah cower before the infidels?" The Judge whipped his hands in the air to stir up the crowd, screaming, "No." He implored the crowd with his arms held wide, the suicide vest glistening in the sun.

"I can't hear you. Do men of Allah cringe before the great Satan?"

The crowd obliged. "NO, NO, NO," they chanted, making the Judge's eyes glow.

A smile flickered across the Judge's face. "I sentence the traitor to death." He grabbed the top of his mother's niqab along with a hunk of hair, pulling her to her toes as he tested the blade, cutting gently through the black garment to rest it against her throat.

The woman wailed, cut short as the Judge sliced her throat like butter. He held the black niqab high as her ample body tumbled down the steps, spraying blood and sending Doug and Ralph stumbling into Nuriddin and Gallouz.

Narin stood stock still, staring at the red polka dots on her scruffy green moccasins. She hissed at the Judge. "You're full of shit with your suicide vest. I bet it's a fake." Narin turned to egg on the crowd, yelling "Fake, fake, fake" and trying to get the crowd to chant along. She got nothing except some murmuring from the spellbound mob.

The Judge choked, gasping for breath, witless with the crowd watching. He tried to speak, but his face wouldn't stay still. His tic rippled as Narin marched up, propped her chin on the top row of pipe bombs, staring into the Judge's unbelieving eyes. She extended her right arm, placed a middle finger on the Judge's nose, and flipped him the bird, hushing the crowd.

The Judge roared and slapped her hand away, the long knife catapulting end over end down the steps as he grabbed for Narin's crotch with both hands.

Narin jumped back and slapped the Judge so hard he staggered sideways, holding his rippling face, aghast as Narin sneered. "No one believes your suicide vest is real. Come on. Show us. You... don't... have... the... balls, do you?"

The Judge stood on his tiptoes, gasping, holding the suicide vest with both hands, fondling the pipes compulsively. "Where's the long knife?" he screamed. "Find the long knife." His hands trembled as he lurched down the steps, looking for the knife. He stumbled over his mother's body and into the street where he grabbed the long knife from the curious ten-year-old in the striped caftan.

The Judge executed an about-face and charged up the stairs with the knife held high like Teddy Roosevelt charging San Juan Hill, his suicide vest rattling as Narin played hide and seek behind Gallouz, Nuriddin, and the boys.

The Judge shifted the long knife to the other hand, shoving Doug aside to thrust and parry as Narin danced away and Doug's pack knocked the Judge sideways. The Judge stood up with a funny look on his face like he remembered what Colonel Beretta said about the pack's contents.

The Judge lowered the long knife, pivoting to address the crowd. "I have a matter of utmost importance to show you."

The Judge turned to the boys. "Put your stuff down here, boys. Okay. Now let's see what's inside. Gross, it smells terrible."

"Look who's talking," hissed Narin like a cobra. "You smell like shit."

The Judge ignored her, peering into Doug's pack. "That really stinks. What did you do?" Ralph shrugged.

"It got dunked in the Euphrates, which stinks like Syria."

"Indeed," said Doug loftily. "I can't imagine there's anything you'd be interested in."

The Judge propped the long knife against his leg as he located the Ram in Doug's pack. He wrinkled his nose as he unwrapped the statue. "I had a nice long chat with Colonel Beretta. He told me all about you two before you took the long way around to Raqqa."

The Judge held the Ram high for the murmuring crowd, the long knife in his other hand. "The infidels have delivered the *Rams in a Thicket* into our hands. But oh, Muslims, our people who lived centuries ago worshiped the Rams as idols and gods instead of worshipping Allah."

Doug whispered to Ralph, "Should I let him know that Allah hadn't been invented yet?" "I suspect the Judge isn't the intellectual type, but maybe Allah wins if the Judge destroys one of the world's two oldest gods," Ralph whispered back as Narin tried to convince Gallouz to make a run for it. Nuriddin was all for it.

"The Assyrians and Akkadians prayed to these idols of war, agriculture, and rain, offering sacrifices." The Judge raised the long knife, screaming at the crowd. "The Prophet ordered all idols destroyed as he destroyed the idols of conquered nations." He set the Ram on the top step.

The Judge slapped the long knife over his heart, overlapping two pipe bombs, bowing. "As Allah

305

ordered." He grabbed the Ram by its head and slammed it on the top step, slashing it with the long knife.

Bits of lapis lazuli flew. Then he severed the goat's golden head and slashed the stems of the golden bough, leaving golden leaves littering the post office steps. The Judge stopped short as his cellphone trilled the *Lone Ranger* song.

"Yo. This is The Judge. Oh, no. You! Yes, Madame. How did you find that out? The fat boys told you. Yes, the girl and the *Rams in a Thicket* are here too. I have this instant destroyed one publicly as ordered by Allah. There are pieces everywhere. It was glorious. You should have seen it... NO, no, I'm..."

The Judge dropped the long knife and put a hand over the phone, whispering. "Sorry. Right away, Madame. I repeat after you. You are a worthless shit... Right, I am a worthless shit, and the *Rams in a Thicket* are worth a hundred of me. The Ram would buy a hundred new tanks. I will deliver the other *Ram in a Thicket* and the infidels forthwith." He snapped the phone shut, muttering, "Fucking cunt bitch."

The Judge picked up the long knife and pointed it at Narin. "You have been saved by the wicked witch of the West." He waved them down the steps. "She will get hers soonest, and then I'll attend to the boys. It's off to the dungeon you go."

CHAPTER SEVENTEEN – THE REHEARSAL

The Judge sat silently as the armored car parked on Raqqa's main square next to what looked like a medieval castle, mini turrets topped with razor wire and bars on every window.

Ralph was sick to his stomach. "What the hell is this place?"

"The women's prison," said Narin. "I was here two months ago, before Papa bailed me out. Forty women in six four-foot-high cages with no food unless its smuggled in. The caliph's father made us wear black slips and nothing else and everyone's available as sex slaves. We starved if our families couldn't pay the ransom."

"We better not have to wear black slips," said Ralph. "But if food can be smuggled in, then maybe we can buy our way out."

"I can't help you there," said Doug. "You tapped me out completely. And I doubt they take credit cards."

"Shut up," said the Judge, swinging open the door of the armored car. "Get out and prepare to enjoy yourselves." He muttered "stupid fucking bitch" under his breath. "It's appropriate to put girly guys and old men in the women's prison. Besides, the warden insisted on hosting you personally."

"What did you do with Nuriddin and Gallouz?" asked Ralph.

"You won't be seeing them again," said the Judge. "They're off to the front lines, a two- man army against the Kurds."

A soldier wearing a balaclava, black beret, black shirt, and black gloves with the fingers cut out reached into the armored car. He grabbed Doug and Ralph by the throat, one in each hand, and yanked them out. "This way, gentlemen," he said.

"Who are you?" croaked Ralph. The soldier sounded like someone they should know. The soldier marched them backward through high doors, following the Judge, who pushed Narin down a hallway as dark as death. They halted before black double doors that would have been invisible except for glistening silver handles fashioned as blindfolded women with swords, requiring considerable care when opening the door.

The soldier held Ralph and Doug tightly, pinching their Adam's apples like squeezeboxes. They stared at his nametag, Arabic curlicues with small print underneath that said "Fakir."

The Judge rapped on the door, holding Narin by the arm.

A memorable voice called, "Enter."

The Judge grasped a silvery handle by the throat and carefully opened the door. Fakir herded Doug and

Ralph into a vast room with cathedral ceilings like a fancy hotel lobby. He flipped them around by the scruff of the neck, and they found themselves under an enormous crystal chandelier. The walls were lined with alcoves framed by marble arches in traditional Moorish style, plastered with posters of Doug and Ralph. Red letters were stenciled across their faces: WANTED.

It took a second to notice that the great room was only the front half of a much larger room divided by floor-to-ceiling bars that acted as a middle wall. Behind the high bars sat six boxes stacked on top of each other, each of them four feet high and enclosed by rebar. The boxes contained women and children in ratty black slips bent double. The stench of corrosive urine lay over the room like a blanket.

Marcy stood on a high dais of marble above a half staircase, glowering with hooded eyelids as the Judge stood rigidly at attention in his suicide vest. Long fake fingernails curled from the slinky sleeves of a black robe embroidered with a rainbow of tiny mosques. She stood regally, staring deadpan and dangerous from a thicket of long black hair as they lined up at attention.

Two diplomas, a fancy gold-and-blue from Notre Dame and a scarlet one from Rutgers flanked a green blackboard. The diplomas were illuminated by laser lights perched on the fancy chandelier. On the far side of the desk sat a purple couch under a sign that read "Reserved for Prisoners Awaiting Execution."

"Welcome, boys. I hope you appreciate the wanted posters in your honor."

"What…" said Ralph. "It's good to be wanted, but how did you…? Oh, the Pez thing in Aleppo. That was a fancy spy camera."

Marcy smiled her famous smile. "Very good, Ralph. I appreciate you bringing the so- called Yazidi Joan of Arc with you." She flipped a hand as if everyone knew Narin was a fake. "Her presence is required by the caliph forthwith, as soon as we get you boys settled."

Narin stuck her tongue out at Marcy, which Marcy ignored. "The caliph is deciding the fate of the Yazidi people, whether they are apostates or fellow Sunnis. He very much wants to meet this Joan of Arc, like it's a theological thing." Marcy shook her mane. "Underage girls will be the downfall of the caliphate." She turned back to the boys.

"As for you old coots, we shall have a grand time." She languidly sliced the air with her fingernails, like a big cat.

"I thought you were supposed to be the big Sharia law hotshot," said Ralph. "How did you to end up as the mere warden of a women's prison, and what's with the gaudy chandelier?"

Marcy put a hand on her hip. "How did you end up *in* a women's prison?" She smiled wickedly. "The chandelier was a gift from an admirer."

Ralph raised little white eyebrows. "I'll bet you've hit the crystal ceiling with ISIS." He peered at the spotlighted diplomas.

Ralph fiddled with his glasses, reading the diploma out loud, "Islamic Law Studies. You'd think a Rutgers law grad would know better than to tangle with the bad boys of ISIS."

"Muath tried to bribe me with the chandelier. The ladies you see and... smell behind me aren't just prisoners. They're held for ransom, sold as sex slaves, or time shared with brave ISIS fighters."

Marcy could tell she had made an impression. "I don't waste money feeding them because starvation instills a sense of urgency in a family raising a ransom. We don't even bother if the woman is from a poor family because they make excellent sex slaves. Men who distinguish themselves in battle can book the woman of their choice by the night. Sometimes entire battalions distinguish themselves in battle, which keeps me busy 24/7." Marcy put a hand to her cheek as if to say "poor me."

"I've expanded into the sale of antiquities, overseeing two of the caliphate's primary sources of revenue. I'm not interested in the third, which is running oil fields. I have to butter up the caliph, get rid of this so-called Judge, and make tons of money for the caliphate."

She laughed shrilly as the Judge blanched. "I like to be up front."

Ralph shook his head, waving a finger at Marcy. "You're such a bigshot with your tacky fingernails, like you trim them with tin-snips and eat puppies." He shrugged his scrawny shoulders. "I suppose that's the point. Big tough Marcy from Joisey."

"Oh, dear Allah, boys, I am so happy to see you." She rubbed her hands together, fingernails flashing like little scissors. She bent and pinched Ralph on his pale cheek, making it glow like an apple.

Ralph squinted at her hair. "So you won the fight against wearing a niqab. The hair looks nice, like a Rutgers sorority girl. Anyway, since we're old friends and all, maybe you can sneak us out of the country."

"We're not looking for a lot of grief," said Doug. You can have the priceless Rambo, the only *Ram in the Thicket* to survive the Islamic State's dumbest judge, and we'll be on our way."

Marcy chortled with pretend laughter. "He's not really a judge, and indeed you'll hand over the *Ram in a Thicket*." She extended her arm and uncurled the long fingernails, beckoning for Ralph to open his bag.

Ralph sighed and dropped the muddy black bag— *kerplop*—on the floor. He stared at Marcy as he slowly unwound the musty clothes from around the Rambo, the striptease annoying Marcy enormously.

Marcy rolled her eyes, jumping off the dais. "You boys won't be going anywhere. You two and the priceless Ram are my ticket out of this stinking prison."

Marcy lifted the Ram, setting it reverently on the white marble dais. She dabbed at it with her sleeve, smearing mud across the colorful appliqué mosques. She gave up trying to clean the Ram but compulsively stroked its head like conjuring black magic.

Marcy leaned forward, whispering, "The caliph offered me the chief judgeship if I captured the Rams and the elusive Western spies known as Ralph and Doug."

Marcy jerked a thumb at the Judge, who was still standing at rigid attention and staring into deep space. "Well, and keep the Judge under control, which is impossible. But two out of three ain't bad."

Marcy tapped a fingernail on Doug's nose. "The Islamic State has suffered a recent scarcity of Westerners, and here you come, relieving the shortage and springing me from this prison."

Doug frowned, rubbing his nose. "I almost hate to point this out, but the Judge destroyed the other Rambo, which means you can't fulfill the caliph's conditions. You only have one Rambo, and you didn't keep the Judge under control. You'll be a prison warden the rest of your natural days. But we're sure the Judge will receive his just desserts for depriving you of your destiny by demolishing the other *Ram in a Thicket*."

They turned in unison to stare at the Judge, who stood shaking in his suicide vest, Narin giggling at his discomfort.

"We'll get to the Judge later," snarled Marcy. "But first we decide the most spectacular means of knocking off an avowed atheist and a so-called religious expert who deems all religions equal. Two nefarious Western spies."

Ralph gasped. "But I'm a fellow American, a bro," he said, smacking his bony chest. "You shouldn't be going off half-cocked, violating the ancient Islamic tradition of hospitality for hapless foreign visitors. And we know each other. We're friends. We traveled together." At Marcy's thunderous look, he backpedaled a bit. "Well, kind of friends. We survived an explosion together. And we had the big party when you burned your passport."

"But you boys didn't burn your passports. You weren't really part of the celebration." "But we took part in the festivities, recording you for posterity." Ralph patted his camera. "You took movies to show back home, didn't you?" said Marcy, snapping her fingers, sparks cascading from her fingernails. "You wanted to exploit the backward foreigners and their curious rituals, to make fun of us."

Ralph laughed half-heartedly. "I took the video as a testament to the ISIS spirit." Ralph pulled out the camera, trying to turn it on. "No!" he screamed.

"Everything got dunked. The camera is ruined."

"And whose fault is that?" asked Doug. "Who turned the boat over?"

"You pulled up the sail, so you turned the boat over. You ruined my camera. My camera!" Ralph sobbed. His suffering was compounded as the lens fell out of his glasses and hit the floor, disappearing as if it never existed. Ralph dropped to his hands and knees, feeling blindly for the lens.

"No," wailed Ralph, peering up at Marcy. "I got great shots of you all. It would have gone viral."

Marcy beckoned with a nasty pointer finger. "Hand over the camera. The SD card probably survived."

Ralph busily kept feeling around the floor, refusing to look at Marcy.

"Slim's video was terrible," she said. "He cut everyone's head off, which was another reason he had to go. I gave Slim the choice of a flying leap or having his head cut off too. Not that he really had a choice."

"I thought you threw Slim off the roof because he was gay," said Doug. "Your lot is real touchy about videographers. Colonel Beretta beheaded one because the poor chap was late for our prison break. His head ended up on a spike at Dabiq city gate."

"Good ole Toulouse-Lautrec," said Ralph, bowing his head, pushing the camera behind him, out of Marcy's sight.

"I am already so tired of you," Marcy screeched. "Go sit on the couch."

Doug and Ralph crept to the purple couch and sat under the big sign that said "Reserved for Prisoners Awaiting Execution."

Marcy scraped her fingernails down the blackboard, standing everyone's hair on end. "Gory plays big on YouTube. But slicing off heads in orange jumpsuits is passé. We've done that so many times no one really cares anymore. Maybe we could boost our audience by executing you naked." She looked Ralph and Doug up and down. "No, that'd be disgusting."

She smiled at their horrified looks, raising an eyebrow when the Judge began to smirk. The smirk was instantly replaced by a mask of terror as the Judge snapped back at attention, shaking as Marcy said, "Watch out, Judge, or you'll be the next one on the couch." She turned back to the boys.

"The preferred way to execute enemies of Islam is good old-fashioned crucifixion. You can't get any more traditional than that."

"As we discussed during our long, intimate bus ride together, ISIS is taking things too far," Ralph said. "You need to modernize, like the Christians, Hindus, and the others did eons ago. You're way behind in the race for civilized behavior."

"Don't tell me," said Marcy, eyes flashing. "I

remember exactly what Mr. Big Religious Expert said." She pointed at Ralph. "ISIS 'observes every murder jot in the Koran literally.' We all clapped, and you said ISIS could unite a schism-proof Islam."

Marcy held her hands wide, fingernails flashing out of fancy sleeves. "You were prophetic, because it's working. ISIS *is* schism-proof, the rallying point for all of Islam. I wrote about it in a feature for *Dabiq Magazine*." She emphasized by scissoring her fingernails, bobbing her head, and swirling her curls. "I thank you. Do you have anything to add?"

Doug and Ralph sat with their mouths open, dumbfounded. Was Ralph of Arabia the prophet of the caliphate by predicting that it would be schism-proof and invincible among religions, all the others having compromised the literal words in their holy books?

Ralph shuddered. "I'd like to argue that the holy books of the Christians and other religions aren't as bloodthirsty as ISIS, but…"

"But you know you can't, not if you're a real religious expert. I ordered Psar to bone up on it. Hey, Psar," Marcy bellowed at a side arch. "Come out here and do a recitation for the boys. The one we talked about."

Psar walked out with his cherubic face sullen, his head bent, and his bright blue eyes staring at the intricate tiles in the floor, refusing to look at the boys on the purple couch.

Marcy clapped her hands, her fingernails rattling. "Lighten up, Psar. It didn't hurt you to memorize a few Bible verses along with the Koran, especially since they enjoy a similar tone.

Now recite!" she ordered.

Psar whisked the red beret off his head as if it would be sullied by a Bible verse. He performed woodenly.

"If your own full brother, or your son or daughter, or your beloved wife, or your intimate friend, entices you secretly to serve other gods, whom you and your fathers have not known do not yield to him or listen to him, nor look with pity upon him, to spare or shield him, but kill him. Your hand shall be the first raised to slay him; the rest of the people shall join in with you. You shall stone him to death because he sought to lead you astray from the Lord."

Psar gave a perfunctory bow, droning, "Deuteronomy 13:7-12 NAB. I don't know what NAB means."

"Go on," screeched Marcy. "We don't have all day."

Psar looked stricken, choking on the words of a false god, the odious, blasphemous, heretical words rising in his throat like bile. He swallowed and said in a monotone voice,

"Suppose you hear in one of the towns the LORD

318

your God is giving you that some worthless rabble among you have led their fellow citizens astray by encouraging them to worship other gods. If you find it is true you must attack that town and completely destroy all its inhabitants, as well as all the livestock. Everyone who would not seek the Lord, the God of Israel, was to be put to death, whether small or great, whether man or woman. Suppose a man or woman among you…violated the covenant by serving other gods…then that man or woman must be taken to the gates of the town and stoned to death."

Psar gulped with relief to be finished with the heathen Bible. "Those were Deuteronomy 13:13-19 NLT, 2 Chronicles 15:12-13 NAB and Deuteronomy 17:2-5 NLT. I don't know what the letters mean or anything else either." He bowed.

"Go on, get out of here," yelled Marcy, shooing Psar out a side arch. "The child has no brain, no understanding, but he can memorize anything, lickety-split. I'm training him to narrate our snuff videos, great roaring stuff from the Koran. But I digress."

"I'm beginning to suspect that you don't play well with others and at heart are a nasty piece of work," Ralph said.

"You silver-tongued devil," Marcy said, laughing. "Does that mean you're tilting toward a favorite way to go?"

"Marcy," said Doug, "I must remark on your

319

kindness, giving us a choice, though I suspect we don't have a choice at all. You'll pick whatever suits marketing…"

"And your videographer," said Ralph flippantly. "Whatever plays in Podunk."

Marcy cackled, skittering her fingernails like castanets. "Thus, it is settled. Crucifixions, filmed at best light." Marcy tilted her chin up, visualizing the setup. "Sunset would be philosophically appropriate, and nicely colorful, and why wait until tomorrow? Let's get it done today."

She turned to point a finger at the Judge. "The problem with a crucifixion is how bored the audience gets standing around for hours watching some guy just hang there. The Judge is talented, making stoning and amputation liven up the proceeding."

Marcy turned to the white-as-a-sheet boys slumped on the purple couch. "The Judge always starts with a little stoning for the pre-crucifixion softening up, beginning with pebbles. In memory of Doug, we'll continue with pub darts. Then we'll incorporate strategic amputations before, during, and after nailing you to the cross. Cutting off a nose to spite a face films remarkably well. The Judge was always an expert at prolonging the amputation process, a finger here, a toe there, half a foot, an arm. One guy lasted a whole week."

"But tell me," she said, as she stepped forward and

raked fingernails down the Judge's face. "What would you recommend?"

A seriously palsied Judge unconsciously raised his hand. "Whatever you want, Madame," he said, his face scrunched into a snarling rictus ribboned with bloody scratches. "Whatever you want."

Marcy smiled widely. "That's very good. You're trainable, not like these old coots and the so-called Yazidi Joan of Arc. Approach," Marcy ordered Narin.

Narin ignored Marcy as if she didn't exist, staring at the two-story stack of prisoner boxes. She'd spent months on the top floor in Box Number Five, living on orange peels that cost a fortune to smuggle in.

The four-foot ceilings forced inmates to stand with their heads bowed and backs bent until they were ransomed or starved to death, which was marginally better than sex slavery by the day or the month. Lying down at night required coordination, the women packed together like spoons on floors covered with sewage.

Going to the toilet meant sticking your butt between bars over the backside of the cage, no toilet paper. The only luxury was rusty water from a bare pipe. The prisoners peed a river while shriveling in their black slips from lack of exercise and food. Pee eddied around the cages and flowed into the dungeon. The only escape was by ransom, as a sex slave, or death.

"The Caliph has ordered Narin's immediate

presence across town," Marcy yelled. "The Judge and Fakir will escort her to the caliph, and I will expect them back within the hour. The sooner Narin visits the caliph, the sooner she can return to Cage Number Five." Marcy smiled sweetly at Narin. "Have a very special day with the time you have left."

She looked at Ralph and Doug. "I can't put the boys in with the women because it would be too dangerous. For the boys, that is. The lack of food pushes the prisoners to cannibalism.

They'd riot when they found you're a dab of gristle and suet." Marcy poked Ralph's tummy with a fingernail.

"I don't believe a word you say, Marcy," Ralph said. "Your prisoners couldn't rip a Kleenex in two, much less two tough old buzzards like Doug and me." Sighting through a curled forefinger, he said, "The women are all bones. None of them are fat and sleek like cannibals."

"Throwing you in with cannibals would certainly go viral," Marcy murmured.

Doug sighed. "I'll humor you and opt for dissection by women in prison. You can title it *Eat Me Up*. That would definitely go viral."

Marcy slung a hand at them, her fingernails sparking. "We'll go the stoning, darts, amputation, and crucifixion route. The videographer will do a light test with you on your crosses as soon as I get rid of the fake

Joan of Arc. Get going, Judge."

The Judge gave a start as his bloodshot eyes withdrew from caressing a sizzling lady bent double in a sheer black slip, her butt framed between the bars.

"Off you go," said Marcy, shooing the Judge, turning him around so he was pointed toward the door.

The Judge toddled off holding Narin's arm as Fakir marched behind them, flexing his hands in the fingerless black gloves.

"Oh, and Judge," Marcy yelled.

The Judge stopped, bumped by Fakir. The Judge turned around with Narin still in hand, the pipes rattling and wires twitching on his vest.

"If you are ever tempted to detonate your so-called suicide vest, please don't hesitate." Marcy clapped politely. "I would applaud if you did the world that one last favor. However, I've always thought your vest was a fake."

"Well, I'll be switched," said Narin. "I told the Judge the exact same thing. Go, sisterhood."

"Shut up, you little twit," said Marcy. "And get thee to the caliph. Shoo, Judge, and good luck with that one."

"I say good luck with me too," said Narin as she disappeared down the long black hall with Fakir closing the big door behind them.

"I wonder if we'll ever see Narin again," said

Doug. "The caliph might decide to keep her."

"Awwad," Marcy yelled, "have Bana and Yana open the dungeon."

A ragged old man in sloppy bib-overalls and knee-high overshoes limped as he herded two hefty girls in flip-flops around the corner of the cages. The girls wore full-length black robes and blue scarves around jolly olive-complexioned faces. They looked like sisters, holding up the hem of their robes as they clomped around islands of muck, heading for the lake of pee in the corner. The old man wore scraggly whiskers with wispy white hair sticking out every which way.

Marcy took a ceremonial key with a big red bow off a wishbone-shaped hook on the corner of her desk and walked to the wall of bars that separated Marcy's opulent office from the odious prison. She punched a button, and a clear plastic curtain slid to the ceiling, creating a vacuum that sucked in the stench of sewage. Doug and Ralph gagged as Marcy inserted the key and pushed open the gate.

The women crouched in four-foot cells with their heads bowed or turned sideways, staring into space like they were drugged, starved, and hopeless. A few women watched Marcy force the boys off the purple couch and herd them inside. The boys choked as Marcy locked the door behind her and dropped the key into her cleavage.

"Follow the walkway to your own private

dungeon," she said, "which unfortunately tends to flood from Pee Lake." A metal walkway bordered the floor-to-ceiling bars, ending at a closed door in the wall next to the glistening yellow lake.

"Bana and Yana," Marcy yelled, "you know where the dungeon is. Right there in the corner of the lake. Awwad, stop being a dirty old man. You're supposed to be supervising Bana and Yana."

Awwad dropped his gaze, swaying, tripping toward the dungeon like a shambling ape.

The girls tiptoed into Pee Lake, grasping a rebar handle on the trapdoor to the dungeon and creaking it open. Yellow liquid with brown streaks slid over the edge, cascading into the dungeon.

"Right. Leave the lid open so the boys can try out the dungeon while you girls go fetch the crosses for the lighting test. Let Zain know we're ready,"

Marcy clapped her hands. "Now, girls." The girls stood like stones.

"Awwad!" shrieked Marcy, sounding like one of the Chipmunks. "Awwad, do your job. Supervise the girls."

Awwad lurched forward, slopping pee inside his overshoes. Rivulets of pee dribbled down his overalls as he splashed over to supervise Bana and Yana.

Doug and Ralph clomped down the metal walkway, stopping at the end where a door opened and an impossibly tiny man emerged, looking through the viewfinder of the world's largest video camera. He stopped abruptly as Doug and Ralph loomed large, peering down at the little man, their pores, ears, and Doug's mop of hair filling his world.

"What is it?" the little man said. "What happened? What is wrong? What—"

"Shut up, Zain," said Marcy. "Get a grip. These are the stars of the caliphate's next extravaganza. Check the lighting when Bana and Yana roll out the crosses, which I suppose will be when Awwad wakes up. Awwad, snap out of it."

"Get down in there," Marcy yelled at Ralph and Doug. "You'll appreciate the cross after your pee-soaked dungeon. Throw your stuff inside."

Ralph looped the garbage bag toward the dungeon. The bag bounced off the lid and landed in the pit, waking a wild-eyed Awwad. Awwad staggered around like he was having a stroke, forcing Bana and Yana into deeper pee as he cursed in an unknown language.

Awwad stood slack-jawed as Doug's pack made a hole in one, like an orange meteor blazing from the sky, landing *kersplash*.

"Bana and Yana, hurry up with the crosses," Marcy yelled.

Bana and Yana huffed and puffed as they pushed

twelve-foot crosses on squeaky wooden rollers across the slippery floor with the tops scraping the cathedral ceiling. The boys stayed high and dry on the walkway.

Marcy watched the crosses grind to a halt on either side of the open dungeon. "Climb up on the crosses, boys, so Zain can get a reading. Awwad, get a hammer and those shiny nails so we get it exactly right."

Zain scooted around like a studious director-producer-cinematographer, paying no attention to the wet floor, slip-sliding as Doug and Ralph tiptoed through Pee Lake and grabbed onto the crosses.

Doug easily swung up onto his cross, posing this way and that on the way up, yelling down at Zain. "My good man, do you think this is my best side? Let me know?"

"This cross is way too big for me," Ralph said. "You'll have to find a smaller cross. I can't reach this one."

"Awwad," screeched Marcy. "Give Ralph a boost up. Awwad!"

Awwad tripped over the dungeon lid and landed with one hand in the muck, dropping the hammer and nails, which seemed to sober him up. He jumped up, shoving a sopping hand on Ralph's butt to boost him up.

Ralph scrambled onto the foot perch, leaning back with his arms held high, barely touching the cross-arm. "See," yelled Ralph down at Marcy. "This cross is way too big for me. Don't you have a carpenter who could fix it?"

"Smartass," said Marcy. "Shut up and let Zain do his work." "You're not a very nice person, Marcy," Ralph yelled.

"Oh, pshaw," said Marcy. "Women of my ilk don't have to be nice, only competent." Doug looked down at Marcy. "May we hop down now?"

"No, you may not," snapped Marcy. "Get up there with the hammer and nails, Awwad. Awwad!"

"Right," said Awwad, on his hands and knees in Pee Lake, looking for the hammer and nails. He slipped as he stood up, standing precariously on one foot with hammer and nails dripping pee. Awwad wiped his nose, slathering his face and raking nails across his cheek. He shook his head, griping as he climbed. He grasped the hammer and slid the nail into the palm of Ralph's hand, raising the hammer to drive it in.

Ralph jerked away, slapping Awwad.

Awwad fell off the scaffolding with a splash, and Marcy screamed, "Guards, guards! Seize that man."

"Very unsanitary," yelled Ralph. "You can get an infection from a nail sopped in pee. And you don't have any guards to seize me. I'm right here on the cross. Where can I run, home to the pit dungeon?"

"There are no guards, Marcy," Doug said calmly. "You have Bana and Yana and Awwad.

You sent Fakir off with the Judge and Narin. No guards, no cigarro."

"Or is pee neutral until it encounters bacteria in the air, and is it subject to the seven- second rule?"

Awwad stormed back up the cross, yelling at Ralph, "Hey, you. You hit me. I'm the boss here. You can't hit me."

Doug sighed. "Your grammar is atrocious, Awwad. Ralph *can* hit you, though you think he's not supposed to, but that's only according to you. According to us, we'd enjoy hitting you, holding you hostage, and escaping."

"Doug," yelled Ralph. "Don't go giving away the plan. You'll upset Marcy."

Marcy held up her hands. "Okay, I'm done here. Zain is finished with the lighting test. Right, Zain?"

"Yes, Mum," said Zain, picking up Doug's accent. "The best light for the crucifixion is when afternoon light flows through high windows yon." He pointed at dingy windows blocking most of the light and then looked at his watch. "It almost three. Five p.m. would be a really good time."

"Sure," said Ralph, flapping his hands. "A really good time for you, maybe. For me, a good time would be tomorrow or the next day. Tuesday next week at five p.m. would find the planets in better alignment, of course, based on the Islamic calendar."

Doug harrumphed. "We may have to start taking them seriously." Ralph sighed. "Would that help?"

Marcy stood musing. "Five p.m. sounds good. By then Fakir and the Judge should be back with Narin, assuming the caliph lets her return. That gives us plenty of time to get ready."

Ralph fluttered his hands. "I'm already taking them seriously. Now what?"

"You're right," said Doug. "Taking them seriously isn't helping at all. So, Marcy, what's for our last supper, the one that's traditional in all cultures? What's on offer? And we'd prefer to eat it topside. The dungeon is too damp for Ralph." He smiled with near sympathy.

"You have anosmia. You can't smell anything," yelled Ralph. Then he paused, incredulous. "You were actually being nice?"

"Sorry about that," said Doug. "I apologize."

Marcy shooed them with her fingers. "Whatever. I'm very late," she said, sounding like South Jersey, daintily holding her nose with six-inch fingernails. "Awwad, do whatever is necessary, security-wise." Marcy sounded stuffy holding her nose. "In a few minutes Slim's replacement will be here to make up Cage Five. And don't be too tough on the boys. The Judge likes starting amputations from scratch."

She let go of her nose and extended her talons.

"Awwad!" she hissed. "The drunken old fool has a fetish for women in black slips. I'd kill the old sumbitch if he wasn't the caliph's father, or maybe father-in-law. He might be both."

Awwad showed up shaky and wild-eyed, his hair sticking out every which way as usual. He mumbled "Yes Mum" as he stuck his thumbs under the shoulder straps of his overalls. "I'm on duty now. Duty."

Enraged and bottled up like a Molotov cocktail, Marcy flipped the key out of her bodice, unlocked the high bars, and sailed through the door to her office. From their high perch, Ralph and Doug watched the odor curtain slam to the floor. A frenetic Marcy hung the red ribbon on the desk hook, grabbed her purse, and ran out, leaving them wondering. Would they get out of this one alive?

CHAPTER EIGHTEEN — THE DUNGEON

Awwad motioned the boys down from the crosses, stomping around the rusty lid and pointing them to the dungeon.

"Didn't you hear the boss?" Ralph asked, hopping down on a dry spot, pushing Doug aside. "We get a last supper, and you have to take care of it."

Doug pushed back, fighting for the center of the dry spot. "We're quite keen to know what's on offer. Ralph likes seafood, and I haven't had a steak for a while."

"Doug's too cheap to buy steak," said Ralph. "Or at least to pay for one. I got roped into buying him one at Everest Steak House in Kathmandu, the only time he ever ate one that I know of. Remember that, Doug?"

Doug looked sheepish. "Yes, well, I'll take a free meal every time, even a last supper. Oh, and Awwad." He gave Awwad the evil eye. "Marcy said we could eat our last meal out here in the open. We don't have to eat in the dungeon."

Ralph tugged on Awwad's overalls. "See what happened when the girls opened the lid? The pee poured in, and it's really icky. We need to get our stuff out of there. In fact, we should eat at Marcy's desk where it doesn't smell so bad."

Awwad cackled. "If it wasn't nasty it wouldn't be a dungeon. Anyway, I don't have a key to Madame's office. They won't give keys to the caliph's papa, Abu Bakr al-Baghdadi senior.

No, no, no. No keys for you, they said. They don't trust the caliph's papa-in-law either, who is also me. The caliph, you see, I call him junior, gets around." Wink, wink. "If you know what I mean. Junior married his sister a couple of times. Just for a few nights. It could have been worse. He's done much worse things than that. Or better, depending on how you look at it."

"Please," said Doug. "Spare us the grisly details."

Awwad cackled. "Oh, no. You'll love the delicious details. Since Mr. Ralph's from Arizona, the caliph wanted me to tell Mr. Ralph about marrying that girl from Prescott. He thought she was the cutest thing. He killed her in his office, so I don't know what else happened."

"Oh my lord," said Ralph, shaken. "The caliph did all that? But he's the spiritual leader of the caliphate. It doesn't seem right."

"That's quite enough," said Doug decorously. "We only asked about supper, assuming poor Ralph can get it down amidst this sinus-rotting stench. What are our choices, and do they include steak and seafood? What do you want Ralph, the usual lobster?"

"That'd be great," said Ralph, brightening up considerably.

Awwad stomped around and splashed the walls in an aren't-you-the-stupid-ones dance, confirmed with a cackle. "You have a choice of cuisine: KFC or Taco Bell."

"You're joking," said Ralph. "That stuff will kill you." Awwad laughed. "You'll still be able to hang on your cross."

"That's a load of cow patties," said Doug. "KFC and Taco Bell wouldn't open their doors in a dump like Raqqa."

"By golly," said Awwad. "You're a smart young feller. We get takeout from Mosul once a month, free delivery with Uber Prime. How'd you know there's no KFC or Taco Bell in Raqqa?"

Doug shook his head sorrowfully. "The world is a book, and those who stay home read but a single page. KFC and Taco Bell aren't stupid enough to open in Raqqa. I'll have a big batch of KFC spicy, extra crispy; coleslaw; and mashed potatoes. And I like the gravy real hot."

"Well, I am guessing it's not too crispy right now." Awwad laughed. "It's been sitting around without refrigeration, and it might be dusty too. Raqqa got hit with a haboob a few days ago, and the coleslaw doesn't look good."

"Yuck," said Ralph. "That's another black mark

against Islamic hospitality, my house, your house, and all that rot. I'll bet you're sinking fast on Trip Advisor. Anyway, I'll have the bean burrito, bean tostada, and crispy taco, though I don't suppose it'll actually be crispy, and I like lots of hot sauce, the hottest fire please."

"Whatever's in inventory, you picky little bitches," said Awwad. "Look at the babes in their cells. They don't get nothing to eat." He shuddered with pleasure. "Peeing. Real skinny. Naked, except for sheerblack slips."

"I see the caliph didn't fall far from the twisted tree," Ralph said.

Awwad turned on Ralph. "You're a pitiful person, picking on a poor old man with a single pleasure left in his lonesome life. You'd be a disgrace to the uniform, if you had one."

At Ralph's surprised look, Awwad said, "We were briefed on you two. We thought it was a big joke, the Marine fetish. But no." Awwad guffawed, slapping his wet leg.

"Yo," yelled a tall blond chap, walking around the cages. "Farid, so good to see you," said Awwad. "I love your work."

Farid twirled over, pirouetting around puddles, bending, kissing the boys' hands. "*Enchanté*. Slim was a fine fellow. Rather too much out of the closet for Raqqa and not good at keeping his mouth shut. But nevertheless, a great artist… All great artists…" Then he stopped like he remembered he should keep his own mouth shut.

"Get in the dungeon," Awwad ordered Doug and Ralph. "Climb right on down in there. I have to help make the girls up properly. I'm expert at nipple blush." Awwad's hands were shaking. "Don't make me make you get inside," Awwad threatened. He suddenly had a shiny handgun in his hand, waving it around like he was deranged, which seemed a good call.

"We wanted to watch Farid at work," Ralph protested. "A tribute to our fallen friend and Farid's mentor."

At this, Awwad pulled the trigger on the little silver gun. *Ping!* The bullet ricocheted off the lid to the dungeon, burying itself at the intersection of the timbers in the closest cross, which stood shivering from the impact.

"Okay, we're going. And who the hell would give you a gun? Anyway, put it down," said Ralph, hands up, stumbling toward the dungeon.

"Welp," said Awwad. "I keep my gun in my overalls, in this little pocket where a hammer goes."

Ralph waved his hands around. "Put the gun away so someone doesn't get hurt. Then we'll retire below. Just leave the lid up because we'll have to pop right back out when the grub arrives."

"Yes, indeed," said Doug. "When the grub arrives.

Go on, Ralph, you first."

Ralph scooted over the lip of the dungeon, turning to hang with his fingers, the rusty edge slippery and yellow. He fell inside, screeching and gagging. "It's horrible, yuck. It's terrible and horrible. Don't come down here. You won't be able to breathe. 'Tis better to die in the open air."

Another ping off the lid, and the bullet whizzed past Doug's ear. "Be a Marine!" Doug yelled. He looped his legs over the edge, smoothly dropping on Ralph's head. "Oh, I suppose you consider this piffle a gas chamber. Perhaps its most propitious that you haven't yet had tea."

"Grack, you're on my head, and already I can't breathe. Scoot off my bag and go sit on your own pack. This is worse than a Chinese toilet. I think there are rats," he squeaked.

"Shut up and find your headlamp before Awwad locks the lid." Awwad slammed the lid over their heads, the compression whooshing their eardrums.

"I'm going to throw up. It's dark."

"Man up, Marine, and find your headlamp. There used to be one in your bag. I have my headlamp, see?" he said, snapping it on and shining it in Ralph's face.

"Hey, you're blinding me. I can't find my headlamp if I'm blind."

Doug panned the light around the six-by-six-foot

pit, the light gleaming off the yellow liquid that streamed like a water curtain down the back side of the dungeon. Two pairs of red eyes glinted back. "Get your light on so we can keep the rats at bay. We may have to swim for it."

"Rats are the least of our worries. I'm tired, and you look terrible, like you're worried."

"To quote the master, *would that help*? Of course I'm worried, you moron. And I know it doesn't help, so what's the plan?"

"I think we should escape. I'm set on that as a plan." Ralph pulled a dripping headlamp out of his pack. "It's too stinky to put on."

"Just put it on. So how do we escape, Sherlock?"

"You asked for it," said Ralph, squeezing pee from the headlamp straps and grimacing as he pulled it over his head. He snapped it on, blinding Doug with his new super-bright LED.

"You win. Your headlamp is brighter. Quit playing around and let's figure out a plan." "There's no rush figuring out a plan. We have hours, and I've had a hard day and need a nap. I almost got my camera confiscated."

"I figured you were putting on an act with Marcy, trying to work the camaraderie shtick." "I lost my last lens," he said, fingering the empty glass socket, "and I'm pooped. I can take a nap and still have time to figure out an escape. Maybe you'll come up with something while

I'm resting, inspired by me sleeping calmly while you panic under fire."

"Two hours is not a long time," said Doug soothingly, like he was dealing with an imbecile. "We need to figure out what surprising thing we can do when Awwad opens the lid. It shouldn't take more than forty minutes to put makeup on forty women."

"Not with Awwad applying the nipple blush. That'll take a couple of hours. So we have time to figure out a really good plan, unless Narin comes back early, and who knows what happens then."

"Narin's not coming back. The caliph's a lech. He'll keep Narin because she looks like that American girl. There was an article with photos in *The Economist*. They look a lot alike."

"What do you know about cute at your age?"

"I still know." Doug shook his head wisely. "If we get out of this one, I'm going find a nice woman to share expenses with on retiredbackpackers.com. Maybe I'll only travel ten months a year."

"I can't believe you'd quit full-time or find a woman who'd go anywhere with you. But future travel plans seem to be shrinking in importance."

"Ten months a year wouldn't be quitting. If I find someone else, you'll have to drag Rabid Rita along to split costs."

"I only called her Rabid Rita once, so stop it. Rita

is only rabid about working out, and anyway she won't travel more than two months a year. She's too independent and doesn't tow well on long trips. She's either working out, hiking, or reading a book, anything that keeps her away from other people."

"Don't you qualify as other people?"

"I'm away most of the time, and absence is the way to Rita's heart."

"What a coincidence. Your absence would strike a major chord in my heart."

"You don't have a heart, you only have a... oh, I am sorry." Ralph had repeated too often that instead of a heart Doug had a money belt.

"Now that you almost mentioned it, the money belt seems less important. We're faceless pawns in unending wars of religion and greed, a world fighting for oil, power, and a license to bully others. The reason for this war will be forgotten, the soon-to-be-dead are dead for no reason at all. Precious wars, when fought, are soon forgot." Doug beamed at his newly made-up quote.

"How morbid," said Ralph, shocked awake. "You gloss over the solace of the religious experience, which helps folks cope with death and makes their lives satisfying."

Doug glared at Ralph, pointing above their heads. "Well, the caliphate is obviously a crock," Ralph added.

"That's the problem. You say religion is a good

thing, but the most devout religion isn't. The caliphate hews to the letter of the Koran while a thousand others have backslid, ignoring the literal words of their holy books. So the backsliders are the good guys?"

Ralph sighed. "Players on a stage, signifying nothing, needing a nap."

"Don't you feel an urgency to get out of here? You only want to take a nap? What kind of Marine are you?"

"A tuckered-out Marine," said Ralph, laying his head on his bag. The stench caught in his throat, causing a fit of coughing as his feet slid into the yellow murk that eddied around the edge of the dungeon.

"You're going to stay awake until you help figure out a plan. Let's recap what we know." Doug shook a finger in Ralph's face. "You will die soon but are just too tuckered to avoid it.

Now that your life is almost over, you're giving up." Doug brought a fist to his mouth like a pretend microphone. "How'd it work out for you, your life and all? Will it be a tragedy when you're gone?"

He swung the fist-mic under Ralph's nose. "Hold me spellbound. Tell me what made your miserable life important, to you or anyone else on the planet."

Ralph lay stunned, head lolling on his pack with his legs sprawled in pee, unresponsive. "Right," Doug said. "You're an AWOL Marine at the exact moment when we have no moments left." Doug shook his head hopelessly. "Okay, I'll go first. I loved walking the cliffs of England from Folkstone to Hastings to Eastbourne, though it's becoming damnably difficult with the new highway. I loved the sea breeze, the hidden coves, the waves crashing, the spray climbing the cliffs, the little harbor towns."

Ralph sat up. "You win. That's really boring. I'm ready to work on a plan." "Sorry to be boring. Pray tell, what indelible memories made your overlong life worthwhile? I wait with bated breath."

"Well," said Ralph, scrunching up his face like he was trying to think. "Girls are indelible memories, the source of a hundred dramas, good and bad. Of course, the travel, world heritage stuff, national parks, the writing, the usual."

"Usual for you and boringly unspecific. I get no feeling from your list, no breezes off the White Cliffs of Dover, no nothing, and you're supposed to be a writer."

"You're a writer whose first book has been in the planning stages for some time now, secondhand except for the quotes you make up. Okay, sunrise after four days on the Inca Trail with Macchu Pichu spread out below, nine days around the Huayhuash in Peru while chewing coca leaves with charcoal to deal with 16,000-foot passes, almost dying from lack of oxygen on the top of Kilimanjaro, my Sherpa porter too altitude sick to make it to Everest basecamp. I'll skip the women, thank you."

"I do appreciate skipping your tragic history with women. So is that all there is?" "Is that all there is?" Ralph peered at Doug. "Are you a Peggy Lee fan?"

"The Americans were invaded by the Brits. It wasn't a vice-versa thing." "So we'll make a plan to keep on dancing."

"We get old, and we die," said Doug. "It's a tradition. So we die now or wait until we're nursing-home ready. It doesn't seem to make it better to know we won't die incapacitated."

"I can't figure out what difference it makes whether you croak at age five or age ninety- five," Ralph mused. "In a split second you go from memories to nothing." Ralph held up a hand in the glare of the headlamp. "No memory of liver spots or anything else. It's good to miss the really-starting-to-go-downhill part," he said, rubbing his neck. "If we aren't crucified now, we'll be forgetting more things than guidebooks. Crucifixion could be a good deal."

Doug shook his head, the headlamp reflecting off the rusty corners of the dungeon. "I'll miss breathing and fun things like that, even if I won't remember them." He shrugged. "Our passing will hardly be a tragedy, except to us. It'll be a boon for my rotten kids."

Ralph sighed. "My death won't be a tragedy for more than five minutes. I have kids from old marriages, who have kids from old marriages, who have kids still too young to make that mistake. I'm the weird old guy who goes to places no one's ever heard of. Boring."

"That's about right for me too."

"Five minutes after a tragedy, it's already a joke. Hey, did you hear about dumb-fuck Ralph, wandered into Syria and ISIS crucified him, literally. How cool is that?" Ralph held up a hand framing a pretend phone screen. "Want to watch it on YouTube? That damn Rambo is lots more precious than we are."

Doug gave a stiff chuckle as the lid to the dungeon clanked up a few inches and suddenly dropped. "When Awwad comes to get us, we'll pull him inside and remove ourselves from the premises. How does that sound for a plan?"

"My sentiments exactly." Ralph gave an arm's-length thumbs-up that cast a shadow like a sailboat on a stick.

Clank, clank! The lid opened to no discernible difference in air quality. Awwad bent over the edge to find Ralph and Doug frozen in place like they'd been caught red-handed, plotting an escape. "Sorry, boys. There's no last supper. The KFC and Taco Bell stuff was rotten. The good news is that Zain found a dozen chrome nails, nicely polished. They'll show up good in your video."

Awwad's teeth chattered with happiness. "I laid the nails out in a row, next to a little sledgehammer." Awwad laughed excitedly, clenching and unclenching his fists. "Unfortunately, taking Narin to see Dad didn't go well. I don't have the whole story, but this is your five-minute warning." Awwad slammed the lid closed.

"With that guy you can't get a word in edgeways," griped Ralph. "You weren't in position. You froze. Why did you just sit there?"

"Same reason you just sat there. Someone forgot to say go, and Awwad didn't lean over far enough. I couldn't reach him to pull him inside."

Doug shook a finger a Ralph. "We have five minutes to come up with a real plan. Not two hours. So we plan, right? Come on Ralph, buck up."

"I hate to be crucified on an empty stomach," Ralph said mournfully. "I was so looking forward to Taco Bell. Damn."

"I have an idea," said Doug. "We never ate the sardines. We still have them, all the way from Aleppo."

"Big deal. A last supper of sardines."

"No, dumb butt. Think about what happens when you open a can of sardines." "Right," said Ralph, inhaling. "You can tell right away whether they're packed in mustard or hot chili sauce. Otherwise, I can't stand sardines."

"Oh, lord," said Doug. "Think about the lid on a can of sardines. We can take Awwad hostage with the jagged metal edge. That will be our big surprise when he opens the dungeon. We come out like Butch Cassidy and

345

the Sundance kid."

"Yeah, but they got massacred, and the movie was a load of crap. It wasn't the whole Bolivian Army waiting for them. Butch and Sundance got their butts shot off by a local sheriff and a couple of deputies."

"Lest we digress," said Doug. "We have no choice. Unless, of course, a brilliant strategist such as your heretofore silent self has a better plan, which in an hour of trying I haven't been able to pry out of your little pea-brain."

"Well, hey, using sardine lids to take Awwad hostage sounds like a hell of a plan. Let's eat the sardines and go from there. We don't want to wait to rip off the lids until Awwad comes back. I mean we need to take the lids off beforehand and have them ready, right?"

"Dear God, why do I ever try? Are you too tired to think?" moaned Doug. "Of course the lids must be ready. So find your sardines and eat up."

"Right. Gentlemen, rev your engines and prepare your sardine lids," Ralph said, rummaging around the limp garbage bag. "The sardine can is what's been hitting me in the butt all week. Here," he said triumphantly, holding the can up, peering, trying to read the label. "Yuck, they're in tomato sauce. I *hate* sardines in tomato sauce."

"For Christ's sake!" Doug stopped, aghast. "You're so maddening that you've gotten me talking religious."

"It's not religious to say 'for Christ's sake.' That's kind of sacrilegious, so for you it's okay."

"Thank you so much." Doug ripped the lid and licked it off, careful not to slice his tongue. He held up the lid and flexed his muscles. "See, I'm armed and ready. When Awwad sticks his head in, we have to decide whether to pull him in or jump out and take him hostage. Which do you think is best?"

Ralph swallowed the last of the sardines and licked his fingers, sniffing. "That was a terrible combination, tomato sauce and pee. We should lock Awwad in the dungeon. So let's pull him in and slice his throat. Well, lightly. We don't want to hurt anyone. And then we get the hell out of Dodge. See, we got a plan."

"Thanks to me. I thought of the sardine lids," said Doug, elevating his nose as he licked each finger. "Stop worrying about the other guy's throat when the other guy is trying to do us in. Slice deep. Slice hard. You're a Marine."

"Yuck," said Ralph. "Maybe I'm not a Marine. I can't imagine the blood, for me or anyone else. You're right, Doug. I am chagrined. I am not a Marine."

"Don't worry," said Doug soothingly. "I know you couldn't cut anyone's throat except your own, accidentally. But your sudden appearance would scare anyone, so you're the diversion. I'll stay out of sight while

347

you jump up and scare him."

Ralph took off the headlamp and shined it on his face, peering as if he could see whether his face looked scary.

Doug was aghast. "What's wrong with you? You're stupid tired or tired stupid. Don't worry, you look scary enough." Doug's headlamp outlined Ralph's ears and bloodshot eyes. His glasses were lopsided with both lenses missing, and his little pink cheeks made him look like a Halloween goblin.

"Get rid of the glasses. They're no good without lenses."

Ralph put a hand on his face, feeling the empty frames. He sighed and dropped the glasses on the floor of the dungeon.

"Good job," said Doug. "So now it's all positioning. I can parry thrusts with my pack, but your garbage bag won't be much help."

"Parry thrusts," said Ralph. He collapsed in the middle of swinging the bag over his shoulder, like he'd been punched in the stomach, floundering in pee. "It sounds dangerous."

"Think c-r-u-c-i-f-i-x-i-o-n in Technicolor. Parrying thrusts is a good thing, so buck up or we're in trouble. You stand in the middle, where Awwad can see you when he opens the hatch. I'll grab his feet from an unexpected direction."

"What direction might that be?" Ralph asked in a daze. "From behind, of course. Are you daft?"

"I might be," said Ralph. "I am tired to the bone."

Doug edged back in the corner as the hatch began to creak open. "Remember the plan!"

Ralph staggered up as Awwad bent down. "Come on out of there," said Awwad. "We're ready for your crucifixion."

Ralph's voice wavered as he held up an arm. "Give me a hand. I fell, and I can't get up." Awwad bent double to clasp wrists with Ralph as Ralph yelled at the top of his lungs,

"Boo!" Then he swiveled his head to flash the headlamp in Awwad's eyes, giving a weak tug on Awwad's hand. Awwad toppled inside, *kersplash,* into the deepest part of Pee Lake, screaming. "You've killed me. I'm dying," Awwad screeched, jumping up with the temple of Ralph's glasses stuck through his hand.

"Aha," said Ralph. "The glasses came in handy."

"Attack," Doug yelled like a banshee, brandishing the sardine can lid and charging. "Cut him, hold him, and grab him. Good one, Ralph," he said as Ralph raked the jagged lid across Awwad's cheek. Blood seeped down Awwad's face like the painting of an old man who'd cut himself shaving.

"Well, damn," said Awwad, holding his cheek, looking at his bloody hand with the glasses' stem through his palm, patting his cheek, staggering to get up, slipping in pee. "I know people. I'm the caliph's papa. You'll pay for this."

"Oh, shut up," said Doug, pushing Awwad, who fell on his face. "See if he has the little silver gun."

"Pull the glasses out of my hand," wailed Awwad, waving his hand with the glasses flopping around.

Ralph yanked the glasses out of Awwad's hand and tossed them into the corner, startling a nest of rats.

Awwad screamed. "I hate rats. Get them away from me."

"Stand still," ordered Ralph, grabbing Awwad and frisking him. He took the little silver gun from the hammer-pocket of his overalls. "Got it," said Ralph, twirling it on a finger, dropping it, scrambling to keep it dry, and slipping it into a back pocket. "Stick him under the hatch," said Ralph, staggering like he was dizzy. "We can get out by standing on Awwad, like on a ladder."

"You can't stand on me," yelped Awwad. "I know people."

Doug scoffed. "Don't worry. You'd make a lousy ladder. What you're going to do is call Bana and Yana to get us out."

"Yeah," said Ralph, pulling himself together like a big tough Marine. "Don't make any sudden moves." He placed the jagged edge of the sardine lid against Awwad's throat, hands shaking with exhaustion.

"You brutes," said Awwad, quaking and rubbing his cheek. "Don't hurt me. And stop shaking. You'll cut my throat."

"Stop rubbing pee in your wound or you'll get an infection," said Ralph. "Staph is nasty stuff, and there are super-bugs everywhere."

"Get on with it," snapped Doug. "Call Bana and Yana."

Awwad staggered up, holding his cheek like he was mortally wounded, weakly yodeling at the open hatch. "Bana. Yana. Come here, girls. Papa needs you." He looked at Doug, leering, "I likes them plump."

Bana and Yana peered into the dungeon, one of them saying, "Right after you fell in we wondered if you needed us."

"Yes, yes, yes," said Doug impatiently. "Now get down here and help us get Awwad topside. He had a nasty accident and needs help. We can't boost him up by ourselves. He's a poor broken-down old man."

Doug gave Ralph a look that said "get ready for new hostages," but Ralph looked beat. His face was drained of color, so white he was almost transparent. He looked every year of eighty, like he might wisp away, so tired he could nap in Pee Lake.

"Here we come," said Yana and Bana. Ralph and Doug jumped back as the girls parachuted into the pit, their black robes billowing.

351

"Well," yelled Ralph, returned to the land of the living by Yana's and Bana's flight that vividly backlit their underwear and knocked Awwad on his butt.

Bana was frozen on all fours, and Yana sat stunned, trying with little success to rearrange her skirt.

"You're wearing Magic Mormon undergarments," Ralph said. "I thought you could only buy them in Salt Lake City."

"How can you tell?" asked Doug, fascinated.

"Did you avert your gaze when the girls came parachuting into the dungeon or did you notice their underwear? The bottoms are like white cotton pedal pushers with a little flap for, as you would say, the naughty bits. You couldn't see the tops, but they'd be a cotton T-shirt with little hearts covering the nipples, men and women alike, which probably isn't a feminist thing. And the Church doesn't like them to be called *magic*."

Awwad groaned, crawling out from under the girls. "When Papa found out how many women were wearing Victoria Secret, he ordered them to wear Mormon underwear for modesty's sake. I thought sheer black slips would be better, but Son knows best. The Church will only sell underwear to registered Mormons, so we had to kill Archibald Hamster of Logan, Utah, hide his body, and order a boxload container of underwear in his name, care of al-Baghdadi, Box 51, Raqqa, Syria…"

"Oh yeah, right, we get it," said Ralph.

"I don't think you do," said Awwad, weaving like a drunk. "Get up, girls. Quit lollygagging around. Papa wanted to make an ecumenical gesture, like making the Church of Jesus Christ of Latter Day Saints a sister religion. We're all people of the Book and hoped to promote solidarity between the caliphate and the Celestial Kingdom, but the Mormons blew us off. I must say they weren't very nice about the whole thing. I think Mitt Romney was behind it, and that's why we've been taking a beating in the media. It was unfair of Kerry to call the caliphate genocidal when we're the world's preeminent holy state, the only one that hews strictly to the word of God Allah. What are you Westerners on about, anyway?"

"Oh, shut up," said Doug, exasperated. "What happened with Narin and the Judge? Did something go awry?"

Awwad shook his head. "Narin escaped and is on the lam, apparently helped by someone who posed as Fakir. The Judge is in big trouble for letting Narin escape. Marcy said we'll have a triple crucifixion, but I don't know where I can rustle up an extra cross."

Doug held his hands up, trying to staunch Awwad in full bore. "Thank you, Awwad. That was very enlightening. Now, Bana, lie down here."

Bana must have hit her head because she stayed on her hands and knees like she was shell-shocked, staring at nothing. Doug reached out, tipped her over, and she fell on her back, twitching.

"Good," said Doug. "You're still alive. Now Yana, you climb up on top of Bana. Yana!"

Yana staggered up and sat on Bana's stomach. She tried to swivel around but lost her balance and rolled into Pee Lake. Yana jumped up with a grimace, climbing on top of Bana as instructed by Doug, making Bana gasp for breath.

Doug rolled his eyes. "Now Awwad, you get on top of Yana. Come on, Awwad. Not on your stomach. Cut it out, Awwad. Lie on your back and quit fooling around. Just think of being in a happy cloud on top of two nicely padded ladies. Awwad! In a happy cloud on your back."

Doug surveyed the stack with his headlamp. "That's a passable ladder." Ralph peered at the stack with his super LED. "That's pretty pretty decent."

"Come on, Ralph." Doug scampered from Bana's shoulder to Yana's shoulder to the middle of Awwad's stomach.

"Ooooof," Awwad groaned.

Doug landed on the edge of the dungeon with his own "Ooooof," slipping and sliding across the top. He levered himself up, brushed pee from his arms and legs, shook his shoulders, and settled the crumpled orange pack on his back, looking around.

Farid had worked his magic, turning Cage Five into lovely women in black slips, though they were still bent double and silent. The only other person in sight was Zain checking lighting and camera angles, sighting the crosses from various vantage points. The posh front of the huge room was empty, but the air sizzled with tension as if Marcy and the Judge might burst through the door at any second.

"We won't have to bother holding Awwad hostage if you hurry up, Ralph. The coast is clear, but it's not going to last," he yelled, bowing to Mr. Zain. "Greetings. It looks like you're ready for an excellent crucifixion. Did you print up a program, something we could take a look at?"

"Help, help," Zain cried. "The prisoners are escaping. Guards, guards!"

"Just pipe down," said Doug, shushing Zain by clamping a hand over his mouth. Zain bit Doug's hand, and Doug screeched as he elbowed Zain on the side of the head, knocking him off the walkway into a deep puddle of pee.

"I'm coming, I'm coming," said Ralph. He threw his bag on the lid, holding on with one elbow as he kicked at something below. "Cut it out, Awwad. You're going to get a foot in the face if you keep that up."

Ralph slid off the top of the dungeon into Pee Lake. "Yuck. I need a nap somewhere dry," he said, scooting on top of the dungeon lid, laying his head on the black garbage bag, exhausted.

"Close the lid before Awwad and the girls climb out. You don't have time for a nap," said Doug. There was an audible *clunk* as Doug threw a sharp elbow at Zain's head and wrapped an arm around his neck.

"Yeah, whatever," said Ralph, rolling sideways with his bag. He threw the dungeon lid closed and rolled back on top.

With Doug's arm around his neck, Zain held up an arm. "Come on, boys. I need this gig. I'm down to my last Syrian pound. My wife was captured by the Kurds, and I've got two days to pay the ransom. If the crucifixion falls through, my wife is kaput." Zain slashed a finger across his throat.

"So," said Doug, swaggering around with his arm around Zain's neck, "we should be choosing between ourselves and your supposed wife in supposed captivity by supposed Kurds. How do we know a single word is true?"

The big front door slammed shut behind Marcy and the Judge, and Marcy raced for the key hanging from the hook on her desk, almost knocking the Ram off the dais. She unlocked the high gate behind her desk as the Judge slumped on the purple couch underneath the sign that said "Reserved for Prisoners Awaiting Execution." He sat, absently rattling pipes, nuts, bolts, and drill-bits.

"Where's Awwad?" Marcy yelled. "Awwad, we have a crucifixion scheduled. Get your butt over here from wherever you are… Ohmigod, the British spy is holding Zain hostage."

"Yes, Madame, and you'd better believe it," said Doug

"I'm in here, Madame," came a muffled voice from the dungeon. "The infidels locked us up. Yana and Bana are here too. Let us out. We can't breathe. We're dying, Madame. Help, Madame."

"I'm coming, Awwad," Marcy called. "Don't worry. Be happy." She pranced down the walkway, slapping at Doug. "Leave Zain alone. He's not your enemy. I'm your enemy."

Doug shrugged, letting Zain go. Excitedly, Zain began videotaping Marcy tiptoeing through pee toward the dungeon.

Ralph levered his weary head off the top of the dungeon, trying to focus on Marcy, fumbling with his back pocket, slowly rolling to his knees and leveling the little silver pistol.

"Avast, ye mateys," said Ralph. "Stop right there." "Oh, pshaw," said Marcy, slapping at the gun.

Ping, Ralph shot a bullet through the palm of her hand.

Marcy grasped her hand, fingernails convulsing as she gasped. "I've been murdered. The little Arizona bastard murdered me."

"Oh, don't be such a wuss," said Ralph, waving

the little gun. "Bravo," said Doug, clapping his hands.

"I'm a little tired," said Ralph, staggering. "No, don't move, Marcy. I'm a sharpshooter, baby. I qualified on the M1 when I was in the fighting 529th Air Force Band."

Marcy lunged at Ralph with her other hand, fingernails slashing.

Ralph jumped back, giving himself a crick in the neck, his head bent as he looked at Marcy cockeyed. "Watch out, Marcy, or I'll drill your other hand. You'll be drummed out of the caliphate if you show up with nail holes in both hands. The stigmata would mark the end of your Sharia court dream." Ralph crouched into a sharpshooter stance, holding the gun with both hands, dead on Marcy.

Marcy did a spin, throwing herself toward Ralph a split second after he nailed her other hand.

Marcy rolled off of Ralph, screaming, "My hands, my hands." She stared down at her shaking hands and thrashing fingernails.

"That wasn't the best marksmanship, Ralph," Doug said stuffily, "shooting off her thumb." Indeed, her left thumb had gone missing, and the stump was disgusting. A bit of bone stuck out and blood gurgled.

"Take this," said Ralph, wearily tugging a handkerchief from his back pocket, handing it to a sobbing Marcy. "Wrap it around your hand to stop the bleeding. Boy, I'm beat." Ralph staggered, collapsing on the lid of the dungeon, rousing Awwad.

The lid thumped. "Let us out." Awwad was obviously standing on the girls. Zain whirled around the edge of the dungeon with the huge video camera, panning Ralph as Awwad thumped inside.

"I'm going to kill you," Marcy screamed. She inspected the handkerchief as she wrapped it around her hand. "If this handkerchief is used I'm *really* going to kill you, Ralph."

"Oh, Marcy." Ralph sighed from his repose on the rusty dungeon lid. "You're so illiteral," he said, languidly dangling the little gun in her general direction.

The Judge jumped off the couch. "I'm here, Madame. I'll save you, and you can save me. What a deal, eh, Madame? We have a deal, right? Madame!"

"Right," said Marcy. "Detonate your vest, now. Now, Judge! Do you hear me? That is the only way to rid the caliphate of the infidel Westerners holding me hostage."

Doug raised a hand. "But, Madame Marcy, wouldn't your death be an obstacle to a Sharia court judgeship?"

"Don't interrupt when I'm talking," she cried. "The Judge is hereby ordered to detonate!" She spat at Ralph. "I'll show you who's a Marine. Maybe we're safe on this side of the bars and maybe we're not. Do what you're told for a change, Judge. Detonate."

"Oh, no," said the Judge. "I'll just pop in and disarm the old coots."

The high front door swept open, spilling Gallouz, Nuriddin, and Narin into the room. "Hey, guys!" said Gallouz. "We've come to rescue the Rambo and the boys. How about

Muath being disguised as Fakir and helping us out, eh? Muath, who'd do anything to get back at Madame Marcy. We need Ralph because Narin has a plan." Then he paused. "Hi, Judge."

CHAPTER NINETEEN – THE PLAN

"You need Ralph," Ralph said sleepily. He tried to focus his eyes, sitting up to watch the fuzzy outline of the Judge pacing up and down in front of the purple couch.

"Watch out," the Judge roared. "I've been ordered to detonate. I might do it. I just might." He fiddled with wires like he was checking connections. His hands were as fluttery as a drunken pigeon as he rattled the nuts, bolts, ball bearings, and drill-bits, shaking the pipes and fondling the electrical bouquet of red wires and yellow tape. A tic had frozen the left side of his face like he'd been harpooned.

"You still don't have the balls, big boy," Narin scoffed. "Perhaps I should say little boy, because I notice you have little hands." She smiled sweetly as she threw down the world's most egregious insult.

The Judge danced around screaming, the side of his head clenched in a tic. "I don't have little hands." He held up his hands, staring at his fingers. "They're not that little. I am killing you all. I am saving the caliphate. I am the big hero."

The Judge reached down and grasped the red lever on the side of the vest, giving it a yank. Everything vanished in an explosion of sticky black smoke, billowing and rolling between the bars and covering the huge room in soot. The concussion knocked everyone flat except the Judge.

The smoke cleared to reveal the Judge staggering around, covered with soot, crazy out of his mind. "Infidels, women, fags! I can't take it anymore."

Smoke poured from his shoulder blades as he lurched around the Ram on the dais like a mime in black makeup, staring at his hands. He was covered with an inch of black ash and his hair stuck straight up. The pipes, after blowing their tops, still vibrated in the frazzled vest.

Everyone was covered with ash on the side facing the Judge, ash coated with crystal from Marcy's chandelier, which had been pulverized by the blown-off ends of the Judge's pipes. Crystal glistened on the vertical lines of soot blown through the bars and across their bodies, making everyone look like zebras, black stripes sprinkled with diamonds.

Doug wiped his face. "Hey, Judge, don't you know suicide vests require periodic inspection? You should have made sure the ends of the pipes were screwed on tight. And you should have double-checked the expiration date on your fancy powder. I assume you found the vest on a bargain table, or maybe it was a reject. You sure got taken by Boko Haram, eh?"

"What will you do with the Judge?" Ralph asked Marcy. "He's still just standing there, like he's frozen, looking at his hands." Ralph did a double take. "I don't think he's seeing a thing. He looks like a stack of charred newsprint. Damn, I need my camera."

The Judge had stopped moving. His shoulders and head were an inch deep in black ash, including his face.

Ralph pulled the camera out of his bag, punched the "on" button, and swore, "Goddamn camera, still not working." He peered through a curled-up forefinger, focusing his right eye. "There are no breath holes in the Judge's soot. He's spontaneously combusted."

Ralph walked over to the Judge and poked him with a finger. The Judge collapsed with a whoosh, sending a fresh coating of ash over the group, knocking Ralph flat

A blackened Narin grabbed the soot-covered Rambo as she rushed with Gallouz and Nuriddin to bend over Ralph. Zain zoomed in for a close-up of the poignant reunion.

"I'm too pooped to pop," said Ralph, lying half comatose, lazily waving the little silver gun back and forth, ignoring Marcy, who stood with tears streaming down her face. Zain filmed her looking like a Madonna, the light from the high windows framing her head with a rosy glow.

"There's no way you're getting out of here," Marcy cried. "And the stupid Judge ruined the prisoners' makeup, so I won't be able to sell a single sex slave. Farid will have to redo the women."

"Hey, don't forget me," said Awwad in a high voice from the dungeon. "I am the nipple- blush artist."

Gallouz wiped Ralph's forehead. "How are you doing, big guy? You look like you need a pick-me-up." Zain zoomed in as Gallouz fumbled in his uniform pocket and pulled out a packet of pills.

"Oh my God, Doug," said Ralph, focusing. "Look at your black hair. You look twenty years younger."

Doug was sooty and snooty. "Well, your whole head is black, and you don't look a day younger. Your ears stick out like a black Dumbo."

"Gee, thanks for that," said Ralph, looking at the white dot in the palm of his hand. "What is this, Gallouz?"

Gallouz chuckled. "Captagon, my man. It's standard ISIS issue. It'll pep you right up. I took one, and it lasted marching fifty miles a day for three days, and I couldn't stop marching. Captagon makes you totally numb and reckless. Man, you'll be something. I mean, if you survive. It might be too much of a strain for an old guy."

"I can't stay awake three minutes, much less three days," said Ralph, peering at the pill. He closed his hand and slumped back on the dungeon lid, asleep, snoring.

"So, Narin," said Doug, "what's the plan? How do we get out of here before ISIS knocks us off? I'm up for anything."

Narin ignored Doug, yelling at Ralph. "Get up and

take the pill like a Marine."

Ralph jerked upright, trying to focus on the pill. "It doesn't look like much. More like a baby aspirin. What's Captagon, anyway?" He popped it into his mouth and swallowed.

"It's a turbo-charged amphetamine," Gallouz said.

"Sounds like fun," said Ralph sleepily.

"Here's the deal," said Narin, bending forward conspiratorially. Zain zoomed in tight, but Narin pushed the camera away, giving Zain a withering look. "Go shoot the Judge. He's at his most photogenic, though maybe looking a little flat." She flicked Zain away with her fingers.

"Pay attention, Ralph," said Narin, slapping him lightly about the face, trying to wake him up.

Ralph jerked upright. "Yeah, what?"

"You bragged about being a pilot and a sailing captain."

"I may have modestly mentioned being a sailing captain and pilot, but I realize they're in my distant past."

Narin rolled her eyes. "You were a pilot at one time, so it's like riding a horse. You need to get back on the horse right now because Turkey is only a twenty-minute flight away. Muath promised to loan us a plane. I don't know if he will, but if he does, you can fly us out of here."

Ralph looked incredulous.

Doug gasped. "Are you nuts? He also said he was a sailing captain. Remember how that turned out? And I know about his landings. Do not risk Captain Ralph, sky pilot."

Ralph mumbled, "You're absolutely right. I only flew a little Cessna. I never flew anything else."

"What's the alternative?" Narin said patiently. "Does anyone have a fast car, slick van, big old truck, or a fleet of motorcycles handy? And how has it worked out for you, escaping Syria through ISIS territory? I could make it to Turkey but not hauling two seniors along."

"Now see here, young lady…" Doug objected.

"You have to pull your own weight," Narin said, "which means Ralph has to fly the plane. So get it together, Ralph. You can do it."

"Right," said Ralph experimentally. "Ralph can do it." He stood up like he was a little less tired, steadying the little silver gun on an oblivious Marcy. He shook his fist anemically. "Let's go, guys, let's go do it. Try doing it, anyway."

"That's the old Marine spirit," said Narin sarcastically. "I'll let the ladies out of their cells, and we'll fly away."

"They'll be lambs to the slaughter if you let those ladies out on the street," Doug said. Narin laughed. "Little you know. The street is far better than sex slavery, starvation, and Awwad. Where're the key to the cells?"

Doug pointed at Marcy and sniffed. "In her bosom."

Narin circled around Marcy, who had nestled her face in her hands, the long, wicked fingernails curled over the top of her head. Marcy had a ragged hole in one hand and a bloody handkerchief wrapped around the other.

Narin stopped in front of Marcy. "I'm going to take the key from your bodice, or you may remove it yourself. Your choice."

Marcy slashed at Narin, who jumped back. Ralph replaced Narin in a blur, pressing the little silver gun to Marcy's temple. "Either I retrieve the key or Narin does Which will it be?" Ralph was in charge, like he'd gotten the second wind he'd never had.

Marcy's head stiffened. "Never," she screamed. "That's millions of dollars in sex slaves and ransomees."

"You have one second. One," Ralph said, then he ripped the front of her dress to the waist.

Doug clapped his hands. "I do declare. Magic Mormon underwear."

Marcy stared down at the key dangling strategically between her Sophia Loren-type breasts. "You ripped my bodice. You shot my hands."

"Oh, please," said Ralph, before she could react, yanking the ribbon from her neck. He tossed the key to Narin. "Better to save two harmless seniors than protect a nasty broad from a ripped dress and minor flesh wounds."

He waved at Zain, who was circling with the big camera.

"You have the most room in your pack, Doug, so you carry the Rambo."

"I see Captagon makes men bossy," Doug said, "kind of a girly effect. You'll owe me even more for carrying the Rambo. Your debt continues to blossom."

A seemingly younger version of Ralph said, "I guess that depends on whether you prefer a knighthood or have instead decided it's beneath you. Your Rambo was massacred, but you can borrow mine even though my debt blossoms forever."

Dozens of women crabbed by in black slips, bent double, unable to walk standing up. "Those are my girls," Marcy screamed. She clutched ruined hands to her chest, smearing blood on her magic underwear. "Bring my girls back. You can't let them go. They're worth millions to the caliphate."

"Don't waste a bullet," Doug yelled at Ralph. "Just poke a pointy finger through her hand. That'll shut her up."

"What?" said Ralph incredulously. "Poke a finger through her hand? This is our old friend, Marcy." He pointed the gun at Marcy's feet. "Shut up, Marcy, or you'll have stigmata on your feet."

Marcy jumped as Ralph patted her on the shoulder. "Don't forget to let Awwad out." He yanked her back as she turned toward the dungeon. "No, you have to wait until we leave. I hope the caliph won't be too upset that you let two old coots lock his papa in a piss-filled dungeon and all your girls escaped.

"We're leaving right now," Doug yelled from the door. "Gallouz got a pickup, and it's out front. Come on, let's go."

Nuriddin and Gallouz beckoned urgently from the door, breaking into laughter at Ralph and Marcy's black soot-covered faces.

"I will get you," Marcy screamed. "You will never escape the caliphate alive." She tried unfurling her fingernails, but her bloody hands were crumpled like claws and covered with soot. She fumbled spastically under the ripped bodice for her phone, snapping it open and punching a big red button.

"All Points Bulletin from Madame Marcy, Sharia law professional and warden of the Mohammed Memorial Prison. Infidel enemy agents, rogue soldiers, and the Yazidi Joan of Arc are fleeing the Mohammed Memorial Prison on Mohammed Boulevard across from Mohammed ISIS headquarters. The Raqqa City Police, the Caliphate Federal Police, and the Brave Warrior Police are ordered to capture the enemy infidels, the rogue soldiers, and the Yazidi Joan of Arc forthwith, if not sooner."

Marcy stared at the phone for a second, struggling with a closing statement, finally saying, "Ten-four," snapping the phone closed.

Ralph yelled over his shoulder as he ran for the door, "You sound like a lawyer, but you've ruined your legal career. You're finished Marcy, and we're outta here, forthwith."

Doug grabbed Ralph's arm in the dark corridor. "We're in the worst neighborhood in Raqqa, the headquarters of everyone out to get us. I hope Narin has a better plan than she's outlined so far."

Ralph slapped Doug on the back. "Don't worry about it. You can trust the new improved Marine. That's me, in case you haven't noticed. We'll melt away before Marcy's Gestapo arrives."

"They only have to walk across the street," said Doug. "They don't even have to run." "Okay. Then here goes the *Butch Cassidy and the Sundance Kid* exit," said Ralph, shoving open the outside door to a complete riot in Raqqa's central square.

"They freed the girls," someone was yelling.

The call echoed around the square. "The girls are free."

A murmur rippled through the crowd and some guy asked, "Free girls?" A lady in black cuffed him and said, "The girls have been freed from that terrible prison."

Women in black enclosed and covered the women and girls wearing black slips, moving them out of the square as Ralph and Doug hurdled down the steps toward an old pickup with a big gun in back. The gun was manned by Gallouz, looking cool in his mirrored sunglasses. From inside the truck, Nuriddin and Narin yelled at Doug and Ralph to hurry up as a squadron of ISIS soldiers marched purposefully across the square toward them.

A little girl on spindly legs ran screaming, chased by a burly Falstaff in a turban who was clubbed by a tall man with a black turban. The little girl was rescued by another woman in a full black niqab.

The ISIS soldiers marched with white tennis shoes flashing in perfect unison as Ralph yelled at Gallouz. "You know how to use that thing?"

Gallouz swiveled the gun at Ralph. "You want a demonstration?"

"They might," Ralph said, pointing at the rapidly converging ISIS squadron. Ralph stuck his head in the passenger-side window of the pickup, motioning for Nuriddin to scoot over as he said to Doug, "Dibs on shotgun."

"Just get in," screamed Narin as Doug and Ralph climbed inside, half sitting on each other to slam the door closed. Narin floored the gas, screeching off and clipping the lead MP as automatic weapon fire began and abruptly ended with a blast that rocked the pickup.

The pickup bounced like a bronco as Narin pointed at a control tower ahead. "See how close we were?"

Ralph curled a forefinger and peered. "The runway is a mile long, right in the middle of town. It must have been here since Raqqa was a village."

"Muath said he'd unlock the side gate, just up ahead," Narin said. "We'll see in a second whether we can just drive in, fly off, and have Turkish shish kebob for dinner."

Ralph's teeth rattled from the jouncing pickup. "If there's something I can fly." On the other side of the airport fence sat a beat-up F-100, an ancient jet with the big hole through the middle, sagging on flat tires.

Ralph shook his head. "I can't imagine how a Cessna would end up in a hellhole like Raqqa. I remind everyone that a Cessna 172 is the limit of my piloting repertoire, some years back."

"If you get us out of Syria," Doug said, "I will forgive you for losing my money belt, without, of course, canceling the debt or accruing interest. Escape would help erase the nightmare of being captured by an assortment of nasty characters, not to mention getting dunked on the Hobie Cat." He smiled as he said it.

Narin swung onto the entrance ramp for the airport, tapping the side gate with the front bumper. The gate swung open and they rolled onto a taxiway, heading for a massive hanger where Muath slouched against the wall. He wore the usual scuffed-leather flight jacket and a garrison cap jutting over his crew cut, staring at them with steel-cut eyes as they rolled up.

"You're not welcome," Muath shouted. "Go away. Madame Marcy called out the troops, and they're on their way. I'd love to torpedo that broad for vetoing an ISIS air force, but capturing public enemies one through five might convince the caliph we really need an air force." Muath glanced at his fancy flight watch. "Marcy will be here in sixty seconds. Consider yourselves captured."

Gallouz laughed as he swiveled the big gun and squeezed a shot off, right between Muath's feet.

Ralph marched up and saluted a shaken Muath. "Sir, here's my private pilot's license. I would like to rent a plane in less than sixty seconds, preferably a Cessna 172."

"You're idiots," said Muath, turning on his heel. He flipped a switch, cranking up the hangar door. "We got nothing. The only Cessna is a 150."

"The 150 is a tail-dragger," said Ralph, "which is unstable and impossible to land in a crosswind without splattering all over the runway, or at least me splattering it all over the runway because in my experience all winds are crosswinds. Anyway, a 150 only holds two people."

"Is everyone still feeling optimistic?" Doug asked. He cupped an ear at Narin and Nuriddin as Gallouz hopped off the back of the pickup. "Hmm? I can't hear you."

"What kind of airplane is that?" asked Ralph as they walked inside. "The wings are below the cockpit, but it kind of looks like a 172."

"That's a Piper Cherokee. It's probably way too much plane for you," Muath scoffed. "Thirty seconds and counting," Narin said.

"I hope it's fueled," said Ralph. "But there's one big problem. A plane this size holds four people max. A Rambo and five people would push the envelope too far. I've seen videos of overweight planes. They're full of fuel and crash at the end of the runway, which means fried passengers, not to mention pilot fricassee. It's a good thing this runway is so long. What size engine—"

"Fifteen seconds and no time left to count," Narin said with steel in her voice. "Do you hear the ruckus outside, the one that sounds like troops lining up?"

"Help me roll it out," yelled Ralph, sprinting to the plane. "Nuriddin, you take the left wing, and I'll take the right wing. Gently now, don't mess up the ailerons."

They pushed the plane through the hangar door and wheeled it onto a taxiway as a hundred soldiers jogged toward them from the administration building a block away.

The troops held their rifles high, commanded by Marcy in a golf cart. She stood tall with her head and shoulders above the canvas roof of the cart. Her driver was Psar, who sat proudly behind the wheel, excitedly accelerating ahead of the troops. Marcy smacked Psar on the head to slow him down, apparently forgetting her crippled hand, screeching as she egged on the troops, fingernails spread like an eagle plunging for the kill.

"Checklist," yelled Ralph at Muath. "Where's the checklist for this thing?"

"There's no time for a goddamn checklist," said Narin. "Get in the goddamn airplane and let's get going."

"Careful of the wing," said Ralph, helping everyone inside. Nuriddin, Gallouz, and Narin crammed into the back seat while Doug sat in the front passenger seat with the Rambo on his lap.

"Okay, I need everyone's weight," said Ralph, fumbling around the instrument panel, looking for the throttle, turning the key, clamping hard on the brakes, the engine coughing and dying.

"Nuriddin and Gallouz, what do you weigh?" Ralph tried the engine again. It caught, coughed, putted, and roared.

Ralph backed down the throttle, letting off the brakes and rolling forward, waving at Muath, who gallantly charged the plane, looking good for Marcy, the troops, and the caliph. He slid harmlessly underneath, looking for an ISIS air force.

Ralph nosed down the taxiway.

Gallouz and Nuriddin shouted over the racket, "Sixty-five… Sixty-seven."

"That's kilos," Ralph yelled back. "Okay. Times two point two equals quite a bit. A plane this size should be able to carry 600 pounds, which is, oh geez, divided by two point two. Say 280 kilos. You two take almost half of that, leaving Narin and Doug and me and the Rambo.

We're way over. We have to get rid of some weight. We'll have to toss the Rambo." "Nonsense," said Doug. "It only weighs a couple of kilos, and it's worth more than we are."

"Not to mention a knighthood," said Ralph sarcastically. "It's not worth our hides if we can't get airborne by the end of the runway. We'll go kersploosh." Ralph picked up the mike. "Alpha Romeo, six seven two six, taxiing for a north departure." He slammed down the mike. "What am I doing?" He peered through a curled-up forefinger, focusing on a connector between the taxiway and the runway, redlining the engine and aiming at the rapidly approaching troops.

Marcy held up a thumb-less hand, standing tall on the golf cart. She ordered the troops to shoulder their rifles, drop to their knees, and shoot the damn plane. But the troops scattered as Ralph roared down on them full bore, clipping Marcy's golf cart and knocking it on its side.

"We have to lighten the plane," Ralph yelled. "It won't lift off with all this weight. Throw out everything that's not nailed down. There's probably an extra radio under the back seat, maybe a shovel, cans of oil, whatever you can find. Throw everything out. Toss that out, Doug." Ralph pointed to a directional finder. "Pry it off the wall."

Ralph spotted an apron leading to the runway and slammed on the brakes, yelling at the passengers as radios, cans of oil, and a shovel bounced around the cockpit. "You have to roll down the windows first."

Doug hurriedly rolled down his window as Ralph made a turn onto the runway in a hail of hardware, including a jerry can. Ralph set the brakes, revving the engine to redline. As compasses and packs flew out the windows, he let off the brakes.

"Still too much weight," said Ralph, as they swerved down the runway. "Get rid of everything, or we don't have a chance. Toss the Rambo, or if you prefer your clothes. In fact, those ISIS uniforms must weigh a ton, so strip 'em off, boys," yelled Ralph as the plane skittered down the runway, too heavy to lift off.

"First my money, now my clothes," Doug griped. "You'll be sorry." Doug unbuttoned his shirt and trousers.

Ralph averted his gaze. "I'm already sorry." He yanked off his shirt with one hand and dropped his trousers.

"You two leave Narin alone back there," he yelled, but it was Narin giggling at Gallouz and Nuriddin, too shy to take off their clothes.

"Don't worry about me," said Narin, tossing a

377

bundle of little green moccasins, tattered blouse, and black tights through the window. She relaxed as Nuriddin and Gallouz contorted to remove heavy black sweaters, camouflage pants, and white tennis shoes, squirming around the cramped bench-seat, trying to avoid giving Narin a glimpse of their junk. They were too shy to look at Narin's underwear that had said "Tuesday" for weeks on end.

"Hurry up," said Ralph, one finger on the wheel as he dropped his shirt out the window, the plane lurching from side to side.

Ralph peered at the end of the runway through a curled-up forefinger. "We have to close the windows before takeoff," he said, finally ripping off his pants.

"Lock the windows," Ralph ordered as clothes fluttered from the plane and the end of the runway loomed large and larger. A ten-foot barricade separated the end of the runway from the adjacent highway.

"Airspeed seventy knots," Ralph yelled.

The barricade loomed as Ralph blindly placed both hands on the wheel, pulling back gently, sick at the thought that the plane would stall. With no time to turn back and land, a stall at this altitude would be fatal. The technical term was crashing and burning.

The plane was sluggish, rising ten feet, falling back, bouncing higher. The wheels rolled over the top of the barrier, cars flashing on the street beneath them as the engine labored to gain another ten feet of altitude, twenty, and then thirty.

Everyone in the back seat was cheering. "We made it," said Narin. "Good on you, my good man," Doug thundered.

"I can't really see," Ralph said, wiping at his eyes, "so if you can all watch for stuff that an airplane shouldn't hit that would be a big help. It's a blur."

"Always has been," said Doug, exceedingly jolly again. "I'm looking forward to calling Ali about the knighthood." He sat proudly with the Rambo in his lap. "Though I am a bit worried about the landing."

"There's another problem about the landing," Narin said. "What's that?" asked Ralph, flying blind.

"We're minutes away from landing in one of the most conservative Muslim countries in the world, sans clothes," Narin said.

Ralph said, "Piece of cake."

THE END

If you liked this book, please leave a review

Also by David Rich:

Sail the World? – An Absurdly True Story, Prequel to RV the World

RV the World, 2nd Ed.

Myths of the Tribe - When Religion and Ethics Diverge

Scribes of the Tribe - The Great Thinkers on Religion and Ethics

Antelopes - A Modern Gulliver's Travels (excerpt below)

Excerpt from Antelopes, A Modern Gulliver's Travels

1

"Where are we?" The plane was dark, with no aisle lights, and the air was smoky, with a bright metallic taste.

Mack elbowed Lucas, sprawled out in the next seat. Lucas had a purple welt across his forehead, and his orange-red hair looked a mess, draping his face like Raggedy Andy, and difficult to make out in the dark. He didn't respond to the elbow.

Mack and Lucas were Arizona Lottery employees, chaperoning eighteen newly minted millionaires in first class to Carnival in Rio. They'd taken off from Caracas at three a.m., on the third leg of their flight. But now it was dead quiet, except for a loud whack in the back, followed by a lighter thump, repeated endlessly. There were no alarms, no cabin crew, and it was freezing cold.

Mack felt his forehead, finding a lump the size of a peach pit. "It smells like an electrical fire," he said, coughing. He looked closely at Lucas's pale face and bloodshot eyes. Probably in shock.

Lucas struggled to sit up. "Where's my big book? You know the one I mean." He looked around. "I'm worried now, mate." He shook his head as though he were dizzy.

"Your millions-of-quotes book? Forget the unimportant stuff and find our hats. We have to look good when we're rescued. Full uniform, you know." Mack brushed a hand over his head, obviously feeling muddled.

"Unimportant to you, not me. Me mum gave me that book."

Mack rolled his eyes. "Haven't seen it. Don't know where it is. Don't care." He felt as languid as silk, floating with no particular place to go.

Lucas looked so pole-axed that Mack felt sorry for him. "You might have dropped it on the floor and it slid somewhere when we...apparently crashed. There's been a lot going on."

Someone pounded on Mack's shoulder with more force than necessary. "Ah, Mrs. Sherman. You can lay off now." Courtney Sherman, one of the eighteen winners, was as round as a cement mixer and twice as strong. Her hair looked like a wig, every strand the same flat black, and she wore a purple blouse under the straps of overalls she'd sown into a long denim skirt. She was looking forward to Carnival as a chance to convert sinners.

She leaned into Mack's face. "Call me Courtney."

"Just a second. I've got a problem here." He turned back to Lucas. "Forget your big book. You couldn't read in all this smoke anyway. And quotes are silly stuff."

"Indeed," said Lucas. "And I quote. 'Be careful; with quotations you can damn anything.'"

"Yeah, and who said that?" demanded Mack.

"Who knows? I don't."

"You remember the quotes but you don't remember who said it? That's bizarre."

Mack grimaced as Courtney bellowed. "You two listen up. Now's the time to say our prayers. Ask the Lord Almighty to spare us, deliver us from this predicament. You're supposed to be taking care of us and you haven't done a thing."

Lucas said, "Cut the religious claptrap—"

Mack held up a hand. "No, Lucas. Let Courtney be." Mack turned to face Courtney, who reminded him of his mother. "I appreciate your concern, but the Arizona Lottery doesn't take sides on religion. But I'd be happy to pray with you while Lucas assists the survivors."

"That's a firm negatory," she snapped. "Lucas must also give thanks that we're alive. Then we can tend to the others."

"We have to check the cockpit, ma'am," said Mack before turning to whisper at Lucas, "Don't trash poor Courtney, you hear?" Then he continued as if he hadn't interrupted himself. "We'll come back and pray if you'd like."

Courtney stood next to Mack with her hands pressed together, clogging the aisle. "Pray first. Time for clear thoughts and clean actions. And a mighty dose of prayer."

Mack sighed, clasping his hands. "Dear Lord, keep us safe in our time of need. And help us get out of whatever mess we're in. Amen." He put his hands down. "Now, Courtney, we need to help the living. You could check out the whack-thump noise in the back, see what's causing that."

Courtney shook Mack's shoulder. "Something's really wrong in back."

Mack unsnapped his seatbelt like he hadn't thought of it before. "I haven't seen the cabin crew since before the crash."

Lucas frowned. "I don't want to read it. But I want to

make sure it's still around. From me mum, you know."

"Stop about the book already. Besides, you're in America, now. Well, South America, I suppose."

"Always was an American. Me mum says so. Even if Immigration doesn't agree. Airplanes have always been trouble." Lucas eyes were out of focus. He looked like an oversized kid.

"Get up." Mack unsnapped Lucas's belt, whipping the cloth cap with the seal of the Arizona Lottery from his back pocket and setting it on his head. He turned to Lucas. "Put your cap on."

"Okay." Lucas jumped up and slapped on his own cap. Lucas stood inches shorter than Courtney. Mack towered over both of them.

Mack said, "We'd better check the cockpit, see what's going on up there. That's where the flight attendants went, before we…landed."

Courtney groaned. "We should all pray and then get everyone out of here. Something might blow up, like ourselves."

"Spoken like a true leader yourself," said Mack. "So why aren't you helping the others? I'm sure Ellen is."

"Who can deal with this mess?" She pointed at the back. The cloud of green smoke smelled poisonous and the seats were cock-eyed. Crazy Peter, the wild blond guy, had barfed on the seat in front of him, purging the drinks they drank with abandon in first class from Phoenix to Miami to Caracas.

Mack sighed. "This is our job, Courtney. So, let's find the crew."

"Before whatever happened, they went up front, into the cockpit." Lucas pointed.

"Yeah, I know that. Something funny with the cockpit door." It was curved forty-five degrees, making the padding look like the inside of an egg. "Let's check it out."

Courtney vehemently shook her head. "But what about the others? We should attend to them first. And don't you find the whack-thump noise rather worrisome?"

Mack waved away the smoke and gently took Courtney's arm, the size of an eight-by-eight, steering her toward the nearest seat. He patted her shoulder. "You have to get out of the way so we can make sure everyone's okay. Help Ellen or stay put until we need you,"

Just then Lucas ran by, ramming the cockpit door with his shoulder. "Oh, sheissarino." He ricocheted backward, fluttering fingers padded with blisters. "Little hot up there. The outside door is the first priority, eh?"

"Whoa, the outside door it is." Mack gave the circular lock a mighty twist, colossal tug, and magnificent jolt. Nothing.

"There's a lock on these things. Right over here, on the underside of the doohickey." Lucas clicked something, and with his left pointer finger twirled the handle, which slid into a groove. The door opened a crack and a torrent of wind tore Lucas's cap off, pasting it against the opposite bulkhead. Lucas was right behind it, spread-eagled. The cockpit door turned pink in the hurricane of air.

Mack yelled, "Everyone out. No time left to screw around." He shoved the door closed, watching Lucas collapse off the wall. "Fine acting."

"I'll deploy the chute." Lucas punched at indentations, buttons, and whatever seemed handy. Still no chute. "Might be a big drop." He pushed the door open a few inches and peered outside. The wind spread his bushy hair into a fantail. "I can't see a damn thing in the dark. Could be a real worry, mate."

"Brilliant. Get a big flashlight, a torch, and let's see how it looks out there."

"Here you go, young man." Courtney shoved a flashlight in Mack's face. "Anything else I can do to help, let me know." She added, "I'll pray for you both," and bowed her head.

"Sure thing, Courtney." Mack elbowed Lucas out of the way and aimed the flashlight through the crack, the wind so strong it seemed to blow the light back inside. Mack grimaced as he stared down, wind whipping his face. "About a ten-foot drop. Not that far."

"Amen." Courtney raised her head and swept toward the door.

"Wait a minute, Courtney." Mack held up an arm, but she ignored it, kicking the door open and plopping down in the doorway. The plane gave a shudder and the whack-thump stopped for a second as the wind became a tornado inside the cabin.

Courtney jumped out and crunched on the ground with a splash. At her unearthly screech, Mack shined the flash down. "Are you okay, Courtney?"

"That's a hearty negativo, son." She leaned on ham-like legs, wallowing in a mud puddle as the wind blew her into the shape of a forty-five-degree butterball.

"Okay. Who's next?" asked Mack as another millionaire walked up.

"Ready, sir," said James Dean. "But I need my hat. I'm

uncomfortable without it, naked, like an undressed deer in season."

"I can identify with that. You help Courtney out of the puddle and we'll look for your hat, and our formal ones too."

During the nationally broadcast lottery drawing, James had imitated his namesake from an old movie called *Giant* and the performance had gone viral. They had to find their official hats because Mack considered them critical to establishing credentials with the locals.

Mack poked James, who jumped cleanly out the door, fortunately landing clear of Courtney.

Mack flashed the light on James, who walked in a precarious tilt around Courtney, trying to see which way she was facing. She looked pretty much the same from any direction.

"Next," said Mack as Lucas pushed two large bundles in his face. "What's this?"

"Supplies. We need more liquor and pillows, blankets, food, and water too."

"We have to get our people off first, and then worry about necessities." Mack crushed the gray cap into his back pocket.

"I'm next," yelled Ef. Everyone knew Ef. He'd collared them all, trying to sell property on the furthest outskirts of Phoenix, where it might grow in a millennium. He was jumping up and down like an elevator, similar to his shoes. "Gotta get someone on the ground with management skills. Someone has to organize this disaster." Ef selling himself long.

"Ladies and children first," said Lucas. "Or can I interest you in desert scrub, hold the utilities?"

"Just trying to help." Ef stood on his tiptoes. "Aim the flashlight so I know where to jump."

"Go ahead." Lucas bobbed the light over the little group below. Ef grasped the edge with his hands, hanging indecisively. Lucas stepped on his fingers.

"Aheeeee—" Ef plummeted into the puddle. He faced off with Courtney as she ransacked the bundles of supplies James had failed to guard.

"Whoosh." The door to the cockpit flared and the other dozen plus millionaires, along with Mack and Lucas, jumped out the door. They fled the puddle to the shelter of strangely shaped rocks. Lucas and Mack adjusted their uniforms and slapped on the cloth garrison hats the airline had made them wear instead of their formal hats. The airline didn't want them mistaken for someone important like a pilot.

Light flickered from the door of the plane, subsiding, then

expanding. Mack pushed Lucas. "Get back up there and see what's happening."

"Go yourself." Lucas clicked the rapidly dimming flashlight on the scene around them. Blond Peter was trying to rollick and roll as if party mode still ruled. But he couldn't compete with the vicious wind. He ran down like a wind-up toy with a tired spring, and his good buddy Chuck was nowhere to be seen. The two of them had celebrated on the flight like Siamese twins. Only seventeen lottery millionaires were left.

Ef was organizing, but it was difficult to tell what. Ellen consoled the bereaved, which included everyone. And Mack stood in awe, distracted by Ellen.

Courtney lectured James that alcohol was not allowed in their new residence, though no one had a clue where that residence was. But it definitely wasn't Rio.

The rest milled around, awaiting Mack's orders, surrounded by hundreds of pinnacles, boulders, and glistening puddles of water that smelled like rotten fruit.

Mack held up his arms. "Listen up. We don't know what caused the crash, but the plane could catch fire at any moment. Lucas will take you to safer ground. Lucas, show the kind people where to go.

"Then I need volunteers to go back on the plane to find available supplies and see whether there are other survivors. We'll try getting to the luggage before the plane explodes or burns." The gangway above them belched a single puff of smoke. "Now men, we're going back in. Volunteers?"

Lucas shone the light on the faces around him. Zero to none volunteered. "You'll have to call the names of volunteers."

Mack said, "Mr. Peter Vittorio, Mr. James Dean, Mr. Roy Jacobowitz, and Mr. Barry McCafferty. Front and center, report for duty." He motioned Lucas to turn the spotlight on the plane as irresistible Ellen stalked forward.

She said, "Now look here, Mr. Steward."

Mack practically stuttered. "I'm not a steward. I'm simply irresistible, make that irresponsible. What I mean is, for some unfathomable reason, I'm responsible for your welfare. So, take care of these poor souls while we try to gather food and look for other survivors."

"No siree, your list of *volunteers* is sexist. You have no women at all. You must include me. Or," Ellen indicated Molly and Betty, "at least one of us."

The others looked elsewhere as Nick, the Serbian Orthodox priest said, "'Adam was deceived by Eve, not Eve by

Adam—it is right that he whom that woman induced to sin should assume the guide lest he fall again through feminine instability.'"

Lucas turned the light on Ellen as she, completely out of character, forwarded a finger signal at Nick.

Mack's heart melted at the sight of Ellen in the harsh light, her filmy blouse caressing the curves above her swirly linen skirt. Then a corner of the plane caught his eye and he understood the whack-thump. "Shine it over there."